# ATONEMENT

USA TODAY BESTSELLING AUTHOR

## T.K. LEIGH

ATONEMENT

Published by Carpe Per Diem Publishing

Edited by: Kim Young, Kim's Editing Services

Image Permission:

IgorVetushko Copyright 2023

Used under license from Deposit Photos

# BOOKS BY T.K. LEIGH

**The Redemption Duet**
Commitment
Redemption

**The Book Boyfriend Chronicles**
The Other Side of Someday
Writing Mr. Right

For more information on any of these titles and upcoming releases, please visit T.K.'s website:
www.tkleighauthor.com

*To everyone who's ever said #MeToo.*

# CHAPTER ONE

## *Londyn*

A t least once a year, my father would preach the parable of the Naked Truth and the Lie. I'd normally zone out at having to listen to the same tale yet again. But this one always fascinated me. A legend about how easy it can be to believe a lie as long as it's cloaked in authenticity and masked in righteousness.

Even though it's been years since I've spoken to him, I can still hear his deep baritone sermonizing to his church, his voice filling the small space.

"One day, the Truth and the Lie meet on a road," he would say as he gripped the lectern, his suit pristine, a cross pinned to his lapel. "The Lie comments to the Truth that it's a marvelous day. While the Truth is suspicious of the Lie, she looks at the sky and sees that it is indeed a beautiful day. So the two walk together for a while until they come to a pool of water.

"Without testing it, the Lie tells the Truth the water is

nice, then suggests they go for a swim. The Truth is suspicious of the Lie once more, but after sticking her toe into the water, discovers it is as the Lie says. The two undress and bathe in the pool.

"Suddenly, the Lie jumps out, dons the Truth's clothes, and runs off to a nearby village. The Truth is furious, of course. So she leaps out and runs after the Lie. But when she reaches the village, the townspeople are horrified at the sight of the Naked Truth. They look away with contempt and outrage.

"At first, the Truth is confused about their reaction. Then she looks down and realizes she's naked, allowing the world to see all her secrets, regardless of how raw and honest they are. Ashamed, she disappears, hiding her disgrace for all eternity, while the Lie, clothed as the Truth, travels the world."

While I've always been drawn to this allegory, I've never truly appreciated the meaning behind it.

Until now.

Now I know what it feels like to beg for help only to have people stare at you with horror and resentment.

I know what it feels like for no one to believe you because of your appearance.

I know what it's like to be sent away in shame.

But unlike the Naked Truth, I won't disappear. Not this time. I'll make sure people have no choice but to face the Truth head on, see the Lie for who he truly is.

Even if I die trying.

# CHAPTER TWO

## *Londyn*

E verything is still, like I'm in a vacuum, frozen in this moment, this turning point in my existence. There's no going back to the life I once knew. Not anymore.

The gunshot echoes in the bakery, the sound lingering, drowning out everything. Birds don't chirp. Children don't laugh. Music doesn't play. There is no happiness in this new reality. Only the cold, hard truth.

But what truth is that?

I hold my breath, waiting for the pain from the bullet to consume me. There's no question in my mind. Jay — *Nick* — ended up the victor in our battle. That seems to be the story of my life — getting so close to having it all, then losing everything I've worked so hard for.

But to my surprise, the pain never comes. Instead, an

anguished cry reverberates against the walls. But it's not mine. It's deep, guttural.

Destructive.

A weight crushes me to the floor, wetness soaking through my dress. Nick's body blankets mine. Blood seeps from his shoulder, his face scrunched up in pain. If it were anyone else, I'd offer words of comfort. Tell him everything will be okay. That I'll call for help.

But after everything I've been through because of *him*, after everything I've lost because of *him*, after all the sleepless nights I've suffered because of *him*, I offer the same compassion he did the night he took everything from me.

Absolutely none.

Shoving him off me, I kick at his shoulder, which elicits a tormented wail. It's vindictive, but I want him to hurt. Want him to suffer. Want him to cry out for help and for no one to come.

Just like I did for years.

I scoot as far away from him as I can, my body trembling from the aftermath of the attack. My heart races faster than I've ever felt before, causing an ache in my chest. What would have happened if I hadn't taken Hazel's advice to learn how to protect myself? Would history have repeated itself? I shudder to think of suffering through that yet again. I barely survived the first time. I doubt I'd be able to do it twice.

But will I be able to survive this?

His distressed moans gradually transition into more of a cackle as he manages to roll onto his side, a hand covering his wounded shoulder, blood seeping through his fingers, the red stark against the cream hue of his sweater.

"You shot me." His voice is breathy and amused, everything about him assured and confident, despite the blood pooling around him, staining the floor. "It's a strange twist, if you ask me." His sinister, blue eyes meet mine, causing bile to rise in my throat. I swallow it down.

"What's that?" I rest my hand on the tile beside me, trying to ward off the lightheaded sensation as the adrenaline slowly leaves my body.

"*You* shooting *me*."

"What choice did I have?"

"That's not what I'm talking about. I'm talking about Medusa being the victor against the final battle with Perseus when he shows up to behead her. Like I said..." He strains to breathe. "Certainly an interesting twist."

"Why? Because you think it's acceptable for men, for society to keep victimizing Medusa when she never did anything wrong? When all she wanted was to be left alone?"

"Is that what you want, Londyn? To be left alone? To be forgotten?" He falls onto his back, his breathing becoming increasingly labored as more blood flows out of his wound. His skin grows paler with each passing moment as he seems to fight losing consciousness.

"Yes," I answer through the tightness in my throat. "That's all I want. To be left alone. To forget I ever met you."

"Oh, come now... You don't mean that. You *needed* me, my fierce Medusa."

"You're delusional. Life isn't like the Greek myths you obsess over."

"You see, that's where you're wrong." A sly smile tugs on his lips as sirens break through the stillness. My pulse accelerating, I dart my eyes to the door, then to the gun still in my hand.

The sirens could be heading somewhere else, but I know better than to think I'll walk away from this with no repercussions. This area of the city is notoriously upscale. I have no doubt someone enjoying their New Year's brunch at the posh restaurant next door probably heard the shot and called the police. Dread settles deep in my stomach at what will happen when they arrive and see a black woman holding a gun, a white man bleeding on the floor.

I quickly drop the gun, kicking it away.

"You can deny it all you want," he continues, his voice becoming more strained, stomach rising and falling with his increasingly labored breathing. "Playing the victim fits the narrative you need, doesn't it? That's been your identity all your life. At least since your mother died. After that, you weren't Londyn. You were simply that poor girl who lost her mother in a horrific church shooting."

He narrows his threatening eyes on me. "I *made* you into the woman you were always meant to be. You may not see it now, but eventually you will." He draws in a shaky breath. "Then you'll finally thank me," he struggles to finish as his eyelids flutter closed, head falling back onto the floor, muscles seeming to give out as unconsciousness takes over.

I stare at him for several moments, debating whether to go over and check his pulse. But then I notice the subtle rise and fall of his chest. I shouldn't feel relief from that. I should want him dead.

But I'd rather him suffer the rest of his life than be able to take the easy way out. He deserves to be held responsible for everything he's done to me. Then maybe I can finally breathe again. Something I haven't been able to do in years.

The blare of nearing sirens snaps me back to the reality of my current situation, the fact that I'm sitting in a room with an unconscious white man who's been shot. Who *I* shot.

I frantically glance around the kitchen of the bakery, unsure what my next move should be. It's not like I can just leave. That would only make matters worse. But *someone* should know what happened. Someone who will understand why I did what I did. As much as I want to believe that person is Wes, he's never been in my shoes. Never been a woman whose life was threatened.

Spying my purse nearby, I grab it and reach inside, retrieving my phone. After tapping on Hazel's contact, I listen to it ring as a strange silence fills the space, the sirens replaced by the distant sound of feet pounding pavement and orders being shouted.

"Come on, Haze," I mutter, nervously glancing at the door, fearing I don't have much time.

Just when I expect her voicemail to pick up, her bright voice greets me instead. "What are you doing calling me when you should be having hot New Year's sex with Wes? And please tell me you two got kinky with those masks."

I don't say anything, swallowing back my emotions at everything that's happened the past twenty-four hours. I'd been excited about the start of a new year, hopeful this was the year I finally took back control. That I'd no longer have to live with the ghosts of my past.

I never could have anticipated not only seeing the one man I hoped to never cross paths with again, but also learning he's married to Wes' sister.

"Lo?" Hazel says when I remain silent. "You okay?"

I look up at the ceiling, shaking my head as I choke out a sob. "No, Hazel. I'm not okay." A dam bursts as all the emotions I've kept inside since seeing Nick last night rush forward.

"What's wrong? What happened?" she asks frantically. "Was last night too much?"

I wipe at my cheeks, trying to calm my cries, the sound of running feet getting louder.

"I shot him."

"Who? Wes? What are you talking about? You're not making any sense. Why—"

"Jay. I shot Jay."

The line falls silent as Hazel processes this. "Jay? How—"

"He was there last night." I squeeze my eyes shut as memories of the gala play before me like a wicked pantomime. How powerful and free I felt, only for it to be shattered in one cruel twist of fate. "He attacked me. He tried to…"

My stomach roils as the familiar scent of citrus and leather surrounds me, burning my nostrils. He's several feet away, but that stench is permanently ingrained in my senses, smothering me, making it difficult to breathe. When I first met him, I loved the smell of his cologne. Now every time I walk by a man who wears it, it makes me want to vomit.

Makes me want to curl up into a ball and disappear.

"It's okay. It'll be okay," Hazel assures me, but her words aren't as certain as I wish they were, especially when I hear pounding on the rear service door, followed by an authoritative voice announcing it's the Atlanta Police.

"Tell Wes I'm sorry," I whisper, guilt rushing through me over the lies I fed him today.

Maybe if I'd been honest, if I'd told Wes who his brother-in-law was, I wouldn't be in this situation. But after everything I endured all those years ago, after everyone who I thought would support me tossed me aside, I swore to never depend on anyone else to fight my battles for me. This was one I needed to fight myself.

One I now fear I'm not meant to win.

"What do you mean? What's going on?" Hazel asks as the door bursts open. Nearly a dozen cops swarm through, weapons raised and pointed at me.

I don't even have a chance to explain myself before the officers rush toward me, knocking the phone out of my hand and forcing my stomach against the floor. A knee in my back keeps me pressed down as someone else brings my wrists together, securing them with handcuffs.

It doesn't matter that I'm not holding the weapon. That *he's* closer. That my dress is covered in blood, so I could very well be injured, too. They don't even take a moment to assess the scene. They don't care. I'm black. He's white.

That's all they need to know.

# CHAPTER THREE

## *Weston*

I glance at my watch, noting the time. Only three minutes have passed since I last checked. I've never been so on edge, so unable to focus. Since Londyn left about an hour ago, I've tried to go through the schematics one of my team members sent earlier in the week, hoping it would take my mind off my excitement — and nerves — about tonight. But nothing seems to work.

It's a blessing in disguise that Londyn had a last-minute meeting this afternoon. Otherwise, I fear she would have noticed my excitability and grown suspicious. Her being out of the condo for a few hours gives me a chance to mentally prepare.

I never expected to be here again. Never expected I'd want to put my heart on the line. Never expected I'd meet someone I could trust with it.

But I never expected Londyn, either. She's the most

amazing, beautiful, unexpected thing to ever happen to me. And I can't wait to start this next chapter in the story of us.

After several more minutes of staring at my tablet with little sinking in, I shove it back into my leather commuter bag, retrieving a small, black velvet box instead. Glancing out the front bay windows of Londyn's condo to make sure she's not home yet, I set it onto the coffee table in front of me and flip it open. My heart fills with love and anticipation when I take in the princess-cut solitaire beaming back at me.

It may be rash, considering we haven't even been together for three months, but we have a connection. One that transcends time. One I didn't think existed.

I stand, briefly closing my eyes, going over the words I painstakingly penned over the past several weeks. I've probably rehearsed this speech a dozen times by this point, but now that I'm mere hours from pouring my heart out and asking her to be my wife, I want to make sure I get this right. Londyn never got the proposal of her dreams prior to her first marriage. It's my hope to give her everything she's always dreamed of this time around. Not only in the proposal, but for the rest of her life.

I clear my throat, then imagine Londyn standing in front of me, her brows scrunched up in confusion about what I'm doing.

"A wise woman once told me that chaos can only truly be appreciated when you understand the calm. That without calm, there would be no chaos."

I pause, picturing her laughing as she asks if that's yet another one of Meemaw's words of wisdom, to which I'll agree it is.

"I've always considered myself fairly calm. Always lived my life according to all the rules I crafted for myself. I've never done anything rash or spontaneous." I pause, my lips curving up in the corners. "And then you happened." I swallow hard, emotion overwhelming me. It doesn't matter this is merely a practice run. These feelings are real. They have been for months now. Even before she decided to take a risk on me.

"You blew into my life like a goddamn hurricane. You shattered the walls of my soul and made me look at the world in a different light. The chaos to my calm. I fought it."

I chuckle at the memory of how much we both resisted falling for each other. Some things you just can't fight. Like the undeniable tether pulling me toward Londyn.

"But with every second I spent with you, I knew one thing was certain. That you're not like any woman I've ever met. I didn't know what to think about what was happening between us, but I liked it, Lo. Hell, loved it. It was different and inspiring and petrifying and just so fucking perfect. I told you the night of our first kiss that I thought you were perfect for me. And over the months, that feeling has only grown stronger. You *are* perfect for me. And the more time we spend together, the more reasons I find that you are the love of my fucking life."

I pause, licking my lips, picturing Londyn overwhelmed with emotion, fully aware of what I'm about to ask.

"From the very beginning, we knew this wouldn't be easy. That we'd face challenges most couples can't even begin to comprehend. But I said it back then and will say it again today and every day for the rest of my life. I don't care about that. I don't care how complicated this gets. I'll take complicated with you over easy with someone else every day."

I lower myself to one knee, reaching out and grabbing her imaginary hand.

"I promise to love you on your brightest of days and your darkest of nights. I promise to always protect you from your demons, both inside and out. I promise to always take care of you, even when you don't think you're worth the effort. I promise to be strong for you, even when you're exhausted from carrying the weight of the world on your shoulders. But most of all, I promise to always be yours. You for me. Me for you. For the rest of our lives. If you'll have me. So please, Londyn Jade Bennett, will you do me the absolute honor of marrying me? Of being my wife? Of completing me?"

A thrill rushes through me as I picture her barely able to form words, tears cascading down her cheeks. But she'll still manage to squeak out a yes as she enthusiastically nods. And there isn't a single doubt in my mind she'll say yes. This time, I won't allow anything to get in the way of marrying the woman of my dreams. I'll be the man she deserves. I'll make her a priority, instead of assuming she'll always be there, like I did with Brooklyn.

I blow out a breath and stand, setting the ring box back onto the coffee table when a loud knocking rips through.

I tear my gaze to the door just as it flies open, slamming into the wall, Hazel storming inside. Before I have a chance to ask what's wrong, she advances, shoving me, the unexpected assault causing me to stumble backward.

"How do you know Jay?" she shrieks, dark eyes wild, expression agitated.

"Jay?" I shake my head, baffled. "Wha—"

"How do you know him?" she repeats even louder.

"She told me about him," I answer quickly, still confused about what this has to do with anything.

"So you knew who he was, yet didn't say anything?" She leans into me again.

I may tower over her short, slight stature, but what she lacks in height she makes up for in determination and tenacity.

I hold up my hands defensively. "All I know is that he was a professor at her college."

"That's it?" Hazel shoots back as Diego darts into the condo and wraps a muscular arm around her waist, attempting to calm her down and peel her away from me. "That's *all* you know about Jay? That he was a professor at her college?"

"Yes. And what he did. Other than that—"

"So you had no idea he was at your fundraiser last night?"

I open my mouth to argue that I've never met the man, then stop, Hazel's statement barreling into my chest like an out-of-control train, her words knocking the wind out of me.

"What did you say?" I choke out.

Her throat bobs in a hard swallow as she nods, her eyes brimming with tears. "He was there."

"No. That's not possible. I know each and every person in attendance. They're all long-time donors. Who—"

"She didn't have time to go into detail. But she said Jay was there. Then she told me…" Her voice catches.

"What is it?" My chest heaves as I step closer.

"He attacked her."

I dig my hands through my hair, doubling over as the truth spears straight through me. My stomach churns, the anger rising in me causing my skin to burn. But the rage isn't solely directed at Jay. It's also directed at myself for being too wrapped up in my life to notice anything was off.

Just like I did with Brooklyn.

"Last night?"

There were times I'd noticed Londyn draw into herself, but I assumed it was due to the memories a masked ball brought forward. Never did I expect it was because I'd brought her into the lion's den, so to speak.

But who is this Jay?

I mentally go through everyone on the guest list named Jason, none of them fitting the picture Londyn painted of this man.

"No. Today," Hazel explains. "She called me a few minutes ago. There wasn't enough time to get all the details. All she said was that he'd found her."

I furrow my brows. "How? She had a meeting with a potential client on a historic renovation." My brain spins as I try to make sense out of everything. "Where is she now? Is she okay?"

Hazel looks from me to Diego. He nods, and she returns her gaze to mine. "She said she shot him. Then she said to tell you she was sorry right before…"

"Before what?" I press, my world spinning out of control. I want to pinch myself and wake up from this nightmare.

"I can't be sure, but I heard a commotion in the background. Sounded like someone shouted Atlanta PD. Then there was a struggle with more shouting before the line went dead. As much as I want to hope otherwise, there's no doubt in my mind. She was arrested. Which would explain why she didn't answer when I repeatedly tried to call her back."

"Why would they arrest her? If *he* attacked *her*, I don't—"

"This may be a difficult concept for you to wrap your privileged head around, Weston, but the criminal justice system isn't too kind to people who look like us." She gestures between her and Diego. It doesn't take a genius for me to figure out she's referring to their Hispanic heritage. "And it's *really* bad to people who look like Londyn."

"Fuck!"

My anger getting the better of me, I turn from her and slam my fist into the wall, but not hard enough to do any permanent damage. At least not to the wall. I shake out my hand, the pain a welcome distraction to everything else.

"That's why I barged in. I saw your car outside and came to get some answers about who Jay is."

"I have no idea who it could be." I blow out a breath and stare into space for a moment, fixating on the small, black box sitting prominently on the coffee table.

"Oh, my god," Hazel breathes, following my line of sight. "Is that…"

"It is," I answer, swallowing hard.

"May I?" She walks toward the box, and I nod. She picks it up, her motions slow and delicate. When she cracks the lid, she inhales a shaky breath. "Oh, Wes. It's stunning."

"I'd planned to ask her to marry me tonight," I admit wistfully. "In the intersection where we first met."

She admires the ring for a few more seconds before closing the box and setting it back down. Then she grabs my hands, giving them a reassuring squeeze. "And you'll still be able to do that. I refuse to believe Londyn went through everything she has, that she's *survived* everything she has, just for this to destroy her future."

I pull away from her and pace. I don't think I've ever felt this helpless before. Even when I watched the woman I thought I was going to marry slide the ring off her finger and hand it back to me. I knew there was nothing I could do to convince her to stay, and it gutted me. But that was nothing compared to this.

It's moments like these I wish Gampy were still alive. He'd know what to do.

"I reached out to a few of my buddies on the force," Diego offers, as if able to read my thoughts. "They said they won't know anything until she's booked and in the system."

"And when I called headquarters, they were less than

helpful," Hazel adds. "Pretty much told me all I could do was wait for her to be allowed to make a phone call and hope she called me."

"We're not fucking waiting," I grit out through the frustration building in my throat. I attempt to slow down my racing mind, needing to think clearly about what I need to do. But I'm so far from thinking rationally right now, it's laughable.

"Do you know any good lawyers?" Diego asks, half-joking, half-serious.

I'm about to tell him the only lawyers I've had any dealings with in the past have been real estate or corporate attorneys. Then I stop myself, recalling my run-in with an old friend several months ago. A woman who Gampy influenced enough to make her want to follow in his footsteps and become an attorney. And not just any attorney. One who also volunteers her time for the Innocence Foundation.

Gampy may not be around to help, but I feel Sophia is the next best thing.

Dashing toward my bag, I retrieve my wallet, flipping through it for her business card.

Once I find it, I grab my phone and punch in her personal number she scribbled on the back of the card. I pray she answers, even though she won't recognize my number and it's a holiday. After the third ring, I expect it to click over to voicemail. Instead, she answers.

"Sophia Mercer."

"Sophia," I breathe.

"Yes…," she draws out. "May I ask who's calling?" Her tone is sweet, yet still polished.

"Weston Bradford. Wes."

"Wes," she exhales, her voice transitioning from professional to more familiar. "I was wondering if you were ever going to get in touch. Truth be told, I gave up hope of hearing from you after Thanksgiving."

"I apologize for not reaching out sooner," I admit through my agitation.

"What's wrong?"

It doesn't matter that we haven't spent any meaningful time together since we were teenagers. She can still sense when things aren't quite right.

"I didn't know who else to call."

"It's okay," she assures me, her tone awash with sympathy. "Just tell me what's going on."

"Do you remember the woman I introduced you to when we ran into each other? Londyn?"

"Your interior designer, right?"

"Actually, she's my girlfriend."

"I had a feeling. Now tell me what happened."

"I don't even know where to begin..." I try to organize my thoughts as best I can. "Long story short, we think she was just arrested. I don't have a lot of information, but Londyn called her neighbor, Hazel." I gesture for her to come closer, putting my phone on speaker. "About five years ago, Londyn was..." I trail off, my stomach tightening at the mere thought. "She was raped by a professor at her college. Said his name was Jay. No charges were ever filed, not for lack of trying, but that's a story for a different day. Apparently, this Jay was also at the fundraiser I hosted last night.

"She never said anything about him being there, so I never suspected anything was amiss. We stayed at the hotel last night. Earlier today, she told me she'd gotten a request from a potential client to meet with her about a historic renovation. Also nothing out of the ordinary for her. So when Hazel and Diego, Londyn's neighbors, came over to tell me they believe she's been arrested, I was surprised."

"Why do they believe she's been arrested?"

"When she called me, she said Jay found her," Hazel pipes up. "That he attacked her and she shot him. Then I heard loud voices in the background, one of them shouting Atlanta PD. We tried calling around to find out what happened, but didn't get far."

"It's going to be okay," Sophia reassures in the same soothing voice I'd heard my gampy use when talking to his own clients and their families. "I'll call around to some of my contacts to see what I can find out. Just give me a few hours to work on this. In the meantime, if she calls you, find out everything you can. Where she is, what she's being booked for, anything. I don't want you to worry. I need you to stay calm and focused. I understand it's a ridiculous request, that you probably feel like your world has been turned upside down, but I promise to get you answers."

"Thank you, Sophia. I can't tell you how much I appreciate this."

"No need to thank me, Wes. This is what your gampy would have done. I'll be in touch soon."

Blowing out a long breath, I end the call, staring at the wall, my eyes glossing over a display of photos of the most important people in Londyn's life. Up until a few months ago, it was mostly comprised of Londyn, Hazel, and Diego, with a few older photos of Londyn and her mother during her childhood. But some have been replaced with selfies we've taken together, as well as pictures of Londyn with my niece, Imogene, and my sister, Julia. Our little family.

"Who is Jay?" I mutter under my breath, partly to Londyn's photo, partly to myself, wracking my brain for someone at last night's gala whose name is Jason and who is also a college professor.

As I continue sorting through every introduction, every

handshake, every conversation, a queasiness overtakes me. I blink, placing my hand on the table to steady myself, my breathing becoming uneven. It can't be. Can it? Am *I* to blame for this? Did I not only bring Londyn into the lion's den, but feed her to the lion himself?

I try to convince myself I'm overreacting, that there has to be another explanation, but I can't ignore the fact that my brother-in-law, Nick, fits that description. At one time, *he* was a college professor. His first name isn't Jason, but his last name does start with a J. Wouldn't Londyn have said something, though?

I fear I already know the answer to that.

A ringing breaks through my thoughts, but it's not my normal tone. I glance at Diego as he looks down at his screen, his eyes lighting up. He taps the phone, bringing it to his ear.

"What did you find out?"

I furrow my brow, pinning Hazel with a questioning stare.

"He called down to the fire station after we got nowhere with the police. Asked if anyone knew of any calls for a gunshot wound. Figured that might help us determine who Jay is."

I nod, returning my eyes to the wall of photos as more and more incidents from the previous night rush back. How Londyn immediately stiffened and clung to me when I introduced her to Nick. How she choked on her Champagne when Julia mentioned he'd been working on a book about Greek mythology.

Can I say with absolute certainty it was because of Nick, though? The mention of Greek mythology could have simply brought forward a painful memory. Couple that with being at a masked ball, and it's no surprise she may have felt uneasy.

I'm doing everything I can to not jump to conclusions, to keep emotions out of this and think about everything objectively and rationally. But with every puzzle piece that snaps into place, it becomes more and more difficult to blame the similarities on something else.

"How do you spell that?" Diego's voice grabs my attention. "And it was a GSW to the shoulder?" He pauses, then scribbles down more information. "Got it. Thanks, man. I appreciate this."

Once he ends the call, he turns around, the notepad in hand. "There were a few gunshot calls today, but the latest one was to the Buckhead Village District."

My breathing increases in time with my pulse, my face heating as a sinking feeling settles within me. Julia's bakery is in the Buckhead Village District. It could just be a coincidence, but I'm starting to think nothing is a coincidence today.

"What happened?" I ask guardedly.

"It was a pretty big deal. Thought it was the start of a mass shooting, so the entire place went into lockdown."

"And the people involved?"

"GSW to the shoulder. They were able to stabilize the victim and transport to Piedmont. Police made an arrest, but my buddy wasn't able to get a name. They're first responders, so they only worry themselves with the person in need of medical attention. But he did get the victim's name."

He pauses, glancing down at the notepad.

"Does the name Domenic Jaskulski ring a bell?"

# CHAPTER FOUR

## *Weston*

I've often heard people talk about feeling like their world has been ripped out from underneath them, but never truly understood what they meant.

Until now.

The second Diego says that name, I feel like I've lost my footing, that I'm slipping away with nothing to pull me back to reality. I didn't want to believe it. Wanted to think it was simply a misunderstanding. I can't anymore.

I blink once. Twice. Then spin around, swiping my wallet and keys off the coffee table.

"Where are you going?" Hazel steps toward me.

"The hospital." I hurry toward the door and yank it open.

"It's not like they're going to let you in to see this guy, Wes," Diego counters, close on my heels.

I pause just before stepping onto Londyn's front stoop,

bringing my eyes to meet his. "They will if he's my brother-in-law."

His dark eyes widen in shock as I turn, darting down the steps and into my car.

I barely register the miles as I speed toward the hospital, wracking my brain for any conceivable explanation for why Nick was shot that doesn't involve Londyn. That it's simply a coincidence Londyn called Hazel to say she shot Jay and that my brother-in-law just so happened to be shot at my sister's bakery in an unrelated incident. Something, *anything* to make this excruciating ache in my chest go away.

I've never felt so torn. I don't want to believe the man Julia's devoted her life to, the father of my niece, could be responsible for Londyn's pain and suffering.

At the same time, I can't ignore the alarming similarities between my sister's husband and the man Londyn described as Jay. They were both college professors at one point. They're both passionate, obsessive about Greek mythology. Still, there's one glaring inconsistency I keep coming back to.

Julia has never lived in Upstate New York, which was where Londyn went to undergrad.

And it's this inconsistency I cling to as I walk from my car and into the hospital, praying my sister hasn't spent the past several years of her life married to a rapist.

When I enter the frenzied, chaotic atmosphere of the emergency room waiting area, the smell of bleach and stale coffee surrounding me, I glance around. What am I supposed to do? Barge through the security door and hope to find Nick's room so I can ask him if he attacked my girl-friend? It sounds so absurd. But for Londyn, I'll do anything.

"Wes?"

I whirl around as Julia rushes to me, throwing her arms around my neck.

"What are you doing here? How did you hear? I was going to call, but I knew you were planning to propose tonight and didn't want to interrupt." The words tumble from her as she all but squeezes the life out of me. When I only weakly return her hug, she pulls back, meeting my confused eyes. "Is everything okay?"

I open my mouth. How can I even attempt to answer that? Things are so far from okay.

"We need to talk."

Before she has a chance to protest, I grab her hand, tugging her away from prying ears and into the crisp, late afternoon air, the sun heading toward the horizon throwing a pink hue over everything.

"Has Nick ever lived in New York?" I demand, my gaze intense.

She blinks, taken aback. "I don't see what that has to——"

"Answer the damn question, Julia!" I roar.

She stiffens, my outburst out of character for me. At least when talking to her. A few passersby glance in our direction, a nurse giving Julia a questioning look. She offers her a smile, wordlessly telling her she's okay, before lifting her eyes back to mine.

"He did."

I expel a long breath, my jaw tensing, processing this information I'd hoped wasn't true. "When?"

"He left that job a little more than five years ago now," she admits timidly. "He taught at a college upstate."

"But you've never lived in New York," I counter, unsure who I'm arguing for — me, Londyn, or Julia.

"I was supposed to, Wes. Don't you remember?"

"I'm sorry. I don't, Jules. I lived up in Boston at that time. We didn't talk like we do now. The only thing I knew was you were pregnant, then had Imogene."

"Don't you remember all the complications I had in my pregnancy? How they found a hole in Imogene's heart that would require surgery within the first few months of her birth?"

I nod.

"That's why I didn't go to New York with Nick. I was on bed rest, so my doctors advised me against traveling. When Imogene was born and needed to have surgery, we decided it was best if I stayed in Charleston so she'd be near her doctor. Nick wanted to stay, said he'd give up his teaching job to be with us, but that job gave us amazing health insurance. So he went back to New York for a second year."

"What did students call him?"

"Wes, I don't—"

"Just answer me," I respond, defeat evident in my tone.

"Professor J. But I guess some of the students he advised or was closer with would call him Jay."

"So it's not short for Jason," I mutter to myself.

"What?"

I snap my head up, having momentarily forgotten I'm not alone. "Has he ever hurt you?" I ask, bile rising in my throat.

"What?" She backs up, defensively crossing her arms over her stomach, shrinking into herself. "Why would you ask a question like that?"

"Just tell me, Jules." I clutch her biceps, not allowing her to escape my questions. "Has he ever hurt you?"

"Of course not." She pulls out of my grip, her eyes on fire. "I don't know where this line of questioning is coming from, but it's pretty shitty timing. My husband was shot during an attempted robbery at my bakery. The only reason he was there in the first place was because I wasn't feeling well, so he offered to go get my paperwork. The last thing I need is my brother, my one source of support, asking questions about the man I'm married to. A man who's currently undergoing surgery to repair damage from a gunshot wound."

She walks to a nearby bench and collapses onto it, burying her head in her hands. "I need your support, Wes." When she finally looks up at me, there's a frailty about her that's a complete one-eighty from the outgoing party girl she was last night. "Not your accusations."

"Who told you it was a robbery?" I ask, widening my stance.

"Does it matter?"

"Yes."

She peers into the distance, pushing out a labored breath. Her normally glimmering, vibrant eyes seem dull, exhausted. "The officer who called to inform me about what happened. Told me they thought Nick had foiled an attempted mass shooting at the shopping district, but on later investigation, it looked to be a robbery gone bad instead."

"And you believed him?"

"Would a cop lie to me about the reason my husband is fighting for his life?"

I give her a knowing look. While our gampy taught us to respect the uniform, he also warned us that there are two sides to every story. To never take everything we're told at face value. To always do our own research and learn all the facts.

Then again, I suppose I'm doing the same thing, believing the narrative Diego, Hazel, and I pieced together based on what little we knew. But Gampy also taught us to trust our instincts. If we're told something is a duck but feel it's a swan, we should go with our gut above all else. Especially when the person telling us it's a duck isn't all that reliable.

"Was anything stolen?" I press.

"I didn't ask. I—"

"Want to know what's a coincidence?" I interrupt, my voice quivering. "And, god, for the past half-hour, you have no idea how hard I've tried to convince myself that's all it was. Just a coincidence. But fuck, Julia." I dig my fingers through my hair, tugging at it. "Did you know Londyn did her undergrad in Upstate New York?"

She lifts her eyes to mine, blinking, remaining silent.

"And did you know she was raped a few weeks before graduating?"

She covers her mouth with her hand, tears falling down her cheeks.

"Do you want to know by whom?"

She shakes her head but doesn't answer. She knows it's pointless. Knows I'm going to tell her anyway.

"By a professor in the English department. A professor who had an affinity for Greek mythology. A professor who was also known as Professor J. Or Jay."

She continues shaking her head, her tears falling more steadily.

"And do you want to know where Londyn is right now?" I step toward her, unable to stop my own tears from escaping.

She peers at me, silently pleading with me to stop. But I can't. As much as it pains her, as much as it pains *me*, she needs to face this truth, too.

"You see, that's the kicker. I *don't know* where she is. Not for certain anyway. But I'm fairly certain she was arrested."

She inhales a sharp breath, eyes wide. "Arrested?"

"Yes. Londyn called Hazel earlier. Told her that Jay

found her…" I take another small step toward her, each of my words seeming to cause Julia physical pain. But not as much pain as Londyn has suffered. "And attacked her. So she did the only thing she could so as not to endure what she did all those years ago." I stop mere inches away, leaning down so Julia can't escape me. "She protected herself and shot him." I linger there for a moment before pulling away.

"So tell me, Jules. Do you think this is all a coincidence? Because if you can think of some other explanation for all these fucking similarities, I would love to hear it. Trust me. I don't want to believe it any more than you do. But if it's true, if he *is* the same Jay who haunts Londyn's dreams, causing her to wake up in a cold sweat screaming, I can't stomach the idea that he's done the same thing to you."

I sit beside her, swiping her hands up and clutching them in mine. "So please, tell me the truth. Has. He. Hurt. You?"

Her lips part as she searches my eyes. There's a vulnerability about her, at complete odds with the strong, confident woman I've known her to be these past several years. In this moment, I see the apprehensive, timid little girl who'd just lost her mother and was now supposed to live with a group of strangers. The girl who would do anything to feel accepted. To feel loved.

Even if it meant covering up the truth.

"Ms. Prescott?" a voice cuts through.

Julia and I simultaneously rise to our feet, shifting our attention to the petite blonde in pink scrubs standing in front of the sliding glass doors.

"I've been instructed to escort you to the waiting area in the surgical unit. It'll be more…private."

"Thank you." She offers a trite smile. "I'll be right in."

"Certainly."

Neither one of us moves as we watch the nurse retreat.

Even when we're alone, we remain silent and unmoving, an invisible wall between us now that I'm essentially asking her to choose me and Londyn over her own husband. How could she not, though, knowing what he's done?

"You should go," she finally says in a firm voice.

"Julia…" I approach her, but she whirls around, holding up a hand.

I stop in my tracks, silently pleading with her. I can't imagine what must be going through her mind right now. If I'd devoted my life to someone only to learn they're not who I thought they were, I'd be confused, too. But something tells me there's more to it.

I rewind to the past few months and the handful of times I've seen her interactions with Nick. She always seemed on edge. She claimed it was because he'd been away on business trips for so long and needed to get used to him being around again. I'm not sure I buy it. If Londyn had been away from me for weeks on end, I wouldn't flinch from her touch or appear inconvenienced by her surprise reappearance, as Julia did with Nick. I'd wrap my arms around her and never let go.

"You can tell me anything, Jules. I'll support you. No matter what. You don't have to go through this alone. I'll take care of you and Imogene. Just tell me what's going on. Please."

She closes her eyes, a single tear rolling down her cheek. Indecision covers her expression, torn between stepping out of the shadows and maintaining the status quo because it's a known quantity.

"It's not that easy, Wes."

"You remember what Gampy and Meemaw always said? 'Sometimes the right path isn't always the easiest.'" I place my hands on her biceps, an urgency in my voice. "Don't take the easy way out. It's okay to take a risk. To do the right thing."

"I don't—"

A loud chiming cuts through the tension. Julia uses the distraction to step out of my hold, nodding toward the pocket where my phone rings.

"Aren't you going to get that?"

I don't move for a beat, then push out a breath, reaching into my pocket and retrieving my phone.

"Who's Sophia?" Julia asks, glancing at my screen.

"Sophia Mercer."

She gives me a questioning look. "The same Sophia Mercer who used to come around Gampy and Meemaw's when we were kids?"

I nod. "She's a lawyer now. I called her to help locate Londyn."

"Then you should talk to her."

"I know. I just…" I look between Julia and the phone, not wanting to leave things so strained.

"You need to be there for Londyn. Just like it's important for me to be there for Nick right now." She smiles sadly, then turns toward the building.

"Is that really what you want?" I call out just before she disappears inside.

She stops, not turning, her shoulders rising and falling with her defeated breath. "When have I ever done what I really want?"

She steps inside, the doors swallowing her, leaving me with more questions than answers.

Answers I desperately need.

# CHAPTER FIVE

## *Weston*

I pace the lobby of the imposing brick building in downtown Atlanta, every second that passes making my anxiety increase. Dozens of people from all walks of life sit in the rows of chairs set up, each of them waiting for news of their loved one. Just like me.

Every so often, I glance at the secured doors, growing more frustrated with every stranger who exits. This has been the worst part of the past eighteen hours. The waiting. The not knowing. The lack of control and not being able to do anything.

When Sophia's familiar silhouette finally slips through the security door, I stop pacing. Hazel and Diego jump up from a few nearby chairs and join me as she approaches.

She tried to tell us it was a waste of time to come down here this morning, since jailhouse bail hearings aren't open to the public like normal criminal proceedings. I couldn't stomach the idea of not being here, though. I needed to show my support, even if I couldn't be in the courtroom. In my heart, I knew Londyn would be able to *feel* my presence. And hopefully that presence gives her the comfort she craves.

"How is she?" I ask urgently, my eyes wild with anticipation. My imagination has run crazy with every scenario about what Londyn could be going through, and it's killing me. I need to know she's okay. Or as okay as she can be, given the circumstances.

Sophia offers a sincere smile as she smooths a few strands of her brown hair behind her shoulder. Her smart pant suit and a few well-appointed pieces of jewelry make her appear somewhat formidable. Not the toothy little girl whose face was always covered in mud I remember from my childhood.

"She's scared, Wes. Lifeless, really. I was able to talk to her for ten minutes before the hearing to get her side of things, and she was...empty. Like simply reporting a summary of events as a detached observer, not someone who'd endured something no person should."

"She shut down," Hazel offers in understanding.

Sophia shifts her eyes to her. "Yes."

"That's how she was when I met her. Depressed, hollow."

"She's not the first client I've had who's reacted this way to such an invasive event," Sophia says. "It'll take some time for the initial shock to wear off, especially considering their history. In my experience, a repeat assault can be even more traumatic. Make the victim feel even more helpless. Trapped."

I nod, crossing my arms in front of my chest, doing my best not to think of Londyn spending the past eighteen hours scared and alone, wondering what was going to happen to her. Wondering if anyone cared what happened to her.

"So what's next?" I ask.

"Her bail's been set," Sophia states in an authoritative

voice. "The DA requested two fifty, but I got them to lower it to one hundred."

I'd prepared myself for this, but it doesn't make it any easier to hear that they believe Londyn to be such a threat to society that they'd set bail in an amount she'd never be able to afford.

"Even though she acted in self-defense?"

"Like I told you," Sophia replies in a soothing tone, "when determining bail, all they care about is her probability of appearing in court to answer for any charges filed against her."

"So what do they need? I assume the great state of Georgia doesn't accept personal checks for that amount of money."

She laughs under her breath, the moment of levity welcome. "You assume correctly. If you want to post a cash bond, it needs to be in the form of a cashier's check, money order, or cold, hard cash. The other option is to put up a property bond."

"We're happy to put up our house as collateral," Diego offers, stepping forward. "We don't want you to feel like you have to bear this burden alone, Wes."

"And I appreciate that." I smile, grateful that, even if Londyn and I had never crossed paths, she still has people in her life willing to help, to go above and beyond. Then again, if Londyn and I had never crossed paths, I doubt she'd be in this situation right now. "But I have the cash. I reached out to my money manager last night to alert him to the situation. He just needs the final amount to prepare the cashier's check."

"Here." Sophia pulls a file out of her bag and hands me a slip of paper. "This is the precise amount of her bond."

I squint at the small type. "If her bail's only a hundred grand, why is the total over one fifty?"

"The state likes to add fees to everything."

"Of course they do," I mutter under my breath as I retrieve my phone from my pocket, then fire off a quick text to my money manager with the full amount. He instantly responds that he'll have it for me to pick up within the half-hour. I shudder to think what I'd do if I didn't have resources at my disposal.

I look back at Sophia. "Now what?"

"Once you've got the money, you'll post bail. Also, you'll need to bring her some clothes to go home in."

"Clothes?"

She nods. "They had to take her clothes as evidence."

"Evidence? Wh—"

"They were covered in blood, Wes."

I squeeze my eyes shut, pinching my lips together.

"Bring the money and her clothes to the bail office," she continues. "After that, they'll have to do a bit of paperwork, so it'll take a few hours for her to be released. Once that happens, they'll alert the police department, which will then send an officer to her house."

"Why?" I demand, my jaw twitching. "Isn't it enough they arrested her for something any reasonable woman in her shoes would do? Now they're sending a cop to her house? Her only place of sanctuary and peace?"

"One of the conditions of her bail is to surrender all of her firearms."

"But she acted in self-defense!" I counter once again, my blood boiling more with every passing second.

"It's useless to get angry over something we can't control. Like I explained—"

"I know, I know," I interrupt with a labored sigh. "That will come out during the next phase."

"Precisely." She smiles compassionately. "Right now, your sole focus needs to be on Londyn's mental well-being. Nothing else. She's going through something most people can't even begin to imagine. The next few days...hell, weeks are going to be trying. It's most likely only going to get more difficult. Just show her you respect her. That you love her. That you *believe* her."

She looks from me to Hazel and Diego, then back at me. "Trust me when I say that this type of case is never easy. There's a reason only thirty-five percent of rapes are reported."

"Thirty-five percent?" I ask incredulously.

"And of that thirty-five percent, only fifteen lead to an arrest. Of that fifteen percent, only ten percent are convicted. So of all the rapes that occur, less than one percent lead to a conviction, a statistic that is so far below the trend for every other crime, it's disgusting. And if you think that's bad, you should look at the same numbers for Hispanic and black women. It's even lower, especially if the perpetrator is white."

"Is this supposed to be your pep talk that this asshole's finally going to answer for his actions? Because if you're trying to cheer me up with these statistics, you missed the mark, Soph."

"I'm not trying to cheer you up. I'm telling you the statistics so you're prepared. And also to explain why the best thing you can do is offer Londyn your unwavering support. To never question her. If she knows you're on her side, perhaps she'll fight even when she's on the brink of giving up. Even when she feels like the world is out to get her."

I struggle to breathe through the lump in my throat.

Hearing these statistics is a rude awakening, shattering the rose-colored glasses I've worn most of my life. I should have known better, especially after all the time I spent with Gampy.

"She's a fighter," I manage to say.

"I know she is. *You* know she is." Sophia squeezes my arm. "Now you need to help *Londyn* see that she is, too."

# CHAPTER SIX

## *Londyn*

I smooth a hand down my sweater and jeans, savoring the feel of the fabric, something I've never truly appreciated until this moment. Until spending nearly twenty-four hours dressed in a scratchy, orange jumpsuit, the material made of the lowest thread count possible. It's no wonder the judge set an unreasonable bail. I actually looked like a criminal when I walked into that courtroom for my hearing. But as Sophia assured me, Wes would get me out. And he did.

In truth, the prospect of seeing Wes is more nerve-wracking than sitting in court and listening to the numerous offenses I'd been booked on. Will he understand why I did what I did? Will he still stand by my side? Or will he be like everyone else in my life and abandon me when I need him the most?

I still don't know what to expect when I see him. Part of

me wonders if this entire ordeal will be easier on both of us if he keeps his distance.

But that's at odds with the part of me that's grown to crave him for my own serenity. My own comfort. My own security. He's done what I didn't think any man would ever do again. He's chased away my demons. I need that more than ever right now.

I struggle to keep my eyes open as I sign paper after paper in order to be released. Once my personal items are returned to me, apart from my clothes that are now considered evidence, I follow the officer's direction toward a solid metal door. When it buzzes, I push it open, making my way down another long corridor before coming to yet another door. I place my hand on the push bar, drawing in a deep breath before opening it.

As I step over the threshold, I squint, the bright lights of the lobby like a spotlight shining directly on me, revealing my sins to everyone waiting. I scan the dozens of people in the sitting area, but it doesn't take me long to spot Wes. The instant my gaze falls on his slumped frame, fingers pinching the bridge of his nose, my heart cracks at the utter despair and exhaustion emanating from him.

Able to sense my presence, he snaps his head up, relief covering his expression when his gaze meets mine. He jumps to his feet, eating up the distance between us in a few long strides. Without a moment's hesitation, his arms swallow me, clinging to me as if I'm his only source of sustenance. His lifeline. His anchor.

I close my eyes, basking in the warmth and familiarity of his embrace. After the past twenty-four hours, I welcome it. But for how much longer will I be able to relish in the love pouring from his heart and into me? I'm free now, but only physically. While Sophia seemed hopeful the DA may not pursue charges, not with a justifiable defense, I'm not so sure. No one believed me all those years ago. What makes me think anyone will now?

"I'm so sorry, Lo." Emotion chokes Wes' voice, his body trembling against mine.

There are no questions about what happened. No accusations about why I lied to him about my plans yesterday. Just unwavering devotion. As always.

He pulls back, but keeps his arms wrapped around me, as if physically unable to release his hold. When he brings a hand to my face, pushing one of my ringlets behind my ear, I melt into his electrifying touch.

"I should have figured it out." Licking his lips, he shakes his head, the lines of his face scrunched up in a mixture of guilt and frustration. "Should have put the pieces together long before now. I knew Nick was a professor, that he taught English and was obsessed with Greek mythology. Never in a million years could I have expected—"

Not wanting to relive the worst moment of my life, I push out of his hold, squaring my shoulders. "It's okay," I say, fighting against the memories, the debilitating fear that consumed me when he had me pinned to the floor.

I thought it was history repeating itself. Instead, I managed to fight. But for what? Will it matter? Will anything be different this time? Or will he get away with it once again?

Unable to peer into Wes' compassionate eyes, I avert my gaze, noticing Diego and Hazel standing off to the side.

"Hey, fighter," Diego says with an encouraging smile, although there's a touch of sadness that typically isn't present.

"Hey, D." I walk into his outstretched arms, allowing him to pull me into his firm embrace. He holds me longer than normal. When he finally releases me, Hazel flings herself at me, squeezing tightly.

"You're okay, Lo," she assures me with a quiver. "You'll get through this." She pulls back, her hands gripping my biceps as she levels a stare on me. "Like I told you the day you walked into my self-defense class… Broken girls turn into warriors. And you're a fucking warrior."

"Thanks, Haze." I try to find some sort of encouragement in her words, ones I once believed. I'm too beaten down to possibly pick up my sword and fight right now.

"I love you, Lo. Always." She holds my gaze another moment, then releases me. "Come on. I'm sure you'd love nothing more than to have a nice long soak in the tub and sleep for a month."

"That may be the understatement of the year." I turn toward the glass doors, desperate for fresh air after spending the night in a cell that reeked of body odor and urine.

Wes is quick to sidle up beside me, placing his hand on the small of my back as he steers me out of the building. It's a small gesture, one most people wouldn't think twice about. But that one gesture means the world to me. His silent assurance he's with me. He's by my side.

I lift my eyes to meet his, dark brown to his vivid blue, and give him a smile. He returns it, all the anguish, despair, and hurt he's endured the past several hours visible. I take a moment to drink in his features, a welcome sight after everything that's transpired. I find comfort in the familiarity of his proud nose, chiseled cheek bones, and the bit of scruff dotting his square jawline.

As we step outside, a chill envelopes me, goosebumps prickling my skin. I wrap my arms around my midsection to fight against the cold air.

"Here." Wes shrugs out of his wool coat and drapes it around my shoulders.

I inhale the familiar scent of wood and spice, pushing away the stench of citrus and leather I thought would be permanently ingrained into my nostrils, mocking and tormenting me. Being wrapped in Wes' warmth offers me a short reprieve, transporting me to before.

Before *he* walked into the New Year's Eve Gala.

Before I tried to take matters into my own hands.

Before history nearly repeated itself.

I wish I could live in that moment. In before. It's where I still had hope. Had love. Had a future.

Now that's all gone.

"I didn't think to grab one of your coats," he explains apologetically. "I was solely focused on getting you out of that place and back home as soon as humanly possible."

I smile, but fear I fall short. "I prefer your coat anyway."

"I prefer you in it, too." He presses a gentle kiss to my forehead, much like my mother used to whenever she sensed I needed a reminder I wasn't alone. "My car is right down the street." He holds out his hand for me.

"You don't have to drive me." I move away from him and toward Hazel.

"Lo…," he begins in a deep voice.

"You've already done more than enough," I continue, not looking directly at him. "You must have a ton of work to catch up on. I don't want to take up any more of your time when Hazel and Diego can drive me."

Wes advances, wearing an expression I can't quite explain. It's almost like a combination of pain and helplessness. "I don't care about that," he declares passionately, taking my icy hands in his, warming me from the outside in.

"I care about *you*, Londyn. Care about making sure you're okay."

I peer into his eyes, wishing I could find comfort in his devotion. But my world's been turned upside down. "I don't think I'll ever be okay again," I admit, much to my surprise.

His strong demeanor cracks at my confession, a single tear sliding down his cheek. "Then let me help you."

"I..." I shake my head, dozens of emotions warring within.

"Diego and I aren't going straight home anyway," Hazel interjects. "We have a bunch of errands to run. And since I'm sure you don't want to go to the grocery store, hardware store, home goods store, and a whole slew of other places right now, you should just let Wes drive you."

She pins me with a stare, silently telling me to cut the shit and let Wes do this for me. During self-defense class, she often berated me for telegraphing my moves before I attacked, making it easy for her to defend against me. I suppose I do that outside of the ring, too.

"Please, Lo," Wes begs.

I look at him as he extends his hand toward me once more, eyes imploring me to choose him. To give him this... Whatever *this* is.

With a subtle nod, I link my fingers with his. He gives me a small smile as he leads me away from the building and toward his car. At one point, his hand wrapped around mine felt so natural. Now everything seems almost foreign. Like Jay — *Nick* — has even tainted Wes' skin on mine.

We approach his car and he opens the passenger door, helping me into my seat as he always does. Once I'm situated, he closes my door, then rushes to get behind the wheel. As he pulls into traffic, I lean my head against the window, focusing on the sights of the city I once viewed as the place of my rebirth. Now it's all polluted.

"Do you want me to put on some music?" Wes asks, breaking through the silence.

I look at him and shake my head before peering out the window again, inching closer to the door. It's a stark contrast to how I normally sit in this car — leaning over the console to be as near to him as possible.

Picking up on my reluctance to talk, Wes doesn't utter a word the remainder of the short drive back to my condo. When he parks in my driveway, I stare at the exterior of the familiar building, everything about it different than when I last saw it. How can that be? How can one man wield so much power over me?

"Come on. Let's get you home."

I nod, unable to tell Wes this isn't my home. Home bears a connotation of safety and security. I'm not sure I'll ever feel that again.

My steps are slow as I follow him into my condo, coming to a stop when Zeus runs toward me, practically jumping on me as he showers me with kisses.

"Hey, boy." I bend down, scratching his head, finding solace in his stinky breath and rambunctious tail wagging.

"Zeus. Down, boy," Wes orders, and his dog complies with his master's command. "Hope you don't mind I brought him here. After yesterday, I needed something to cheer me up, and, well… Dogs are great for that."

"I'm glad he's here." I shrug out of his coat and hang it up in the foyer before stepping farther into my house.

Everything looks exactly as it did when I left. Then why does it feel different? Like there's a darkness hovering in the air and clinging to the walls.

"Would you like some tea? Or a whiskey? Maybe a little of both?"

I face him, but maintain my distance. "I just want to soak in the tub for the next week. I need to wash—" I stop short, unable to finish my statement. I don't need to. Wes knows what I was about to say. That I need to wash *him* from my body.

"Understood." His Adam's apple bobs up and down in a hard swallow, the pain on his face unmistakable. "You start drawing a bath. I'll bring you up some tea. Then I'll order us some sushi. Or Korean barbecue. Or pizza. Or even a combination of all three. Whatever you're hungry for, I'll make it happen."

"Thank you," I say, then turn.

"Hey, Lo?" he calls out as I'm about to head up to the second floor.

I pause, glancing over my shoulder, our gazes locking. "Yes?"

With slow steps, he walks toward me. I fully face him, my breaths coming quicker, as always seems to be the case whenever he's near. Then he wraps his arms around me. This embrace is markedly different from the way he hugged me in the jailhouse lobby. That one was more relieved, laced with desperation. This one is more comforting and affectionate.

He places a soft kiss on my forehead. "Everything's going to be okay," he murmurs.

I exhale, melting into him, breathing in his scent. How can one man be so perfect? How can one man read my mind and know exactly what I need when I don't even know myself?

This was all I wanted from my father and Sawyer when I told them the truth, yet I never got it. But Wes remembers. It's such a small thing, but it speaks volumes as to his character. That despite knowing who Nick is, he's still here. He's still with me. Just like he promised.

"Thank you."

"You for me, Lo."

I pull my head away from his chest, meeting his eyes. "Me for you."

"For the rest of our lives." He leans in, placing a delicate kiss on my lips before dropping his hold. "I'll be right up with your tea."

# CHAPTER SEVEN

## *Weston*

I watch as Londyn drags herself up the stairs and disappears into the master bedroom. And that's exactly what it feels like. Not like she's making a conscious decision to put one foot in front of the other. It's like she has to force her body to move forward and not wallow in the present. Or the past. I hate it. Hate seeing her like this. Hate not knowing what I can do to fix it.

Resisting the urge to scream in frustration, I make my way into the kitchen and grab the tea kettle, filling it with water before setting it back onto the stove and lighting a burner. I try to concentrate on the mundane task and not Londyn, but that's easier said than done.

In the six months I've known her, I've never seen her so broken, so depressed, even when she finally shared the secrets of her past.

The sparkle in her eyes is gone. Her smile, on the rare

occasion she offers it, feels contrived. She's just a lifeless shell, the soul of the woman I'd do anything for a distant memory.

I knew this wouldn't be easy. That things wouldn't go back to the way they were. But I didn't expect her to look like the life had been sucked right out of her. Like she's forcing herself to go through the motions of living until she gives up. What I wouldn't give to make Nick suffer as Londyn is now. To inflict the same pain, the same emptiness. To make him live in a perpetual state of fear that today is the day his past finally catches up to him.

All I can do is pray he'll get what he's due. That karma will eventually pay him a visit.

At the whistle of the kettle, I snap out of my increasingly angry thoughts and turn off the burner. After steeping some green tea and adding a touch of honey, the way Londyn prefers it, I head upstairs.

As I approach the open door to the master bathroom, I pause, not wanting to sneak up on her, the sound of the running bath water drowning out my footsteps. I linger in the doorway, watching as she slides off her jeans, leaving her in a cami and her panties.

Sensing my presence, she turns toward me. I inhale a sharp breath, my grasp on the mug loosening, causing it to fall to the tile floor and shatter around me.

"Londyn…," I quiver, my gaze glued to a huge red and purple area spanning her hip.

I blink, the mere idea of what could have caused that making bile rise in my throat. I scan the rest of her frame for any other bruises. My blood boils when I notice the imprint of a hand on her bicep, as well as more around her wrists that I hadn't seen earlier with her sweater on. But now that she's practically naked, they're glaring.

"It looks worse than it is," she says weakly, but doesn't look directly into my eyes. She forces her lips into a smile, then grabs a towel, bending down to clean up the tea and broken glass. I notice her wince, the movement causing her pain.

"What did he do?" My jaw tightens, nostrils flaring.

I know he attacked her. She'd told Hazel that much. But now that I see physical proof of his assault, it only increases my hatred for this man and the justice system that, instead of getting her help, locked her up. Treated her like a criminal.

The injustice infuriates me.

She straightens, her dark eyes imploring me. "Wes, please."

"What. Did. He. Do?" I demand once more, my voice strained.

"He did enough, Wes," she retorts, throwing the towel to the floor. "Okay? He did enough. That's all I'm ready to tell you right now. So I'd appreciate some space. What happened yesterday… The things he said… The things he did…" She squeezes her eyes shut and draws in a deep, steadying breath before returning her pained, empty gaze to mine. "It's the last thing I want to talk about. All I want right now is to scrub every inch of my body and forget. So please… Let me forget."

"I don't know if I can, Lo. It's killing me not to know what he—"

"If you think it's killing you not to know what he did, imagine how it must be for me to be forced to relive it." Her voice comes out strong and determined, echoing against the tile in the bathroom. "Imagine what it's like to not only have to suffer through it once, but again. And again. And again."

I part my lips, struggling to find the words to convince

her that talking about it will help her heal. But then I remember Sophia's admonition from earlier. That the best thing I can do is give her my unwavering support. So that's what I do.

"I'm sorry, Lo. I didn't think—"

"I know." She offers me a smile, almost like she's trying to comfort me when I'm the one who should be comforting her. I just don't know how. Don't know what to do or say to make this better. Will things ever get better? Or are we a ticking time bomb? "I just can't relive it right now. Okay?"

"Okay." I nod, a heaviness settling on my chest.

All my life, I've been a problem solver. That's why I've always enjoyed my line of work, particularly the technical aspect of designing buildings. Whenever faced with a problem, I could come up with a myriad of solutions.

But this?

I have no solution. No way to solve it.

"I'll get you a fresh cup of tea," I say.

"You don't have to."

"Yes, I do. I can't do anything else to make this better, and it's killing me. So let me at least make you a tea. Please?"

Her eyes glisten with tears, and she nods. "Okay."

"Okay."

After pushing the towel and broken glass into the corner for the time being, I head back down to the kitchen, trying with everything to erase Londyn's battered and bruised body from my memory. But I can't.

Jaw clenched, I grip the edge of the counter, heat rushing through me. I've never considered myself a violent man. As Gampy often reminded me, the pen is mightier than the sword. But right now, I'd give anything to finish the job Londyn started.

Spying a whiskey bottle, I grab it, pouring a healthy

portion into a rocks glass. I bring it to my lips, downing practically the entire thing in three gulps, wincing through the burn. But I need it. It takes my mind off the excruciating pain wrenching my heart. Slamming the glass onto the counter, I pour more liquor into it. I don't care that it's a little after noon on a Saturday. I need this right now.

I'm about to take another large swallow when my phone pings in the pocket of my jeans. I pull it out, expecting a text from Hazel or Diego checking in on Londyn. Instead, it's from my sister.

JULIA:

> Thought I'd let you know that Nick's surgery was successful and the hospital will be releasing him tomorrow. He'll be reevaluated once the swelling goes down to determine if he needs shoulder replacement, but for now, they're hopeful he'll heal completely. Wasn't sure if you cared, but figured I'd update you either way.

I grip my phone, my anger rising yet again. I fight the temptation to text back and tell her how nice it is that Nick's injury will heal when Londyn may never recover from what he did.

But I don't.

I click off the phone, about to shove it back into my pocket, but stop myself.

Julia's still my sister. Based on the stories Londyn told me about how conniving her professor was, I can't shake the feeling he may have manipulated Julia, too. As much as I hate the idea of her taking his side, I need to try with her. So instead of ignoring her, I unlock my phone and type out a quick reply.

ME:

Are you okay?

The message is marked delivered, then read. A text bubble pops up below my message. Several seconds pass as I await her response. Then the text bubble disappears for a bit before reappearing. This goes on for several minutes before her reply finally comes.

JULIA:

Yes.

I contemplate calling her out on the fact that she'd typed out a different response before changing her mind, but I don't want her to shut me out altogether. Just like I have to hold onto hope that Londyn will get through this, I have to hope Julia and I do, too. That Julia will realize the truth. That she won't allow her desperate need to be accepted to control her like it has most of her life.

Shoving my phone back into my pocket, I heat up the kettle again. Once it boils, I prepare a fresh cup of tea and carry it upstairs.

When I enter the bathroom this time, Londyn's in the tub, her body hidden beneath a blanket of bubbles. Her eyes are closed as she leans her head against the marble ledge, a look of serenity washing over her. Not wanting to disturb her, I gingerly set the mug on the counter and retreat, padding back down the stairs, allowing Zeus to remain at his post outside the bathroom.

Feeling like it should be after one in the morning instead of the afternoon, I collapse onto the couch, the past twenty-four hours catching up to me as exhaustion consumes me. I lay my head on the accent pillow, immediately enveloped in Londyn's familiar scent. I close my eyes, swallowing through the tightness in my throat at the mere thought of how frightened she must have been when I introduced Nick at the masquerade ball. And I did nothing to help her. Missed all the clues. And I'll have to live with that the rest of my life.

Hundreds of scenarios about what happened in that bakery fill my thoughts. Each one is more agonizing and debilitating than the previous. My anger and rage over the situation growing with every heartbeat, I jump up and storm back into the kitchen to pour yet another whiskey. Alcohol won't solve anything, but I need something to numb the pain.

After I slam back another large gulp, I take a deep breath to pull myself together, then head upstairs to check on Londyn. When I enter the bedroom, it's dark, all the lights off, a few towels discarded on the floor. Londyn's curled up on what has become her side of the bed, Zeus snuggled up with her, offering her all the comfort he did me when I first found him. Her cheeks are wet with tears, body trembling through her silent cries.

I thought staring into her vacant, lifeless eyes was the hardest thing possible. Then when I saw her bruises, I didn't think things could get much worse. But this... Watching her break down and not being able to do anything destroys me. I wish I could flip a switch that would make everything okay. Prepare a magic potion that would transfer all her pain to me. But that doesn't exist.

So I do the only thing I can to let her know I'm here for her. That I'm not going anywhere. That I support her.

Grabbing the blanket off the foot of the bed, I unfold it, draping it over her. Hesitantly, I crawl onto the mattress behind her, expecting her to ask me to leave her alone.

But she doesn't.

Finding my hand, she links her fingers with mine,

bringing my arm over her frame and squeezing tightly. I mold my body to hers, burying my head in her hair, relishing in the feel of her.

"I'd take away your pain if I could."

"I know."

# CHAPTER EIGHT

## *Londyn*

"**A**re you sure you don't want me to go with you today?" Wes asks Monday morning when he walks into my kitchen after showering.

Since New Year's Eve, I haven't stepped foot inside his house. I used to spend most of my free time there. But that was before.

Now, I need the security of my condo. A place that's never held any trace of *him*. Luckily, Wes didn't question my reluctance. Instead, he brought a few things over to my place, including Zeus, which I'm grateful for. While I've always loved animals, I never understood how people considered them a form of therapy. Until now.

Whenever I was on the verge of a breakdown these past few days, memories of the attack threatening to drown me, Zeus seemed to sense it, nuzzling me and providing the comfort I needed.

"You've already done so much," I respond with a smile.

"And I've heard your phone ringing off the hook with what I can only assume are work calls. You can't put your life on hold for me."

"But I would, Lo." He narrows his gaze on me, voice laced with sincerity. "You know that."

"I just want life to get back to normal. Or as normal as possible, all things considered. And that means getting back to work."

"Okay," he says with a long exhale. "If that's what you want."

"It is."

It doesn't make sense for me to ask him to give up another day of work so he can sit in the waiting area of Sophia's law firm while a detective interviews me. He needs to go on with his life. Just like I need to go on with mine, even though my life bears little resemblance to what it was mere days ago.

"Then I suppose I should get going." He leans down, brushing a soft kiss on my temple. When he pulls back, his eyes meet mine. "Want me to pick up dinner on the way home? Or I can cook something."

"Actually, I might hit up the grocery store and get some things. Cooking might be a nice distraction for me."

"If you're sure."

"I am."

"Okay." He turns from me and whistles for Zeus to follow, which he obediently does. As he's about to open the door, he stops, facing me once more. "I almost forgot."

"What?"

"This." He reaches into the inside pocket of his coat, revealing a slim box.

"Wes," I sigh, "I don't—"

"Please, Londyn…" He may be giving me a gift, but I

can't shake the feeling this is more for him than me. His way of feeling like he's doing something. "Let me do this for you."

"Okay." With a slight smile that offers the barest hint of assurance, I take the proffered box.

When I open the lid, I squeeze my eyes shut. He never ceases to amaze me with his ability to know exactly what I need.

"Wes…," I half-breathe, half-choke out, returning my gaze to the contents. A delicate chain made to look like snakes ends in a glittering pendant with Medusa's face, her bold and powerful eyes prepared to turn everyone who crosses her to stone.

"I went back and forth over this. Wasn't sure if you'd want it. If you'd be able to stomach wearing what some might say could be a reminder."

He extends his hand toward me, silently asking permission. Without saying a word, I hand it to him, nodding. He carefully detaches the stunning piece, setting the box on the counter, then steps behind me. When he brushes my curls to the side, a shiver rolls through me, as innate and uncontrolled as my heart beating or my lungs drawing in oxygen. A response my body is pre-programmed to have whenever he's near.

He leans closer, the heat of his breath on my skin causing my pulse to increase. I swallow hard, a dozen sensations fighting for attention within me. Sensations I didn't think I'd experience again. Sensations I thought I'd shut off as I simply drifted, unfeeling, through the motions of life.

Apparently, Wes possesses the key to the "on" switch.

When he finishes and steps in front of me, I glance down at the medallion sitting just above my cleavage, Medusa's eyes two glittering emeralds, diamonds sparkling on the pendant and snake-like chain.

"It's breathtaking, Wes." I meet his affectionate gaze. "And perfect."

He takes my left hand in his, brushing his thumb along my knuckles, paying particular attention to my ring finger. Then he shifts his eyes toward mine again.

"I know this is difficult. That you probably feel like you're being torn in a thousand different directions. I can't stand here and pretend to have the faintest idea of what you're going through. And I can't even begin to understand how difficult what you're about to do will be.

"When you told me what happened all those years ago, I'd never been so angry before in my life. Not just at *him*, but at the system that failed you. That treated you like the predator instead of the victim. And that's why I wanted to give you this necklace. Why I felt in my soul you should wear it. Despite everything Medusa went through, she was a fighter. Even after her death, her powers remained. Some would argue they were even more potent."

His Adam's apple bobs up and down, chin wavering as his voice becomes choked with emotion.

"So it's my hope that this necklace helps you draw the strength Medusa possessed. Helps keep your demons at bay. Helps serve as a reminder of just how fucking amazing you are. Today, and every other day you feel lost."

Overwhelmed by his gesture and reassurances, I clutch his cheeks in a fierce grip, pulling his lips toward mine.

Since I was released on Saturday, Wes has been hesitant around me. The most intimate thing he's done has been kissing my forehead or a slight peck on my lips. But I need more. Need to drown myself in him.

"Kiss me," I beg.

A flicker of uncertainty crosses his expression, seemingly torn between giving me what I need and not doing anything that might upset me. But his undeniable craving for me wins out.

With nothing short of raw desire, he loops an arm around my waist and yanks me close. His breath warms my lips, anticipation coiling inside me as I wait for my first taste of him in days. The seconds stretch as the space between us slowly evaporates, my heart hammering in my chest.

When his mouth finally lands on mine, I sigh. It's a light connection at first, like our first kiss all those months ago, both of us testing the waters. And just like that first touching of our lips, sparks shoot through me, hunger blooming from my core and spreading through me like a wildfire.

Arching into him, I swipe my tongue along his bottom lip, eliciting a groan from him.

"God, honeybee. I needed this."

He presses his lips more firmly against mine, opening his mouth, our tongues tangling in a soulful dance as he kisses me with desperation. With admiration. With veneration. In his kiss, he communicates everything words alone cannot. That words will never be able to convey.

Over the course of the weekend...hell, our relationship, he's repeatedly told me he's with me. That he'll stand by my side through it all. But as I bask in the way he reveres me, the way he gives me every last part of him, I physically *feel* the meaning behind his repeated assurances.

I breathe into him as I give him all my anguish, pain, frustration. And he offers me his strength, courage, and fortitude, bringing me back to life after days of wondering if any of it is worth it. In this moment, I know it is. Know that Wes is worth fighting for. His kiss is the reminder I need that things *are* different this time around. That I have people who believe me on my side.

I needed a few days to fully process everything. Now that

I have, I'm ready to fight again. Like Hazel reminded me... Broken girls turn into warriors. I'm ready to pick up my sword and slay my dragon.

Wes' desperation slows as he reluctantly pulls his lips from mine, peering down at me with a hint of a smile.

"I love you, honeybee. Me for you."

"You for me," I answer. "For the rest of our lives."

He nods. "No matter what."

# CHAPTER NINE

*Londyn*

"How are you holding up?" Sophia asks, wrapping her arms around me the second she walks into the waiting room of her posh office in downtown Atlanta located mere blocks away from my old office building. I even drove past the intersection where, on a fateful day back in June, I met the man who would change my life as I know it.

"Better than I thought I'd be," I tell her.

She pulls back, meeting my eyes, keeping her hands on my biceps. "That's wonderful to hear." She drops her hold, gesturing toward the hallway. "Let's go talk for a few minutes while we wait for Detective Trager. She's from the Special Victims Unit of the Major Crimes Division. They were going to send the detective they'd originally assigned to the case, but I insisted on someone from Special Victims due to the nature of the incident."

"That's good, right?" I ask as I follow her.

"Yes. These detectives have gone through extensive training on how to work with victims of sexual assault."

I briefly close my eyes, relief filling me that this won't be like it was all those years ago. I subconsciously bring my hand up to my necklace, running my fingers over the pendant. Like the real Medusa, it seems to possess some sort of mystical power I can't explain, making me more confident and assured than I thought possible after everything.

"That's beautiful," Sophia remarks as she gestures to a chair at a large conference table in her corner office, downtown Atlanta buzzing a dozen stories below us. She arches a perfectly manicured brow. "Wes?"

"Yes." I drop my hold on it, removing my coat and settling into my chair.

"He's a good man."

Sophia sits beside me, writing the date and my name on a fresh page of a yellow legal pad. "Now, we've already gone over some of this when we spoke on the phone yesterday, but I want to reiterate to just tell your story. Everything you say today will be a part of the investigative report. If at any point I don't like the questioning, I'll say so. I'm here to watch out for your rights. But it's my hope that, by being forthcoming and honest, they'll realize you were well within your rights to do what you did and the DA will decline to pursue charges. Okay?"

I draw in a deep breath. "Okay."

"Good."

There's a knock, and we look toward the door, a blonde in a sleek pencil skirt and pressed blouse opening it.

"Sophia, Detective Trager and Detective Stocker are here for your ten o'clock."

She stands, brows furrowed as a petite woman with

brown hair and a large man with a shaved head walk into the room.

"Detectives. I was under the impression we would only be meeting with Detective Trager due to the sensitive nature of the case."

The woman parts her lips to respond, but the male detective interjects. "Which is why Detective Trager is here. But the captain requested I also attend to make sure we dot all our i's and cross all our t's. As you know, this has become a high-profile case. Not only with the media initially thinking it was another mass shooting, but also since the victim married into the Bradford family. There's a lot of pressure from above my pay grade to ensure no mistakes are made."

I look at Sophia, my stomach churning at the idea of having to tell him all my secrets. It doesn't help that he bears a striking resemblance to the officer who took my statement all those years ago when I first tried to turn Nick in. I fear history will repeat itself. That this detective will also discount my story and find me at fault.

"Of course, we can easily do this down at the station instead."

I bring my hand back up to my necklace, rubbing the outline of Medusa's snakes and glittering eyes, willing her to work her magic and turn him to stone.

"Here is fine," Sophia says with authority, gesturing to a few chairs across the table for them to sit. "This is my client, Londyn Bennett."

The woman smiles warmly at me, extending her hand. "Detective Anabelle Trager."

"Nice to meet you," I say as we shake.

Once she releases my hand, I look at the other detective, who barely acknowledges me with anything more than a curt nod. Instead, he opens a file, his eyes scanning what I recognize as a police report.

"Now, your lawyer has advised you regarding your rights, correct?" he asks, uncapping a pen. "That everything you say here today will be part of the record and can be used during court proceedings?"

"Yes."

He finally looks at me. "And you're willing to voluntarily answer questions regarding the events that occurred at The Mad Batter bakery in Buckhead on January first of this year. Is that correct?"

"Yes," I repeat, trying to subdue the nervous fluttering in my stomach.

"As I mentioned to Detective Trager yesterday," Sophia begins, "my client would also like to make a statement in support of a sexual assault charge against Mr. Domenic Jaskulski."

Detective Stocker peruses the police report. "The victim?"

"In a matter of speaking, I suppose."

He pauses for a moment, then leans back in his chair. "We'll see if the facts warrant it. Let's start with how you know the victim."

Sophia opens her mouth, but Detective Stocker cuts her off before she can utter a single syllable.

"I understand your client's version of events may not paint him as the victim," he states in a patronizing voice that makes my skin crawl. It reminds me of the way Nick spoke to me. "But according to the police report, Mr. Jaskulski was the one who was wheeled out of his wife's bakery on a stretcher with a gunshot wound to the shoulder. So right now, he *is* the victim."

He floats his stare toward me. "I'll ask again. How do

you know the victim?"

I steal a glance at Sophia, noticing her jaw tightening, her lips forming a thin line as if biting back a snarky reply. She meets my gaze, giving me an encouraging nod.

"He's married to my boyfriend's sister."

He's about to write this down, then stops, lifting his eyes to mine. "Mr. Jaskulski is married to Julia Prescott. Her brother is—"

"Weston Bradford," Sophia interjects.

Detective Stocker draws in a long breath, looking from Sophia to me, then jots down Wes' name. I'm not sure if he's surprised Wes would date someone like me or if there's a different reason for his reaction to this information.

"So Mr. Jaskulski is your boyfriend's brother-in-law."

"Yes, but I didn't know that until a few days ago. I knew him in a different capacity."

"How?"

"He was an English professor at my undergrad university in Upstate New York."

"Was he your professor?"

"No. When we first met, I didn't even realize he was a professor at my college."

"And when was this?"

"I graduated six years ago this coming May, and we met my senior year."

"How did you meet?"

"At a coffee shop a few blocks from campus."

"How would you describe your relationship with him if he wasn't your professor?"

I worry my bottom lip, fingering my Medusa pendant, drawing in her strength to talk about my relationship with Nick. "We started as two people who happened to frequent the same coffee shop. But at some point, we crossed the line to something else."

"Something other than friends?" Detective Stocker asks, a single brow arched.

I swallow hard. "Yes."

He scratches something down on his pad, then returns his hardened stare to me. What I wouldn't give for Detective Trager to ask these questions instead. "And was he married when you became something other than friends?"

I look down, fidgeting with my hands, the same guilt that plagued me in the months following his assault returning with a vengeance. I should have put a stop to things between us the first time Nick tested the waters into more dangerous territory. When he'd asked me if I'd ever had an orgasm after I'd mentioned I didn't feel like I was married due to the lack of intimacy in my marriage. His question had caught me off guard, a voice in my head screaming at me to retreat, to make up some excuse about needing to get to class.

But the way he looked at me was thrilling, unlike the way anyone had ever peered at me before. Even Sawyer. He only looked at me like a means to an end. And that was how I felt. Like a piece of property he bartered for. Not someone he promised to love and cherish, as his vows stated.

So instead of nipping the conversation in the bud, I humored him, a need to feel wanted and desired by someone burning inside me.

Biggest mistake of my life.

"It's okay," Detective Trager encourages in a gentle tone. "We're all human. We all make mistakes. It's imperative we understand the precise nature of your relationship with Mr. Jaskulski."

"Yes," I answer firmly. "I knew he was married."

"And despite knowing he was already married, you slept

with him?" Detective Stocker counters, his question seeming more like an accusation.

"Bryant, I—" Detective Trager interjects.

"My client never said she slept with him," Sophia argues at the same time, preventing me from answering. "I'd appreciate it if you didn't put words into her mouth."

"Let me rephrase," Detective Stocker says without apology. "Were you romantically involved?"

I pinch my lips together, ruminating over a response. Our relationship is difficult to explain and probably even more difficult for someone to understand. But was it romantic? Maybe I thought so at the time. Now I see it for what it was. Insincere. Manipulative. Deceitful.

"No. We were both married."

Detective Stocker looks up from his notes. "You were married, as well?"

"Yes."

"And did your husband attend the same university?"

"No. He was a pastor of a church in Virginia, so he stayed there while I completed my education."

"I see." After making a few more notes, he sets down the pen, leaning back in his chair. "Would it be accurate to say you formed a…close relationship with Mr. Jaskulski during your time at school?"

I look at Sophia for guidance, who nods.

"Yes," I answer firmly.

"But you didn't have an affair."

"No."

"Were you ever intimate with him?"

"Not willingly."

He stares at me for several moments, an expression that's a combination of arrogance and disbelief on his face.

"Did Mr. Jaskulski rape you at college?" Detective Trager asks sympathetically.

"He did."

"Do you have a copy of the police report of the incident?"

"There isn't one," I reply, running my clammy hands over my jeans.

"*Did* you go to the police?" Detective Stocker snips, his tone heavy with skepticism, at complete odds with the kind nature of Detective Trager's questions. It's like a perverse version of good cop-bad cop, one I sense is completely unintentional. Detective Stocker isn't a bad cop. He's just an asshole.

"I did," I answer, trying not to sound too defensive, as Sophia had instructed yesterday.

"So you went to the police about this rape, yet they didn't find your story believable enough to so much as file a report?"

Sophia's on her feet immediately, hands pressed against the table as she leans forward, eyes narrowed on the detective. "Detective Stocker, my client and I would appreciate it if you didn't pass judgment over an incident that happened almost six years ago. If my client claims she was raped, she was raped. As Detective Trager can attest to, thanks to her extensive training, this kind of treatment is the precise reason many women *don't* report sexual abuse.

"My client has shown incredible strength in not only answering your questions today, but also when she first tried to seek justice. Her story was ignored, like so many other women's stories are. Instead of promising to investigate the matter, the officer asked what she was wearing. How much she had to drink. If she'd done anything to make him think she'd wanted to have sex with him.

"How would you feel if your daughter were sitting in this chair? Would you ask her these same questions? Or would you promise to do everything in your power to seek justice?"

The detective opens his mouth to respond, but before he can, Detective Trager places her hand on his arm, stopping him.

"My colleague and I apologize." She gives me an encouraging smile. "I assure you. We're not here to pass judgment." Her eyes float back to Detective Stocker's, her voice almost like a warning. "Just to get to the truth."

"Thank you." Sophia retakes her seat, exuding nothing but confidence.

"Why don't we move to the present," Detective Trager suggests. "I think we've established how Ms. Bennett and Mr. Jaskulski know each other."

"I agree," Sophia states.

"How did—" Detective Stocker begins, but Detective Trager interrupts, much to my relief.

"When did you realize Mr. Jaskulski's connection to your boyfriend?"

"New Year's Eve."

"And how long have you been dating Mr. Bradford?" she asks.

"Technically only since October, but I've known him since June."

"In what capacity were you acquainted with Mr. Bradford before you started dating?"

"He was a client. I'm an interior designer. But as we spent time together, we became closer."

"And in the past seven months, you didn't realize who his brother-in-law was?" Detective Stocker cuts in. "Didn't you hear him mention his name? If I heard someone I'd been dating refer to their brother-in-law and the name was the same as someone who'd assaulted me, I'd certainly question it."

I shrug. "I had no reason to. He goes by Nick, not Domenic. I figured it was short for Nicholas. And since Wes' sister's last name is Prescott, not Bradford, I assumed it was her married name. Instead, Julia insisted on keeping her birth mother's last name, since she's adopted."

"Prior to this, did Mr. Bradford know of your history with his brother-in-law?"

"Not that it was him, but I told him of the assault."

"And he didn't think to mention his brother-in-law's name was the same as that of your abuser?"

"He didn't know, either."

"You never told him his name?" Detective Trager presses, brows furrowed.

"Around campus, he went by Professor J. Or Jay to his friends. So I knew him as Jay. Trust me. I would have much preferred to learn this piece of information instead of looking up at the gala and being blindsided."

"And this gala was this past New Year's Eve?" Detective Stocker inquires.

"Yes."

"Did you share this information with Mr. Bradford?" Detective Trager asks.

"No."

"Why not?" Detective Stocker presses.

"I felt like Julia deserved to know the truth first. After all, she's married to him."

"A reasonable explanation." Detective Trager shoots Detective Stocker a look of reproach before turning her attention back to me. "What led you to The Mad Batter Friday afternoon?"

"Julia mentioned she planned to head in for a few hours

to get some paperwork done. I thought it would be a good opportunity to talk to her about her husband. Nick had said something the previous night that made me wonder if he'd assaulted her, too, so I wanted to ask her. Or, at the very least, warn her, I guess." I chew on my bottom lip. "To be honest, I'm not quite sure *what* I was thinking at the time. Just that I needed to do something."

"What happened when you arrived?" she asks.

"Julia wasn't there." I swallow hard, my mouth suddenly dry. I reach for the water bottle in front of me, my hands shaking slightly.

"How did you get inside?" Detective Stocker presses. "According to the police report, the bakery was closed."

"It was," I respond after taking a long swallow of water. "The rear service door was unlocked. I knocked, but there was no answer. Since I noticed her car parked out back, I knew she had to be there, so I walked inside, calling her name. Instead, Jay... *Nick* was there."

"What happened next?"

I take a moment, doing my best to unscramble my thoughts. Everything seemed to happen so fast, it felt like a dream.

Or a nightmare.

"He figured out I was there to tell Julia the truth."

"And how did he respond?"

"He claimed he'd already told her. Or at least told her he'd slept with a former student at his college. Which, in his convoluted brain, is probably what he honestly believes. He tried to convince me he didn't do anything I didn't want, even if I refused to admit it to myself. I told him he was delusional to think I actually wanted him to assault me like he did."

"What was his reaction?" Detective Trager asks, fully

engaged in the conversation, whereas Detective Stocker simply seems to write down anything that can paint me in a negative light.

"He pressed his body against mine, pinning me to the wall." I squeeze my eyes shut, bile rising in my throat. When a hand grasps my forearm, I jump, gaze flinging wide.

"I'm sorry," Sophia offers quickly, scanning my face to make sure I'm okay.

I look from her to the detectives — one peering at me with distrust, the other with compassion. I'd give anything to stop all of this right now. But I didn't come this far just to retreat. I need to see this through. Need Nick to finally be held responsible for what he's done.

"He threatened to silence me if I dared tell anyone what really happened. So, at my first opportunity, I ducked out of his grasp. I made it a few feet before he tackled me to the floor. I tried to fight him, to defend myself, but he had me trapped on my stomach, my wrists bound in one of his hands over my head. With the other, he…"

I squeeze my eyes shut, the scene flashing before me, torturing and tormenting me when I'd love nothing more than to forget everything. To erase it from my memory.

"It's okay," Detective Trager assures me.

I glance at Detective Stocker, who looks uncomfortable. Imagine how it must feel to have to tell it. I doubt he has the ability to sympathize, though.

I draw in a calming breath and return my gaze to Detective Trager. "I was wearing a dress, and he…" I push down the nausea from the memory of Nick's hand traveling up my thigh. I uncross and recross my legs, feeling the ghost of his touch on my skin, making the hair on my neck stand on end. "He touched me."

"Where?" Detective Stocker asks.

"Between my legs. He pushed my underwear to the side and…" I pause, taking a moment to get my emotions under control. "He fondled me. When his grip on my wrists weakened momentarily, I took the opportunity and elbowed him in the nose. Then I scrambled for my purse."

"Your purse?" Detective Stocker frowns. "Why didn't you just hightail it out of there? The last thing I'd do if my life was in danger, as you make it seem, is grab my purse."

"To make it to the exit, I'd have to get past Nick. My purse was close, and my gun was in it."

"So you made the decision to go for the gun instead of trying to get away from the man who'd assaulted you years ago and threatened to do so again?" he presses, skeptical.

"Again, Detective Stocker," Sophia begins, a trite smile on her face, "I'd request you not jump to judgment. My client isn't a trained law enforcement officer able to make quick decisions when her life is threatened. She did what she thought was best."

"So arming yourself was the best course of action?"

"At that moment, yes," I answer before Sophia can.

"Do you always carry a gun?" he asks.

"Yes. Or I did, before I was ordered to surrender them. I have a Georgia Weapons Carry License."

"And why do you need to carry a gun?"

"I didn't realize someone had to have a reason," Sophia remarks. "Last I checked, this state doesn't seem to care the reason for carrying a gun, just that those who want to do so go through the appropriate training. My client was well within her rights to keep a weapon in her purse."

He pins Sophia with a pompous glare, obviously not appreciating the way she spoke to him as if he were a child, something I imagine she did intentionally.

"So you decide to go for the gun," Detective Trager interjects. "Then what?"

I place my hands in my lap, reliving the most frightening moments of my life. In retrospect, it was probably only a matter of seconds between the instant I felt the cool metal of the gun against my hand to the shot ringing out in the air. But the struggle had felt like it lasted hours.

"Once I pulled the gun out of my purse, Nick knocked it out of my grasp. I went after it."

"Instead of using the opportunity to escape?" Detective Stocker brings up yet again.

"I—"

Sophia raises her hand. "We're done answering that question, Detective," she admonishes before shifting her gaze to mine, silently telling me to continue.

"We both went for the gun," I correct. "After that, it all happened so quickly."

"Just tell us what you remember," Detective Trager encourages.

"It's just snapshots, really. Like a time-lapse. I remember going for the gun, but Nick tackled me back to the floor. When I saw the gun nearly within my reach, I did everything I could to grasp it, but he had the same idea. The second I grabbed the gun, he did, too. I refused to release my hold on the handle. In the melee, I somehow managed to roll over onto my back.

"As we struggled for control, I used all the strength I had to point it away from me."

My throat tightens as I'm transported back to those few awful seconds, how close I was to joining my mother. A few tears escape my eyes, and I swipe them away, but the more I talk, the more tears fall.

"I never intended to shoot him. I just wanted to get away.

To be free of this person who's hung over my life like a shadow the past several years." My lower lip trembles, and I bite it, attempting to reel in my emotions, an impossible task. "I didn't even know where the gun was aimed when the shot rang out. Until Nick collapsed on top of me."

"As you can see, it's clear my client acted in self-defense," Sophia begins very matter-of-factly, but Detective Stocker holds up his hand, cutting her off.

"Save your arguments for the judge, Counselor. My only job is to ascertain the facts."

"I'm fully aware of what your job entails, Detective. And because you're under a duty and obligation to investigate criminal accusations, I'd suggest investigating Mr. Jaskulski's crimes."

"Your client admitted the assault happened in New York. That's out of my jurisdiction."

"She also made a statement that he assaulted her here in Atlanta. Last I checked, that's well within your jurisdiction."

"I'm not so sure I'd categorize his actions as assault."

Detective Trager opens her mouth to speak, but Sophia beats her to the punch. "No? How would you feel if someone had you restrained on the floor and slid their hand between your legs? Does that not qualify? Correct me if I'm wrong, which I'm not, but penetration isn't necessary for a sexual battery charge. According to the Georgia statute, sexual battery occurs when the offender intentionally makes phys- ical contact with the intimate body parts of another without consent. My client's statement supports the charge. Not to mention, I noticed the photographs taken of the bruises on her hip, arms, and wrists when she was booked are attached to that police report you have there. Those most certainly corroborate her story."

"I don't—"

"Of course we'll investigate," Detective Trager interrupts, which elicits a scowl from Detective Stocker, obviously incensed that she'd dare question his authority. "The Atlanta Police Department wants the people of the city to feel confident that all accusations of criminal behavior will be investigated. Particularly accusations of sexual assault."

"That's all my client asks. That the police department takes her accusations just as seriously as they do other crimes. Just as seriously as they're taking the aggravated assault charges against her."

"Of course." Detective Trager smiles once more.

"Thank you. If you have any further questions, we'll arrange another time to get together. My client's already been through more than enough these past few days."

Detective Stocker opens his mouth but is interrupted again by Detective Trager. "I can understand how mentally exhausted you must be." She stands, extending her hand across the table. "Thank you for your time."

"Of course." Sophia rises and shakes her hand.

I do my best to appear calm and composed as Detective Stocker pushes out of his chair, pinning me with an annoyed glare before walking out of the office.

The second I'm alone with Sophia, I sink into my chair, exhaling my held breath.

"You did great, despite everything." She grasps my hand and squeezes. "I'm so sorry Detective Stocker was here."

"It's okay," I assure her with a small smile. "I've dealt with people like that my entire life. Pretty sure most women have."

"You're right about that," Sophia mutters just as a knock cuts through, followed by the door cracking open, Detective Trager sticking her head back in.

"Attorney Mercer?"

"Detective Trager." She waves her in. "Did you need something?"

She steps inside, closing the door behind her. "I want to apologize for Detective Stocker's behavior."

"I will admit, I was rather surprised to see him here."

"Captain's orders. Once he learned about Mr. Jaskulski's connection to the Bradfords, he insisted. I think it was to nip any possible accusations against him in the bud."

"Why would he want that?" I ask, dread settling in my stomach.

"Because the Bradfords have a lot of pull in this city and tend to dangle political donations like candy in front of a toddler. At least Lydia Bradford does. I just didn't want you to think your story fell on deaf ears. I heard you. And I'm going to do everything I can to make sure I'm not the only one."

# CHAPTER TEN

## *Weston*

I tap my fingers against the cool wood of my desk, staring out the floor-to-ceiling windows in my office overlooking downtown Atlanta and Centennial Park. It's been over three hours since I walked away from Londyn. Each minute I don't hear from her only causes my mind to run rampant with every scenario possible. I just pray her interview went well. That they listened. That they believe her.

"Mr. Bradford, did you hear me?" my assistant's voice cuts through, snapping me back to the present.

I look away from the window, meeting Mia's kind, green eyes as she stands in the doorway. "I'm sorry. What was that?"

"It's your mother."

I roll my eyes. Mia's more than aware of my preferences regarding my mother's phone calls. "Tell her I'm in a meeting."

"She's not here. Or on the phone. She…" She trails off, chewing on her lower lip as she rocks on her heels.

I straighten, squaring my shoulders. "What is it?"

"She's… She's at a press conference. It's live right now."

My heart drops into the pit of my stomach. Sure, there could be any number of reasons my mother would be at a press conference, usually something to do with one of her so-called charity projects that in reality are solely for media attention. But I can't shake the feeling in my gut today's is different.

Turning toward to my computer, I type in a quick search. I click on the first link and am taken to a live webcast of a press conference, the exterior of police headquarters prominent in the background.

"Shit," I mutter.

"I'll give you some privacy," Mia says, about to excuse herself as a tall, graying man in a suit walks up to the podium.

"Stay. You need to see this. If it's about what I think it is, you need to be informed."

Mia nods, stepping up behind me. "Yes, sir."

I return my attention to the screen, raising the volume as the man begins to speak.

"Thank you for being here. My name is Zachary Matthews. I'm a captain with the Major Crimes Unit. As you may or may not be aware, there was a shooting in the Buckhead Village District on New Year's Day. A single gunshot was fired at approximately 3:12 on Friday afternoon, causing panic to spread through the district, many stores putting their lockdown procedures into effect. After a canvass of the area, the police were able to pinpoint the location to The Mad Batter, a bakery owned by Julia Prescott."

The camera zooms in on Julia standing off to the side, an

expression on her face I haven't seen in years. It reminds me of the one she wore during her first society tea or party. Like a deer in the headlights. Like someone desperate to scream out and beg for help but has somehow lost her ability to do so. Like she's shut down and is simply going through the motions, doing what's expected of her.

A caged bird once more.

"On the afternoon of January first, Ms. Prescott's husband, Domenic Jaskulski, was in the kitchen of The Mad Batter collecting paperwork for his wife when a woman entered. After a brief altercation, the woman fired a gun she'd concealed, hitting Mr. Jaskulski in the shoulder."

The camera moves to Nick sitting in a wheelchair, a sling wrapped around his arm, pained expression on his face. My mother stands beside him, forced tears sliding down her cheeks. I have to hand it to her. She puts on a damn good show. And that's precisely what this is. A show.

"Mrs. Lydia Bradford, the victim's mother-in-law, has prepared a statement on behalf of the family during these trying times, so I yield the floor to her before opening up for questions."

The captain steps away as my mother walks toward the microphone. With her hands on either side of the podium, she squeezes her eyes shut, drawing in a shaky breath as she feigns trying to summon strength.

"First, I want to thank the incredible medical staff who worked tirelessly on my son-in-law so that he can still be here with us today. If it weren't for them, I don't want to think about what would have happened." She chokes out a sob that's a fake as her nose. As much as I want to storm down to the police station to set the record straight, I need to be here. Need to watch this. Need to know what she's doing. "The woman responsible for nearly taking my son-in-law's life,

Londyn Bennett, is loosely connected to the family. For the past several months, she's been dating my son, Weston." She shakes her head sadly. "I tried to warn him about her."

"Warn me?" I seethe through my clenched jaw, rage bubbling inside me with every word my mother says, every lie that falls so easily from her lips. "About what? That she's black?"

Mia places a reassuring hand on my shoulder, trying to calm me. I don't think anything can calm me now. Not when my mother is defaming my girlfriend for the world to see.

"Call it mother's intuition," my mother continues with a slight laugh. "Sometimes you just get a feeling that something's not quite right. And from the moment I met Londyn Bennett, I knew something about her seemed off. I didn't want to be right. After all, my only hope is that my son finds the happiness he deserves."

"Yeah. As long as it's with someone who has the right pedigree," I scoff.

"Unfortunately, my son couldn't see what I did. That Londyn Bennett was only after his money."

I stare at the screen, trying to figure out what game she's playing.

"Publicity stunt," Mia mumbles, as if able to read my mind.

While she may merely be my assistant, she probably knows more about the Bradford family than anyone else. I suppose it's part of her job. And part of that job is knowing exactly who my mother is. About her desperate need to constantly be in the public eye, just to remind everyone in Southern society that she's still relevant. That she still has a certain level of importance and power in the caste system she's created with herself at the top.

"Mrs. Bradford," a reporter calls out from the assembled

masses, interrupting her. "I truly am sorry for your family's struggles and pray for your son-in-law's speedy recovery."

"Thank you."

"I was hoping you could clarify something for me, though. Why would Ms. Bennett shoot Mr. Jaskulski?"

The captain jumps in front of the microphone. "All questions should be held until Mrs. Bradford has finished with her statement. At that point, I'll be happy to share what I can about the case."

"That's quite all right." My mother smiles politely at the captain before returning her attention to the reporter. "I'm more than happy to answer. And the answer is I don't know. You'd probably be better off directing that line of inquiry to Ms. Bennett herself." She shifts her gaze to the rest of the reporters. "Now, as I was saying—"

"It's my understanding Ms. Bennett *did* make a statement to that effect." The reporter looks down at the phone in her hand. "According to my source, Mr. Jaskulski was a professor at the university Ms. Bennett attended and sexually assaulted her approximately five-and-a-half years ago. Would either you or Mr. Jaskulski care to comment on this allegation?"

Captain Matthews jumps in front of the microphone once more. "Like I said…" The slight waver to his voice gives the impression that the inquiry caught him off guard. "All questions should be held until the end. I—"

"No," my mother snips authoritatively, stepping in front of the captain, almost pushing him aside. "I'm happy to comment on this baseless accusation. That is the problem with this whole 'Me Too' movement," she says, using air quotes, her nose turned up in disgust. "All you have to do is cry rape and people drop everything. But you've all heard the story of the little boy who cried wolf. You cry wolf enough times with no evidence to back it up, eventually people will stop believing. And that's the case with any supposed rape of Ms. Bennett. It's just her crying wolf. Her way of trying to justify her otherwise illegal action of shooting my son-in-law. She nearly took away my granddaughter's father," she chokes out.

Truthfully, she deserves an award for this performance. If I didn't know any better, I might believe her emotions are real. But she's using this to garner sympathy as the doting mother-in-law when, in reality, she never cared much for Nick. Can't say I blame her. Not now anyway.

"If her aim was just a few inches lower, he wouldn't be with us. My daughter would have to bury her husband. My granddaughter..." She dabs at her eyes. "Well, I don't even want to consider the idea of my granddaughter growing up without a father. This is a tragedy, something I don't wish on my worst enemy. But our family is extremely resilient, especially in the face of adversity. We'll bounce back from this stronger than ever. For now, we ask you keep Julia, Imogene, Domenic, and even Weston in your thoughts and prayers during this very trying time."

The picture of poise and sophistication, she steps back from the podium, allowing the captain to answer the myriad of questions the press now fires at him. But I can't listen anymore.

I bang on the keyboard, closing out of the webcast, my jaw ticking as I glower at the blank screen with animosity, as if it had something to do with my mother's vindictive actions.

"Should I prepare a statement?" Mia asks after several silent moments.

I shake my head, feeling like the rug's been pulled out from beneath me. I should have expected something like this, considering who my family is. I didn't realize it growing up, but as I got older, I learned the Bradford name was as powerful in the South as the last name Carnegie once was in steel country. I should be happy reporters didn't swarm the jailhouse Saturday morning. Thankfully, the holiday worked to our advantage.

Not anymore.

I'm about to respond to Mia when my cell rings on my desk. I glance at it, assuming it's Londyn. Instead, I see my father's name flash on the screen. It certainly didn't escape my notice that he was nowhere to be found during my mother's press conference. But it didn't surprise me. He normally keeps as much space between them as possible, unless absolutely necessary.

"I'll give you some privacy," Mia offers, then slips out of my office, closing the door behind her.

"Dad," I answer, a touch of hesitation in my tone.

"I assume you've seen." His voice is deep and slightly gravelly, yet exhibits the same smooth, Southern accent I have.

"She couldn't keep her mouth shut about this? Did she really have to paint Londyn in such a horrible light?"

"That's your mother for you. She's always been a big fan of the Danish Gambit in chess. This is just her striking first and striking hard. Not against you, Wes, but against the media circus that was sure to follow once word about the parties involved became public."

I blow out a laugh. "Danish Gambit, huh? So... What? I'm just supposed to accept it and watch as she declares checkmate in a matter of only a few moves?"

"I didn't say that," he replies slyly. "I taught you how to play chess, son. What's the one thing I told you about opening with the Danish Gambit?"

I sigh, pinching the bridge of my nose, not seeing how

this is relevant to my current predicament. Still, I humor him. "You either win spectacularly or fail miserably."

"Precisely. And if you ask me, your mother is set up to fail miserably."

"How? By telling everyone who will listen that my girl-friend is lying? That she's crying wolf, as she put it?"

He chuckles to himself. "Just like your mother, you often focus on the negative and forget the positive."

"And what's that, Dad? What could have possibly come out of that ridiculous publicity stunt that would be considered positive?"

"Didn't you hear that reporter? She knows Londyn's side, something I can tell you Captain Matthews definitely wanted to keep from the media."

I straighten, peering into the distance. "How do you know that?"

"I may have overheard a conversation between him and your mother. And based on that conversation, I may have reached out to some of my contacts in the media."

"*You* were the source?"

"Would you be surprised?"

I stand, walking to the windows of my office. "Actually, no. But if you were just going to leak information to the media, why put up with Mom's press conference in the first place? Why didn't you just stop it from happening?"

"You and I both know nothing could have stopped her from doing something like this eventually, Wes. She craves being the center of attention. It's just who she is. I figured it best to let her put on the show she desperately needed, but also throw her a curveball. That's what the leak was. A curveball. One she failed to hit. Her bashing the 'Me Too' movement?" There's a hint of amusement in his tone. "Trust me, son. That will backfire. Your mother thinks she holds a great deal of influence over powerful people here in the great state of Georgia, but that movement will eat her up and spit her out. And I hope to have a front-row seat for the barbecue."

I take a moment to process his words, trying to find some sort of reassurance in them. As always, I'm left with more questions than answers.

"Why do you stay married to her?" I ask after a pause. "Even when I was a kid, I could tell you didn't love each other. Hell, I was barely a teenager when you added the second wing of the house so you could have separate living quarters. I don't think I've seen you in the main part of the house in years."

He exhales a deep sigh. I picture him pinching the bridge of his nose, as I've witnessed him do on more than one occasion while sighing in such a manner. "It may be difficult for you to understand because times have changed, but this sort of arrangement was all I knew. My father never married for love. He did so for power. Was paired with a woman who had something to offer, like an influential family. Same with me. Your gampy may have grown a bit…eccentric in his older years, but when I met your mother, he was an extremely influential man. Which made your mother appear to be a great match for me. At least according to my parents. So we were married."

"And neither of you cared? I can't believe Gampy and Meemaw would be okay with their daughter marrying for anything less than love."

"As you know, your mother can be very headstrong. She may not have loved me, but I can attest to the fact that she absolutely fell in love with my bank account. So we were able to convince everyone, including her parents, that we were the perfect couple. Still do."

"That's so…sad," I say, unable to stop myself.

"Like I said, different times." There's a wistfulness in his tone. "But I'm glad you and Julia didn't follow the same path."

He clears his throat. "Now, I think it advisable for you to spend a few hours and touch base with clients, assure them it's still business as usual. Would you like me to reach out to a few myself?"

I consider his offer. What impression would that give people that I still need my dad to help in moments of crisis? A few years ago, he stepped back from the day-to-day running of the firm, leaving it to me to handle. So that's what I need to do here.

"Thanks for the offer, but I'll take care of it myself."

"Good. I'm proud of you. And for what it's worth…" He trails off.

"Yes?"

"Well, I've never liked that smug husband of Julia's."

"Do you… Do you think he's hurt her?"

"I'd like to think she wouldn't stay with him if he had. That doesn't sound like the Julia I know."

"But you saw the press conference. That Julia wasn't the same Julia."

"I know. Which was why I came back from Aspen with your mother when I was supposed to head to Pebble Beach for the month. To keep my eye on Julia. Just like you need to do with Londyn."

I close my eyes, finding comfort in his words. Something I didn't think possible after witnessing my mother's press conference. But that's always seemed to be my father's role in our lives. Whenever my mother threatened to destroy everything, he would come in and mitigate the damage.

"Thanks, Dad."

"I'll let you get back to work."

"Thanks," I say again, about to end the call when I stop myself. "Hey, Dad?"

"Yes?"

"If you were to finally leave Mom, I can guarantee you'd have my and Julia's full support."

He belts out a full belly laugh I usually only hear during the firm's Christmas party when he dresses up as Santa for all our employees' children. "Duly noted. Unfortunately, some things are easier said than done."

I nod, knowing all too well how he feels.

# CHAPTER ELEVEN

*Weston*

I stare up at the imposing brick façade of the house that never felt like home, despite having everything I could want at my fingertips. Welcoming light glows from several windows, giving off the impression of warmth and comfort. It's all a front, a way to make our family appear happy. But I was never happy here. The only place I felt an iota of happiness was with Gampy and Meemaw.

After taking a minute to steel my nerves for what I came here to do, I slide out of my car. Ever since my failed engagement to Brooklyn, I've done everything in my power to avoid my mother as much as possible, but I need to confront her over her latest publicity stunt. My father may think he mitigated any damage by leaking Londyn's statement to the press, but I couldn't face Londyn without knowing I stood up to my mother. Let her know my loyalty can't be swayed, no matter what she tries.

As I approach the front door, it swings open, my parents' housekeeper, Lila, greeting me with a warm smile.

"Good evening, Mr. Bradford. May I take your coat?" she asks, stepping back, allowing me to enter the high-ceilinged foyer. "Get you something to drink perhaps?"

I'm sure I look a sight after the past few days of barely sleeping. Couple that with spending all afternoon on the phone with several of the firm's largest clients, ensuring them it's still business as usual, and I'm nearing the end of my rope.

"I won't be staying long. Is my mother here?"

"They're in the den."

"Thank you, Lila."

"Of course, sir."

With determined strides, I make my way through the large living area and past the formal dining room, everything pristine and perfect. Exactly like the public's perception of my family. But I know the truth. Our sins are masked with piety, our crimes with charity.

Stepping over the threshold into the den, I focus on the high-back chair by the fireplace, my mother's usual spot, a queen on her throne.

"Weston, darling. What a pleasant surprise." She treats me to a fake smile.

"Is it really?" I continue toward her, eyes on fire. "Something tells me you fully anticipated my—"

I come to an abrupt stop as I pass the couch, taking in the rest of the room.

"Nick," I sneer, my blood boiling. "What are *you* doing here?"

"Recovering, Weston," he answers with a pompous smirk I'd love nothing more than to wipe off his face with my fist.

"You couldn't expect me to travel back home. Not in my condition." He gestures to his sling.

"Domenic will be convalescing in Atlanta," my mother explains. "In this house."

"*What?*" I counter, eyes wide.

"The doctors said he'll be out of commission for the next six weeks. Not to mention the physical therapy he'll require in order to repair the damage that horrible woman caused." Her lower lip quivers.

"The cameras aren't around, Mother. You can drop the act."

"What act is that, Weston?" she asks, holding her head high, spine stiff, shoulders squared. "That I'm beside myself with grief over the idea that something could have happened to Julia's husband? Where's *your* compassion?"

"Trust me. I'm just as beside myself with grief over what happened." I turn my glare on Nick. "But not for him."

My animosity grows with every minute I'm forced to be in the same room with him. The thought of Julia having to endure this nearly breaks me. That's when I realize she's not here.

"Where's Julia?"

"She and your father went to Charleston to pack up a few things and get Imogene," my mother answers with an air of authority. "They'll be back on Wednesday. They'll stay here while Nick recovers and for the duration of the criminal proceedings."

I do my best not to react. My mother must be in her glory at the idea of being at the center of a sensationalized trial. I'm not sure I should be the one to break it to her that less than one percent of all criminal proceedings actually end up in trial. The DA hasn't officially filed charges against

Londyn…yet. I'm still holding out hope they won't. That after Londyn's statement and the leak at the press conference today, they'll see it's a losing case and decline to prosecute her.

"And Julia's on board with that? What about Imogene's schooling?"

My mother waves a hand. "I called in a favor with the headmaster of the academy here. They're happy to have Imogene as one of their students."

"What about Julia's business? Her test kitchen is in Charleston, not here."

"After what happened, it's probably best for her business that she stay here. Wouldn't you agree, Weston?" my mother presses.

"Plus, I couldn't stomach the idea of something happening to my family if I allowed them to remain in Charleston without me there to protect them," Nick adds. "There's no telling who might target them."

"I'm fairly certain they'd both be much safer in Charleston than here with you."

"Oh please," my mother interjects with a dramatic roll of her eyes. "You can't seriously believe what that homewrecker told you." She stands from her chair, sauntering toward me. "Because that's all she is. A homewrecker. A woman who preyed on a vulnerable man at a difficult time in his life. And when things didn't go as planned, she did the one thing she could. Accused him of rape. And, sadly, she's manipulated you, just like she did Nick. What's it going to take for you to see that?"

I force a smile, undeterred by her words. "And what's it going to take for *you* to see that *he's* manipulating you, just like he did Londyn. And Julia."

She opens her mouth to protest when a knock sounds. We both turn to face Lila, who stands in the open doorway.

"Pardon the interruption, Mrs. Bradford, but Detective Stocker is here to talk to Mr. Jaskulski. He called earlier."

"Of course," Nick says in an authoritative voice, preventing my mother from doing so.

I can only imagine the tension that will pervade this house the longer Nick and my mother remain under the same roof. They're both arrogant. Both pompous. Both have egos bigger than the entire state of Georgia. I give it a week until they're at each other's throats.

Then again, maybe that's not a bad thing.

"I apologize for intruding on your recovery," a tall, stocky man with a shaved head says as he walks into the room. "If it were up to me, I wouldn't have bothered you with this at all, but after the leak to the media, I've been ordered to do my due diligence and question you regarding the perp's statement."

"So if no one had let it slip that he'd raped a woman, you wouldn't have done your due diligence?" I narrow my gaze on him as I widen my stance. "Makes me question the integrity of the police department."

The detective bristles at my comment. "And you are?"

"Weston Bradford."

His eyes flicker with recognition. He knows exactly who I am. And not that I'm simply Nick's brother-in-law, but that I'm dating the so-called "perp".

"Well…," Detective Stocker begins nervously, looking between me and Nick. "Perhaps I should come back at a later time when we can talk more candidly." He starts to turn, but Nick interrupts.

"Right now is fine." His smug eyes meet mine. "I have nothing to hide." He turns his attention back to Detective Stocker. "Like my brother-in-law should know, there are two sides to every story. And I'm certain that's exactly what Ms.

Bennett fed you. A whopper of a story. I'm more than happy to set the record straight, once and for all."

I'm not sure I can stand here and listen to Nick spin what I imagine will be quite the story without wanting to put my fist through his teeth. Or, at the very least, the wall. But I need to know what he says. It can only help Londyn with any potential defense.

"Let's start with how you're acquainted with Londyn Bennett," Detective Stocker begins once he's situated in a chair across from the couch where Nick currently reclines. "She claimed you met when she attended college in Upstate New York."

Nick nods. "That's correct."

"And what was the nature of your relationship?"

"Platonic. We were regulars at a coffee shop a few blocks from campus. Over the weeks of constantly running into each other, we formed a friendship."

"Even though you're a married man?" Detective Stocker asks with a raised brow.

"My intentions never veered into anything less than honorable where Ms. Bennett was concerned. I was married. She was married. But we were both away from our respective spouses, so I suppose we found a camaraderie in each other."

"And why wasn't your wife with you?"

"She'd given birth earlier in the year. Imogene was born with a hole in her heart that required surgery soon after birth. It was in her best interests that she remained in Charleston, close to her medical team, at least until she was on a better path. I initially hated the idea of being away from my wife and daughter, but my job provided excellent health insurance, which was necessary considering the high cost of her lengthy hospital stay."

"And was this your first year at this university?"

"Second."

"Was your wife with you the previous year?"

"No. She'd gotten pregnant prior to our scheduled move to New York. At her eighteen-week checkup, they'd noticed some abnormalities in Imogene's heart. Due to the high-risk nature of the pregnancy, Julia thought it best to stay in Charleston where she had access to her doctors. Not to mention the hospital was within minutes of our home, something she wouldn't have in the small, rural town in New York."

"I see."

"I suppose that's why I felt a connection to Ms. Bennett. She was away from her home and husband, as well. It was refreshing to have someone to talk to about my struggles."

The detective jots down a few more notes before looking up. "And is that all you discussed with Ms. Bennett? Just your struggles?"

"Mostly, yes. Sure, I shared my knowledge of Greek mythology with her, and she shared her passion for art history with me, since that was her major, but like I said, our relationship had always been platonic. At least until the masked ball."

"Masked ball?"

"Every year, the arts and humanities department hosted a masked ball for its outgoing seniors. It was tradition for all the professors and their spouses to attend, as well."

"And what happened at this masked ball to cause things to change between you?"

"I wanted to do something nice for her before she graduated. She was fascinated with a historic home on campus that only faculty members had access to. I'd gotten the keys from the dean and took her to see it after the ball ended. She did have quite a bit to drink. In retrospect, that's probably what made me brush off her overly amorous ovations toward me as we toured the house. Now, I will admit that, prior to this evening, Londyn had attempted to goad me into discussing topics I didn't feel were appropriate, considering my position as a faculty member."

I bark out a sarcastic laugh, the notion that Londyn was the one who preyed on Nick ridiculous. When three pairs of eyes fling to mine, I cover it up with a cough.

"I apologize," I mutter, not wanting to do anything to jeopardize my ability to remain. "Got something stuck in my throat."

"Like I was saying," Nick continues, seemingly annoyed, "some of Ms. Bennett's topics bordered on inappropriate. As such, I took the necessary precautions and alerted her advisor, the chair of her department, as well as the dean of the College of Humanities of the situation."

"If I were to reach out to the dean, would he or she corroborate this?"

"I don't see why not. It was standard protocol to document any conduct deemed inappropriate. As a newer professor, I was adamant about following protocol. I didn't want to get fired and lose our health insurance for something that was not my fault. It's my understanding they're obligated to keep all administrative records for seven years, so they should still have it on file."

"Was any disciplinary action taken in response to your complaints?"

"They weren't complaints, per se. Just making them aware of the situation. I don't know." He blows out a breath. "I had this strange feeling in my gut about the reasons behind Londyn's sudden desire to discuss my sex life. Couple that with the fact I'd noticed her lingering in the hallway outside my office. Then in the building where I held one of my lectures, which was across campus from the art department. Then again roaming the faculty parking lot. I just wanted to make sure it was documented in case things went awry."

My jaw aches from being clenched so tightly. But I remain silent, even though it's killing me. I have to hand it to Nick. He certainly weaves a compelling story. But this is nothing more than a massive fabrication.

"If Ms. Bennett had begun to act inappropriately around you, why go out of your way to take her to this historic house on campus?"

On a deep inhale, his expression morphs into one of feigned regret as he peers into the detective's eyes. "I've asked myself that countless times since that night. I don't have a good answer. It's no excuse, but being hundreds of miles away from my wife and baby took its toll on me. Despite Ms. Bennett's inappropriate behavior, I came to…depend on her for that connection. I regret it now, but back then, being able to talk to someone who understood what I was going through helped me durings those difficult times."

"What happened between you and Ms. Bennett on the evening of the masked ball?"

"Earlier that night, Julia and I had received news of a setback in Imogene's progress. I can't remember what it was now. At the time, there were so many. Thankfully, Imogene is now as healthy as every other six-year-old girl, even if she'll never be able to be an Olympic runner. But back then, it seemed we had to endure a constant cycle of one step forward, two steps back. So when Ms. Bennett kissed me… I don't know." He exhales deeply. "I knew it was wrong, knew I should push her away, but it felt so good to feel something other than the heartache of not knowing if my daughter would see another birthday."

"Did anything else happen?"

He nods, squeezing his eyes shut for a protracted beat. When he finally returns his gaze to Detective Stocker, his expression is pained.

"I'd give anything to have a do-over of that night. But all I can do is move forward."

"Did you have sex with Ms. Bennett that night?"

"Yes."

"At any point, did Ms. Bennett say or do anything to indicate she didn't want to have sex? Or had she revoked her consent?"

"Absolutely not," he answers without a moment's hesitation. "I would never touch a woman like that. She'd initiated things. If she'd told me to stop, I would have. I have a daughter. A wife I respect. I don't rape women."

"Was your wife aware of what transpired?"

"I told her the following morning. I'd regretted my actions immediately. All I could think was that my wife would leave me and forbid me to see my daughter again. I couldn't stomach that. So I told her everything, preparing for the worst. But Julia… She's such a graceful, benevolent woman. She found it in her heart to forgive me. In exchange, I swore to her that I'd come home once the semester was over and find a job in the Charleston area, even if it wasn't teaching. And that's precisely what I did. Stopped teaching and started working as a PR consultant instead."

"Did you have any communication with Ms. Bennett afterward?"

"No. Those few weeks between the ball and graduation, I did everything to avoid her, which wasn't difficult, considering it was finals. Once I submitted my final grades, I moved out of my apartment and returned to Charleston. I hadn't seen or spoken to her until this past weekend."

Detective Stocker scribbles on his pad. "Prior to that, were you aware she was dating your brother-in-law?"

He smiles shyly, a new look for him. "I know it sounds ridiculous, but I had no idea. Sure, I'd heard Imogene, Julia, and Wes refer to her as Londyn, but it never crossed my mind."

"Even after commenting on the sketch I did of her?" I mutter.

Nick shifts his pretentious eyes to mine. "If I recall correctly, I'd commented on that sketch after getting off a long flight from Europe. You'll have to excuse me for not putting the pieces together in my jet-lagged state." His words come out biting.

"Completely understandable." Detective Stocker shoots daggers in my direction before looking back at Nick. "How did you react when you realized who your brother-in-law was dating?"

"To say I was shocked would be putting it mildly."

"You said you'd told your wife about the affair. Did you tell her who you'd had an affair with?"

"Just that she was a student."

"When you saw Ms. Bennett on Thursday evening, did you say anything to either your wife or brother-in-law about your previous relationship with her?"

"It was New Year's Eve. I didn't want to ruin their night by laying that on them. I decided I'd wait until the following day. Unfortunately, I never got the chance." He brings his free hand to his bandaged shoulder.

"Let's move on to what transpired at the bakery. Why were you there?"

"Julia was sleeping off a hangover, but I knew she wanted to go in to get some paperwork done." He blows out a laugh. "The downfall of owning your own business. There's no such thing as a day off. Since she was still sleeping, I took a drive to the bakery for her."

"She was still sleeping at three in the afternoon?" I ask in disbelief.

"It was New Year's Day." He chuckles, leaning closer to Detective Stocker. "My wife can't handle her liquor like she could during her younger years."

"We all have to get old some time," he retorts with a smile.

"But that's not like Julia," I protest, my arms crossed. "Even with her worst hangover, she tends to be up around six-thirty or seven. Says it's her internal clock. The only time in recent history she's slept like that was when she had a root canal and was drugged up afterward."

"Well, she was asleep, Wes," Nick answers, clearly annoyed. "Why would I lie about that?"

"You tell me."

"Let's get back to the bakery," Detective Stocker suggests, ignoring my insinuations. "It was closed for business that day, correct?"

"Yes. Julia gives her employees all major holidays off, even if all the other restaurants and shops are open. Says it makes them more loyal and appreciative."

"And do you have a set of keys?"

"I grabbed hers."

"What entrance did you use?"

"The rear service door."

"Did you lock it after you entered?"

"I assumed I'd be in and out in less than five minutes, so I didn't see the point."

"And where were you when Ms. Bennett arrived?"

"The bathroom. When I finished up, I returned to the kitchen to see her standing in the doorway of Julia's office."

"What happened next?"

"I'm just so relieved *I* was the one who was there, not Julia. If she were…" He trails off, biting his lower lip, laying it on thick.

I struggle to understand how this detective can actually believe this story. Shouldn't he be trained to pick up when people aren't being sincere? Even if I didn't know Nick as well as I do, which isn't *that* well, I'd still question his honesty. It all seems so over the top. So dramatic. So disingenuous.

"I'd hate to think what would have happened." Nick returns his eyes to the detective. "She wouldn't have been able to thwart her attack."

"What do you mean by that?"

"Londyn Bennett is not right in the head," Nick replies quickly, his comment directed at me. Then he addresses Detective Stocker once more. "The night I slept with her, I'd told her it was a mistake. But she wouldn't listen. Even begged me to leave my wife for her. So when she saw me again, she probably viewed it as her opportunity to finally have me to herself. Hell, I wouldn't put it past the girl to have targeted Julia and Wes just to get back at me for my rejection."

"Even nearly six years later?" Detective Stocker asks.

"In my experience, hell hath no fury like a woman scorned," Nick answers. "And I certainly scorned Ms. Bennett. But she was a mistake, one I haven't made again. Since then, all my time and energy has been devoted to doing everything in my power to make my wife happy. And we're exceedingly happy. I can't allow anything to come between us again."

"I understand." He offers a compassionate smile. "I hate to ask for details, but I need to know the sequence of events that led to the shooting."

Nick closes his eyes, covering his shoulder with his free hand, wincing, as if in pain. "It's all still a blur."

"Do you remember if she was holding the weapon when you returned to the office?"

I roll my eyes. I may not know much about the law and interrogating a witness, but that seems like a leading question if I ever heard one.

"Now that I think about it…" He opens his eyes. "She was. I'd never been so close to a gun before. I remember thinking that I couldn't let this woman come between me and my family. That I couldn't let Imogene grow up without a father. So I took a chance and knocked it out of her hand. She lunged for it. I lunged for her. There was a struggle for control, but we both ended up grabbing the weapon at the same time. Unfortunately, I didn't have as firm a grip as I thought, and she shot me." He pats his shoulder. "Good thing I showed some resistance, though. If I hadn't, I wouldn't be here right now."

"We all must thank God for this miracle then," Detective Stocker says.

"We have every minute." My mother clasps her hands together, looking upward, as if in prayer.

"At any time, did you threaten Ms. Bennett?" he asks. "Or sexually assault her?"

Nick's mouth falls open, aghast. "Never. Not several years ago. And not now."

"When Ms. Bennett was booked, she had visible bruises on her wrists, arms, and hip. She claims you gave them to her. Is that true?"

"Maybe. Like I said, we struggled for the gun. I lunged for her and tackled her to the floor. It's possible I may have caused some bruising during our struggle. It wasn't intentional. And it certainly wasn't the result of any alleged sexual assault. I don't harm women."

The detective scribbles down a few additional notes in his pad before flipping it closed and standing. "This has all been extremely helpful. I'm sure you want to get some rest after what I imagine has been a rather difficult several days. I'll finish my report tonight, then send it to the DA's office. They may reach out to you if they have any additional questions or need clarification." He reaches into his pocket and pulls out a business card, handing it to Nick. "In the meantime, if you think of anything else that could be helpful in the prosecution of this case, please let me know."

"Thank you so much for all you're doing to help keep my family safe," my mother adds. "The Bradford family plans to make a large donation to the local Law Enforcement Officers Memorial Fund as a show of gratitude."

"Or a bribe," I cough, knowing all too well how my mother works.

She shoots me a glare before fixing her expression to the one she's mastered throughout her life. Eyes interested. Smile soft, but not overly enthusiastic. Not a single hint of emotion on her face.

Brushing off my remark, the detective scans the room, avoiding my stare. "Thanks again for your time. I'll show myself out." With that, he turns, no one saying a word as we listen to his retreating footsteps, followed by the front door opening and closing.

"Well...," my mother begins brightly, standing. "That went much better than I expected. I doubt that girl has a leg to stand on now."

"I couldn't agree more." Nick shifts his attention to me, smiling smugly.

"Bullshit," I mutter under my breath, my lip curling in

disgust when I see how proud they both seem to be with whatever just went on here.

"Do you honestly believe *her* lies?" he scoffs. "If that's the case, you're dumber than I thought. She's nothing more than a liar. A thief. A troubled woman so desperate for attention she'd fabricate an outrageous story."

For the past half-hour, I've kept my anger relatively in check, even when listening to Nick spread obvious lies about Londyn. But I can't hold back anymore. Nick doesn't deserve to be catered to. He deserves to suffer just like Londyn has suffered these past few days…hell, years.

My nostrils flare as heat washes over me, rage burning my veins. Not thinking and only reacting, I rush toward him, my feet moving of their own volition.

"That was *bullshit*, and you know it!" I roar as I wrap my hands around his throat.

Nick's eyes widen, his arrogance replaced with a new expression. Unease. Trepidation. *Fear.*

"Is this all a goddamn joke to you? So help me God, if you've done the same thing to Julia, a bullet to the shoulder will be the least of your concerns."

"Weston!" My mother shrieks, indignant, gliding across the room toward me. "What are you doing?" She attempts to pry my hands off Nick as he struggles below me, but she's no match for my strength. "I didn't raise you to act so… barbaric! All the more reason for you to get as far away from that woman as possible. Look at what she's done to you!"

"Done to me?" I repeat, my wild eyes shooting toward hers, my entire body shaking with fury. "What she's done to me? Do you want to know what she's *done* to me?"

My jaw tightening, I peer down at Nick, his fingers clawing at my hands as he struggles to breathe, his face turning from red to purple. With one final squeeze, I release my hold on him, and he takes a gasping breath. I spin from him, pinning my mother with a hardened stare.

"That woman has done nothing but teach me something you couldn't even fathom understanding. She's taught me about grace. About forgiveness. About unconditional love. She did all that, despite listening to your hate-filled words. Despite all your friends turning up their noses at her. Because of her, I'm a better person. Because of her, I know what true love feels like. And true love includes standing by someone's side when they're at their lowest of lows. Which is exactly what I plan to do."

I storm out of the den, needing to put as much distance between me and this woman as possible, the mere sight of her and Nick making my stomach churn.

"If I were you, I'd rethink your allegiance, Weston!" she calls out before I can disappear down the hallway. "If this is the path you choose, you could lose everything."

I hesitate, then peer over my shoulder. "If I don't choose this path, I'll lose everything. That woman *is* everything to me. And she's worth whatever price I have to pay."

My mother crosses her arms in front of her chest. "We'll just have to see about that, won't we?"

# CHAPTER TWELVE

## *Londyn*

**M**usic blares through my AirPods as I apply another coat of paint to a dresser I plan to turn into a kitchen island. It's been ages since I've spent any time in my garage, considering I'd moved most of my projects over to Gampy and Meemaw's house, where Wes built me the workshop of my dreams. To be honest, my up-cycling business has been the last thing on my mind lately.

But today, I don't feel as dejected and beaten down. I actually feel…optimistic. Not only because of Detective Trager's promise to make sure my version of events is taken seriously, but also the reporter at Mrs. Bradford's press conference asking about Nick's assault. It gives me hope I'll finally get justice. That someone will finally believe me.

"Ms. Bennett?"

I whirl around, surprised to find Detective Trager standing outside the open garage door. I remove my earbuds, clicking off the music on my phone.

"I'm sorry. How long have you been standing there?"

"Not long. Only a few seconds." She smiles warmly. "What is all of this?" Her eyes float to the multiple pieces of furniture set along the perimeter of the over-stuffed garage, all of them in various stages of repair, from being a piece of junk I found on the side of the road to being completely refinished and available for purchase.

"I up-cycle furniture." I remove my safety glasses and work gloves. "It started as a hobby, but eventually turned into my own business."

"Impressive. I can't even pick out paint colors for my bathroom, so this just boggles my mind."

"I've always loved art. Designing furniture is just another form of art."

"I can see that." She brings her blue eyes back to mine.

"Is there something I can help you with?" I ask when she doesn't immediately say anything further.

She clears her throat. "I'm sorry for bothering you at home. I just wanted to talk to you face-to-face."

"Should I have my lawyer here?"

"No. I'm not here to ask you any questions. I felt I should come and tell you myself."

"Tell me what?" I ask cautiously.

She chews on her bottom lip, then pushes out a long breath. "I tried. I really did. But the DA and captain had already made up their minds before I even interviewed you this morning."

I close my eyes, swallowing through the frustration building in my throat. I doubt she's about to tell me the police and prosecutor had their minds made up that Nick was the one at fault. Detective Trager's expression wouldn't be so morose if that were the case.

"They're filing formal charges against me," I say, more resigned than anything.

"I'm sorry. I truly am. I thought they'd see that it was a losing case, but they disagree."

I knew this would probably happen. While Sophia had told me that there was a chance they would decide not to prosecute once I made my statement, luck has never exactly been on my side.

"And my complaint against Mr. Jaskulski?" I ask, almost hesitant to hear her response.

She sighs, then subtly shakes her head. She doesn't need to say anything. That one gesture alone tells me everything I need to know. No charges will be filed against him.

History repeating itself.

"I'm so sorry, Londyn," she says, stepping toward me. "I tried to tell them there was a strong case against him. But I don't get to make that call. Only the DA does."

"I should have expected this," I remark dejectedly, not sure if I'm talking to her or simply berating myself for being foolish enough to have hope.

"No, you shouldn't have," she insists. "It shouldn't be this way. No woman should have to go through what you did only to be told it doesn't matter."

"But it doesn't. Nothing will ever change. And men like Nick will keep doing it because no one tells them they can't."

"I'm sorry I couldn't do more, Londyn."

I smile, but it wavers. "You did more than any other police officer ever has."

"And for that, I'm sorry." She holds my gaze another moment, then steps back. "I won't intrude on your evening any further. I just felt you deserved to hear the truth from me, not learn about it on the news tomorrow."

I nod. "Thank you."

"Of course."

I stare into space as she makes her way out of the garage and into her sedan, not snapping out of my trance until her car disappears from view. When it does, I exhale and head back toward my project, hoping it will help take my mind off everything.

Looking at my phone, I'm about to restart my music app when I spy the Facebook icon in the bottom left corner. I shouldn't do this, should avoid all social media, as Sophia recommended. But my curiosity gets the better of me. I click on the app, navigating to the page for the local network that aired the press conference earlier.

As expected, the video is pinned to the top of their page, having generated tens of thousands of views and comments in just a few hours. I should close out of the app right now, but I can't help myself, scrolling through comment after comment, each one causing my stomach to churn. I almost can't believe some of these are real, that someone could be so cruel.

But I know they can be. I've endured some sort of cruelty and hate most of my life.

Just not like this.

*Another example of the mainstream media trying to interfere with justice being served.*

*Londyn Bennett is just another lowlife trying to escape responsibility. She's ruining this man's life with this false accusation.*

*She needs to be locked up and held accountable for her false accusations. She can't get away with this.*

I do my best to steady my hands, becoming increasingly despondent with every comment. This isn't boosting my drive to fight. All it does is make me want to give up.

"Honeybee?".

Quickly clicking off the screen, I whirl around to see Wes lingering at the entrance to the garage.

"I'm glad to see you're back in your workshop. Doing something that brings you joy."

I glance at my half-finished project. A few minutes ago, it *did* bring me joy.

I'm not sure anything can anymore.

When I don't say anything, he runs his hands through his dark, disheveled hair and takes a few steps toward me. "Did you happen to see—"

"Your mother's press conference?" I interject. "Sure did."

He hangs his head, shaking it. Then he grabs my hands, running his fingers over my knuckles. "I'm so sorry. I had no idea she was going to do something like that. It was just a publicity stunt. Nothing she said meant anything. Nothing she said changes anything."

I inwardly laugh at the irony. "It changes everything, Wes."

He tilts his head, brows scrunched. "What do you mean?"

"Exactly what I said." I pull my hands from his, increasing the distance between us. "I thought things would be different this time. Thought someone might finally believe me. Thought someone would finally fight for me. But I was wrong. It doesn't matter how hard I fight. There will always be someone who wants to keep me down. It's useless to keep trying." I start to turn from him, but his voice stops me.

"Do you remember what I told you right before we made love the first time?"

I close my eyes, my chest tightening. I can't bear to say the words. But I don't have to.

"That I wouldn't let you push me away," Wes states, advancing toward me and clutching my cheeks in his hands. The feel of his flesh on mine is familiar, yet heartbreaking at the same time. "That I'd fight for you. That I wouldn't let you fall. Those words were true then. And they remain true today. I won't abandon you when you need me the most. I hate that you have to go through this. I'd give anything to be in your shoes. To be the one with his freedom on the line."

"But you're not, Wes!" I pull away from him, tears spilling over my eyelids and down my cheeks. "I'm the one he attacked." I point to my chest, my voice echoing against the cement floor. "I'm the one who defended myself. Because of that, I could go to prison. And not just for a month or two. With all the charges they can file against me, I could be looking at twenty years!"

"But you gave your statement this morning. And it was leaked to the media. I'm sure it's only a matter of time—"

I burst out laughing, the sound borderline maniacal. "Do you hear yourself, Wes? So what if I gave my statement? So what if the media knows? The media isn't the DA! The media isn't the judge! My statement won't change anything. The DA already made up his mind the second I was booked. Nothing I say, nothing I do, nothing *anyone* does will make a fucking speck of difference. Do you want to know the only thing that *does* matter?"

"What's that?" he asks cautiously.

"This, Wes." I extend my arm, pointing to my flesh. "This is the only thing that matters. That I'm a black woman who made the mistake of carrying a gun to protect herself and dared to fucking use it against a white man!"

"Londyn…" He advances toward me once more, anguish

covering his expression. And I hate that. Hate that this is hurting him.

And it will only get worse.

What will it take for him to see reality? That I'm facing an uphill battle I most likely won't win?

I hold up my hand, preventing him from taking another step. "Do you remember telling me that story about Eli? How Gampy fought until his dying day to get him justice for a crime he didn't commit? And he couldn't."

"Your case is different than Eli's," Wes urges.

I smile sadly. "You're right. It is. Because I *did* commit this crime. I *did* shoot Nick. And I'm going to have to live with that for the rest of my life." I pause, my throat closing up, as if not wanting to play any part in my next statement. "I can't let you do that, too."

I manage to look into his eyes, the blue that was once piercing and vibrant now dull, all the life slowly leaving them. I hate that I'm the cause of it, but it has to be this way. If I'm going down, I can't bring him down with me.

Lowering my head, I scurry away in a desperate attempt to put as much distance between us as possible.

"So that's it?" he thunders, his voice rattling the furniture. I'd never heard him speak with such passion and fury before. It causes me to stop in my tracks. "You're just going to give up? You're going to let *him* win?"

I face him, my eyes flaming. "I'm not letting *him* do anything. But I can't fight against a system that was put in place to keep someone like me down. Do you think this is what I want? Because this is *killing* me."

"Then don't give up! Fight! Don't become another statistic! Be the strong Medusa I know you are."

"Even Medusa lost in the end, Wes. You weren't there this morning. You didn't have to sit in a room with a pompous detective and listen to him poke holes in your story and justify Nick's actions. I had so much hope, ya know?" My fingers instinctively go to the pendant around my neck. "After you gave me this necklace, I really thought things would be different. That someone would listen." I drop my hold on the medallion and wrap my arms around my stomach, fighting against the sudden chill enveloping me. "But they never will. I'm exhausted from trying to fight for justice in a system that will never care about me. That still treats people who look like me like property, not a person." I draw in a deep breath, the atmosphere in the room shifting. "I'm just..." I shake my head. "I'm just too tired, Wes."

An exhaustion unlike any I've felt before washes over me. It's not physical exhaustion, although that certainly comes into play, too. It's mental and emotional exhaustion.

For over five years, I've held onto hope that karma would eventually come to get Nick. It was the only thing that kept me going. Now, I'm forced to admit the truth I refused to for so long.

That he's won.

That he'll always win.

With slow movements, I turn from Wes again, each step taking more and more out of me. More of my fight. More of my faith. More of my hope. Until all that's left is a shell of the person I once was.

"You may have given up, but I haven't," Wes states when I reach the top of the stairs leading into my condo.

I stop, but don't look back at him.

"Do you want to know what keeps me going?"

"What's that?" I ask in a soft voice.

"This, Londyn."

I slowly look at him, my breath catching when I see he's

holding a small, black box, a gorgeous diamond solitaire displayed prominently, the overhead lights reflecting in it.

"This is what keeps me going. The idea that, once this is all over, I'll be able to get down on one knee and ask you to be my wife."

I squeeze my eyes shut, my heart physically aching. If he thought this would make me reconsider, he's wrong. It only makes this even more painful than it already is.

"I planned to ask you New Year's Day. I was so fucking excited to see this ring on your finger, Lo."

"Wes, please...," I beg, each word he says like another knife in my heart.

"We may have gotten off course. You may think things have changed, but they haven't. I *still* want to get down on one knee and ask you to be my wife. I *still* want to see this ring on your finger. And I *still* want to stand before God and all the important people in our lives as we become one."

I swipe at the tears falling steadily down my cheeks, wanting to run, but at the same time clinging to every word he says.

"I won't stand here and tell you everything will be okay. I don't know if it will. It kills me to see you hurting like this and not being able to do anything to fix it, except love you with every beat of my heart. Except stand by your side, even when you push me away. Except fight for you, even when you don't think it's worth it. Because let me tell you something, Londyn..."

I shift my gaze back to his, swallowing hard.

"You *are* worth it. And nothing you say will make me think otherwise. Nothing will break this tether binding me to you. You for me, Lo. For the rest of our lives. Even if we're apart, you will still own me. Own my body. My mind. My heart. And I wouldn't have it any other way."

I part my lips, his passionate plea rendering me speech-less. It would be so easy to get swept up in his words, to believe that things will work out. But we've lived in the clouds most of our relationship. We can't afford to do that anymore.

*I* can't afford to do that anymore.

"I'm sorry, Wes," I squeak out, the pain in my throat excruciating. I part my lips, attempting to find the words I need to tell him it's not worth it. But my brain physically won't allow me to say them.

Instead, I continue up the stairs, slamming the door behind me.

# CHAPTER THIRTEEN

## *Weston*

"Londyn!" I bellow, frustration washing over me. Feeling like nothing I say or do will get through to her, I punch the wall. "Goddammit!"

Pain pulses through me, my hand throbbing. I shake it out, hoping I didn't break a bone. Even if I did, I'd welcome the agony. It takes my mind off the anguish in my heart.

"If you need something to hit, I've got a gym next door with all the punching bags you could ask for."

At the sound of the thick Brooklyn accent, I spin, Diego standing in the open door to Londyn's garage, arms crossed.

"Might not be a bad idea after today," I admit, attempting to compose myself.

"Figured. Or maybe I could offer you a beer instead."

I glance up at the staircase to Londyn's condo, hating to walk away with things unresolved.

At least unresolved in my head.

"Give her some space," he encourages me. "She'll come around."

"I hope you're right." I exhale a long breath, shaking my head as I shove the ring back into the inside pocket of my jacket. I don't even know why I brought it with me today. It's almost like some higher power thought it might come in useful.

They were wrong.

"Trust me," Diego says as I walk toward him. "I've been in your shoes."

I stop, furrowing my brow. "You have?"

"Sure have. Come on." He slaps my back. "I'll tell you all about it over a beer."

He steers me out of the garage and up the walkway toward his condo.

"Make yourself at home," he instructs once we enter, gesturing toward a couch against the far wall.

I continue into the open living area, feeling like I'm in Londyn's condo, except in reverse. Even the décor seems to be in her style. Comfortable and homey with a modern flair. I stop by a display of photos hanging over the couch, chronicling Hazel and Diego throughout the years. A few wedding photos. Some of Diego at one of his fights. Of him in his firefighter gear.

As I reach the last few photos, I stop, staring at an image of two young boys.

"That's Evan and Benjamin," Diego explains, handing me a beer.

"Hazel's kids?"

"Yes," he states, then slowly brings his beer to his mouth before adding, "And my nephews." He takes a swig.

I dart my wide eyes to his, taken aback by this.

"Did Londyn ever mention what happened to Hazel?"

He lowers himself to the couch, and I join him, more than intrigued by this revelation.

"She mentioned she was in an abusive relationship. That she tried to leave, but her husband shot her and her sons before he turned the gun on himself. Hazel was the lone survivor."

"Her husband, Carlos, was my brother."

My heart drops. "I had no idea."

"Suffice it to say, things weren't always great between Hazel and me, especially after everything that happened." His Adam's apple bobs up and down, sadness washing over his expression. "Hell, for the longest time, she couldn't even stand the sight of me. She refused to spend time with anyone who had any connection to Carlos or the life she had before that day."

He rests his forearms on his knees as his lips curve up in the corners, a nostalgic gleam filling his eyes. "I'd always had a thing for Hazel. We grew up in the same neighborhood in Brooklyn. Went to the same high school. But I was more reserved than my brother. More focused on my training."

"For MMA?"

He nods. "I'd hoped to fight professionally. Had a manager and everything. He told me I showed more promise than any of the other guys he'd managed. That seeing my name in lights wasn't a pipe dream."

"What changed?"

"With what? My fighting? Or Hazel?"

I shrug. "Both, I suppose."

"My priorities changed. When Carlos did what he did, when I got that phone call…" His strained voice trails off as he swallows. "I was beside myself. And torn. I knew I should mourn my brother, despite his horrible decision. But he wasn't my focus. Hazel was. It was my attempt at cleaning up my brother's mess, as I'd done most of my life. At the beginning, that's what Hazel was to me. One last mess to clean up. Then my conscience would be clear and I could stop feeling guilty about what Carlos had done."

"And how did she respond to being one last mess?"

"I wasn't about to tell *her* I thought she was a mess," he jokes, shaking his head as he takes a long swallow of his beer. "I may take risks on the mat, but I don't have a death wish."

I laugh, grateful for the break in tension, then turn my expectant eyes toward him. "So how did she go from not wanting anything to do with you to being your wife?"

"It wasn't easy. After everything went down, she shut out everyone. She was in a dark place."

"Yet you still persevered."

"Hazel may be stubborn," he says with a gleam in his eyes, "but so am I. If she truly didn't want anything to do with me, I would have respected her wishes. I'm not one of those guys who thinks they know what's best for everyone. But I knew Hazel. And I knew if I showed her the patience she deserved, she'd come around. Make no mistake. It killed me to stand back and watch her self-destruct. I'd never felt so helpless before in my life."

I briefly close my eyes, nodding, knowing all too well how he must have felt. It's how I've felt since Hazel stormed into my condo and I realized the truth.

"But I also knew Hazel needed to work through this in her own time and on her own schedule. There's no hard and fast rule about how long you should take to mourn the loss of a loved one. Especially your own sons. So I did what I felt was best. I gave her time." He gives me a knowing look.

I pick at the label on the beer bottle. "You heard us?"

He barks out a laugh. "Pretty sure all of Atlanta heard you two."

I lean back on the couch, staring straight ahead. "I just don't know if I can walk away. She's in a pretty dark place, too."

"I'm not telling you to walk away. I'm just saying that maybe you need to give her some time. And some space. She's going through something none of us can truly understand. Trust me, it kills me to watch the life slowly drain from her. And if it's killing me, I can only imagine how it's eating you up."

"I've always been a problem solver. But I have no idea how to solve this one. It makes me feel...powerless." I shake my head. "I never should have let her leave that day. I could have prevented all of this. Then things would be the way they were. We could be happy. I could have my Londyn back."

"You have to stop thinking that way. She *did* leave. You can't bully your way into her life in the hopes of things going back to the way they were before. Forget about before. Before is gone. A distant memory. A mythical place that you'll never see again. And the Londyn you knew, the one you fell in love with?" He raises a brow. "She's gone, too, Wes. This entire ordeal has changed her. You don't endure something as traumatic as Londyn has and come out of it the same."

"But that's the problem," I interject, my voice becoming louder. "I don't *know* what she's endured. She refused to talk about it, leaving me to just my brother-in-law's obviously twisted version of events and my own imagination."

He places a hand on my shoulder. "She'll open up to you. In time. It took me a while to figure that out with Hazel. I blamed myself, too. I still struggle with it. Still wish I had seen the signs earlier. But that's the thing about women like Hazel and Londyn. They are strong and fierce. They refuse to rely on someone else's sword to save them because they have their own. They won't tell you about the demons plaguing them. They prefer to fight them on their own terms. In their own way. In their own time."

"So I'm just supposed to sit on the sidelines while she breaks down? She needs to know people care. She *deserves* to know people care. That we believe her. That we support her."

"And you still can. But do it in a way that shows you're listening, that you respect her wishes, her *need* for space."

"But—"

"I get it, Wes. Believe me. We may come from different backgrounds, but you and I aren't all that different. Like you, I've always considered myself a problem solver. If I see something wrong, I fix it. Being faced with a situation you have absolutely no control over… It's the worst feeling in the world. If *you* feel like you have no control, imagine how Londyn must feel right now. I guarantee it's a lot worse than you."

"Which is why I want to be there for her."

"And you can be. By listening to her. By not telling her you think you know what she needs better than she does. By giving her some semblance of control over her life. Give her back the control to make decisions."

"Even if they're the wrong decisions?" I quip, my question coming out more biting and arrogant than I intended. But I can't help myself.

"It may be the wrong decision in your eyes, but in hers, this is what she needs. Remember back in the summer after she told you the truth about her past? You gave her space. Didn't you?"

I squeeze my eyes shut, slowly nodding.

"And how did that end up?"

"She eventually came around."

"Exactly. Because you respected her wishes. Because you gave her the control to decide her own fate. Because you *listened*. Do that again, and I know she'll come around again." He brings his beer back to his mouth, taking a sip. "Trust me on that."

# CHAPTER FOURTEEN

## *Londyn*

"You ready?" Hazel asks Friday morning as I descend the stairs into the kitchen where she and Diego wait, both of them dressed for the occasion — a button-down and dark jeans for Diego, a black dress for Hazel. It's a strange sight, considering neither of them typically wear anything other than jeans or workout clothes. Then again, today will be anything but typical.

"Ready as I'm going to be," I say with a smile, shifting toward the full-length mirror in the living room for one last check of my appearance.

I push a few curls out of my eyes, then smooth a hand down my cream blouse, adjusting the deep purple pants. These once fit perfectly, but now there's room around my waist. Evidence of my lack of appetite this past week.

It's been four days since I've seen Wes.

Four days since he poured his heart out to me, showing me the engagement ring he bought.

Four days since I pushed him away to protect him from being pulled down with me.

Four days that I've questioned whether I did the right thing.

At first, I was surprised he didn't rush after me, bang on the door, demand I listen.

Then I remembered how he gave me space all those months ago after I'd finally shared my past. He'd given me time to realize that what we have is bigger than my deepest fears. To show me he'll respect my wishes, despite the personal cost to him.

I have no doubt he's doing the same thing now.

Once I'm content with my appearance, I turn toward Hazel and Diego, nod, then we all leave my condo.

The car is eerily silent as Diego drives us toward the courthouse, all our minds and hearts consumed with what the day will bring. The second that gun went off and Nick collapsed on top of me, I knew there would be no avoiding this. It doesn't make it any easier to accept that no one believed me.

Again.

Justice isn't blind. She's dead, run over by power-hungry men.

As we near the downtown area where the courthouse is located, my heart rate increases, palms becoming sweaty. I close my eyes, taking several deep breaths to calm my nerves. Sophia told me today is only a formality. That it'll be over in five minutes. But in those five minutes, I'll have to stand before a judge as a slew of charges are read against me, then enter a plea.

"Holy shit...," Hazel exhales, cutting through my thoughts.

I peer out the window as the courthouse comes into view,

trying to make sense out of the scene in front of me. This isn't a typical Friday in downtown Atlanta. There has to be something else going on.

Hundreds of people are assembled in front of the court-house, with even more overflowing across the street in Liberty Plaza and by the capitol building. Most of them are women, many of them holding signs.

"What is this?" I ask, wondering if they're protesting some statute the governor is slated to sign into law today.

But when I scan the messages scrawled on the poster boards, I know that's not why they're here. That *I'm* why they're here.

*BELIEVE WOMEN.*

*I DON'T WANT A RAPE WHISTLE. I WANT CHANGE.*

*IF YOU ARE NOT OUTRAGED, YOU ARE NOT PAYING ATTENTION.*

*YOU ARE NOT POWERLESS.*

*#LONDYNSTRONG*

*WE WILL NOT BE SILENCED.*

*THE WAY I DRESS IS NOT A YES.*

*I MARCH SO MY DAUGHTER WILL NEVER HAVE TO SAY #METOO.*

With each sign I read, the more I'm overcome with emotion, tears welling in my eyes.

All week, I thought I was alone. Thought no one could possibly comprehend what I'm going through. Sure, Hazel,

Diego, even Wes have done everything to remind me that they support me, believe me. But it still felt as if the world was against me.

Until now.

"You okay, Lo?" Hazel asks, peeking back at me from the front seat of Diego's truck.

"I just... I didn't expect anything like this to happen," I answer with a quiver, dabbing at my eyes.

"People were outraged after the DA held that press conference saying he was filing charges against you but not Nick the Prick. This case has certainly caught the public's attention, and not because of the fact that the media initially thought it was some mass shooting at a public shopping district. Because of *your* story, Lo. All these women want justice for you." She reaches for my hand, squeezing it. "Like I've told you, you are not alone." She holds my gaze for a beat.

"I'll drop you off here and come find you once I park," Diego interjects as he comes to a stop in front of the courthouse. He jumps out of the truck, rushing around to open my and Hazel's door.

The second I step onto the sidewalk, cameras flash around me, hundreds of people calling my name. It was one thing to see it all from the comfort of Diego's truck. Now that I'm in the midst of it, now that I hear their words of encouragement, now that I see the hope and determination in everyone's eyes, I'm overwhelmed with an emotion I can't quite describe.

"What am I supposed to do?" I whisper to Hazel, blindsided by this show of support.

"Just wave, I guess."

So that's what I do. Once Diego drives off, I raise my arm, waving at the assembled crowd as I mouth *thank you*.

Then we turn, making our way toward the entrance of the building as Sophia comes rushing out.

"Oh, good. You're here. It's all pretty incredible, isn't it?"

"It is," I admit as she escorts us toward the front of the security line. "Will it help my case at all?"

Once our purses have been scanned by the X-ray machine and we've cleared the metal detector, Sophia faces me. "Public opinion *can* be helpful. And I'm sure it makes you feel somewhat vindicated. But I won't lie to you. People on the street can shout and protest all they want. Once you're inside that courtroom, all that matters is the evidence."

"Oh." My shoulders fall, any hope I'd felt evaporating as quickly as it appeared. I know all too well the evidence against me is pretty ironclad. Any proof of my version of events is weak, at best. Apart from a few bruises that can be explained as simply an indication of our struggle over the weapon, it's my word against his. And Detective Trager made it pretty clear they believe him, not me. At least the DA does.

Sophia clutches my hand, squeezing it. "Have faith. This is far from over."

I grit a smile as she leads us through a maze of hallways, people assembled around each of the various courtrooms, checking a screen with docket numbers outside each door. I barely pay attention as she explains what will happen for what feels like the tenth time. I nod every so often so she doesn't think her words fall on deaf ears, but my mind is elsewhere.

"This is us," she announces as we come to a stop outside a pair of double wooden doors.

I glance at the screen to the right, my last name at the top of the docket list.

"Court will open in about ten minutes. I already talked to the clerk. She'll call us first, since I have another hearing scheduled for eleven. If you want to freshen up or take a minute, the ladies' room is right around the corner." She points in the general vicinity.

"Thanks." I begin to turn.

"I'll come with you," Hazel offers just as her phone rings. She pauses, looking at the screen. "Hold on. It's Diego."

I nod, standing off to the side, listening to their conversation in Spanish. Then she lowers her cell, covering the microphone. "He can't find the courtroom. He somehow ended up over in the civil court. I'm not surprised. This place is like a friggin' maze."

"It's okay. Go find him."

"I'll be right back." Returning the phone to her ear, she walks back the way we came, rattling something off in Spanish, probably making some joke about his horrible sense of direction.

Once I'm certain she's headed the right way, I excuse myself from Sophia, walk down the corridor, and slip inside the bathroom. All the buzz from the busy courthouse disappears behind the closed door, silence surrounding me.

I make my way toward one of the stalls and lock myself inside. Closing my eyes, I draw in a deep breath, taking a minute to collect myself without Hazel, Diego, or Sophia psychoanalyzing every single facial expression, blank stare, or long exhale.

After several deep breaths, the sound of the door opening cuts through, noisy conversations from the corridor filtering in. I snap my eyes open, glancing at my watch. Five minutes until court opens.

Pulling myself together, I step out of the stall and move toward the line of sinks. After washing my hands, I check my

reflection one last time, then make my way out of the bathroom at the same time as the door to the men's room across
the corridor swings open.

I glance up, about to excuse myself, coming to a hard
stop when my eyes lock with the individual exiting. My brain
tries to tell my legs to put one foot in front of the other and
leave, but I'm frozen, the familiar scent of leather and citrus
like an evil spell cast over me.

On instinct, I reach for the Medusa pendant. My good
luck charm. My talisman.

Despite the way I pushed Wes away, I still find myself
reaching for this necklace whenever I need reassurance. And
right now, as I stare into Nick's cold eyes, a sly smirk playing
on his lips, I need that reassurance.

The door to the ladies' room opens, hitting me, and I
snap out of my stupor, jumping to the side.

"Ah, there you are, darling," Nick booms. I follow his line
of sight, watching as Julia emerges.

"Julia…," I exhale, momentarily forgetting everything
that's transpired. "How are you?"

She glances at Nick, as if tempering her response. Then
she holds her head high, avoiding my gaze. "As good as can
be expected."

"Are you sure?" I press, unable to stop myself.

On the outside, she looks the same as always. Blonde hair
impeccable. Stylish clothes. Makeup carefully applied. But
there's a nervousness about her, at complete odds with the
woman who's become like a sister to me over the past several
months.

"Of course we are." Nick turns from me, his intent gaze
focused on Julia, a silent warning in his eyes. "Let's get back
to your mother and father. No need to worry them about
why it's taking so long."

Without protest, she nods, allowing him to lead her away from me.

"What did he do to you?" I whisper to myself as they retreat. And there's no doubt in my mind he's hurt her. Maybe not physically, but he's manipulating her mentally. I know it.

As they're about to round the corner, Julia glances back at me, our eyes locking. It only lasts a second, but in that moment, I can practically hear her cries for help, begging for someone to finally see the truth. To see the monster hiding behind the perfectly groomed blond hair, dapper suit, and cunning smile.

Or do I only *wish* I could?

# CHAPTER FIFTEEN

## *Londyn*

"All rise."

I follow Sophia's lead, standing as a short, balding man in dark robes enters the courtroom and makes his way toward the bench. Once he's seated, the bailiff indicates it's okay for everyone else to re-take their seats.

As I lower myself back to the long, wooden bench that reminds me of an uncomfortable church pew, I glance around the courtroom, as I'd been doing prior to the judge entering. I shouldn't feel downhearted over the fact that Wes isn't here. I didn't exactly invite him or make him feel like I wanted him to come. But a part of me hoped he'd be here anyway. It would make the fact that Nick and Mrs. Bradford sit less than twenty feet away, their eyes trained on me as if I'm some sort of hardened criminal who should never see the light of day again, more bearable.

"That's us." Sophia touches my arm, and I snap my eyes toward her.

With an encouraging nod, she stands, and I do the same, my heart thrashing in my ears as I follow her up to the defense table.

I remain standing beside her, as she'd instructed, when I sense a shift in the room's energy. I subtly glance over my shoulder, expecting to see Nick glowering at me with his vindictive smile. Instead, I watch as Wes strides into the courtroom, bypassing his family and sitting directly behind me. He meets my gaze, his blue eyes comforting. Relief rolls off me, a warmth filling me at the thought that he *is* here. That he *hasn't* given up on me.

"Appearances?"

At the sound of the judge's voice, I face forward once more.

"Sophia Mercer for the defendant, Londyn Bennett, Your Honor," Sophia states firmly.

"Bridgette Hawkins, Assistant District Attorney, Your Honor," a tall woman adds from the table on the opposite side of the courtroom. The stack of files in front of her gives the impression I'm just one case of many she has to deal with today.

"Thank you. Now, Ms. Bennett," the judge says, turning his attention to me for the first time. "I'm sure your attorney already explained what's going to happen today. I'm going to read off the charges the District Attorney's office has filed against you. All you'll need to tell me is if you plead guilty, not guilty, or some other plea you've discussed with your attorney. Do you understand?"

I nod. "Yes, Your Honor."

"Splendid." He lowers his glasses in front of his eyes,

bringing up a piece of paper in front of him. "On the charge of aggravated assault, how do you plead?"

I swallow hard, my mouth growing dry. It doesn't matter how many times Sophia told me that this is simply a formality. It's still nerve-wracking to stand up here and hear these charges against me.

"Not guilty."

"On the charge of reckless conduct, how do you plead?"

"Not guilty," I say again.

"On the charge of criminal trespassing, how do you plead?"

"Not guilty."

"On the charge of battery, how do you plead?"

"Not guilty."

"And on the final charge of pointing a weapon at another, how do you plead?"

"Not guilty."

"Thank you, Ms. Bennett. The record shows you've entered your pleas knowingly and willingly." The judge shifts to address Sophia, peering over the rim of his glasses. "I assume you'll be filing pre-trial motions."

"Yes, Your Honor."

"Okay." He looks to the woman sitting at the desk to the right of the bench. "Let's put this over for pre-trial—"

"If I may interject, Your Honor," the ADA interrupts, standing.

"Yes, Ms. Hawkins?"

"I've been in discussions with the victim and his family. This is a bit of a unique situation because of the close relationship between the defendant and the victim's family. According to the victim, Mr. Jaskulski, Ms. Bennett is involved in a romantic relationship with his brother-in-law, Weston Bradford. While this case wouldn't fall under the statutory definition of family violence, thus necessitating some sort of order of protection for the duration of the pending criminal proceedings, there is also a prior romantic relationship between the victim and the defendant, as well as evidence of prior stalking while the defendant was a student at the university where the victim taught. As such, the prosecution requests an order of protection be issued in this case for not only the victim, but also his wife and minor child."

I blink, turning my eyes to Sophia, a question in my gaze. She subtly shakes her head before addressing the judge. "Your Honor, that's a bit excessive. As Assistant District Attorney Hawkins admitted, there is no statutory obligation to issue any sort of protective order. This is Ms. Bennett's first offense. She's never received so much as a parking ticket before this. Not to mention, the prior relationship included Mr. Jaskulski sexually assaulting my client, which will be the basis of our defense to the charges. At this point, issuing a protective order would just be punitive."

"Duly noted, Attorney Mercer. But in this case, I'm inclined to agree with Assistant District Attorney Hawkins. While I am aware of the defendant's accusations of sexual assault, the parties do have a history I can't ignore."

The clerk extends her hand toward the ADA, who provides her with several pieces of paper, which I can only assume are the protective orders already drawn up and awaiting a signature.

"Okay, Ms. Bennett. I'm signing three temporary protective orders here. One for Domenic Jaskulski. One for Julia Prescott. And one for Imogene Jaskulski. These are no-contact protective orders, which means you cannot contact these individuals in any way whatsoever. If you happen to be in the same restaurant, you're the one obligated to leave. They are not. From this moment forward, you must remain at least fifty feet away from them at all times, with the exception of any court proceedings. These will remain in effect for a year, but may be extended or terminated early if warranted. Violation of these protective orders is a misdemeanor punishable by up to twelve months incarceration. Do you understand?"

I look at Sophia, who nods for me to agree.

"Yes, Your Honor."

I stare blankly ahead as the clerk, ADA, and Sophia discuss a date for pre-trial motions. Once we're dismissed, I follow Sophia away from the table and out of the courtroom.

Growing up, I truly believed in the concept of everyone being innocent until proven guilty, probably naïvely so. But I somehow held onto hope that guilty people would be punished for their crimes, innocent people set free.

Now I've finally realized that's not how the justice system works. I saw the way everyone in that courtroom looked at me the second my case was called. They'd already made up their minds without hearing a single shred of evidence.

Why even bother fighting?

"Don't let this affect you," Sophia whispers once we slip out of the double doors. "I'll be filing several pre-trial motions. Some I can file right now. Others I'll have to wait until after the prosecution has shared their evidence with me prior to trial. However, I expect to hear from the ADA assigned to this case this afternoon. They'll want to make a deal as quickly as possible so they don't have to go through the discovery process."

"A deal?"

She nods. "A plea bargain. I know it's not what you want, and I promised I'd fight for you all the way to the end, but we also need to be realistic. This first deal they make will most likely be the most attractive. But like I said, I will fight this thing to the bitter end, if that's the decision you make. If you ask me, the battle's just begun. Okay?"

I draw in a deep breath, trying to find comfort in her reassurance. With every setback, it's becoming more and more difficult. It's not like I've spent any time with Julia or Imogene since New Year's Eve anyway, so this shouldn't bother me. But to know the judge believes my actions warrant protection makes me think that, no matter what I do or say, he'll only hear that a black woman shot a white man.

"I have to get to my next hearing," Sophia says, glancing at her watch. "I'll be in touch soon. If anything comes up or you have any questions, just give me a call." She grabs my hand and squeezes, then runs off into another part of the courthouse.

"You okay?" Hazel asks, approaching with Diego.

I grit a smile. "Yeah."

"Day drinking?" She arches a brow.

"Sure."

I allow her to lead me away from the courtroom, and we successfully navigate the various corridors back toward the main rotunda. Everything looks just as it did when I first walked into the building, yet everything's changed. Especially my optimism.

"You two wait in here and I'll grab the car," Diego directs as we approach the front doors. "I'll text when I'm about to pull up."

"You sure you won't get lost this time?" Hazel jabs, placing a hand on her hip.

Diego rolls his eyes, leaning toward her, his expression devilish. "Watch that smart mouth."

"And here I thought you loved my smart mouth."

"You know I do." He places a short but full kiss on her lips. "Be right back." Turning, he skirts through the steady stream of people coming into the courthouse, then disappears through the glass doors.

"Come on. Let's sit." Hazel grabs my hand, tugging me toward a set of benches off to the side. I walk with her a few steps, then stop in my tracks when a familiar silhouette approaches. He stops, too, just as uneasy about our surprise encounter. Although it's difficult to truly call this a surprise, considering he did show up to my arraignment.

"Hey," Wes says, cutting through the tense silence between us. He runs his long fingers through his dark hair, making my hand twitch with an urge to do that myself.

"Hey," I respond timidly, rocking on my feet.

"How… Um… How are you?"

I peer into his eyes. Ones that were once vibrant and full of life seem deflated. His suit is disheveled, his normally crisp tie loosened.

"Good. You?"

"Good." His lips lift into a hint of a smile, but sadness still envelopes him. From his slumped shoulders, to the bags under his eyes, to the slight quiver of his chin. "Actually, that's a lie. I'm not good."

"Neither am I," I admit, much to my surprise. That's always seemed to be Wes' superpower. His mere proximity causes me to confess my darkest secrets, succumb to my deepest desires.

"Oh, shoot!" Hazel's voice forces my head toward her, reminding me we're not alone. Another one of Wes' superpowers — making me forget everything and everyone else. "I think I left my, um…pen in the courtroom."

I look at her, brows furrowed. "Your…pen?"

"Yeah. I'll go check."

"It's just a pen, Haze."

She scurries away, waving me off. "It's my favorite one. Wes, wait with her for me, would you?"

I steal a glance at him, his gaze focused on me and nothing else, stripping me raw, yet making me feel more hope than I have in days.

"I'd be happy to."

# CHAPTER SIXTEEN

## *Weston*

I watch as Hazel runs off, leaving me alone with Londyn for the first time since Monday.

All week, I've thought about what I'd say once I saw her again. Nothing seems appropriate right now, not after watching her being accused of baseless crimes in court, then being forbidden from having any contact with my sister and niece. It took every ounce of resolve I possessed to not fly across the courtroom and strangle Nick as he flashed his vindictive smile in my direction when the prosecutor requested those protective orders.

Shifting my eyes toward Londyn, I take in her appearance. She looks as beautiful as ever, but something's off. She doesn't belong in this place. Doesn't deserve to go through this after everything else she's endured. Frustration builds in my throat for what feels like the hundredth time in the past week over the fact that I can't do anything to stop this out-of-control train from careening off the tracks.

"You wore your necklace," I finally say.

Her fingers go to the pendant. "I haven't taken it off since you gave it to me." She meets my eyes, a small smile playing on her full, glossy lips I've dreamt of kissing every second of our separation. "Except to shower, of course."

"Of course." I shove my hands into my pockets, shifting my weight on my feet.

I hate this tension surrounding us. I didn't even feel this uneasy around her when we first met. Or during that first dinner my sister planned in order to force us to spend time together. Or during those early days after she agreed to help with Gampy and Meemaw's house as more than just my interior designer.

"Is it me, or is this more awkward than a first date?" I blurt out after several moments of strained silence.

Her shoulders relaxing, she laughs, the sound like music to my ears. "It is." She tilts her head, pinching her lips together in a playful pout. "Then again, I'm not sure what we'd classify as *our* first date."

"We kind of just fell into us, didn't we?"

"We kind of did," she admits with a tremble.

It takes everything I have to not wrap my arms around her, pull her into me, and never let go. Just like it's killed me to keep my distance this week. But she needed space. Needed to know I'll respect her wishes and won't assume to know what she needs better than she does. Needed to know I respect her desire to maintain control of her life.

But she also needs to know I still support her, something I was able to demonstrate by being here today instead of golfing with a client who's on the brink of taking his business to another firm, costing mine ten percent of our annual earnings.

The truth is, even if it cost my firm 100 percent of its annual earnings, I'd still be here.

"So…" She clears her throat. "What would you call our first date?"

"That's a tough one, considering our path has been anything but traditional. In my line of work, when faced with a problem, it's best to look at the necessary elements. We should do the same here."

"Okay." She smirks, an easiness about her I haven't seen in what feels like forever. Almost like the past week never happened. Like we're still the same people we've always been before our world crashed around us. "What are the essential requirements for a date to be considered a date?"

I briefly tap on my bottom lip, as if deep in thought. "First and foremost, there needs to be some sort of offer and acceptance."

She arches a single brow. "That sounds like a contract."

"True. But you can't classify something as a date if you just so happen to be at the same place at the same time."

"I suppose that rules out our first encounter."

I chuckle. "It certainly does. As much as I enjoyed that first meeting, I don't consider that a date. More like a…very interesting plot twist."

She barks out a laugh, the sound strange in a place where guilt is decided and freedom erased. "A plot twist? So that's what I am to you?"

"Perhaps." I lean down, inhaling her comforting scent, and lower my voice. "But you're the best kind of plot twist. I never saw you coming, Lo." I adjust my stance, our bodies a breath away. Electricity hums in the space between us. "The second I did, I knew I'd do whatever it took to keep you in my life. Still will."

She briefly closes her eyes, seeming to bask in my reassurance before stepping back. "What's the next requirement?"

I cross my arms in front of my chest. "Some women may not agree with this, but the man should pay."

She parts her lips, as I knew she would, but I hold up my hand, cutting off her protest.

"I understand this whole feminism thing, and fully agree that women are equal to men. Hell, if you ask me, women far exceed men in many areas."

"Nice save," she remarks flirtatiously.

"Still, I like to think chivalry isn't completely dead. So for it to count as our first date, I would have had to pay for you."

"I suppose I'll let you have that one. For now." She winks. "What else?"

I relax my stance. "This is where it gets trickier. Or at least more specific. For it to be a date, I believe a man should compliment her appearance."

"Is that right?"

I nod, edging toward her. "Absolutely. There should be no doubt in her mind he thinks she's the most beautiful woman in the room…hell, the most beautiful woman he's ever seen."

Her gaze lifts to mine, peaceful and serene. "That's how you've always made me feel. Like I'm the most beautiful woman you've ever seen."

"That's because you *are* the most beautiful woman I've ever seen."

I rake my gaze over her appearance. From the ringlet curls framing her face and cascading past her shoulders. To the depths of her dark eyes that once hid secrets from me but now gladly allow me to see their pain. To her full, glossy lips that I've been lucky enough to taste on an almost daily basis.

But it's not just her outer beauty that's drawn me to her from the beginning. It's the beauty found underneath that's always spoken to me. Since our first encounter, I felt in my heart she was different. Felt her pain, her anguish, but also her strength.

She inches closer, barely a breath separating our bodies. But that small space may as well be an ocean for all I'm concerned, the wall she erected a barrier I'm not sure I'll ever be able to scale again. But I can't lose hope. Just like I gave her space all those months ago after she told me about her past, I'll do the same now. She eventually realized what was right in front of her. I pray she will again.

"If that's the case, our first date couldn't have been before the county fair. If memory serves, that was the first time you complimented my appearance. When you helped me out of your sister's car, I believe."

"You have no idea how many times I wanted to tell you before then," I admit, resisting the urge to cup her face in my hands and pull her lips toward mine. "Since I met you, I haven't thought about another woman. Even when we tried to keep our relationship strictly professional."

My heart warms at the memory of how hard we both fought this attraction. But there are some forces too powerful to resist. And that was Londyn. Our lives collided in a way I never imagined. Regardless of how it all ends, I'll never regret running into a torrential downpour to help a complete stranger.

"I think you and I both know our relationship has never been professional," she says in a soft voice.

"I do." I gradually lean toward her, but still don't touch her.

"What else needs to be present for a date to be considered a date?"

I clear my throat, straightening, but not pulling back too much. "It probably goes without saying that he's nervous."

She cocks a brow. "That's a requirement?"

"For a first date. It's like a job interview. You can have all the confidence in the world, yet still be nervous you'll say the wrong thing and ruin your chances. If you ask me, the stakes are even higher on a date."

"Higher than job security?"

"You can always apply for a different job. But a first date with a woman who completely steals your breath?" I shake my head. "You only have one chance to get it right or risk losing the best thing that could ever happen to you."

"Did I make you nervous when we first met?" She bats her lashes.

"That may be the understatement of the year," I respond with a laugh, then lower my voice. "And if I'm being honest, you still make me nervous, Lo."

She tilts her gaze toward mine. "Still?"

I nod. "Or maybe scared is a better word."

"What are you scared about?"

I reach for her hand, grateful when she allows me to take it. I study her skin against mine. Dark against light. Two polar opposites. Two different worlds. Yet we somehow found each other. Somehow fell for each other.

"Losing you, Lo," I say past the lump building in my throat, the mere idea like a knife through my heart.

"Wes…," she begins with a sigh, pulling her hand from mine.

"So when you take into account all of that…," I interject before she can list all the reasons I should keep my distance. I know her concerns. It doesn't mean I can accept them. I doubt I ever will. "I'd argue our first date was on the Ferris wheel."

"The Ferris wheel?" She scrunches her brows. "I'm not sure that qualifies. Hell, I was practically coerced into getting on that dang death trap by Imogene." Her expression falters briefly at the mention of my niece.

"You could have walked away."

A contemplative look crosses her face before she blows out a breath, shaking her head. "No, I couldn't, Wes. From the beginning, I've been completely powerless when it comes to you."

Easing toward her, I bring my hand up to her cheek. "And I've always been utterly powerless when it comes to you, honeybee," I admit, my lips descending toward hers.

She closes her eyes, jutting out her chin in preparation for my kiss. But at the last minute, I shift gears, feathering my lips against her forehead before dropping my hold on her.

She snaps her gaze to mine. "Wha——"

"You need space, and that's what I'm giving you. When you're ready to fight for yourself, for *us*, I'll be here." I leave one last kiss on her forehead, lingering for several long seconds as I breathe in her powdery fresh scent before pulling back.

Spying Hazel off to the side, I give her a grateful smile, then turn, making my way toward the glass doors.

Just as I'm about to push through them, Londyn's voice stops me.

"Hey, Wes?"

I pause, glancing over my shoulder.

She hesitates, chewing her bottom lip. "Do you... Do you want to come over tomorrow? Maybe grab lunch or something?"

My shoulders fall, relief rolling off me. "I'd love to."

# CHAPTER SEVENTEEN

## *Weston*

I sit on my couch Friday night, sipping on a scotch, watching a news report of the peaceful protest at the courthouse earlier today. When they segue to yet another story on the Buckhead shooting and the woman responsible, I change the channel, not wanting to sit through a reminder of what's going on. To most, it's a sensational story. To me, it's a cruel reality.

Navigating toward my movies, I search for something that's heavy on the humor and low on the drama. There's one movie that always fits the bill. One movie my sister and I would watch whenever we needed a pick-me-up. *Ferris Bueller's Day Off*. We all wish we could have one day to abandon responsibility. If there were any day I wish I could do just that, it's today.

It's strange to watch this now that I'm no longer a teenager. Back then, I thought the premise was entirely believable. From stealing your parents' car. To sneaking into a five-star restaurant. To dancing on a float during a parade in downtown Chicago. But that's the thing about being a teenager. You haven't really experienced life yet. You *can* believe in the ridiculousness of a John Hughes movie because the real world hasn't left you jaded and without hope.

What I wouldn't give to go back to that innocence. To believe in the goodness of people again.

Just as Ferris tries to convince the snotty maître d' that he's Abe Froman, the Sausage King of Chicago, my doorbell rings. I sit up, furrowing my brow. It's after ten o'clock at night. No one stops by this late. Hell, no one stops by at all, apart from Londyn. Or my mother.

But if it were my mother, she'd incessantly knock on my door, telling me she knows I'm home because she sees my car. So that leaves only one other possibility.

Jumping to my feet, I hurriedly make my way to the door, not even stopping to check the peephole before opening it. The second I do, my expression drops in surprise.

"Jules?"

She spins to face me, eyes wide, mouth agape, as if startled to see me, despite it being my house.

I tried to talk to her at court, but my mother and Nick ushered her out of there before I could. My only comfort was the look of reassurance from my father, silently telling me he had it under control.

"I-I'm sorry for just dropping in on you like this," she says in a small voice.

Her eyes appear vacant, her skin lackluster. It looks like she hasn't slept in days. I don't blame her. I really haven't, either.

"I didn't know if I should even come over, but I needed to get out of that house for a bit." She pulls her oversized sweater closer into her body. "Can I… Can I come in?"

"Of course." With a smile, I step back and allow her inside the house that was once her second home. It still could be if she needs it.

I follow her into the kitchen. Skirting around the island, I grab the bottle of red wine and hold it up.

"Would you like a glass?" I ask.

She exhales, her shoulders seeming to relax. "I'd love one. Especially without judgment."

I grab a glass out of the cabinet and pour the liquid into it before handing it to her. "Mom still thinks it's reckless to take care of a child and enjoy a glass of wine?"

She rolls her eyes as she swallows a healthy sip. "Now I remember why I was so desperate to go away to college, even if it was to one of her choosing. Living in that house is like a prison." She stops short, eyes flinging wide, her breath hitching. "I mean…"

"It's okay," I say, not wanting her to feel bad for her slip. I'm just glad she's here. "How did you get out tonight?"

She crosses an arm over her stomach. "I lied and said I needed to swing by the bakery."

"Well, I'm glad you're here."

"Me, too." She smiles, life returning to her eyes. She's still not the same Julia, but she's not the scared woman I saw earlier today, either.

"Want to sit?"

Nodding, she follows me into the living room. I lower myself to what's always been my spot on the couch, Julia sitting on the opposite end of the sectional in hers. The only thing missing now is Imogene.

And Londyn.

"Shitty day?" Julia comments, her focus on the television.

"What makes you say that?"

She nods at the screen. *"Ferris Bueller's Day Off.* That was our go-to movie after a crappy day."

I sigh, swiping my nearly empty glass of scotch off the coffee table, finishing it. "It's been a pretty shitty week, to be honest."

"It sure has." She takes a long gulp of her wine.

I glance at her, hesitating, a thousand questions swirling in my head. But I don't want to do anything to chase her away now that she's here. The heavy stuff can wait. For now, I just want to enjoy watching a movie with my sister. Like we used to.

Our conversation remains light as the movie plays, mostly reminiscing about the memories it brings forward. Like the time she stole our father's car and drove to Savannah for the day. Or the time we both skipped school to catch the Braves home opener. Or the time we threw a party at our house when we thought we had it to ourselves, only for our parents to come home after their flight was canceled due to a huge snowstorm up north.

With each memory, our laughter increases, reminding me how important she is to me. Ever since Julia arrived at our house all those years ago, we've had a bond that transcends that of brother and sister. I have to believe it's this bond that will help us get through this, too.

Once the credits roll, Julia reluctantly pulls herself to her feet. "I should probably get back before Lydia sends out a search party."

I stand, walking beside her as she makes her way toward the kitchen. "Probably not a bad idea."

After she rinses out her glass, she sets it on the drying rack, then heads toward the foyer. As she approaches the front door, I reach past her to open it, then face her.

"I'm really glad you stopped by tonight. You're welcome anytime. You know that, right?"

"I know." She lingers in the doorway for a protracted moment, not wanting to leave, but not able to stay. Suddenly, she throws herself at me, flinging her arms around my waist and hugging me tighter than she has in recent memory. Probably since Gampy and Meemaw's funeral. "Thank you, Wes. You're a good brother."

I squeeze her, wanting her to feel love that doesn't come with any conditions attached, as so often seems to be the case with my mother. And I get the feeling may also be the case with Nick.

"I love you, Jules. No matter what."

"No matter what," she repeats, savoring in my embrace for a beat before pulling away, swiping at the tears that had escaped. "Thanks again." She gives me one last smile, then steps into the chilly night air, tugging her sweater against her body as she walks swiftly to her car.

I watch her, hating the idea of sending her back to that house with Nick and my mother. After everything that's transpired, I have questions. And a premonition that only grows stronger with every passing minute.

"Are you okay, Julia?" I shout when she reaches her SUV.

She stops, glancing over her shoulder. "What do you mean? I—"

"Are you okay?" I repeat, striding down the walkway toward her. "You can talk to me. About anything. About Nick. You can *trust* me. You don't have to keep it all hidden because you're worried about what Lydia will say."

"And I appreciate that," she counters, squaring her shoulders and looking straight ahead. "But there is nothing to talk about."

"Nothing? So there's nothing going on with Nick? You never picked up on anything…off about him?"

"Off?" She scrunches her brows. "What do you—"

"Has he ever touched you in a way you didn't like or that wasn't appropriate?"

"Of course not!" she exclaims, but doesn't look me directly in the eyes.

If I didn't know Julia as well as I do, maybe I'd let it go. But after growing up together, I can tell when she's lying. When she's hiding something. And there's no doubt in my mind she's lying to me. The way she chews on her bottom lip and fidgets with the hem of her sweater makes it obvious.

"Look me in the eye and tell me he's never touched you," I demand. "That he's never hurt you."

"Don't be ridiculous, Wes."

"Do it, Jules." Jaw clenching and expression tense, I lean toward her. "If he's never hurt you, this shouldn't be a problem."

"Please, Wes." She keeps her head lowered, shaking it, the truth clear in her silence. But she still refuses to admit it.

"Say it, Jules," I continue, not letting her get away so easily. "Tell me he's never touched you without your consent."

She digs her hands through her hair, still shaking her head, each word I utter seeming to cause her more and more anguish.

"That you honestly believe his story," I growl, my voice growing louder. "That Londyn came on to him and shot him as some sort of woman-scorned revenge bullshit! Because if that's what you believe, if that's the truth, you should have no problem looking me in the eye and saying so."

"Wes, please…"

"Goddammit, Julia!" I don't think as I clutch her biceps

with a harsh grip, the trauma and stress of the past week catching up to me. "Just fucking tell me the truth already!"

"Don't touch me!" she cries out, wiggling in my grasp, pure terror covering her face.

The reality of what I'm doing washing over me, I snap out of my trance, quickly dropping my hold. The instant she's free, she spins around and flings her car door open.

In all my thirty-six years, I've never touched a woman like I just did Julia. My stomach tenses, throat constricting.

"Julia, I'm so—"

She quickly lifts a hand, preventing me from getting any closer to her. "Just stop, Wes. Please." She draws in a deep breath as she rubs her arms. "I know you mean well, but I am begging you." She slowly lifts her eyes to mine. I've never seen her so tortured before. "You have to stop asking questions. You're not helping matters."

I blink, her words catching me off guard. They could mean so many things. "You don't have to go back there. You don't need him. Don't need any of them."

She pulls her bottom lip between her teeth to stop her chin from quivering. "I wish it were that simple, Wes," she admits, tears streaming down her face, an odd look for a woman who's always hidden her emotions behind a locked door. "But it's not. I..." She trails off, the words stuck in her throat. "I'm sorry."

She climbs into the car and slams the door, then cranks the ignition, peeling down my driveway and off into the night.

# CHAPTER EIGHTEEN

*Londyn*

I stare at the pad in front of me, notes from my conversation with Sophia scrawled on it. It's been an hour since her phone call, and I still struggle to comprehend the reality that this is what the ADA calls their best offer. I figured I'd plead to one of the misdemeanor charges, have to do some community service, perhaps probation. But this? This doesn't seem like a bargain at all.

In exchange for pleading guilty to aggravated assault, they'll drop all the misdemeanor charges. They'll also recommend a much lighter sentence than the twenty years I could potentially face. One year in prison, suspended after six months, then five years' probation.

My initial response was to not take it. Why would I? I didn't do anything wrong. Didn't do anything any other woman in my shoes wouldn't do.

But can I really put my freedom at risk in the hopes the

judge or jury believes my story? Or do I just accept defeat and take the offer, since it's most likely the best I'll get?

A knock on my door cuts through my thoughts. I look at it, a heaviness settling over me, knowing all too well it's Wes here for our lunch date. I'd looked forward to seeing him... until Sophia called.

With slow steps, I make my way to the door, still not sure what to tell him about Sophia's phone call. He'd appeared so hopeful after I asked him to lunch today. This will surely eviscerate that. Just like it did to my optimism.

"Wes, I—" I begin, pulling the door open before snapping my mouth shut when I see it's not Wes at all.

In fact, it's someone I didn't think I'd ever see again. Someone I never *wanted* to see again.

"Surprised to see me, Lo?" Sawyer asks, a righteous expression etched on his face.

All I can do is stare at the man who looks as out of place on my front stoop as a rainstorm in the desert. I once thought him to be attractive. Chiseled jawline. Kind eyes. Charismatic smile. But the kindness and grace he purports to possess during his weekly sermons is simply a mask. Sawyer Ross is no more compassionate than I am guilty of the crime of which I'm accused.

A movement over his shoulder catches my attention. I glimpse toward it, blinking when I notice my father standing at the bottom of the steps. I expect to see disappointment, like I did the last time I saw him. Instead, there's something else. Remorse? That can't be. Can it?

"Aren't you going to invite us inside?" Sawyer pulls my attention back to him.

But he doesn't wait for an invitation, pushing past me and into my condo, ignoring my wishes, just as he did during our marriage. He failed to take into account one important thing, though. I'm *not* the same person I was during our marriage. I've grown. Matured. Learned to speak up for myself. And that's precisely what I intend to do now.

Spinning on my heels, I storm toward Sawyer as he makes himself at home, setting his briefcase down on my kitchen table before removing his wool coat and draping it over one of the chairs.

"What are you doing here?" I demand as my father slowly makes his way into my condo, silently observing his surroundings.

"Is that any way to greet someone who might be willing to help?" Sawyer turns toward me, smiling slyly.

"Help?" I place a hand on my hip. "Like you did all those years ago when I told you what happened to me? Because if that's the same kind of help you came to offer, I—"

"It's in your best interests to listen to what I have to say, Londyn," he interjects with a reproachful glare. "Unless you *want* to spend the next several years of your life in prison."

I should kick him out. Kick them *both* out. But what if Sawyer really can help me? Over the past several years, he has proven himself to be quite influential. Has associated with people in powerful positions. Maybe he'll use his influence to help me. But at what cost?

"May I?" He gestures toward the couch, but his request is simply a formality. He doesn't wait for my response, walking toward the couch and sitting in my spot. It's the side of the couch I've always sat on, even when we were married. And he knows it.

He smirks, confirming my suspicions that he chose that spot intentionally, to maintain control. Then he nods toward the reading chair, indicating where I should sit, a king holding court.

But I'm no longer one of his subjects.

My head held high in defiance, I cross my arms in front of my chest. "I'll stand."

He glowers at me for several long moments, then shrugs. "Suit yourself." He settles into the cushions. "Your case has made quite the splash in the headlines these past few days."

"Yes, it has. Which explains why you're here. To cash in on that publicity."

He feigns indignation, his hand going to his heart. "How could you say that? Like I told you, I'm here to help."

I roll my eyes so hard, I'm positive they're about to pop out of their sockets. "And like *I* told *you*, you didn't seem interested in helping me all those years ago, Sawyer. No. You used me as a way to garner sympathy. Make you out to be the victim. Isn't that right?"

"Do you think I *wanted* to admit to the board of the church that my wife left me after sleeping with another man?"

"For crying out loud! You *actually* believe that? That I would lie to you? Make up some story just to cover up an affair?"

"You *did* lie to me, Lo. Almost got away with it, too, if it weren't for Mrs. Leonard seeing you leave the abortion clinic."

I tilt my head back, summoning the strength to get through this. "You're ridiculous, Sawyer. No better than the asshole who actually *raped* me."

I notice my father flinch, then squeeze his eyes shut as he scrubs a hand over his face. It's only been a few years, but he looks as if he's aged fifteen, his normally dark hair now showing signs of gray. Sure, he's in his fifties and it's expected he'd have gray hair by now. But the lines around his eyes and heavy bags beneath them make it appear he hasn't slept a wink since I left. I want to feel bad for him, go to him and make sure he's okay. But he chose his side. And it wasn't mine.

I point between them. "You're both manipulative pricks who will do or say anything to get what you want. To get people to do what you want. I may have fallen for it when I first agreed to the ridiculous idea of marrying you instead of someone who loved me. I won't do it again. So let's get this over with. I'm not exactly in the mood for a trip down memory lane right now."

I keep my gaze trained on them, my chest heaving, doing my best to show them I'm not that same girl. Sawyer returns my glare, probably expecting it to have the same effect it once did and I'll back down. Not anymore. That girl died years ago.

"If you must know," Sawyer begins after a beat, "I just came from a meeting with the District Attorney. He told me the ADA has made an offer." He cocks a brow, awaiting a response, to which I nod. "Well, I'm here with an even better one."

"How? My attorney said it's the best one they could make, all things considered."

"And that's true. But as you may be aware, the DA has his sights set on the governorship next year."

"So I've been told." I rub my arms, a chill tricking down my spine.

He crosses a leg, resting his calf on his opposite thigh, spreading his arms wide as he leans against my couch, an air of superiority about him. "There's quite a large black population in Georgia, isn't there?"

I don't respond, not liking where this is going.

"District Attorney Ambrose is more than aware that his chances of winning the election are slim if he doesn't have the black vote."

"And you'll help with that." My words come out as a cross between a question and a statement.

"I will. In exchange for him dropping all charges against you, which will help him garner the black vote even more. It'll be like it never happened. We'll go back to the way things were. You'll come home to Virginia and fulfill your promise to me."

"My promise to you?" I repeat, unsure I'd heard him correctly.

This must be some sort of dream. Or nightmare. I must have fallen asleep on the couch. There's no way my father and Sawyer would appear on my doorstep after nearly six years of no communication, apart from the monthly letters my father sent that I never opened. There's no way Sawyer would want things to go back to the way they were. That's absurd.

"Precisely. You'll act the part of my wife, like you promised."

"Why? Why is this so important to you? Last I checked, you seemed to love milking the idea of having an estranged wife who lost her way. You still constantly bring me up in your sermons to get people to supposedly pray for you every goddamn week."

"Lo," my father interjects in his deep baritone that once read me Bible stories as I fell asleep. "Don't take the Lord's name in vain."

Of course he wouldn't speak up to defend me. It would be to scold me, even though I'm nearly thirty years old.

"I'm sorry." I glower at him for a beat, then return my

eyes to Sawyer. "To get people to pray for you every *fucking* week." I shift my gaze to my father, smirking. "Is that better for your pious ears?"

I expect him to appear annoyed or offended. Instead, a soft chuckle vibrates through him, which he tries to mask with a cough. It strikes me as odd. Couple that with his look of remorse when they first arrived, and it has me second-guessing things. But that still doesn't mean I can forgive him for his failure to stand up for me all those years ago. The scars he caused are just as prominent as the ones Nick left.

"It doesn't look good when I tell people I'm estranged from my wife." Sawyer's voice forces my attention back to him. "Sure, divorce doesn't carry the stigma it once did, but there are still some people who…take issue with the fact that I haven't fixed our marriage. If we're being honest, I'm lucky my church kept me on after what you did."

"Oh, you mean refuse to carry the baby of my rapist?" I retort with a trite smile.

He avoids my eyes, knowing it's the truth.

"That's right. You left that part out when you informed the board, didn't you?"

If I hadn't gotten curious in the months following my move to Atlanta, I probably wouldn't have learned that. But feeling homesick one day, I'd tuned into his Sunday sermon he streamed online, just like I did every Sunday while I was away at college. And that's how I learned he never admitted the full story to his church or the board. He let them believe the baby I aborted didn't belong to my rapist, but to Sawyer, a fact that was scientifically impossible. That didn't matter to him. He twisted the truth to fit his needs, as always.

"That's irrelevant now. What's done is done."

"You're such a goddamn hypocrite," I mutter under my

breath, then straighten, hearing my father's warning in my head. "Sorry." I glance at him before shifting my eyes back to Sawyer. "Such a *fucking* hypocrite."

Unfazed, he stands, towering over me. "You can think that all you want, but the truth remains." When he advances toward me, I back up on instinct, needing to keep my personal space. "I have the power to help you. I do this for you, you agree to return to Virginia and be my wife again."

"And what do you get out of it?"

"What do you mean?"

"Exactly what I said. You don't help anybody unless there's something in it for you. So what's in it for you? Money? A staff position if the DA wins? What?"

He pauses, lips pinched into a tight line. "The past few years, I've been teaching at Living Gospel, where I studied myself."

I nod. "I've heard."

"Then you may have also heard that the president is step-ping down. My name's been tossed around in consideration."

I stare, unblinking, feeling like I've traveled back in time to the day my father called me into his office. Sawyer had a similar story back then, too.

"Unfortunately, the board has brought up my supposed marital...issues as a problem."

"Let me guess. The two of you got together and figured all you had to do was convince me to come back and play the dutiful wife so you could get the job, right? Without a single regard for what I want?"

"I'm not asking a lot of you, Lo. Just to fulfill the vows you made to me."

I bark out a laugh. "*My* vows? What about *your* vows to *me*?" I step toward him, eyes wild. "To love me in sickness and in health? To honor me? You threw those out the window at the first opportunity to garner sympathy from your church. And you're doing the same thing now. That's the only reason you're here. Because you saw the protests on TV. Saw the thousands of women assembling to support me. You must hate that you had nothing to do with it. That there are women now marching across the country *for* me! Because they *believe* me. Because they *are* me. They've been where I am and feel strongly enough in a cause to make their voice heard. Something you wouldn't have the first clue about. You may put on a good show when the cameras are on, offer a sympathetic ear to another mom whose son was another unfortunate victim of driving while black, or walking while black, or pretty much breathing while black. That doesn't change the fact that the only cause Sawyer Ross actually believes in is Sawyer Ross."

He stares at me, mouth agape, taken aback by my outburst. As is my father. These are words I never would have spoken if I hadn't somehow found the courage to walk away from my sheltered existence. If I hadn't decided enough was enough and taken back control of my life. If I hadn't walked into that first self-defense class and met Diego and Hazel. They're my family now. Not these two imposters.

"Regardless of any supposed support you may think you have," Sawyer continues, his words laced with superiority, "according to the DA, you're on the hook for up to twenty years in prison. It's a blow to your defense that they didn't find your claims of sexual assault reliable, refusing to file charges against the man you shot. So your chances of actually prevailing if you take this to trial?" He arches a single brow. "They're not good." He gestures toward my TV as a national news network covers a protest in Seattle. "All these protests, all these marches… They're not going to help you. It's just noise. Trust me. In a few weeks, your name will no longer be in the headlines and they'll find something else to protest. Like the DA said. The evidence against you for aggravated assault is compelling. While the evidence against Mr. Jaskulski for sexual assault is weak, at best. But I can help you. If you help me."

With determined strides, he makes his way toward the kitchen table and opens his briefcase. After withdrawing a few papers, he returns, handing them to me.

"What's this?" I ask, my eyes scanning the documents.

"An…agreement of sorts. It's not legally enforceable, per se, but I thought it best to detail what I expect from you. I've come up with a list of things I'll need from you in order for the board at the college to believe our reconciliation is authentic. Some rules, I suppose."

"How do you expect this to work? You left out quite a few details when you informed the board at your church of our separation. My case has made national news. I'm sure someone will have doubts."

"It's all in the agreement, but I'll need you to make a confession to the church corroborating Mr. Jaskulski's version of events."

I toss the papers back onto the table. "You said yourself this isn't enforceable."

"True. It's not. But I still expect you to adhere to these… requests. Tit for tat, Londyn."

"And if I don't follow these so-called 'requests'?" I ask, using air quotes.

"Simple. I'll cease all cooperation with District Attorney Ambrose's campaign. Do you know what he'll then be free to do at that point?"

"What's that?" I ask in a shaky voice, although I already know the answer.

"He'll be free to refile charges against you, especially if new evidence comes to light. Like my corroborative testimony regarding your affair with the man you almost killed."

"So you're offering me to exchange one prison sentence for another. At least with the plea deal the ADA offered, I'd only have to serve six months. Your deal doesn't sound too attractive next to that."

"I'd be hard-pressed to call living with me a prison sentence. You'll be free to do whatever you please, including your little interior decorating and furniture hobby."

"It's design," I correct.

"Excuse me?"

"I'm an interior *designer*. Not decorator. There's a big difference."

"If you say so." He waves me off, as if my life's passion is inconsequential compared to his. "Regardless, I believe my offer is much more attractive than the one your attorney relayed to you. Or did she not tell you all about the possible ramifications of a felony conviction on your record?"

My expression falters. "She did," I admit in a small voice.

"Then you know it's not only your freedom at stake, but also your livelihood. I'm not sure many people will want to hire an interior *designer* with a felony conviction on her record, especially one for a violent crime like aggravated assault. And with a gun, no less. If it were me, I wouldn't hire you. But if you accept my offer, it will all…" He snaps his fingers, "disappear."

As much as I hate to admit it, Sawyer has a point. Since my arrest and the subsequent media attention, I haven't received a single sale from my up-cycling business or an inquiry for my interior design services. I'd like to blame it on the post-Christmas lull, but that's probably only partly to blame.

I chew on my bottom lip, considering the pros and cons of each option.

Option one: Fight this all the way to trial. Pro: Being found innocent and going on with my life. Cons: A drawn-out trial that could result in conviction and being sentenced to a lengthy prison term. Not to mention all the financial ramifications.

Option two: Take the plea bargain. Pro: Only serve six months in prison. Cons: Serving six months in prison, as well as having a criminal conviction for a violent felony follow me around the rest of my life, which could make it difficult to gain new clients or get a job if I end up having to close my design business.

Option three: Accept Sawyer's offer. Pros: Have the charges against me dropped. Be able to keep pursuing my passion. Cons: Confess to an affair I didn't have in front of Sawyer's entire church. Leave behind the life I've built for myself.

Leave behind Wes.

"Can I have a day to think about it?" I ask, bringing my gaze back to Sawyer.

I shouldn't even be contemplating his offer. But it provides me a way to avoid serving any actual time. To keep my business up and running. To continue pursuing my passion.

"There's a lot to consider."

"I can do that." He closes his briefcase, leaving the papers on the table for me to peruse. Then he shrugs his jacket back on. "I'll pick you up tomorrow at eleven."

"Pick me up? For what?"

"Church. Your father's delivering a guest sermon at Elevate Life Church. The service starts at noon."

"I don't think that's such a great idea."

Church was once a part of my weekly, if not daily, life. But that was before. Since walking away from Sawyer and my father, I haven't stepped foot in one. Haven't felt like worshiping a God who allowed two men to turn their backs on me.

"Please, Lo," my dad implores, standing and timidly approaching me. "It was the church your mother went to when she was younger. It would mean a lot to her if you were in attendance."

My confusion only increases with this piece of information. "She grew up in Atlanta?"

He nods. "She did."

I stare into the distance. How did I not know that? Then again, I was so young when she passed away. After that, I saw how much it pained my father to talk about her, to be reminded of everything he lost. Instead, I let her live on in my own truncated memories, never pushing to learn more about the woman who's become more like a ghost over the years.

"Okay." I draw in a shaky breath, my palms growing clammy over the idea of going to church. "I'll be there."

My dad offers me a sad smile as he reaches out and grasps my hand, the contact taking me by surprise. "Thank you. It means a lot. More than I think you realize."

He holds my gaze for a beat, then Sawyer clears his throat, breaking the moment. My dad tears his hand from mine, an unspoken apology in his gaze as he heads toward the foyer.

"And be sure to dress presentable," Sawyer admonishes as he opens the door.

I'm about to argue that I'll dress how I want. But when I see Wes just outside, hand raised as he's about to knock, any protest is ripped from my throat, panic filling me.

"Can I help you?" Sawyer asks, stance wide, arms crossed, as if this is his domain.

Wes looks from him to me, then back again, confusion wrinkling the lines of his brow. "Who are you?" he demands, his refined Southern drawl exhibiting an edginess I typically don't hear.

"I'm her—"

"Wes," I interject, jumping to diffuse the situation. Placing my hand on his elbow, I gesture toward my father standing right behind Sawyer. "This is my father, Marlon Bennett." I draw in a deep breath before shifting toward Sawyer and gritting a smile. "And this is Sawyer Ross. Sawyer, Dad, this is Weston Bradford." I pause. "My boyfriend."

No one says anything for several protracted moments, my heart hammering in my chest so loudly, I'm pretty sure everyone can hear. I glance between Sawyer and Wes as they glare at each other.

"Well, that puts us all in a bit of a conundrum then." Sawyer looks from Wes to me.

"Why's that?" Wes loops his arm around my waist, holding me protectively. I once loved when he held me like this, staking his claim. Now it makes me feel guilty for all the secrets I've kept.

Including the biggest one I fear he's about to uncover.

Sawyer's expression falls, causing an icy chill to rush down my spine. Nothing good ever follows *this* look. It's cold. Conniving. Calculating.

"Because I'm her husband."

"You mean *ex*-husband," Wes emphasizes, albeit warily. "She told me all about you."

"Apparently not *all* about me. Because it seems she left out one rather important detail."

"And what's that?" Wes peers into my eyes, silently pleading for an explanation.

I wish I had one.

Sawyer smiles smugly. "She never filed for divorce."

# CHAPTER NINETEEN

## *Weston*

Heat washes over my face as I waver on my legs, feeling like the rug was just ripped out from under me. I tell myself to think rationally. That there must be a reason for this. But what?

Why wouldn't Londyn mention she was still married? Why didn't she file for divorce and end it?

"I understand what a shock this must be," Sawyer continues with a look of superiority I'd love to punch off his face.

"She referred to you as her ex. And based on the way you tossed her out, I don't blame her."

"I didn't toss her out. I gave her a choice."

I hate everything about the way he glowers at her, as if silently chastising her, reminding her of her place. It makes the hair on my nape stand on end. She attempts to slink away, but I tighten my grip on her.

"It's a good thing she never filed for divorce, though. Because I'm here to rectify things."

"Rectify things?" I shift my attention to Londyn, brows furrowed. "What is he talking about?"

Londyn pushes away from me, increasing the distance between us, a thousand apologies written within her deep, dark eyes. This isn't a woman who would deceive me about being married. If she didn't file for divorce, she had a damn good reason for it. Based on the vibes Sawyer gives off, I have a feeling I know what that reason is.

"Wes, I—"

"I'm good friends with the District Attorney," Sawyer interrupts before Londyn can get more than a few words in. "He's agreed to drop the charges if I help with his campaign. Help him win the black vote. And like I told Londyn, I'll only stick my neck out like that if I get something in return."

He doesn't need to spell it out. I know exactly what he hopes to get out of Londyn in return. The same thing that started all of this for her years ago. He just wants a woman to play the part of his wife.

"You're not seriously thinking about taking him up on that, are you?" I ask urgently, barely able to say the words through the tightness in my throat, as if my body fights against the mere idea.

She parts her lips to speak, but before she can, Sawyer cuts her off. Again.

"Trust me. This is a much better deal than her attorney was able to get. At least with me, she'll avoid prison. She'll avoid charges altogether."

"They made an offer?" I ask her directly, something it appears Sawyer is incapable of doing.

She smiles sadly through tight lips. In that one gesture, I know it wasn't an offer worth accepting. At least not when there's a better one dangling in front of her, even if it's from a man who will only use her.

"Sophia—"

"One year of incarceration, suspended after six months, and five years' probation in exchange for a guilty plea to felony aggravated assault," Sawyer speaks over her yet again.

It reminds me of how Nick is around Julia. I never noticed it before. But that was before I had the rose-colored lenses I tended to view the world through smashed to pieces. Now I see things I was blind to. Like the way Nick seemed to constantly cut off Julia when she started to speak. The way he'd pull her into his body, his hold not protective, but possessive. The watchful way he'd peer at her. I once thought it was because he was so in love with her that he couldn't stand not looking at her. Now I know the truth. It was all a way for him to retain control over Julia.

And Sawyer is just as manipulative.

He may never have laid a hand on Londyn, may not have left any visible bruises, but there's no doubt in my mind that the ones he left below the surface are still struggling to heal.

"They'll drop the rest of the charges, which are only misdemeanors anyway. Still, she'll have to carry around a felony conviction for the rest of her life, something that could affect her ability to get a mortgage, a job, find clients for her dream business she's just started."

"That's it?" I direct my question to Londyn. "That's the best offer they could make?"

"I—" she begins, and as expected, Sawyer doesn't let her finish.

"If you care about her like you purport to, why wouldn't you want her to take my offer? She'll be free. Never have to serve a single day in prison." He crosses his arms in front of his chest.

I lean into him, incensed that this man has the audacity to show up and blackmail Londyn into returning to the life she fought to free herself from. "And *because* I love her, I won't let her do that." I take her hands in mine, praying the connection I still feel is strong enough for her to realize she doesn't need to do this. "I told you I'd fight for you, honey-bee," I say in a soft voice. "And I will. You can't go with him."

"So you'll send her off to prison?" Sawyer booms. "Nice way of showing your supposed 'love'," he quips, using air quotes.

I drop my hold on Londyn and advance toward Sawyer, my eyes on fire. "At least I believed her when she told me what Nick did. I didn't blame her for being unfaithful when nothing could be further from the truth."

"That's in the past." He waves me off, stepping away from me. "All that matters now, all that's important now, is that I can help her. Do you want to see her locked up? Have you ever been to a jail or prison? Trust me. It's not some-where I'd want to spend a day, let alone six months."

"And after the way you treated her, I wouldn't want Londyn to have to endure living in the same house as you," I retort.

"She knew what she was getting into when she agreed to marry me," Sawyer insists.

"Is that right? So you told her from the beginning that she'd be no more than a piece of property to you?" Spittle forms on the corners of my mouth as I straighten, looming over him by less than an inch, but I'll take any advantage I can get right now. "That she was nothing more than a means to an end? Something you could exert absolute control over?"

He opens his mouth to protest, but I cut him off, giving him a dose of his own medicine.

"At least I treat her like a human being," I bellow, pointing to my chest, my voice carrying through the condo, probably even outside. "I *love* her like a human being. And because of that love, I'll fight for her. Because of that love, I won't let her accept your offer. I won't let her return to that life. I—"

"*Enough!*" Londyn shrieks, sharp and cutting.

I snap my mouth shut, everyone shifting their attention to Londyn as she stands there, eyes clamped shut, fists clenched, chest heaving. She takes several moments to pull herself together, then pins Sawyer and me with a venomous stare.

"This isn't a decision for either of you to make." She points between us. "Neither of you gets to tell me what I will or won't do. I'm not a fucking child. I'm a grown-ass woman who happens to have a brain on her shoulders. One who is capable of making a decision without some *man* telling me what's best for me. Because neither one of you cares about that. Have you even listened to yourselves? It's me, me, me, me, me! You mask *your* needs by saying it's best for me when neither one of you seems to have a fucking clue about what's best for me."

"Londyn, I—" I begin, but she holds up her hand, silencing me. I step back, guilt festering inside me. I'd been angered by how dismissive Sawyer was of Londyn's wishes. But by trying to speak for her, I'd also rendered her mute.

Just like Sawyer.

"Either way I look at it, I stand to lose something I've fought to have for years." She looks at Sawyer. "Freedom." She briefly shifts her eyes toward her father. "A family." Then she turns toward me, a small smile tugging on her lips. "Love." Her voice quivers, eyes glossing over for a second before her stare hardens again.

"So if this is the last decision I get to make for the foreseeable future, *I'm* the one who's going to make it. Not you." She shoves her finger into my chest before fixing her fiery gaze on her father. "Not you." She points at him before turning her ire on Sawyer. "And certainly not you. I just…" She shakes her head, at a loss for words. "Just get out of my house," she says in a pained voice.

I study Sawyer, wondering how he'll respond to her demand. He doesn't strike me as the type of person who'd follow anyone's orders.

"Londyn, I—" Sawyer begins, but she remains steadfast in her resolve.

"Now," she demands.

He hesitates a minute, then nods at her father, both of them retreating. I stand back, watching them leave, vindicated by her dismissal of them.

"That includes you, Wes."

I dart my gaze to hers, brow furrowed. "But—"

"You don't get to tell me what to do, either."

"I didn't mean—"

"I know," she admits with a sad smile. "But I need to make this decision on my own. I hope you can respect that."

My shoulders dropping, I briefly close my eyes. I'd spent this past week giving her space so she didn't think I was making decisions for her. To give her some semblance of control in a life that's spinning out of control. As much as it pains me, I need to give her this, too.

"I can."

On a long exhale, I start to leave, but change course,

making my way toward the kitchen table, reaching into my jacket.

"What are…" She trails off when I pull out the little box I've been carrying everywhere lately and set it on the surface.

"Maybe this will help."

"Wes…" My name on her lips is a cross between a plea and a benediction.

"I meant what I told you the other night. I'll go into battle for you, no matter the cost." I hold out my hand, urging her to grab onto it, needing that spark of electricity that comes to life whenever our skin touches.

She floats her eyes to my hand, as if it holds all the answers. "I know you will."

She places her hand in mine, our fingers locking together. I squeeze, trying to give her everything I have. My strength. My determination. My love.

Then, reluctantly, I pull away from her, leaving her alone in her condo, praying she chooses to fight. And not for me. But for her.

"It'll never work out," a snide voice says as I continue down the walkway.

I stop, turning toward where Sawyer stands beside a dark SUV.

"Just because *you* refused to treat her like she deserves, don't be so sure I will," I retort, erasing the distance between us. "I actually care about her. I actually *love* her."

He smirks, tilting his head to the side. "You say that now. But do you love her enough to raise a black baby with her?"

I blink, his question catching me off guard. "To be honest, that's never crossed my mind. I don't care what skin color our baby will have. All I care—"

"Well, you *should* care. You *should* be thinking about it. If you haven't figured it out by now, not being white in this country isn't exactly a walk in the park. It's hard. And tiring. Are you ready to allow your son or daughter to run to the local convenience store for a candy bar and worry the entire time about whether they'll make it back home?"

"We haven't discussed having children, but no matter what, I'll teach our son or daughter how to be strong, brave, and resilient." With each word, my voice grows louder, my passion and determination mounting. "I will raise *our* baby. White. Black. Brown. Red. Yellow. I don't care. That baby will be *our* baby. And I pray there will come a time when people will look *beyond* the different colors of our skin and only see the love we share. Only see that love is love, regardless of the colors involved. And the love I have for that woman..." I point toward her house, my chest heaving through my labored breathing. "Nothing will scare me away. You can't bring up how difficult our lives will be in the hopes of chasing me off. I know it won't be easy. It hasn't exactly been all fun and games up to this point. But through it all, do you want to know what I've done?"

He simply stares at me, not uttering a single word.

"I've stayed by her side. I've supported her. I've *loved* her. Something you couldn't even begin to know how to do. You may think you have the upper hand, that you'll be able to convince Londyn to go back home with you. And maybe she'll agree to your ridiculous proposal. But I won't stop fighting for her. You can take her back to Virginia, but I won't stop. You can do everything to hide her from me, to mold her back into a puppet who does everything you ask, but I. Won't. Stop. And that's a goddamn promise."

I spin on my heels, storming toward my car, slamming the door behind me. With my hands on the wheel, I take a few moments to compose myself and slow my racing heart before cranking the ignition. I'm about to put the car into drive when I glance at Londyn's condo, noticing her standing just inside her front door, watching me, probably having overheard what just transpired.

Her lips lift in the corners as she meets my gaze.

I don't know what's going to happen with us.

But it's that one look, one smile, that gives me hope this hasn't all been for nothing. That we'll get through this, too.

# CHAPTER TWENTY

## *Londyn*

"He was a cute kid, for what it's worth," Hazel offers later that evening as we watch one of the earliest interviews the media did with Sawyer in the days following the church shooting.

Even as a boy of eleven, he was extremely charismatic, talkative, charming. I was always the opposite, even before I lost my mother. More reserved. Cautious. Contemplative. It's not that I was shy. I just chose my words and interactions wisely. Unlike Sawyer, who became the poster child for the tragedy.

People's hearts went out to the poor boy who no longer had a father. It was his first taste of stardom. I still struggle to rationalize the Sawyer who held my hand as I watched them lower my mother's casket into the ground with the Sawyer who, mere hours ago, all but blackmailed me to be his wife.

Again.

"He was. Sweet, too. Always looked out for me." I exhale

deeply. "What happened?" I ask under my breath, more to myself than Hazel.

"People change, Lo. It's part of life. You're not the same girl you were back then, are you?" She nods at my laptop screen as a much younger version of myself huddles next to my father, who's beside himself with grief.

She has a point. People *do* change. I've changed. So has Sawyer. Unfortunately, he didn't change for the better.

In the following years, his pseudo-celebrity status as being the poster boy of that shooting ended up going to his head, especially as he forged a career as a pastor and, eventually, civil rights activist. Although I still struggle to truly call him an activist.

"I hate this." I hit the spacebar on my laptop, pausing the screen just as the camera pans to a younger version of Sawyer looking upon me with affection, arm draped around my shoulders. I'd hoped watching some of these videos would help me make my decision. Instead, it's only amplified the mess I'm currently in.

When Hazel came over and I told her everything that had transpired, she certainly voiced her opinion about Sawyer's offer. And just as I did with Wes and Sawyer, I told her this was my decision and it was important I explore *all* my options, regardless of how crappy she thought they were.

And just like any good friend would, she understood, spending the past several hours listening to me discuss the pros and cons of each with as little judgment as possible.

"You know the theory behind the Butterfly Effect, right?" Hazel asks.

"I do." My lips curve up slightly as I'm transported back to last summer. To installing insulation with Wes in what would become the primary bedroom of Gampy and Meemaw's house. How he'd equated my leaving the only life

I'd ever known as the first flap of the butterfly's wings, which set into motion the chain of events that would eventually lead to our meeting.

At the time, I found it sweet and romantic. But I'd ignored the most important aspect of the Butterfly Effect. That a single flap of a butterfly's wings could eventually lead to a massive storm, upending everything in its path.

"Everything has a cause and effect," Hazel states. "So you need to decide what effect is most important to you. You're here in this precise moment. You can't control anything that's happened prior. The storm's already brewing. The way I see it, you have three choices."

She points to the first piece of paper, where I'd scrawled out the list of pros and cons of accepting Sawyer's offer. "Do you run in the opposite direction, knowing you'll never be happy again?" She turns her attention to the next sheet of paper, which lists the pros and cons of accepting the plea deal. "Do you seek refuge away from everyone and everything you hold dear, thinking it's the safest bet?" She brings her gaze toward mine, her eyes determined. "Or do you take a risk and ride out the storm, knowing there's a chance it may bypass you altogether? But also that it might destroy everything you've built?" She takes my hands in hers. "Do you fight, Londyn? Or do you give up?"

I chew on my bottom lip, shaking my head. If she thought her little analogy would help, she was mistaken. Nothing I do seems to make this decision any easier. There's so much at stake.

"I need to get out of here," I announce, pulling my hands from hers and standing.

"Where are you going?" she asks as I grab my keys off the entryway table.

"For a drive. I just need to clear my head. And I can't think here. It's too…foggy."

She rises to her feet, making her way toward me. "Are you sure you're okay?" She runs her hands along my arms.

"I'm sure." I offer her as reassuring of a smile as I can muster right now. "I just need space to breathe."

"I get it." She pulls me in for a hug. "Just be careful."

"I will." I relish in her embrace for a moment before stepping away and heading out of my house.

A few streetlights illuminate the quaint neighborhood, the occasional childish squeal or dog barking cutting through the stillness. Other than that, everything is normal. Peaceful.

At complete odds with my mind.

I slide into my car and pull away from my condo, the burden weighing me down gradually lightening. It's a little thing, but I forgot how much I enjoyed the freedom of driving. Since everything happened with Nick, I've barely driven myself anywhere. But now that I'm behind the wheel, can make my own decisions about where to go, I feel a sense of freedom. Do I really want to give this up?

For the next several hours, I drive around the city with no direction in mind. But I don't care. There's a comfort in being able to decide if I should turn left or right. If I should push my luck and go more than five miles above the speed limit. If I should stop and check out some of the Christmas lights that should have been taken down a week ago.

At some point, I find myself in a section of town I'm not all too familiar with, but one I keep passing. Convinced I'm lost, I pull to the side of the road and grab my phone to check the GPS. Just as I'm about to punch in my home address to get my bearings, I stop myself, peering at the steepled, brick building just up the block. It's not the fact it's a church that catches me off guard. It's *what* church.

Elevate Life Church.

My mother's church growing up.

Maybe there's a reason I ended up here. Maybe my mother had a hand in steering me here during my moment of crisis. Maybe she knew I needed direction. Forgiveness. Clarity.

I navigate my car into the church parking lot and kill the ignition. The instant I step out into the crisp air, beautiful music surrounds me. The parking lot is mostly vacant, apart from a handful of cars, which leads me to believe it's simply a choir rehearsal, not a Saturday evening service.

A force pulling me forward, my legs are on autopilot as they carry me up the short flight of stairs and toward the large, white doors. I half expect them to be locked. But as I tug and it opens, I smile, remembering my father's words that God's house is never locked. Even after the shooting that took my mother's life, he refused to lock his church, despite the fact it could have prevented the loss of life on that fateful night.

I wouldn't be surprised to learn he still refuses to lock the doors.

My steps light, I walk through the modest lobby. It's a stark contrast to the over-the-top, extravagant look of Sawyer's church, everything showy and flashy, a disgusting display of money. Apparently, Sawyer must have been sleeping the day we learned about greed or avarice being one of the seven deadly sins.

Just before I enter the sanctuary, I pause, my eyes falling on a series of portraits of previous pastors. I stop at one of the man who served as pastor in the seventies when my mother was a little girl. I can almost picture my grandparents walking with her, dressed in her Sunday best, white gloves on her hands and a respectable hat pinned to her curls. I don't remember much about my mother, but the image of her in my mind right now is incredibly clear.

I slowly make my way into the main church, the music growing louder. Doing my best to remain as quiet as possible so as to not disturb the rehearsal, I slip into one of the pews and inhale a deep breath, a feeling I can't quite explain washing over me.

Something drew me to this particular place tonight when I could have ended up anywhere in the Atlanta area. As I listen to one of my mother's favorite hymns, I know in my heart there was a reason a force bigger than myself intervened and pulled me to this building.

I've avoided God and religion for years now, everything Sawyer and my father did leaving a bad taste in my mouth. But maybe this is what I need. After all, my father often told me that religion and God are different things to different people. That God is whatever that person needs Her to be at that time in their life. And right now, what I need is some higher power where I can put all my troubles. Where I can let go. Where I can breathe again.

Where I won't be judged for my mistakes.

I tilt my head back, closing my eyes, allowing the mercy and forgiveness inside these four walls to feed my soul with positive energy and hope. Lately, I've run low on faith. Hell, since Nick's attack, my faith in anything, in anyone, has been questionable, at best. Maybe that's the problem. Maybe I need to find my faith again. To feel some sort of grace again. To feel *human* again.

"Reminds you of her, doesn't it?" a deep baritone cuts through my moment of self-introspection.

I jump, flinging my eyes toward the source, gaping when I see my father sitting beside me. I stare, dumbfounded, unsure how to respond or what to say. There's so much I *should* say now that I have the opportunity. For years, I imagined what I'd tell him if we were ever in the same room again. But now that we are, I don't have it in me. I'm just so tired of fighting.

"I can't really remember her that much," I answer curtly.

He leans forward, resting his forearms on his knees, briefly hanging his head. "That's partly my fault." He lifts his eyes to mine. "I should have spoken about her more. It just hurt so much, ya know?" His voice wavers with emotion as he draws a deep breath. "And the older you got, the more you looked like her. It only made me miss her even more."

I stare forward, not responding. How am I supposed to react to this little trip down memory lane? I'm not sure it's a trip I want to take with him. Not after everything.

I'm about to get up to leave, my moment of clarity officially ruined, when his voice stops me.

"Lollipop…"

Inhaling sharply, I whip my eyes to his, my throat tightening at the memory of my childhood nickname. He hasn't called me that in ages. I didn't think I'd ever hear it again.

A pained expression crosses his face as he peers at me, his eyes swirling with something that borders on regret. It reminds me of the way he looked at me earlier today. But now it's even more pronounced.

"Don't take Sawyer's offer," he whispers.

I blink several times. Did I hear him correctly? I thought he'd *want* me to take his offer and return home. He was the one who told me to tell him yes all those years ago. To promise my life to him. To sacrifice my happiness for his. Why would he sing a different song now?

Then again, as Hazel reminded me, people change. Maybe my father has changed, too. Maybe he's been living these past several years burdened with regret and remorse.

"I messed up, Londyn. Well, more than messed up." When his sad eyes lock with mine, I settle back into my seat. "And I fear you'll never forgive me for my actions. You probably shouldn't. I can't go back and change what I've done. That ship has sailed. But I *can* do everything to ensure you have the happiness you deserve going forward. And you deserve to be happy, Lo. Deserve to be loved. And there is absolutely no question in my mind that Wes loves you. If you ask me, *that's* something worth fighting for."

He licks his lips, collecting his thoughts. "What I saw today, the *love* I saw today, doesn't come around often. Once in a lifetime if you're lucky. Don't throw it away."

I nod, looking forward once more, unsure how to respond to his unexpected speech. I wish it were as easy as he makes it sound. Wish I could take a risk. But love doesn't have the power to fix everything.

"What do you think she would have done if she were in my shoes?" I ask after a beat, not having to clarify who I'm referring to. He knows.

"Your mother would fight," he replies without a single hesitation. "It's who she was." He chuckles under his breath, a gleam of nostalgia filling his gaze. "From the minute we met, she had this spark. This life. If she wanted something, she'd stop at nothing until she achieved it. You're a lot like her in that respect."

"I'm not a fighter," I say dejectedly. "For years, I've barely been able to keep my head above water."

"That's not true, baby girl. You may think you were barely hanging on, but you used every ounce of courage you had *to* hold on when the world tried to throw you off. You *fought*. And I know you've got the strength to fight your way through this, too."

When he reaches for my hand, I allow him to take it.

"I can't tell you what to do. I *won't* tell you what to do. Not anymore. If the past several years have taught me anything, it's that you're more than capable of taking care of yourself and making your own decisions. But what I will tell you is that I *know* you are one of the strongest, most courageous, resilient women I've ever known. No matter what you choose, know that I am so proud of who you are."

He stands, sliding out of the pew. He's about to turn to walk up the aisle when he pauses.

"I'm sorry I didn't believe you."

His apology hanging in the air between us, I squeeze my eyes shut. For years, I'd hoped to hear him say those words, thinking it would be a magic pill that would fix everything. That it would erase the shame, inadequacy, and disgust I lived with.

"Why didn't you?" I choke out, glancing back at him.

"I wish I had a good answer." He smiles sadly, scrubbing a hand over his weary face as he fully turns toward me. "I don't. And there's no excuse that could possibly make what I did right. I still struggle to fully understand it myself. The past few years, I've started attending meetings…"

I cock my head to the side. "Meetings?"

"For families of sexual assault victims."

"Oh."

This is more surprising than his admonition I not accept Sawyer's offer. I grew up in a world where there was a stigma attached to so much as the mention of therapy. Where we were supposed to look to God for guidance. This proves my father truly isn't the same man he once was.

"A common theme among those of us who initially didn't take the complaints seriously is that we didn't want to admit that something so horrible could happen to someone we cared about." His voice catches as tears well in the corners of his eyes. "I didn't want it to be true, Londyn. It was easier to believe Sawyer's version of events instead of having to admit something so horrible happened to my baby girl." His voice rises in pitch at the end. "To my lollipop."

"I wish we could all be so lucky. I wish I could just turn it off and claim it didn't happen like you did."

"I'm not saying what I did was right. It wasn't. And this isn't an excuse. I just…"

He heaves a sigh as his eyes shift upward. His lips move, as if uttering a prayer. I'd seen him do this several times a day during my younger years whenever he was faced with a problem he wasn't sure how to solve. He claimed he was having a conversation with my mother, who always seemed to have all the right answers. Maybe she has them here, too.

Finally, he returns his dark gaze to mine. "It's no secret that I'd been living in denial for ages. I'd been stuck there since your mother's death. In a way, it was easier to deny what happened than accept it."

"But what about me? Did you not stop to think what your denial did to me?"

He erases the space between us, lowering himself back to the pew as he clutches my hands in his. "Every day of my life. Not a single hour has gone by that I haven't thought of it. Haven't regretted it. I've never been a good father to you. I realize that now. And I must live with what I've done for the rest of my life. But *you* don't have to pay the price for my mistakes.

"When Sawyer came to me all those years ago with his proposition, I should have told him no. You deserved the same kind of love your mother and I shared. But somewhere in the back of my mind, I thought by encouraging you to accept his proposal, knowing you didn't have feelings for him, that I was protecting you from suffering the heartache I did when I lost your mother."

He hangs his head. "In reality, I should have protected you from him. He had me fooled. Had all of us fooled. I didn't realize that until today when I saw the way Wes looked at you. *That's* what you deserve, lollipop. I've already taken so much from you. Sawyer's already taken so much from you. Don't let him take even more."

# CHAPTER TWENTY-ONE

## *Weston*

I stare at my tablet, stylus in hand, reviewing the notes I've made about a new business plan that could keep our earnings what they were before the great exodus, as I've started calling all the firm's clients who have taken their business elsewhere over the past several days.

But as has been the case all week, my focus is somewhere else. This time, it's not just on Londyn, but also Julia. I'd attempted to reach out earlier to apologize for the way I ambushed her last night. As expected, she refused my call, sending it to voicemail after a single ring. All I can do is the same thing I've done with Londyn... Let her know I'm here for her whenever she's ready to talk.

A gentle rapping cuts through, and I shoot my eyes toward the front door. Just like last night, there's no incessant nagging from my mother announcing that she knows I'm home, meaning it can only be one of two people — Londyn or Julia.

Lifting myself from the couch, I stride toward the foyer and check the peephole. When I see Londyn standing on the front step, I quickly open the door, drinking in her appearance. It doesn't matter how long we've been together. Every time I lay eyes on her still feels like the first, her beauty ramming into me like a semi, leaving me breathless.

"Hey," I say.

"Hey," she responds timidly, shuffling her feet as she avoids my gaze.

Dread settles in my stomach that she's here to tell me she's made her decision, and it's not me. I'd like to think she wouldn't take Sawyer's offer, that the price she'd pay for her freedom is too steep. But after this week, I'm no longer sure of anything.

"Are you okay?"

She chews on her lower lip. "Can I come in? I'd rather not have this conversation on your front stoop."

My Adam's apple bobs up and down in a hard swallow. "Of course." I step back, allowing her to walk into my house.

It's only been a little more than a week since she was here last, but this feels...different. I wish it didn't. Wish we could go back to being who we were when we left to go to the New Year's Eve Gala. Then again, those people are gone. All we can do is embrace who we are today and try to move on. Together.

I hope she finally wants to move on together.

"Do you mind?" she asks, gesturing to the half-full glass of scotch on the coffee table as she settles on the couch.

"What's mine is yours."

"Thanks." Grabbing the glass, she throws back a large gulp, almost finishing it off.

"Do you want more?" I ask guardedly, sitting beside her.

"No." She blows out a nervous laugh. "It's probably best I keep a clear head so I can get through this."

I nod, my chest tightening, anxious about what she's here to tell me. I just want to remain in this place where I still have hope for a future between us. I fear that hope is about to be torn to pieces, along with my heart.

"He commented on my mask," she says after what feels like an eternity.

I furrow my brow, shaking my head. "What do you—"

"Jay... Nick. Whoever." She waves her hand around, looking forward for a beat before returning her eyes to mine. All week, they've been lackluster, the spark gone. But now, they're...haunted. "When I saw him at the New Year's Eve Gala," she adds in explanation. "He said it was fitting."

I remain silent, resisting the urge for the thousandth time this week to drive over to my parents' house and use Nick's face as a punching bag.

"You have to understand what a shock it was, Wes. That's why I didn't say anything to you that night. Or the next day. Medusa may have been cursed with the power to turn men to stone, but the sight of him, the realization that he's married to Julia, turned *me* to stone."

"What else did he say to you?" I ask through a clenched jaw.

She shrugs, pinching her lips together. "He was the same manipulative asshole. Tried to tell me everything I've been through was necessary to get me to where I am." She laughs under her breath, then tilts her head. "Do you want to know the really fucked-up part?"

"What's that?"

"He truly believes he *helped* me."

"Helped you?"

"That's how delusional he is. He thinks by raping me, he

freed me from the life I'd been living. Gave me my wings." She turns her steely gaze back to mine. "Then he said he did the same thing to Julia."

I squeeze my eyes shut. While I already sensed that was the case, I hoped I was wrong. Hoped there was some other explanation.

"That's why I lied to you, Wes." Londyn grasps my hands in hers. "Why I told you I had a meeting with a client when my plan was to drop in on Julia at the bakery. I felt like I owed it to her to talk to her first. To *help* her." Her gaze shifts over my shoulder, that haunted expression returning. Then she pulls away, a chill seeming to wash over her as she wraps her arms around her body. "But Nick was there instead."

"What happened?" I ask, my voice strained.

She shakes her head, closing her eyes, anguish covering her expression. Neither one of us utters a syllable for several long moments as I silently beg her to finally put me out of my misery. I can't go on like this anymore. Can't constantly wonder what happened in the bakery, each scenario my brain comes up with worse than the previous.

On a long inhale, she returns her tear-filled eyes to mine. "He figured out I was there to tell Julia."

"And how did he react?"

"He claimed he wasn't concerned because he'd already told her some convoluted version of the truth. I mean, not that it was me, per se, and not that it wasn't consensual, but he'd obviously manipulated her into believing his version of events." A contemplative expression crosses her face. "But I think somewhere in the recesses of his subconscious, he knew she might question his claims… Especially when I mentioned you."

"Me?"

"You're a chink in his armor, Wes. The Typhon to his

Zeus. He may be able to exert control over Julia in a lot of aspects. But when it comes to you, he knows he can't."

I process this, praying Londyn's right. Then maybe I'll be able to get through to my sister. Break the hold Nick seems to have over her. Even if she can't see it.

"What happened next?" I ask.

"He told me he'd do whatever it took to protect the life he built. Pinned me against the wall, trapping me. I was eventually able to duck under him and get away. I didn't get far before he tackled me to the floor."

Several tears cascade down her cheeks as she stares straight ahead, recalling what I can only assume to be one of the most terrifying moments of her life. And I hate that I wasn't there for her. Hate I didn't put the pieces together sooner and figure it out.

"He had me in the same exact position he did all those years ago," she continues, her voice low. "I tried to buck him off, but that only made him more…enthusiastic."

"Jesus," I grind out as I run a hand over my face. I draw in a deep breath to calm myself, but it doesn't work. Nothing can erase the picture in my mind, causing my blood to boil.

"His mistake was loosening the grip he had on my wrists when he ran his hand up my thigh and…touched me."

I clench my fists, a pain unlike any I've experienced repeatedly jabbing me like a knife to my heart. Still, it's nothing remotely close to what Londyn endured that day. Hell, every day for the past five-and-a-half years.

"I never should have allowed you to be in that position, Lo."

"This isn't your fault, Wes." She grabs my hands again, brushing her fingers over my knuckles, offering me the reassurance I should be giving her right now. "I don't want you to think it is. *I'm* the one who kept the truth from you. *I'm* the one who thought it was a good idea to talk to Julia. And *he's* the one who tackled me to the floor. He expected the same girl I was back then. But thanks to you, I'm not that same girl. Back then, I had nothing to fight for. I do now. So that's what I did. Instead of giving in, I fought with everything I had. I fought for *you*. For us."

The corner of her mouth quirks up into a small smile, a glimmer of hope in her eyes.

"You saved me, Wes. You gave me the strength to break free from him. And when he knocked the gun out of my grip, *you* gave me the strength to not only retrieve it, but also make sure the barrel wasn't pointed in my direction when it went off. For that, I'll always be eternally grateful. You gave me something to fight for."

I look down at our joined hands, my heart full of an emotion that's so much bigger and more poignant than love. But I don't have another word for it.

"I love you, Lo."

"I know you do. And in my darkest moment, when I was ready to give in, it was your love that pushed me to fight. To survive. And that's what I need to do now. Survive."

Pulling her hands from mine, she reaches into her purse and withdraws the velvet box I'd left her earlier today. She stares at it, seemingly torn. My throat tightens, chest squeezing as I plead with her to keep it. To return it to her bag.

But she doesn't.

With a tear-filled gaze, she holds the box toward me. "I want you to have this back."

My shoulders fall, an anguish unlike anything I thought possible rolling over me like a wave, drowning me, making it difficult to breathe. I knew it was a long shot to convince her to keep going, especially considering Sawyer can offer her something I can't. I'd simply hoped our love was strong enough.

"And for you to hold onto it," she adds.

I fling my eyes to her. "Hold onto it?"

"Yes." She treats me to a brilliant smile. "When this is all over, I want the proposal you promised me the other night. If that's still what you want," she adds quickly. "I'm sorry I didn't tell you I'm still technically married to Sawyer. I should have. I just… I wanted to move on from my past, and if I'm being honest, the thought of facing him in court frightened me."

"I don't care about that." I cup her cheek, my grip tight, my stare intense. "All I care about is having your present."

"And it's yours, Wes." She curves into me, her mouth close to mine, sending a spark through me. "I choose *you*, Wes. I choose to fight. I choose to survive. For you."

"No, Lo. Not for me. This time, you're fighting for you."

"And for us," she declares with determination.

"For us."

"Us," she says again, inching closer, anticipation coursing through my veins.

When she's a whisper away and I can almost taste her kiss, she stops, a slight smile playing on her full lips.

"Is this okay?" she murmurs.

I can't help but chuckle lightly at the reminder of our very first kiss all those months ago. But this time, our roles are reversed.

"Yes," I say, a teasing quality to my tone.

"Good." Edging toward me, her mouth touches the corner of mine, the contact as light as a breeze. When she pulls back, I groan, desperate to feel her, to have her, to consume her. But I also want this to last. Want to stay in this moment when it's just us. No past. No future. Only us. Only this love.

She creeps back toward me, her lips covering mine in a fuller kiss. But it's still not deep enough, still not enough to satisfy this insane craving coursing through me.

"Is this okay?" she asks, her mouth still hovering over mine.

"Yes," I exhale breathily.

She places her hand on my shoulder and brings her body on top of mine, straddling me. Desire settles deep in my belly when her warmth wraps around me, causing me to harden even more. Pulling back, she locks her eyes with mine, her tight ringlets creating a cocoon around us, shielding us from the real world, blocking out any negativity.

"Is this okay?" She circles her hips against me.

I place my hands on her waist as I lose myself in her. "God yes."

"I was hoping you'd say that."

# CHAPTER TWENTY-TWO

## *Londyn*

I slam my mouth against Wes', not a single ounce of hesitation in the way I coax his lips open, begging for entry. Begging for him. He's only too happy to allow me in. To give me what I need, what I crave, what I demand.

When my tongue slides against his for the first time in days, peace washes over me, all my worry about whether this is the right path disappearing. Like Gampy said, "Sometimes the right path isn't always the easiest." The path I've chosen certainly won't be easy. But in my heart, I know this is the one I'm meant to travel. With Wes by my side. And there's no question in my mind that he'll be by my side every step of the way. That even if I try to push him away, he won't stop fighting for me. He won't stop supporting me. He won't stop choosing me.

It's time I finally choose me, too.

Panting, he breaks our kiss, twisting a hand around my hair. His unshaven jawline scrapes against my skin as he trails desperate kisses along my mouth, the roughness reinvigorating me.

"Wes...," I moan through my labored breaths.

"Yes, honeybee?" he replies, pulling away for a beat before returning his attention to my neck, his teeth and tongue two of the most delicious torture devices I've ever known. The things this man can do with a quick nip followed by a little suck should be illegal.

I turn my blazing eyes toward his. "Take me to bed."

His lips quirk into a mischievous smile. "Gladly."

Swiftly, he flips me off his body and onto my back. He hovers over me for a beat, making no attempt to hide his need tenting his sweatpants. Then, as if I weigh nothing, he scoops me into his arms, rushing through his house and taking the stairs two at a time.

After crossing the threshold into the master bedroom, he carefully lowers me to my feet, then steps back and admires me as the atmosphere shifts from sexy and playful to deep and poignant. He cups my cheek, and I relish in the warmth of his flesh against mine.

"I love you."

He's said these three words to me countless times. But after everything we've endured this week, they mean so much more than they ever have. It's more than a declaration. It's a promise. A commitment. A solemn pledge.

"And I love you."

He briefly closes his eyes, the tension that had built inside him visibly evaporating, his muscles relaxing. Then he hooks his arm around my waist, pulling me against him as he covers my lips with his, his kiss telling me everything that words alone cannot. That I'm the air he breathes. The blood in his veins. The love in his soul.

And he's all those things to me, too.

A hand on my hip, he guides me toward his bed. This is a dance we've done dozens of times, but it feels like the first time all over again. Butterflies flit relentlessly in my stomach, a thrill rushing through me at the prospect of what we're about to do. At what I'm about to experience.

And that's what being with Wes is like. A journey. An adventure. An experience.

When the backs of my legs hit the mattress, he treats me to a devilish smirk before dropping to his knees. With slow movements, he unzips each of my boots and removes them, tossing them to the side. I expect him to stand, but he doesn't. Instead, he remains kneeling before me and grabs my hips, drawing my body closer to him. His gaze unwavering, he lifts the hem of my sweater and traces a line with his tongue along my waist.

"Wes…," I moan, his delicate touch like the strike of a match, a wildfire spreading through my core.

He grasps the button of my jeans and unfastens it before lowering my zipper in an agonizingly languid pace. Each second is pure torture, my body craving, demanding, to feel him on every inch. To succumb to his touch. To drown in his love.

"Mmm…," he groans as he flicks his tongue along the band of my panties. "Do you know my favorite part of your body?"

"What's that?" I whimper, my nerve endings stirring and tingling.

"This." He drags a finger along the skin just above the waistband of my panties, his touch intoxicating and invigorating. "This right here is my absolute favorite part of your body."

"Why?" I ask, digging my fingers into his thick hair, needing to feel grounded when I'm on the edge of falling.

"If there were a mirror in front of you, you'd see why."

He presses his mouth against the spot near my hipbone. The one that drives me wild. The one he *knows* drives me wild.

"The expression on your face right now." His tongue swirls against my skin as he hooks his fingers into my belt loops and pushes my jeans over my hips. "It's pure fucking heaven."

I step out of my pants, placing my hand on Wes' shoulder to help me balance. Once my legs are bare, he returns to me. I close my eyes in anticipation of his tongue along my waist once more, gasping when I feel the heat of his breath between my legs.

"God, I've missed your scent," he groans, moving his mouth against me, making me wish he'd already taken off my panties. But at the same time, I like this, too. Like the buildup. The seduction.

Too soon, he pulls back, pinning me with a sensual look. "Sit on the bed," he says in a soft voice that oozes with sex and authority.

I do as he requests, lowering myself. Before I can shift toward the headboard, he grabs my ankles, hooking my legs over his shoulders. With a devilish glint in his eyes, he presses a hand against my chest, pushing me back onto the mattress.

Propping myself up on my elbows, I meet his eyes, my breath catching as he gradually runs his hand up my calf, over my knee, up my thigh, the inches separating his fingers from my apex feeling like miles.

Finally, he nudges my panties aside, his thumb ghosting against me. I collapse onto the bed, my eyes rolling into the back of my head as I savor that first contact.

"Oh god," I moan as he spreads my slickness around. I

move with his rhythm, urging him to keep going, to keep touching me, to never stop touching me.

"What do you want, honeybee?" he asks as he plants several kisses along my waist.

"You," I pant, then cry out something incomprehensible when he pushes a finger inside me.

"How do you want me?"

"Any way you want," I answer, my brain mush.

When he removes his finger, I fling my eyes open, peering at him with disbelief. I squirm, attempting to squeeze my thighs together to find some sort of release, an ache building inside me I don't think will ever go away.

"You're in control, Lo. You call the shots. So..." He smiles slyly. "What do you want me to do? Did you like when I fingered you?"

I nod.

"Words, Lo. I need your words."

"Yes. I liked it when you fingered me."

"Good." He waggles his brows. "I liked it, too." He pushes my panties aside, circling my clit once more. "I *really* fucking like it. Love seeing how wet you are. How wet *I* make you."

"Take off my panties."

"Your wish is my command." He moves my legs off his shoulders, his hands gliding up my thighs before hooking into the waistband of my panties and sliding them off. Once he tosses them onto the floor, he returns to me, draping my legs over his shoulders once more. "Now what?" he asks, the warmth of his breath so close to my center making me wild with need.

"Your mouth. On me."

"Where, Lo? Your knee? Your foot?"

"You know where."

"Perhaps. But I want to hear you tell me. Like I said, you're in control. You call the shots. You tell me exactly where you want my mouth." He licks his lips, his tongue swiping against my clit. The contact is faint, but it sends a shock wave through me.

"On my pussy. With a finger inside me."

"That's my girl."

He grips my thighs, spreading them farther apart. I watch as Wes' mouth descends toward me. There's something so erotic about observing that first lick. And that's all it takes for me to succumb to him. I fall back onto the mattress, closing my eyes as he tastes me, devours me, worships me.

"You're so fucking sweet," he groans, his breaths coming in pants, mirroring mine. "So fucking perfect. So fucking mine."

I move my hips faster against him, that familiar sensation settling low in my belly. But that's not how I want this to go. And I'm the one calling the shots. So just before Wes sends me past the point of oblivion, I thread my fingers into his hair, pushing him away.

"Inside me. Now."

My desire coating his lips, he grins a lazy smile. "Yes, ma'am," he says, playing up his sweet, Southern accent.

Climbing to his feet, he rips his t-shirt over his head at the same time as I tug off my sweater and unclasp my bra. I crawl on the mattress toward him, my fingers finding the waistband of his sweatpants.

"As much as I love a hot guy in a pair of sweats, they've got to go." I shove them down his legs.

Once he kicks them off, he wraps an arm around me, supporting me as he lays me on the bed. His lips feather against mine as he brings his erection up to me.

I moan, the anticipation ready to undo me, but just as

he's about to thrust inside, I place my hand on his chest, stopping him. He peers at me, questioning.

"You said I get to call the shots."

"I did."

"Then get on your back." I curve toward him, nibbling on his earlobe. "I'm on top this time."

I don't think I've ever seen Wes move as quickly as he does when he flips onto his back, taking me with him. I land with a grunt, the sudden movement surprising me. But when the initial shock wears off, I straighten, dragging my fingers down his chest. A hiss falls from his throat, his eyelids fluttering closed.

Leaning down, I take his bottom lip between my teeth. "Eyes. On. Me," I demand in a flirtatious voice.

His grip on my hips hardens, his length twitching beneath me as he snaps his gaze back to mine.

"I think I like this side of you." He digs his fingers into my hair, pulling my mouth toward his.

"You like it when I tell you what to do?" I waggle my brows.

"I like that you feel comfortable enough around me to tell me what you want."

"Good. Because right now, I want you."

I press a kiss to his lips, then sit back, scraping my nails down the hard planes of his chest, leaving red marks in their wake. When I reach his arousal, his breathing becomes more uneven, hooded eyes staring back at me with a heady expression of adoration and raw hunger.

"But first, I want to repay the favor."

"Favor?"

I nod, wrapping my hand around his erection. I inch my mouth toward him, swirling my tongue along the tip.

"Fuck," he exhales, jerking at that first contact.

Emboldened, I drag my tongue down his length, then take him into my mouth, my motions slow as I worship him the same way he always does me.

His eyes find mine as he tightens his grip in my hair, guiding me, thrusting his hips in time with my movement.

"God, baby. I love your mouth. Love your body. Love your fucking tongue."

His words encouraging me, I increase my pace and relax my jaw, taking him deeper with each motion. When I gently bare my teeth, he yanks me off him, chest heaving.

"I can't hold off much longer, so unless you want me to come in your mouth, get on me right now."

His carnal words cause my pulse to skyrocket, a delicious shiver coursing through me.

"Impatient much?" I tease as I make a show of wiping my bottom lip.

"For you?" He draws my lips toward his. "I have absolutely no patience. No control. So take it all, Lo. Take what you need."

I capture his mouth with mine, circling my hips against him as pleasure builds deep within me, touching parts of me I didn't know existed. I fear the second he's inside me, I'll lose all control. But there's no one else I'd rather lose control with. He's my alpha and omega. My heaven and hell. My beginning and end.

And I'll gladly walk through the flames of hell for a single taste of heaven.

Lifting myself up, I bring his erection to my entrance, not looking away from his eyes as I ease him inside. When he's as deep as he can go, I pause, neither one of us moving or breathing as we revel in the sensation, as if it were the first time.

Then we exhale simultaneously, and I bury my head in his neck, breathing in his scent.

"I've missed this," he murmurs huskily, a hand affectionately splayed on my back, fingers moving in slow circles.

"And I've missed you." I treat him to a soft kiss. "I won't shut you out again."

"Promise?" He rests his hand over my heart.

I nod, mirroring his gesture on his chest. "Promise."

"Good."

He circles his hips, encouraging me to move along with him. But we keep our hands in place, him holding my heart, and me his. Just like we promised last week at the gala. Him for me. Me for him. For the rest of our lives.

And right now, I truly believe that. Truly believe this *is* for the rest of our lives. Truly believe we'll navigate the obstacles in our way and come out stronger on the other side.

Heavy breathing fills the room as we indulge in each other in a way we never have. From the beginning, Wes has always had a unique ability to make me feel loved and respected, yet still desired and craved. The way our bodies seem to be in tune with each other is something I didn't think possible. But even without the fast motions, without the hunger-filled words, I'm on the brink of falling over the edge, the love flowing out of his heart and into my soul propelling me higher than I've been before.

"Let go, baby," Wes says through his labored breaths. "Fall with me."

That's all I need to let go, my body trembling as I come undone. I seal my mouth over his, tongues tangling and hearts racing. He breathes into me as he jerks through his own release, kissing me with desperation. His grip over my heart tightens until he reaches the point of oblivion, every muscle in his body giving out.

He collapses onto the mattress, his heart hammering against my hand. He gradually eases himself out of me, shifting our bodies so we're both on our sides, facing each other. And still, through all this, we keep our hands over each other's chests, our hearts beating as one.

"You're my love story, Lo," he murmurs as he feathers a delicate kiss against my lips. "My beacon. I was lost at sea until I found you. You helped guide me home. The second we met, I knew the journey I'd been on had ended. And the real one had begun." He presses his lips firmly against mine. "With you."

I melt into his kiss, basking in his love, his determination, his strength. I thought running away from love was the only option.

Now, I pray our love is strong enough to help us through the storm threatening offshore.

# CHAPTER TWENTY-THREE

## *Londyn*

I stare at the clock on the wall over my sofa, my stomach in knots. I shouldn't be this nervous. I've chosen this path for a reason.

That still doesn't make this any easier, though.

A warmth approaches from behind, two strong, loving arms wrapping around me.

"I'm here," Wes croons into my ear. "I'm not going anywhere."

I close my eyes, indulging in his reassurance before turning in his embrace. "Thanks for being here." I drape my arms on his shoulders, smiling up at him as I toy with a few tendrils of hair hanging over the collar of his crisp, button-down shirt.

He leans down, placing a soft kiss on my lips. "Are you sure you don't want me by your side when you tell him?"

"I need to do this on my own. Need to show him he doesn't dictate my life anymore."

"Okay. But if anything happens, I'll be right upstairs."

A determined knocking echoes through our moment of serenity. We simultaneously fling our gazes toward the door, my pulse immediately kicking up. I tell myself it'll all be over soon. That I just need to get through this. Then I'll finally be free.

"I suppose that's my cue to disappear," Wes states.

"I suppose it is," I say with a sigh.

Pinching my chin, he draws my lips toward his. "Thank you for choosing me," he murmurs before sealing his declaration with a kiss.

I sigh into him, momentarily forgetting that Sawyer's currently standing on the other side of the door. Momentarily forgetting about the nerves working their way through me over how he'll react to my decision. Momentarily forgetting about the uncertainty of what my future holds. Nothing matters right now. Except the love pouring from Wes' simple kiss.

"It was never a choice with you."

"And it was never a choice with you," he replies, leaving me with one more kiss.

When Sawyer knocks again, this time more urgently, I step away from Wes, giving him a reassuring smile. He reaches for my hand, brushes a delicate kiss on my knuckles, then retreats up the stairs. Once he's disappears, I take a calming breath, holding my head high as I make my way toward the front door and pull it open.

The second I do, Sawyer pushes past me and into my condo, an air of superiority about him.

I meet my father's eyes and we share a moment, his expression searching for an answer as to my decision. When I wink, his shoulders fall out of relief. He links his pinky with mine, the contact surprisingly comforting, considering less than twenty-four hours ago, I never wanted to see this man again. But after last night, I can't help but appreciate him for finally apologizing. We have a long way to go to repair the damage his past actions have caused. But I have to believe this is a step in the right direction.

My father holds my gaze for a heartbeat, then releases my pinky, gesturing for me to walk ahead of him into my living room.

"I assume you've signed," Sawyer declares, as if the idea of me *not* signing is preposterous. To most, it would be, considering the price I'd pay by not agreeing to his proposition.

But if I did agree, the price would be much higher.

I turn toward the kitchen table and grab the file folder. "I have." I hand it to him.

"I knew you would. You may put up a fight, may claim to have changed, but you still lack any conviction." With a cocky smirk, he opens the folder. The arrogance vanishes from his face, dark eyes flinging toward mine. "What's this?" he demands in a growl.

I square my shoulders, reminding myself that I'm not the same girl he used to boss around. Who he used to issue ulti-matums to. Who he used to control.

"Divorce papers."

"Divorce?" he repeats, the word seeming foreign on his tongue.

"Yes. My lawyer will be filing those tomorrow, but as a courtesy, I thought I'd show you what you'll have no choice but to agree to."

He scoffs. "You forget who holds the upper hand here. I'm not the one with the possibility of prison time hanging over him."

"And that's precisely why I'm *not* agreeing. It's simply a

possibility. I know the truth. And deep down, you do, too. I did what any woman in my position should be able to do against some pompous man who thinks he can do whatever he wants and get away with it. So I'm choosing to fight. Not just for myself, but for the thousands of women who are too scared to speak up. Who have spent all their lives being intimidated into silence. Like you did to me for years. I'm done being silent. Done living according to everyone's expectations.

"You came here in the hopes of finding the same girl who agreed, without protest, to marry a man she didn't love. That girl died. I've had to face several hard truths about myself. Some good. Some not so good. But I've learned one thing…"

I glance to my father before returning my heated stare to Sawyer.

"I'm a fighter. Just like my mother. And I'd rather fight for my freedom than trade it away for a lifetime with you. Hell, for even just a day with you. Because that is a sentence worse than prison." I edge closer to him, lip curling up in the corner, lowering my voice to barely louder than a whisper. "*You* are a sentence worse than prison. One I have no interest in serving. So get the fuck out of my house."

His jaw clenches, his grip on the proposed divorce settlement agreement tightening, causing the papers to crinkle. I don't know how much time passes as I glare at him, neither one of us backing down. It's probably only seconds, but it feels so much longer, the only sound in the room that of the clock ticking.

"You want to go to prison?" Sawyer finally says. "Fine. Be my guest. But mark my words." He glowers, malevolent eyes piercing me. "You chose wrong today."

"No, Sawyer. I didn't. I chose wrong when I agreed to play the part of your wife. Today, I finally chose right."

Five years ago, his disdainful stare would have probably caused me to back down. Apologize. Grovel for forgiveness. Not anymore. That version of Londyn is gone. No more will I do what's expected of me because of some misguided belief it's the way to repay the universe for sparing me in the shooting that took my mother's life. She would have wanted me to live, to fight. That's what I'm finally doing.

"You'll regret this. Trust me on that." He spins from me, storming toward my front door.

"The only thing I regret is marrying you," I call out after him. He doesn't respond, continuing out of my condo and slamming the door, causing my heart to skyrocket for a beat.

Once he's gone, I close my eyes, exhaling a long breath, everything peaceful. And not just in my house. My mind and soul are finally at peace.

"I'm proud of you, Lo," Dad says.

I open my eyes, offering him a smile. Reaching for his hand, I squeeze. "I'm proud of me, too."

"You okay, honeybee?" Wes asks, rushing down the stairs, coming to a stop when he sees my father is still here. He raises a single brow, giving me a questioning look.

In all the excitement of reconnecting yesterday, I forgot to mention the role my father played in helping me realize what's important.

"Better than ever."

"Good."

"Well…" My father clears his throat, dropping his hold on me. "I still need to get to the church to deliver a sermon."

"Do you mind if I don't go, Dad? Religion and me, well… We're not exactly on good terms these days."

"I'm probably partly to blame for that. But I understand." He smiles weakly. "If you're willing, perhaps we can get together for dinner tonight? Or sometime this week? I'd like to get to know you again." He shifts his hopeful gaze to Wes. "And get to know the man who seems to have captured your heart."

I look to Wes, who nods subtly.

This must be what trust looks like. I don't have to utter a single syllable about the breakthrough I had with my father last night. Wes trusts my decision, no matter what it is. It's refreshing, especially after a marriage to a man who never allowed me to make a single decision of my own.

"Tonight is fine. I'm sure you need to get back home."

He hesitates, rocking on his heels. "Actually…" He runs a hand over his short, graying hair. "I think I might stick around here for a while. If that's okay with you. I wasn't there for you when you needed me. I want to rectify that. Or at least try to."

I have every reason to hate this man. To shut him out and never speak to him again. But through all the trials in my life, I've learned the power of forgiveness. Life is too short to hold grudges. People change. And there's no question in my mind that my father has changed. That he's no longer clinging to the ghost of my mother, refusing to move forward.

"I'd like that."

"Good." He squeezes my arm, then steps back and looks at Wes. "You take good care of my girl."

"Londyn does a good job of taking care of herself," Wes responds, wrapping an arm around my shoulders and pulling me against him. "But I'm more than happy to fill in the gaps."

"That's all any of us can do." He smiles sadly as he looks

back at me, his expression a mixture of relief and regret. Then he turns, making his way out the door.

Once we're alone, I face Wes. I don't say anything right away. Just look at him, a strange feeling enveloping me.

"You're not having second thoughts, are you?" he asks.

"No way." I curve into him. "But this feels...different."

He arches a brow. "Different?"

"Don't worry. It's a good different. A great different. I never really had a chance to stand up for myself to Sawyer before. Instead, I just kind of...disappeared. That's part of why I never went through the trouble of filing for divorce. I didn't exactly have the money and knew Sawyer would make it as impossible for me as he could. But mostly, I was scared of seeing him again. Of confronting him. Of him making me feel so small and powerless."

"You're not small. *He* is. Any man who treats a woman the way that asshole treated you isn't worthy of so much as an ounce of your worry. He may never have left bruises on your skin, but what he did was just as bad."

I draw in a shaky breath. "I see that now, especially when I have such an incredible man."

He leans down, his lips caressing mine. "I'll do anything for you."

"Good. Because right now, I need something." I waggle my brows, the atmosphere becoming playful.

"And what would that be, Ms. Bennett?"

I lift onto my toes, dragging my tongue along his neck, nibbling on that spot just underneath his earlobe that I know drives him crazy. "You. Naked. In my bed." I return my eyes to his, watching as his gaze darkens, a wicked smile curling his lips.

"Your wish is my command."

# CHAPTER TWENTY-FOUR

## *Weston*

"Uncle Wes!" an excited squeal echoes the instant I step into Julia's bakery Monday afternoon, the familiar aroma like coming home after a long absence.

Before I can react, a pair of tiny arms fling around my waist, squeezing tightly. I look down at little Imogene, my heart expanding. It's amazing what somebody who doesn't even weigh forty pounds can do to you.

Smiling, I tousle her curls, then lower myself to peer into her eyes. "Hey, peanut. How are you?"

"I'm good." Her smile falters. "I've missed you."

"I've missed you, too."

"And I miss my bedroom at your house. Can't I come and live with you instead of Grandma and Pappy?"

My chest squeezes. What I wouldn't give to have both Imogene and Julia under my roof. That way, I could be confident nothing would ever happen to them. But things are complicated. How do you explain that to a six-year-old, though? How do you tell a little girl the man who reads her bedtime stories and plays tea party with her hurts people?

That he may have hurt her mother?

"You need to be with your mama right now. She needs you, pipsqueak."

"I'm not a pipsqueak anymore," she pouts. "The doctor said I grew four whole inches this year."

"Four inches?" I reply in faux wonder. "Better slow down. Or soon you might be taller than your mama."

"She certainly doesn't have far to go there."

I look away from Imogene, watching as my sister takes several timid steps toward me, wiping her flour-covered hands on the white apron strung around her waist.

"Hey, Jules." I straighten, smiling.

"Hey, Wes." She lifts herself onto her toes, wrapping her arms around my neck. I pull her toward me, hugging her as I always do. But today, she remains in my embrace a bit longer than normal. She squeezes me a bit harder than normal. She seems a lot sadder than normal.

I wasn't sure how she'd react to seeing me today, especially after my repeated attempts to get in touch with her this weekend, all of which she ignored. I half expected her to kick me out of the bakery. Hell, I didn't even know if she'd be here, but I figured it wouldn't hurt to try.

"How are you?" I ask when she pulls back.

"Okay. You?"

I run my fingers through my hair. "Okay."

We both stare at each other for a while. I don't think I've ever felt this uncomfortable around her, not even when Mom first brought her home and told me she was my new sister. But now, I don't know what to say.

"Can we—"

"Do you want—" she says at the same time.

We both stop, laughing nervously.

"You first," I tell her.

"Do you want to sit and talk?"

I nod. "I'd like that."

She smiles, then crouches down to Imogene's level. "I need to talk to Uncle Wes about something important. It's grown-up stuff."

"Are you going to swear a lot? Is that why you don't want me to hear?"

Julia chuckles, life returning to her green eyes. "I'm going to try not to. I'm running short on dollar bills for your swear jar."

"That's because you've been swearing a lot lately, Mama."

Julia glances at me for a beat, worry flickering in her expression before looking back at Imogene. "I know, and I'm sorry. I'll try to do better."

"I don't mind. It means more money for me."

"Do you think you can sit at your table and practice some of your math problems?"

"Can I have a peanut butter and jelly cookie if I do?"

"Of course, sweetie." Julia beams, the affection she has for her daughter oozing from every inch of her. "Now go on. I'll come check on you in a few minutes."

"Okay!" She spins, her curls bouncing with her move-ments, returning to the table in the corner, coloring books, crayons, as well as a few workbooks and pencils littering the surface.

"Did she start school?" I ask, watching as she flips open a workbook.

"Today was her first day."

"How's she handling everything? The change of schools and all that?"

She exhales deeply. "Kids are resilient. More so than adults."

"We've been around a lot longer. Old habits die hard."

"They sure do," she retorts, a contemplative look pulling on her brows for a moment. Then she snaps her gaze back to mine. "Want a coffee or something?"

"Coffee sounds great."

"I'll be right back. Grab us a table, will ya?"

"You got it."

I make my way through the bakery, a few dozen people lined up to grab some lunch and a sugary concoction. As I do, I steal a glimpse behind the counter and into the kitchen. My steps slow, my skin heating over the idea that, just a little more than a week ago, this was the scene of Nick's assault on Londyn. I try to not get worked up over it, but it's hard.

"Here you go," Julia sings, snapping me out of my thoughts. "Strong with a hint of cream. Just the way you like it."

I take the mug from her. "Thanks."

"You bet."

I lead her toward an empty table. It's secluded enough that we can talk candidly without curious ears eavesdropping, but still allows us to keep Imogene in our sights.

I hold out a chair for Julia, then skirt around to the other side, lowering myself into my seat. I take a sip of the coffee, savoring the familiar, nutty flavor. I don't know what it is about the coffee she sources, but there's nothing like it anywhere else in the South.

After another sip, I set my mug onto the surface, meeting Julia's gaze.

"Jules—" I begin.

Just like before, she speaks at the same time.

"I'm sorry."

We both laugh, breaking the tension.

"Normally, I'd let you go first," I say, reaching across the table and clutching her hand in mine. "But I'm the one at fault here, Jules. Not you."

"I shouldn't have gone off on you," she protests. "I'm an adult. I should have handled the situation better."

"No. *I'm* the one who should have handled the situation better. I guess all the stress caught up to me and I snapped. Unfortunately, you were the only one around, so you bore the brunt of it. For that, I'm sorry."

"You did what any good brother would. If I were in your shoes, I'd question things, too."

"But you told me at the hospital there was nothing… questionable going on. I should have believed you."

She smiles sadly. "I'm glad you didn't."

I swallow hard, but don't press her. If I do, I fear she'll cut ties with me altogether. Or worse, Nick will make her. I need her in my life. Need to provide her some sort of escape. Some sort of semblance of normalcy. All I can do is be here for her and pray that by doing so, whatever chains Nick has wrapped around her will weaken. Now that I know he sees me as a threat, that's precisely what I plan to do.

On a deep inhale, she pulls her hand away from mine, bringing her mug to her lips. "No one else has."

"Has what?"

"Asked me anything. Of course, Mom refuses to even consider Londyn's version of events." She pauses, pressing her lips together, hesitating. Then she leans toward me. "Promise you'll watch out for her."

"I am."

"Mom's got it out for her."

I roll my eyes. "She's just pissed I'm not dating someone with good 'breeding', as she'd put it."

I expect Julia to laugh at this, as she typically would, but she doesn't, her expression remaining serious. "I mean it, Wes. Some things I've overheard..." Her brows scrunch together as she peers into the distance before looking back at me. "When you were seeing Brooklyn, she was pissed you weren't dating someone with good 'breeding'. This is something...more."

"What have you overheard?"

"Just some things that don't make sense. She's never been Nick's biggest fan. But the second she learned Londyn was the one who shot him, she rushed to support him. Booked the first flight back to Atlanta from Aspen."

"He *is* her son-in-law. For better or for worse."

She pinches her lips together. "That's the thing. She didn't care he was shot *until* she found out who shot him. It's like she was...happy about it. I just have a bad feeling in my gut that she'll do whatever it takes to force her from your life. And she's using this to achieve that."

"I don't know, Jules," I say after a beat. "Sounds like a lot of effort for what? So I'll stop dating her?" My voice lacks the conviction I wish it had. This is exactly something my mother would do, as my father reminded me last week.

"I know it sounds crazy." Julia laughs under her breath. "I've tried to tell myself that dozens of times. Just...keep Londyn close." She lowers her head, fidgeting with her mug. "Despite what my actions may indicate, I do care about her."

"She cares about you, too. She just wants *you* to be safe."

"Imogene is safe. That's all that matters right now."

I nod, following her gaze as she glances in my niece's direction. "What have you told her?"

"Nothing. She's young. She doesn't need to be saddled with all of this."

I arch a brow. "And Nick's injury?"

"I told her Daddy hurt his shoulder. One day, I'll tell her everything."

"Everything?" I ask, unable to stop myself.

"I hope to. Someday."

"Someday is better than no day."

Her expression lights up at the memory of yet another one of Gampy and Meemaw's words of wisdom.

"Yes, it is."

"So…" My voice brightens. "What size shirt do you wear?"

"Shirt?" she asks, confused.

"Yeah." I bring my mug to my lips. "I need to know what size to order when I buy you a shirt that says 'I still live with my parents'."

"Asshole," she mutters, grabbing a sugar packet and throwing it at me.

"But you love me." I waggle my brows.

She draws in a deep breath, fighting the grin crawling across her face. "Always." She reaches across the table, holding out her hand.

With a smile, I place mine in hers, squeezing. "Always, Jules."

# CHAPTER TWENTY-FIVE

## *Londyn*

The aroma of bacon envelopes me the instant I turn the corner into my kitchen, a growl rumbling from my stomach. I pause, unable to stop from smiling at the scene that greets me. Londyn stands at the stove, pushing the crackling bacon around a frying pan, dressed in one of my oversized t-shirts. Her tight curls are piled on top of her head, a pink headband securing any flyaways away from her face.

Over the past three weeks, this has been the precise scene that's greeted me every weekday morning. After my alarm goes off, we make love before I jump into the shower. By the time I get out and dress, Londyn's already made her way downstairs to cook breakfast. I've never asked her to, and certainly don't expect it. I'm happy with a bowl of cereal or a bagel. But I love walking into my kitchen to see her here. Makes this house feel like a home. I thought it felt like a home whenever Julia and Imogene stayed with me.

I was wrong.

I hadn't realized something so profound and impactful was missing until Londyn barreled her way into my life. Now I can't imagine my world without her, regardless of the obstacles we'll have to face in the weeks and months ahead. That doesn't matter. Moments like this make it all worth it.

Luckily, we haven't had many obstacles to face these past few weeks. As Sophia predicted, court proceedings are a lot of hurry up and wait. Since Londyn turned down the DA's initial plea offer, they've been going through the discovery process, sharing any and all evidence with Sophia for Londyn's defense. There have been a few small victories with certain pieces of evidence being excluded, which has given Londyn hope that she has a fighting chance to beat this. Luck finally seems to be on our side. I hope it stays there.

Sauntering up to Londyn, I pull her against me, her back to my front, her body molding perfectly against mine.

"Mmm…," I moan, feathering kisses along her neckline. "I love that smell."

She giggles, the sound lighthearted and devoid of any anxiety. It's almost like we've gone back to the way things were before. But they're even better, our connection impenetrable.

"Who doesn't love the smell of bacon?"

"Communists," I joke back. "And probably vegans, although I've known a few who've admitted to loving it, too. But that's not what I'm talking about anyway."

She spins in my embrace, draping her arms around my neck, batting her lashes. "It's not?"

I slowly shake my head, eyes flaming, my arousal springing back to life, even though it hasn't yet been an hour since the last time I was buried deep inside her. "No, honeybee." I bend toward her, feathering my lips against hers. "I was talking about you. Powder, lilac…just a hint of sex." I grind my hips against hers. "Makes me want to cancel all my meetings and spend the day in bed with you."

She playfully swats me away. "Fiend. The only reason I still smell like sex is because I haven't showered yet. Someone can't seem to keep his hands off me first thing in the morning and insists on marking me like a Neanderthal."

"Perhaps." I waggle my brows. "But I didn't hear you complaining. If memory serves, all I heard from you was 'Oh, Wes. Yes. Right there'," I jest, doing my best Londyn impersonation.

She pushes against me again, but I don't let her escape, drawing her closer.

"Come on. Admit it. You like it when I go all caveman on you."

Rolling her eyes, she wiggles away, returning to the stove. With a quick glance behind her, she tosses me a "Maybe" before removing the bacon to a waiting plate.

I head to the one-cup brewer and make a cup of coffee, then sit at the eat-in kitchen island, savoring that first sip. I tap on my phone, bringing up my calendar for my day packed with meetings, including a pitch to yet another one of the firm's long-term clients. And like with all them lately, what was once just a formality, since it was a given the firm would win the contract, is now an actual pitch.

"Busy day?" Londyn asks as she sets a plate with two eggs over easy, bacon, and toast in front of me before sitting in the chair beside me with her own plate.

"It seems they're all busy these days. If I'm not trying to convince old clients to stay on, I'm reaching out to potential clients in the hopes of making up the shortfall."

She offers a sad smile, averting her gaze. "I'm sorry."

"Hey." I cup her cheek. "You have nothing to be sorry about. I said it months ago, and I'll say it again. If these assholes are considering pulling their accounts because my girlfriend isn't white or because I choose to stand by her when she says some asshole assaulted her, I don't want to do business with them in the first place." I stare into her dark pools, wanting her to see the truth in my words.

Then I drop my hold on her, placing a napkin across my lap. "If anything, this has been good for the firm. I said when I took over that I wanted to bring it into this century with new and innovative ideas. This has brought a vulnerability to the forefront I hadn't noticed before." I slice into one of the eggs.

"And what's that?" she asks over her coffee mug.

"That the firm has been relying on the same few dozen clients for over ninety percent of its revenue for too long now, often turning down new clients. Not to mention, with the economy as it is, a lot of our former clients are trying to cut costs and have decided to hire their own in-house architects. So now's the perfect time to explore some ideas that have been simmering for quite a while now."

She shakes some hot sauce onto her eggs, then cuts into one. "What kind of new ideas?"

I smile. "Historic renovations."

She tilts her head to the side. "Is that right?"

"There's quite a big market for it. And it's something I've always wanted to get involved in. Like you, I've always been fascinated by history. How every building has a story to tell. My father always shot down the idea of adding it as one of our firm's services, but… I don't know." I shrug. "I loved renovating Gampy and Meemaw's house with you. It was the first historic project I'd worked on since leaving Boston. And remember how you gave me that whole spiel about doing one thing every day that brings me joy and maybe my job wouldn't suck so much?"

"I do."

"I think this might be the answer. It's time to stop depending on the relationships my father forged and build my own."

"I'm proud of you, Wes." She offers me a heartfelt smile, squeezing my thigh. "Life without passion isn't a life worth living."

I lean toward her. "Good thing I have you then. Because I'm extremely passionate about you." I brush my lips against hers.

"Such a charmer," she jokes.

"Always." I wink, then glance at the TV in the living room as the morning news plays on the screen. I'm about to return my attention to my breakfast when I do a double take.

"What's wrong?" Londyn asks, following my gaze. When she sees, her fork clatters onto the plate and she pushes out of her chair, her legs on autopilot as they carry her into the living room.

I follow, grabbing the remote to raise the volume, the newscaster's animated voice filling the room.

"For those viewers not familiar with this case that's gotten national attention over the past several weeks, this is Sawyer Ross. He's married to Londyn Bennett, the defendant in this case."

"*Was* married," I mutter under my breath.

"Although Sawyer Ross is well known in his own right as being an influential civil rights activist, often advocating for men and women of color who've been discriminated against."

"Yeah." Londyn crosses her arms in front of her chest.

"When it serves to get his name in the headlines. Otherwise, he doesn't give a shit. Pious asshole."

The newscaster flashes a congenial smile as she turns from the camera and toward Sawyer sitting on a couch catty-corner to her chair. "I have to say, I was somewhat surprised to learn that the Buckhead shooter is your wife."

"As was I," Sawyer offers.

"Do you believe this is just another case of racial discrimination by the police?"

"Actually, I don't. That's why I'm here. I've toiled over this for weeks now, but I feel it's my duty to set the record straight about Londyn Bennett, considering all the conflicting reports out there."

I notice Londyn's muscles clench, her breathing growing faster. I wrap my arm around her, wanting to turn this off. She doesn't need this. Things have been going so well. She's reconnected with her father, often meeting him for lunch when I'm at work. She's even started working on her up-cycling business, having moved a lot of her materials from her tiny garage into mine, spending hours a day in there. I fear this will set her back yet again.

"According to some of our sources, Ms. Bennett has claimed she acted in self-defense," the reporter says. "That the man she shot had sexually assaulted her in the past, which sparked quite a few 'Me Too' protests across the country recently."

"And I can absolutely empathize with a woman who *has* been sexually assaulted. But Londyn Bennett hasn't."

"What a fucking asshole," Londyn spits out.

I pull her closer, wishing I could put a stop to all of this. But I can't. All I can do is offer her my support, prove to her that I'm still here, that I'm not going anywhere.

"What kind of insight can you offer us as her husband? It's my understanding you've been estranged for nearly six years. Is that correct?"

"Not by choice. In fact, I took a trip to Atlanta a few weeks ago, hoping to reconcile."

"Even with the charges against her?"

"You can't just turn off love, ya know?" He swallows hard, a forced expression of heartache crossing his face.

If I hadn't interacted with him, I might believe it. But I've seen firsthand that he's nothing but a fake, an opportunist, a man who is so desperate for attention and fame that he'll throw anyone under the bus in order to achieve it.

Like he's doing to Londyn right now.

"We were childhood friends."

"You both lost a parent in the infamous Virginia church shooting, correct?"

"Yes. And I suppose it was that event that kind of… connected us. From an early age, I knew I wanted to spend the rest of my life with her. I mean, when we were kids, it was just a cute thing. But as we both matured, I fell for her. Hard. It was like my heart physically beat for her and her alone."

"She was your soulmate." The host places her hand over her heart, giving Sawyer a sympathetic smile.

"Does she actually believe this shit?" Londyn hisses.

What can I tell her right now to make her feel better? I wish I could encourage her not to worry about this, but I refuse to lie to her. Sawyer did threaten she'd regret her decision to serve him with divorce papers. I have a feeling this may have been his Plan B all along.

"She was. Still is. And because of that, I tried to give her everything she asked for. Sure, we married young, but we were in love. Why wouldn't we get married? I will admit, those first few years were difficult. She hadn't yet finished college, and I was all too happy for her to complete her degree, even if it meant living apart for most of the year."

"She didn't go to college close by?"

He slowly shakes his head. "In retrospect, I should have done the right thing and sacrificed my job to go with her. Because that's what a good husband does. Makes sacrifices for those he loves. I thought our love was strong enough to endure any separation. Unfortunately, I misjudged Londyn's commitment to me. I didn't realize it at the time, but the reason she'd insisted on returning to that same college was because she'd been having several affairs, including one with a professor."

"And that's Domenic Jaskulski, correct? The man she's accused of shooting?"

"That's correct." Sawyer's chin quivers as he looks upward for a moment, as if collecting himself. "When I learned the truth, I blamed myself. Convinced myself that if I'd been more present, she wouldn't have felt the need to stray. Londyn was deeply troubled."

"Troubled?" the host asks, brow scrunched. "How so?"

"She never got over losing her mother. She constantly placed the blame for her failings or mistakes on other people instead of accepting responsibility herself. Her therapist insisted it was common in children who'd experienced a traumatic loss. That they often lied or made up stories because it was better than the reality of their lives. But despite the years she spent in therapy, she never seemed to make any notable advances. Always insisted there was nothing wrong with her. That she didn't need therapy."

"Is he fucking shitting me right now?" Londyn chokes out, muscles tensing.

I can physically feel her frustration and anger radiating through her. What I wouldn't give to haul Sawyer back here on a silver platter for Londyn to give a piece of her mind. Or use as a punching bag. Instead, I just hold her tighter, not letting go for anything.

"How tragic." The reporter shakes her head. "But it says a lot about your character for agreeing to deal with that."

"I loved her. But it just wasn't enough."

"So is it your belief that Ms. Bennett made up the story about Mr. Jaskulski assaulting her?"

"I know she did. She'd gotten caught and needed to lie her way out of it."

"Gotten caught?"

He nods. "A member of my church saw Londyn leaving a…clinic. After I confronted her, she admitted that she did, in fact, terminate a pregnancy. Told me the last thing she wanted was to carry my child. I should have known something was amiss when she kept putting off changing her last name officially."

I tighten my grip on Londyn when her body trembles even more violently. It takes everything I have to keep myself from putting my fist through the television. But that won't solve anything. I just can't wrap my head around why a national news network would invite this guy to be on their morning talk show and take his version of events as gospel. Simply because he's supposedly a man of faith he should be believed over Londyn?

"An affair is usually the death knell in many relationships, but I was willing to work through it. Willing to work on being a better husband. But she didn't seem interested in that. One night, as I worked on my sermon for the following week, she left. Didn't even leave a note. In the years that followed, I tried reaching out to her countless times, but every attempt went unanswered."

"Then it must have been a shock to learn she shot Mr. Jaskulski a few weeks ago."

"That may just be the understatement of the year." He chuckles, flashing a charismatic smile that's no more real than the Loch Ness Monster. "And while I want to believe my wife, I see the damage my reluctance to come forward has done. A man could have lost his life because of her lies, her disconnection from reality. She needs to be held responsible for her actions, not be allowed to throw around some baseless accusation of assault. She's gotten away with her lies long enough."

"I can't tell you how much we appreciate you taking the time to talk to us and our viewers today. And for giving us some insight into who exactly Londyn Bennett is. I can only imagine the strength it took for you to reopen these old wounds."

"As difficult as it has been to come to terms with this, to finally speak out, I needed to. I'd never forgive myself if she walked free to do something like this again. To ruin another man's life."

The host offers Sawyer a warm smile, reaching out and squeezing his hand before turning her attention back toward the camera. "Next up," she begins, her voice bright and chipper, "a woman who decided to say yes for an entire year. Stay tuned to see what she learned about herself and society."

Pointing the remote at the screen, I turn it off, neither one of us speaking for several seconds. Up until now, it's been a he-said/she-said scenario that could go either way. With the public outcry and benefit of the #MeToo movement supporting Londyn, Sophia has been optimistic things had turned the corner in our favor. I fear Sawyer's interview may have far-reaching ramifications.

"He's going to testify against me," she murmurs.

I spin her so she's facing me. "You don't know that."

"You heard him when I served him with the divorce papers," she counters. "He said I'd regret it. This was his plan all along."

I pinch my lips into a tight line, not wanting to tell her I had the same thought. "This is just one interview on a morning talk show. Not exactly *60 Minutes*."

"But it's out there. People don't care about the truth these days. Only what improves ratings. And that…" She points to the screen. "That just boosted their ratings big time."

I smooth my hands down her arms. "He's pissed he lost. I've known guys like Sawyer my entire life. All they care about is the win, not the people they hurt along the way."

"And he's going to win, Wes. How can I compete with all the lies he just spouted? I can't."

I grab her chin, forcing her eyes to mine. "You don't have to. Like you said, they're just lies."

"But no one will see that," she counters. "That man is a fucking pastor."

I smirk, trying to lighten the mood. "Definitely not two words I ever thought I'd hear in the same sentence."

Her demeanor momentarily cracks before her expression hardens once more. "He holds a great deal of influence and credibility. This isn't he-said/she-said anymore. It's my word against the world. At some point…" She trails off as she pushes away, wrapping her arms around her stomach. "It's like the Naked Truth and the Lie."

I approach, brows scrunched. "The what?"

"An allegory my father would talk about in his sermons."

"What's it about?"

"It tells the story about the Truth and the Lie. The Truth is initially suspicious of everything the Lie says. But every time the Lie speaks, the Truth confirms what he says is true. Eventually, the Lie convinces the Truth to go for a swim, so they both disrobe. Once the Truth is naked, the Lie steals her clothes. The Truth goes after him, but when she reaches the nearby village, all the townspeople look away, unable to stomach the sight of the Naked Truth. Ashamed, she hides away for all eternity as the Lie parades around as the Truth."

She blows out a long breath. "I fear my truth will suffer the same fate. That people will be disgusted by it and instead believe the lie parading around as the truth."

I do my best to keep my emotions in check, although it's becoming increasingly difficult. I wish there were something I could do to make this hurt less. Wish I could do something to make her forget. Wish there were someplace we could go where our troubles would disappear, even if for just a minute.

"Go shower and pack a bag," I say with authority.

She snaps her gaze toward mine. "Pack a bag?"

"Yes. We're getting away."

"I can't leave the state. It's a condition of my bail."

"And we won't. But we're getting out of the city."

"What about work? And your meetings?"

I shrug, playing down the stress filling me at the prospect of blowing off yet another meeting. But Londyn needs me more.

"My team can handle it. It'll be fine." I pull her into my embrace. "Being with you right now is more important."

"I'm fine, Wes. I—"

"I won't be going into the office today no matter what you say. So you can either come away with me for the weekend or not. But I'd prefer if you do."

She pouts, feigning irritation. "You can be quite frustrating at times."

"And stubborn." I wink. "Don't forget stubborn."

"Fine." She huffs. "I'll go shower. But whatever tricks you have up your sleeve better be worth you ditching work."

I bury my head in her neck. "You will always be worth it."

# CHAPTER TWENTY-SIX

## *Londyn*

"Where are we going?" I ask as Wes pulls the Range Rover off a familiar exit, driving roads I can probably navigate blindfolded after traveling this same route countless times over the past several months.

Reaching across the center console, he squeezes my hand, his eyes momentarily locking with mine. "Home."

Sighing, I rest my head back against my seat, a weight lifting off me. I didn't think a house could fill me with so much serenity, but it does.

"Home," I repeat, closing my eyes, keeping my hand enclosed in his.

And that's precisely where it stays as my surroundings transition from the densely populated region of Atlanta and its suburbs to the more rural area of Gampy and Meemaw's lake house.

When Wes pulls down the familiar dirt drive after an

hour, I can't stop the smile that lights up my face. Zeus can't contain his excitement, either, tail wagging and mouth panting as he tries to weasel his way into the front seat from where he's been resting in the back.

The instant we round the bend and Gampy and Meemaw's house comes into view, peace washes over me, all the troubles weighing me down evaporating. Now I understand why Wes and Julia wanted this house back so badly. There's something about it, a sort of magic it holds.

Here, our troubles disappear.

Here, nothing else matters.

Here, we can be free.

Coming to a stop, Wes puts the car in park, then jumps out, making his way around to the passenger side to open my door. I don't even have a foot on the ground before Zeus leaps out and makes a beeline toward the front porch, happily sniffing all the familiar smells.

I inhale a deep breath of the fresh air, the sun shining through scattered clouds.

"I love this smell," I murmur, allowing everything about this place to fill me with the strength I need right now.

When I sense a warmth beside me, I glance toward Wes, his gaze focused on me.

He brushes a few tendrils of hair out of my face, his touch thrilling me. "Reminds me of us."

"Not your childhood?"

While the scent around here reminds me of us, too, my memories don't go nearly as far back as Wes' do.

"No." He cups my cheeks. "Not anymore. That's how deeply you've burrowed your way into my soul, Londyn. Despite having spent the past thirty-six years of my life without you, the second you stepped out of your car to help with the insulation and drywall, wearing a tank top and a pair of cut-off shorts that should be illegal, I knew that no matter what happened, you'd leave a permanent mark on this place." He grabs my hand and places it over his chest. "And here, too, Lo. You will always be here. No matter what."

With slow motions, his lips descend on mine, covering and consuming them. His kiss is unhurried, languid, as if we have all the time in the world. As if this is the first of many kisses he'll bestow on me over our lifetime. As if our kisses aren't numbered.

"I never could have imagined you if I tried," I murmur once our kiss comes to an end.

"I'll take that as a compliment." He winks.

Placing a hand to my lower back, he leads me toward the porch, the lantern over the door like a beacon, welcoming us home after too long away. Exactly as I imagined it would when I designed this house. At that time, I didn't picture myself still here. But as Wes unlocks the front door and we step inside, memories of renovating this house with him playing in front of me like a home movie, there's nowhere else I'd rather be.

"Welcome home, Londyn," Wes murmurs into my ear.

I turn around, draping my arms over his shoulders. Standing on my tiptoes, I brush my lips against his. "Welcome home, Weston."

"Come on." He leads me down the hallway, through the kitchen, and out onto the screened-in back porch. Opening the screen door, he hooks it against the porch railing, a detail I insisted on so I could still do my favorite thing. Sit on the top step with Wes at my side.

Zeus darts between us and out into the meadow, barking and chasing away a few birds.

"Silly dog," Wes comments as he helps me sit, then brushes a kiss to my temple. "Be right back."

I watch as he disappears into the house before shifting my eyes back out over the property. A couple hundred feet to the left is the large lake where Gampy taught Wes to swim. Mature trees offer shade on hot, summer days, but now, in the dead of winter, their branches are devoid of most of their leaves. Around the other side of the lake is the horse paddock and stables that Wes turned into a state-of-the-art workshop for me. I grow giddy with excitement over the idea of spending a few hours in there this weekend. But I grow even more giddy over the idea of just spending time with Wes here. To go back to our roots. To forget for a minute.

A warmth across my shoulders pulls me out of my thoughts. I look to my left as Wes wraps a blanket around me, then holds out a beer.

It transports me to the first day I helped him install the insulation and drywall. After a hard day's work, I sat in this precise spot as Wes approached, handing me a bottle. Who knew that one beer would change everything?

"Figured you could use one today, even if it's only a little past noon."

I laugh under my breath. "I certainly could."

He lowers himself beside me, and I grab one side of the blanket, wrapping it around him, as well, before resting my head on his shoulder.

"So many memories of this place," he murmurs absent-mindedly.

I take a sip of my beer, then set it beside me, snuggling into Wes. "Tell me another story about your grandparents."

He peers into the distance with a contemplative expression. "Gampy could be a bit...hard-headed."

"Must run in the family," I remark, playfully nudging him.

"I suppose. I just like to think he had strong beliefs, which he absolutely did. When he made up his mind, there was no convincing him otherwise. Which was difficult when he got into an argument. On the other hand, Meemaw was always this compassionate, sympathetic individual. They both were, but Meemaw wasn't all that stubborn. And she had no problem admitting when she was wrong."

He furrows his brows, as if trying to pull a memory back to the surface. "I remember this heated argument Gampy and Dad got into one time when he dropped me off here for a weekend. I'm not even sure what caused it, but I think it was about money or something because I distinctly recall my dad kept mentioning a penny."

"They were arguing over a penny?"

He shrugs. "I was probably only eight at the time. It was right before Julia came to us, if I remember correctly. Anyway, Dad left angry. Gampy stormed through the house angry. Everyone was just…angry. Except for Meemaw. Gampy always said she was the sun to his rain. That she helped him see things more clearly. Eventually, she talked some sense into him, then made him call my dad to apologize. Of course, he grumbled about it, but still, no one could tell Meemaw no."

"I imagine not."

"So, after having a few glasses of scotch, he called my dad. And do you want to know what Gampy's apology sounded like?"

"What's that?" I lean closer, consumed by this story. Or maybe I just love the sound of Wes' voice as he reminisces about his childhood.

He takes a long pull from his beer, then wipes the residue

from his lips. He clears his throat. "'James,'" he begins, doing what I assume to be his best Gampy impression, the Southern twang even more pronounced, "'it's Connie. You know that place I told you to go? Well, if you haven't gone yet, don't go.'"

I burst out laughing, the sound echoing against the nature surrounding us, causing a flock of birds in a nearby tree to take flight. "I assume your gampy told your father to go to hell."

Wes nods through his own chuckles. "You assume correctly. So there you have it. A stubborn man's apology. Over the years, it became a running gag amongst all of us, including Julia, even though she wasn't around when it happened. Any time Julia and I would argue about something and then apologize, we'd do so in Gampy's way first before apologizing for real."

"He sounds like he was quite the character."

"He certainly was."

"I don't have any memories like that of my dad," I murmur.

Wes doesn't say anything, just leans down to kiss my forehead, squeezing me tightly.

"It's like he did everything to avoid me after my mother died."

"It couldn't have been easy on him."

"No. Especially considering the older I got, the more I resembled my mother. If you look at photos of us when we're around the same age, you probably wouldn't be able to tell us apart. Everyone always called me her mini-me, and I truly was. I was 100 percent my mother's daughter. Straight down to *my* stubbornness." I shake my head, worrying my bottom lip. "Is it horrible that I still find myself angry with my father, even though I can see he's trying to make amends?"

"It's going to take more than just a few weeks to build back everything that was lost between you two. Things like that don't happen overnight. You can't just flip a switch and forgive him. Forgiveness happens in increments, not all at once. At least that's my experience."

I nod. "I think it's just some of the guilt ingrained in me from a lifetime of being a pastor's daughter."

"That's your problem, Lo."

I tilt my head. "What is?"

"You need to stop thinking of yourself as a pastor's daughter. Or a pastor's ex-wife. Stop basing your identity on somebody else's. You're not just a pastor's daughter. You are so much more than that. You probably never felt that way growing up. And after seeing the way Sawyer treats you, I am absolutely certain he made you feel even more insignificant."

He grips my face, so much power and control emanating from his fingertips. But at the same time, also love and devotion.

"You are an incredible woman," he continues. "You are a survivor. A warrior. A fucking goddess. You've been dealt more shit than most people can even wrap their heads around, but every time, instead of allowing it to consume you, you walked through the goddamn flames with a look on your face that said 'That's all you got?' So don't allow yourself to feel guilty for needing time to forgive your father. *You* make the rules now. This is *your* life. No one else's."

I swallow hard, the dedication and zeal in his statement moving me in a way I didn't think words alone ever could. "I like the sound of that," I say through the thickness in my throat. Then I touch my lips to his. "But when this is all over, I'd like for it to be *our* life. Together. As one."

His muscles relax as he presses his lips more firmly against mine, coaxing my mouth open. He breathes into me, his tongue tangling with mine in a way that makes me feel as if he's giving me life. And that's what he's done from the beginning. Gave me life. Brought me back from the empty existence I'd been living. Reminded me what it's like to live. To laugh. To love.

Ending the kiss, his eyes bore into mine. "As much as I love the sound of that, it will still be *your* life. Even when you have my last name — and god, Lo, I am *dying* for you to have my last name — I still want you to live your own life. And I'll still live mine. But we'll live them together. Kind of like…ski tracks."

I shake my head, confused. "Ski tracks?"

"Yeah." He grabs my hand and flips it over, tracing his finger along the few lines in my palm. "Every person takes a different route down the mountain. But when you're at the very top, you can see how often the various tracks intersect, even though each person took their own journey to the bottom. Like with us." He holds my hand tightly. "We're both on our own journey. Some journeys we'll take together. Others, we'll need to do on our own." His lips slowly edge toward mine. "But when they do intersect, I guarantee it will be…"

"Magic," I breathe as his mouth closes over mine.

"Exactly, honeybee. Magic. What we have is magic. And I promise I will do everything I can to ensure the magic never dies."

# CHAPTER TWENTY-SEVEN

## *Weston*

A sliver of sunlight stirs me awake the following morning, and I stretch, pulling Londyn's naked body into mine. I nuzzle her neck, drawing in a deep inhale of her addictive scent. It brings me back to the day we first met. I'd found her scent intoxicating back then. And once I got a taste of her lips, I knew I was done for. There's magic in her kisses. The perfect medicine for my soul.

"Morning," Londyn says in a raspy voice.

"Morning, beautiful," I murmur, kissing her neck. "Have I told you lately how much I love waking up next to you."

"Mmm-hmm," she moans as she wiggles her ass against me, causing my erection to harden, as if it needs any help. "I quite enjoy it myself." She sighs and links her fingers with mine, resting my hand over her stomach. "So, what do you feel like doing today?"

I push her onto her back and hover over her, staring intently into her dark eyes that are lazy from sleep.

"A little of this…" I lower my mouth to her breast, circling her nipple with my tongue. She arches into me, her lips parting with her increased breathing.

I place my knee between her legs, spreading them apart as I lick my way from her chest and down her stomach. "And a little of this…" I dip my tongue into her belly button before continuing past her waist, settling between her thighs.

With a devilish grin, I lift my eyes to meet hers, my body throbbing when I see the raw need and hunger covering her. Then I grip her hips, urging her closer to my mouth. "And a whole lot of this."

When my tongue flicks her clit, she exhales, digging her fingernails into my scalp as she moves against me.

"That feel good, baby?" I ask between licks.

"God yes."

I glance up, pleasure visible in the lines of her face. I slip a finger inside, then another, stretching and massaging her. I doubt I'll ever get my fill of this woman. She's a drug, one I can't resist, desperate to experience that unbridled bliss only being with Londyn can give me.

And I'm only too happy to do everything in my power to make her feel that same euphoria.

It doesn't take long for her muscles to tighten, her breaths coming in shorter pants, her face scrunched up, as if trying to prolong this feeling. But I won't let her. She deserves to feel good. Deserves to fall over the edge.

"Let go, baby. Let me feel you." I return to her, pressing my tongue even more firmly against her clit, then suck gently. Like a bomb detonating, her body convulses beneath me, her cries echoing in the stillness of the morning as wave after wave of ecstasy courses through her.

When her tremors wane, I crawl up her frame and slam my mouth against hers. She bites my lower lip, a pleasurable ache settling deep within me. One I doubt will ever be satisfied. But if there's anyone who can, it's Londyn.

"Inside me," she orders breathily, wrapping her legs around my waist. "Now."

"Yes, ma'am." I leave her with a kiss, leaning back and bringing my erection up to her.

Our gazes locked, I ease inside her, savoring every millimeter until I'm fully seated, staying still for a beat. Londyn arches her back, a ray of sunlight casting along her lustrous body as she closes her eyes, relishing in the sensation.

"Open them, baby," I growl, running my hand along her torso.

She follows my request, meeting my stare, our connection unbreakable. Slowly, I begin to move inside her, wanting to take my time.

She grabs the back of my head, forcing my lips to hers. "I love you, Wes," she breathes as she circles her hips against me, everything about her so damn perfect. From the way her body molds to mine. To the way her kisses light me on fire. To the way her heart loves me, even after being betrayed in the worst way possible.

And it's that betrayal that makes her love feel even more powerful. She could have kept her heart locked up tightly. And she certainly tried. But I felt it that first day. We were made for each other. I've never been so sure of anything in my life.

"I love you, honeybee," I declare.

With each thrust, each kiss, each scrape of her fingernails down my spine, my pulse increases. I lean into her touch, something as insignificant as a breath against my skin igniting me, my nerves overly sensitive.

When she takes my lower lip between her teeth again, I groan, increasing my motions until I can no longer hold back, my release overtaking me.

"Fuck," I grunt, thrusting into her a few more times, then collapse on top of her, sated and content.

"I'm sorry," I struggle to say through my ragged breathing. "I'd hoped to give you another one, but I couldn't hang on. That's what you do to me, baby. You make me lose all fucking control."

She giggles as I nip at her throat. "A feat for a man who likes to stay in control of everything."

"True. But I enjoy losing control with you."

She wraps her arms and legs around me, her warmth causing me to stir yet again. "I can tell. Now get off me so I can go clean up."

"Only if I can join you." I waggle my brows.

"Shower?"

"A nice long shower. Because I plan on making you dirty again before it's all over."

"I like the sound of that." She presses a light kiss to my lips just as a rustling sounds from the front porch.

We stiffen simultaneously, flinging our gazes toward the windows.

Normally, I'd blame it on the fact that we're surrounded by nature. It's not the first time an animal has made itself welcome on either one of the porches. But when the front door opens, I go into defensive mode.

Jumping out of bed, I tug on my pants, wondering why Zeus isn't barking or growling at whoever it is.

Heavy footsteps grow closer as they storm up the stairs and down the hall. Then the bedroom door flies open, Imogene barreling into the room. Her blue eyes light up in excitement when she sees Londyn, who hastily attempts to pull the duvet up to her neck.

"Miss Londyn! I've missed you so much!" Imogene jumps onto the bed and flings her arms around her, as if there's nothing wrong with her being here.

As uncomfortable as it is, Londyn's state of undress isn't what leaves her in shock. It's the fact that she's not supposed to be within fifty feet of Imogene, let alone in the same room.

She looks at me, questioning, as she weakly returns Imogene's hug. All I can do is shake my head, mouth agape, no answer forthcoming. I wish I had one.

More footsteps grow close, and I whirl around. Julia comes to an abrupt stop when she sees Imogene on the bed with an obviously naked and confused Londyn.

There was once a time this wouldn't have been an issue, apart from the awkwardness of my niece bursting in on us when we're naked. Now there are court orders preventing us from spending time together. From enjoying this house as I pictured we all would.

"Imogene, sweetie, I think we may have woken Uncle Wes and Miss Londyn." Julia plasters a forced smile onto her face, not wanting to let on to her daughter that anything's amiss. "Why don't we go downstairs and visit with Zeus? You were just mentioning how much you miss him."

"Okay!" Without a single word of complaint, she bounces off the bed, darting from the bedroom, her feet pounding down the stairs.

Julia looks at me, her lips parted, as if on the brink of saying something.

"I'm sorry" is all she can muster before spinning around, closing the door behind her.

A heavy silence settles in the room as Londyn and I stare at the closed door. I'd brought her here to forget everything for a minute. Now all her troubles are back, reminding her there's nowhere she can go to escape them.

"What are we going to do?" Londyn asks after a few seconds.

I scrub a hand over my face, returning to her and sitting on the edge of the mattress. "We can't all be here."

"*You* can," she reminds me with a sad smile. "But I can't."

"Which means I can't, either. I go where you go, Lo. Plain and simple."

I blow out a breath, my anger toward Nick growing with each passing second. His request for a protective order was bullshit, and he knows it. I'd understand the purpose behind it if Londyn were actually a criminal with a history of violence. She's not. She's a woman who protected herself. Yet she's the only one being punished.

"I'll go talk to her," I declare. "See if we can work out something."

"I'm sorry, Wes. This whole situation… It sucks."

"I won't disagree with you. But for now, we'll abide by every court order in place. Soon, this will all be over and we'll be able to go back to normal."

Tears threaten to spill over her eyelids and down her cheeks. "What is normal?"

I wrack my brain for the right answer. But as seems to be the case lately, I come up empty. "I wish I knew. But we'll find some sort of normal. Together." I press a kiss to her lips, then stand, grabbing a t-shirt from my bag. I pull it on and step out into the hallway, closing the door behind me.

As I'm about to pad down the stairs, I stop in my tracks at the sound of Imogene yelling and crying.

"But you promised me!" she shrieks.

I retreat, hiding behind the wall, but shift my body so I can still see them.

While Julia and Imogene have spent months under my roof in the past, I've never witnessed them argue. Not like this. She's only a few months shy of her seventh birthday, so she still has her moments, as any young child does. But she's also a very reasonable little girl. This is out of character for her.

"I know I did, sweetie. But we can't stay." Julia crouches down and attempts to pull her daughter in for a hug, which she pushes away from.

"Why? Why can't we? We stayed with Uncle Wes and Miss Londyn during Thanksgiving! And Christmas! What's different now?"

I can see the weight on Julia's shoulders as she pinches the bridge of her nose. "Everything's different now, baby. I wish it weren't. God, do I wish things weren't. But right now, we need to go back home."

"To my *real* home?" she asks, placing her hands on her hips.

"It's too long of a drive. Maybe we can go for a few days next weekend."

Imogene glowers at Julia, her tiny hands fisting. "I hate it here! And I hate you!" She whirls around, storming down the hallway, the screen door off the back porch slamming behind her.

If I felt bad about this mess before, I feel absolutely horrible now. I can deal with disappointing my sister. I hate letting down my niece.

"You can come down now, Wes," Julia says after a few moments, the defeat audible in her tone. "I know you're up there."

Blowing out a long breath, I step onto the landing, then shuffle downstairs. "You heard me?"

"You're not exactly stealthy. Doesn't help that the floorboards in this house are on the creaky side. Unless you know where to step," she adds, but her words lack their normal teasing nature.

"I take it Imogene isn't happy about being in Atlanta." I run my fingers through my hair.

"She's having a difficult time lately." She stares out past the back porch.

I follow her gaze, able to make out Imogene sitting under an overgrown oak tree, arms wrapped around her knees. Zeus remains at her side, nuzzling her.

"She hates having to wear a uniform to school. Even worse, it's a dress." She playfully rolls her eyes before her expression becomes serious once more. "She misses home. The way things were before…" She trails off. "Well, before."

"I think we all do."

"I should have checked with you first, but it never crossed my mind. I'm so used to being able to come down here whenever Imogene asks that it didn't even register you and Londyn might be here. I didn't see your car out front, so—"

"I put it in the garage last night since they were predicting rain."

"I figured. I'll just… I'll figure out something else. Maybe book a hotel suite downtown. Go for a mani-pedi. Call it a girls' weekend."

"I'll reach out to Mia and have her arrange something for you," I offer. "Tell her to charge it to my account."

"I can take care of it, Wes."

"Please, Jules." I touch her arm. "Let me do this for you."

Closing her eyes, she nods, blowing out a long breath. "Okay."

I pull her into my arms and kiss the top of her head.

"You're a good brother, Wes."

"I love you, Jules. I'll do anything for you." I peer down at her. "You know that, don't you?"

Chewing on her lower lip, something akin to indecision flickers within. Then she releases a sigh, stepping out of my hold and avoiding my eyes.

"We'll get out of your hair. Let you enjoy your weekend." She starts toward the back door.

I part my lips, wanting to tell her she doesn't have to go. But she does. And there's nothing I can do about it.

As she's about to step out onto the back porch, she pauses, glancing back at me. "Maybe the three of us can get together for dinner on Monday night?" She lifts a brow.

"Three of us?"

"Yeah. You, me, and Imogene. Like old times."

"I'd like that."

"Me, too." She returns my smile, then continues onto the porch and down the stairs, slowly walking across the yard.

I watch as she talks to Imogene for a minute, who grudgingly pulls herself to her feet. After showering Zeus with plenty of hugs and kisses, she follows Julia to the front of the house and into their car.

Once I hear the crunching of tires kicking up dirt, I blow out a breath and turn, about to head up to the master bedroom, but pause when I notice Londyn standing halfway down the stairs.

"Is Imogene okay?" She fidgets with the hem of my oversized t-shirt she threw on.

"She'll be okay. I told Julia to book a hotel suite downtown on me."

She nods, drawing in a shaky breath before blurting out, "I'm sorry I destroyed everything."

I take the steps two at a time to get to her and cup her cheeks. "Don't you dare say that. Don't you dare *think* that."

"But you're sacrificing so much by being with me. Losing so much. Clients. Your sister. Your niece. Is it really worth it?"

"Yes, it is," I reply intently. "A hundred times, yes. It is worth it. *You* are worth it. You think I'm losing so much by being with you. But I'd lose more by *not* being with you. Don't you dare ever think otherwise. Okay?"

Her eyes trace over mine, as if searching for any hint of reluctance on my part. But she won't find any. Not when it comes to her.

I lower my lips to hers, trying to erase any question of my devotion. She's stiff at first, at war with herself. But she eventually melts into me, her body molding to mine. When I pull back, the concern and uneasiness has vanished, a look of adoration in her eyes as she gazes up at me.

"Still game for a shower?" I ask, a single brow cocked.

She gives me a flirtatious look. "Still game to make me dirty?"

I draw her back to me, squeezing her ass. "Always, darling."

# CHAPTER TWENTY-EIGHT

## *Weston*

"How was everything?" Miss Clara approaches the same booth Gampy used to always request whenever we came here all those years ago. The table may have been swapped out and the booth reupholstered, but it's in the same spot with the same exact view of Main Street out the large windows.

"Absolutely terrible," I joke, throwing my napkin onto my plate that once held Miss Clara's meatloaf and mashed potatoes, another one of Gampy's favorites.

"I see that. Just like your gampy. Y'all say the meatloaf is terrible, yet you order it every single time. And eat every last bite, too, I might add."

"Just hoping it'll eventually get better."

"Yeah. Yeah." She rolls her eyes, taking my plate as she turns toward Londyn. "And how about you, dear? Did you get enough?"

"You may just have the best chicken pot pie I've had in quite some time."

"And the collards?"

"Almost as good as my mama's."

"Well, I'll take that as a compliment. Because if you ask me, everyone's mama makes the best collards." She winks. "Now, what do you two say to some peach cobbler?"

The bell over the door chimes, announcing a new arrival. Clara glances toward it, about to tell whoever to sit wherever they'd like, as she always does. Instead, her expression hardens into an annoyed stare. It's a stark contrast to her typical hospitality.

"Well, well, well…"

When I hear that familiar voice, I know precisely what caused Miss Clara's reaction. I look past her as Grady Stowe saunters toward us, the same lackeys who'd been with him at the county fair following dutifully behind.

"I'd heard you brought that girl back to town, but didn't think it possible."

"Why?" I glower. "Think your threats last summer really had any effect on me? Hate to break it to you, but I've spent plenty of time here since then. We both have. Together." I reach across the table, squeezing Londyn's hand.

"Not talking about that, Wesley," he says with a heavy drawl.

I fight against the wince wanting to break free. I've always hated when people called me Wesley, especially when they intentionally did so just to piss me off. Like Grady always did throughout our childhood and adolescence.

"Then what *are* you talking about?"

"The fact that you brought her here given who she is."

"And who *is* she?" I sneer.

"A fucking criminal who belongs in prison for trying to kill a good white man."

When he leers at Londyn, she doesn't back down, pinning him with a penetrating glare, almost urging him to make a move he'll regret.

"Although, if I'm being honest," he continues, "I kind of wish you *did* kill him. Then the state could get rid of one more useless nigger whore."

I've heard people talk about seeing red when in a fit of rage, but never truly understood what they meant.

Until now.

It's not red they see.

It's the manifestation of drawing blood.

My ears pound, my body shakes, my face burns hotter than the sun.

I'm usually a pretty even-tempered guy. I don't fly off the handle all that easily. But when it comes to Londyn, I don't think, just react. So when Grady calls her such a derogatory name, I do what I wanted to all those months ago.

And this time, Londyn doesn't stop me, watching with interest as I shoot to my feet and reel back in one swift motion, my fist connecting with Grady's jaw, a crack echoing around us.

A few surprised gasps can be heard before the diner goes silent. Grady remains motionless for a protracted moment, massaging his jaw. Then he looks back at me.

"Is that really the best you got? Come on, man." He punches his chest. "Let's settle this. Right here. Right now."

"I don't think so," Miss Clara's voice cuts through as she pushes her way between us. She turns to Grady. "Get out of my restaurant. I've put up with your shenanigans long enough, and I won't do it anymore. So get on. Find somewhere else to spend your money, because it ain't welcome here no more." She stands her ground, eyes unwavering, almost urging him to say something in response.

I widen my stance, ready to jump into action if he tries anything. Luckily, he doesn't, backing down after a protracted moment.

"You'll regret this, Clara," Grady hisses. "I'll spread the word around town that you cater to criminals."

"You mean like your entire family?" she scoffs, then waves him off. "Now get, before I call the sheriff."

He hesitates for a minute, every other diner holding their breath as they wait for his next move. Finally, he turns, storming toward the front door, his friends falling in line behind him. Just before he's about to disappear, he pauses, his eyes finding mine.

"You better watch your fucking back, Bradford. I saw some of the shit people are posting online about your girl. Wouldn't want history to repeat itself, would you?"

"What do you—" I begin just as Clara interrupts.

"I told you to get. Or do you want to add trespassing to your list of achievements?" She places a hand on her hip, everyone watching the exchange with wide eyes. This is probably the most exciting thing to happen in this town in quite some time.

He flips her off and stomps onto the sidewalk, silence falling over the normally lively family restaurant.

After several moments of awkward tension, Miss Clara claps her hands together, her expression brightening. "I think we could all use some peach cobbler," she says to everyone in the small diner. "Peach cobblers all around. On the house."

That's all people need to hear to return to their conversations and meals, chatter filling the space once more.

"Are you okay, dear?" Miss Clara asks Londyn as I slide back into the booth, still seething.

"I'm fine." She forces a smile.

"Don't you pay no attention to him." Miss Clara squeezes her hand. "He's not a good person. Never has been. Never will be. He doesn't speak for me or anyone else in this town, ya hear?"

Londyn nods. "Thank you."

"Anytime, dear. Now, let me get you two some cobbler." She scurries away, making her rounds through the restaurant to check on everyone.

Once we're alone, I grab Londyn's hand, wishing I could do or say something to make her feel better. It seems we've been riding a tumultuous rollercoaster these past several weeks. For every up, there's an even bigger down.

And since yesterday, it feels like we keep falling with no end in sight.

"I'm so sorry, Lo. The things he said…"

"I should have known something like this might happen, especially here."

"But it shouldn't."

She shrugs, turning to look out the window. The street is busy for this small of a town. Then again, it is Saturday, and this is the only area to shop or grab a bite to eat.

Noticing Londyn's gaze fixated on something, I follow her line of sight, spotting a couple around our age walking hand in hand. There's nothing remarkable about them. Except they don't have to hide their affection from anyone out of fear that some racist asshole might attack them for the simple reason that they fell in love with someone of a different race.

"What do you think he meant?" she asks, returning her eyes to mine. "About history repeating itself. What did he mean by that?"

"I'm not sure," I reply just as Miss Clara swings by,

carrying two plates of peach cobbler, the vanilla ice cream on top already starting to melt.

"Here you go," she sings, setting them down in front of us. "Enjoy."

She's about to walk away when I stop her.

"Hey, Miss Clara?"

"Yes, dear?"

I glance at Londyn, then back at her. "What did Grady mean about history repeating itself?"

"Oh, you know how he can be," she says dismissively. "Probably talking out of his behind, as always."

"Clara..." I narrow my eyes on her. "I don't think that was it. He's talking about something in particular, isn't he?"

She worries her bottom lip, glancing around the restaurant. Then she heaves a labored sigh. "Well, you'll just be able to read about it online, so I may as well tell you the correct story." She motions for Londyn to scoot over, sitting beside her.

"Did your mama ever talk about Penny?"

"Penny?" I swallow hard.

Londyn's intrigued eyes meet mine, obviously remembering the story I'd told her yesterday. How I thought Gampy and my father had been fighting over money. I'd thought it strange to argue over something as insignificant as a penny. What if it weren't a coin, but a person?

"I figured she wouldn't," Clara says. "It was a difficult subject for your grandparents. Hell, for everyone around these parts. At least the good people."

"Who was she?"

"You know your grandparents fostered kids when your mama was younger, right?"

I nod.

"Well, Penny was one of them. Normally, the kids only

stayed a few months while they waited for a more permanent placement. Except Penny. Your grandparents took a liking to her right away, agreed to foster her as long as she needed."

I sense this story doesn't have a happy ending. "What happened to her?"

"Depends on who you ask. Most people these days have finally come to terms with the truth, but back then, they were happy to turn a blind eye to this sort of thing. This was the early 70s, so things were much different. Especially if a white person were to date someone black. Like Penny did."

"Oh." Out of instinct, I clutch Londyn's hand in mine.

"If you think people are less than accepting now, it was even worse back then. Sure, the Civil Rights Act had been passed and racism was supposed to be dead—"

"It'll never be dead," Londyn says softly. "Not when it's so deeply entrenched in this country's roots."

Clara nods. "You're right about that, sweetie. In the 70s, racial tensions were pretty high, especially in this small town." She peers out the window. "I'll never forget the day a teenager rushed into the diner when my mama still ran it, God rest her soul. There had been a car wreck about a half mile up the road. He'd asked us to call an ambulance, said a man was badly injured. I was about to do so, but my mama placed a hand over my wrist, stopping me. Then she asked the boy what color the man was."

"Why would that matter?" I ask, although I already know the answer.

"It always matters," Londyn says. "Even today."

"Up until that moment, I'd always thought my mama to be a good Christian woman. Always advocating how important it was to help those less fortunate than us. Which was why she often donated excess food to the local shelters. Little did I know that she'd only donate to *white* shelters."

"So I take it most people in town didn't like the idea of Penny dating a black boy," I comment.

"Certainly not, but that didn't bother her one bit. Nothing seemed to bother her. She marched to the beat of her own drum."

"Who was the boy?" Londyn inquires.

"As you know, your grandparents spent the summers here," she says to me before looking back at Londyn. "Samuel's mama worked as a housekeeper at their house. And Samuel helped take care of the grounds. Mowing the grass. Fixing things that needed fixing."

"Whenever Gampy let him," I joke, knowing how my grandfather could be.

A smile lights up her face. "He wanted to help them out. They were good people. Proud people. Samuel's mama, I believe her name was Abigail, had lost her husband a few years prior, so money was tight. From what I understand, your gampy offered to help with her bills, but she wouldn't have it. Didn't want people to think she was looking for a handout. So he hired Samuel, as well. Every day, he spent hours with that young man, showing him how to fix things. How to be the man of the house."

"That's admirable," Londyn says in awe. "Especially considering the time."

"That's Conrad Hammond for you," Clara states with a wistful look. "Always helping where he could. With all the time Samuel spent at the house, he started to notice Penny. Their friendship grew over the course of a few summers. And for the longest time, Penny and Samuel stayed just that. Friends. Despite your mother's constant teasing about being friends with a black boy, let alone 'the help', as she referred to him," she adds under her breath with a roll of her eyes.

"So she's always been this way?" I remark.

She considers my question for a beat, then shakes her head. "Not always. When she was younger, Lydia would play with Abigail's kids, since your meemaw was more than happy for her to bring her kids with her to the house. But once Lydia hit adolescence, she changed, like most teenagers do. Girls are mean. There's so much peer pressure to fit in. And back then, there was peer pressure to be on the…correct side of certain issues."

"And she never outgrew it," I comment, filling in the blanks.

"I think some people are born with hate in their heart. It's not for your gampy's and meemaw's lack of trying. Back then, they weren't as vocal as they were in their later years, due to your gampy's job at the prosecutor's office, then as a judge. But they were still good people. Didn't make a ruckus when they learned about Penny's relationship with Samuel. Just warned her to be careful, that people may not be as understanding as they were." She briefly closes her eyes as she draws in a deep breath. "But what those boys did…"

"What happened?" I ask again.

Shaking her head, she returns her haunted gaze to mine. "It was a week or so before Labor Day. One morning, your meemaw came into the diner looking for Penny. She hadn't come home the night before, which was unlike her. Claimed Lydia had seen her sneak out to meet Samuel at one of their usual spots. When your meemaw went over to ask Samuel, he claimed he hadn't seen Penny since the previous afternoon."

"Did Penny sneak out to meet him?"

Miss Clara nods.

"Why did she have to sneak out? You said my grandparents didn't mind so much."

"And they didn't. But people around town did, so they were never able to go on real dates together."

"Why not?"

"A lot of establishments in the South refused to serve interracial couples during that time," Londyn explains.

"That's right." Miss Clara nods. "The only reason anyone around town even knew about Penny and Samuel was because of Lydia. She couldn't resist poking fun at her to all her friends."

"Was Penny ever found?" Londyn asks.

Clara pinches her lips together. "Later that morning, Penny's unconscious body was discovered on the riverbank. Her clothes were torn. There was blood between her legs. It was obvious what had happened. Everyone was outraged. It didn't matter these same people had spoken ill of Penny mere hours ago, made fun of her for daring to date someone other than a white boy. Now that she'd been hurt, presumably by a black man, the town rallied behind her while she lay in a coma in the hospital."

"Was Samuel arrested?" I ask.

"The police never got the chance. People in town took justice into their own hands."

"Oh god." Londyn covers her mouth with her hand.

"They beat Samuel to death, then burned down his mama's house while the rest of his family slept. His mama and most of his siblings were able to get out in time, but…" She trails off, eyes glistening with unshed tears. "A little girl died in the fire. Only four years old."

"No…" Londyn's lower lip quivers.

"Was anyone ever arrested?"

Clara gives me a pointed stare. "What do you think?"

My shoulders fall. "No."

"Correct."

"What about Penny?" Londyn asks, wiping her eyes. "Did she ever wake up from the coma?"

"She did. Tried to tell the police what really happened that night, but no one wanted to hear it, although I think we all knew she was telling the truth. It was easier to believe the contrary."

"And what did she say happened?" I ask.

"According to Penny, she snuck out to meet Samuel, as Lydia claimed. But along the way, she was…intercepted."

"Intercepted?"

"By a bunch of boys around Penny's age. Teenagers. Troublemakers. And the head troublemaker?" She pauses. "None other than Edward Stowe."

I cock a single brow. "Stowe?"

"Grady's father. He'd always had an eye for Penny. I could be wrong, but I think he finally snapped over the idea that she chose a black boy over him."

"What did he do?"

"Penny claimed he assaulted her." She lowers her voice. "Raped and beat her before leaving her for dead."

"Was he arrested?"

"Of course not. It was the word of a white boy against a dead black boy. Who do you think they believed?"

"Even with Penny's statement?" I press.

"The police claimed she was scared of retribution, which was why she tried to blame Edward when, according to the authorities, an 'upstanding citizen from a good white family' wouldn't do what Penny alleged." She uses air quotes, her tone dripping with sarcasm.

"Such bullshit," I mutter under my breath. "What happened to Penny?"

Clara heaves a sigh. "Once she was discharged from the

hospital, she was removed from Gampy and Meemaw's care."

"Why?"

"Child Services claimed it was due to insufficient supervision. Even went so far as to terminate their status as foster parents. But I think they did so because your grandparents allowed Penny to carry on with Samuel instead of forbidding it. Other than hearing she'd been placed with a family in Savannah, I don't know what became of her."

"Gampy and Meemaw must have been devastated," I remark, mostly to myself.

"They were definitely rattled by everything. Which was probably why that was the last summer they spent here." She nods at me. "Until you were born."

I shake my head, sitting back in the booth, the ice cream now melted in a pool around the untouched peach cobbler. "Why is it like this? Why do people hate? Why do people judge based on someone's skin color?"

On a deep inhale, Clara slides out of the booth, slowly rising to her feet. "That's the million-dollar question, my dear Weston. One I don't think we'll ever have an answer to. All we can do is love as fiercely as possible in the hopes of drowning out all the hate in the world."

# CHAPTER TWENTY-NINE

## *Londyn*

I can't stop thinking about Miss Clara's story. It's not the first one like that I've heard. Growing up, it seemed everyone had some footnote they'd share about their own experiences with racism. While the town where I spent most of my younger years was predominantly black, I still took these things to heart. Knew it didn't matter that laws had been passed to supposedly protect people of different races and ethnicities from discrimination. It still happens. It always will.

Needing to do something to take my mind off everything for a minute, I slip out of bed and pull on the pair of yoga pants I'd discarded on the floor last night. After shrugging on a hoodie, I slide on my sneakers and grab my phone. Then I scribble out a quick note.

*I'm in the workshop. If you wake up and miss me, feel free to join me.*

*I love you.*

I leave it on my side of the bed, pausing to appreciate how peaceful Wes looks as he sleeps. Then I make my way out of the bedroom, down the stairs, and out the back door, Zeus following dutifully behind me.

"It's a chilly one, isn't it, boy?" I say to him as we travel the familiar path from the house, the flashlight on my phone illuminating the way.

Once I reach the old stable-turned-workshop, I open the door, ushering Zeus inside ahead of me. I flick on the lights, peace enveloping me as I take in the unfinished projects scattered around the vast space, everything exactly as I left it the last time I was here a few days before New Year's Eve.

A part of me doesn't want to touch anything. Wants to keep it like it is, if only to have one place I can go where I can pretend things are the way they once were. Then again, Gampy and Meemaw's house offers me that. Once Julia and Imogene left earlier, I hadn't thought much about my troubles, thanks to Wes. It wasn't until we ran into Grady at the diner that I was reminded of my current predicament. That's the healing power this place possesses. It truly is magic.

"What do you think, boy? Work on the wine bar or the dresser?" I glance at Zeus, who gives me a disinterested look before finding his doggie bed in the corner, curling up in it.

I chuckle. "You're a horrible assistant, bud. I may have to give some serious consideration to replacing you. But I think the wine bar."

I look at the battered secretary desk, something that's a dime a dozen at flea markets. Most people find them useless due to their tall frame and the drop-down leaf that serves as an unstable writing surface. But despite its uselessness as a desk, it's the perfect piece to turn into a wine bar.

Over the years, it's become one of my top-selling items, people often special ordering one even when I'm out of stock.

Popping in my earbuds, I navigate to one of my favorite playlists on my phone and blast the music. It only takes a matter of seconds for me to lose myself in my project. To quiet my mind as I focus solely on the task at hand, tuning out the rest of the world.

It's not until Zeus tugs on my pant leg that I take a break from sanding. "What is it, pal?" I ask, removing my earbuds, expecting him to answer me.

He darts away, growling and barking as he runs in a circle.

"What are you doing? You rarely even bark when someone rings the doorbell. Why now?" I remove my gloves and protective glasses, dropping them onto a nearby work-bench before grabbing my phone and following Zeus toward the door. "Do you need to go out?"

Bringing up the flashlight on my phone, I open the door for him. The second the door is cracked enough, he bolts out and along the path toward the house. I attempt to keep up, coming to a dead stop when I see what has Zeus on high alert.

Actually, I'm not sure that's entirely true.

I *feel* what has set Zeus off before I see it, the scorching heat warming my skin, even from several hundred feet away.

"No," I breathe, a chill trickling through me, despite the heat. "No. No. No. No!"

I take off running. Not thinking, not feeling. Just reacting to the sight in front of me, not wanting to believe what my eyes tell me is happening. This can't be real. It must just be a horrible nightmare, brought forward because of Clara's story earlier. That has to be it. I must be dreaming. I'll soon wake up enclosed in Wes' embrace as he chases the nightmares away.

But as I break into a fit of coughing from the smoke the wind has kicked up, I know it's not simply a nightmare.

Gampy and Meemaw's house is fully engulfed in flames, red and orange stark against the night sky.

"*Wes!*" I bellow, praying he somehow got out before the flames overtook the house.

Panicked, I do the only thing I can think of. Fingers trembling, I somehow manage to dial 9-1-1 as I frantically run around the property, coughing and fighting against the smoke, searching for any sign of Wes.

"9-1-1. What's your emergency?" a voice answers instantly.

"Our house is on fire!" I yell, my throat tightening when some of the wood planks of the front porch cave in, sending sparks and embers flying, Zeus scrambling away. "Oh god. I think he's inside."

"What's the location?"

I press my hand to my forehead as I rattle off the address, my pulse racing faster than it ever has.

"Fire personnel are on their way. I need you to remain where you are and not enter the building. Do you want me to stay on the line with you until they get there?"

I stare into space, helplessness washing over me as I watch flames consume more and more of the house. I want to tell her no, that I need to get into the house to do every-thing I can to help Wes. But if I do, fire personnel will have two people trapped inside. If by some miracle Wes *is* still alive, that may just cost him his life.

"It'll be okay," the woman assures me. "According to my computer, their ETA is just under four minutes."

"Four minutes…" I blink slowly.

I doubt it's been more than two minutes since I stepped out of the workshop. Yet in those two minutes, I've watched the flames destroy more and more of the house.

"There may not be much left," I choke out.

I sink to the ground, understanding how Wes must have felt when he learned I'd been arrested. At least he could do something to help me. He bailed me out. Was there for me when my life had been turned upside down. But me? I can't do anything to help. Other than pray.

So, for the first time in years, that's what I do. I close my eyes and pray, hoping with everything I have that some higher power will intervene and save the man I love. That we didn't come this far, didn't overcome obstacle after obstacle, to lose now.

When a blaring siren cuts through the roar of the fire, I snap my eyes open as a pair of fire engines round the dirt path and pull up in front of Meemaw and Gampy's house.

"I'll let you go," the dispatcher says as I jump to my feet.

I don't even acknowledge her, all my attention focused on the firefighters in full gear scrambling out of the trucks.

"You're the one who called?" one of them shouts at me, jogging up to me.

"Yes."

"Dispatch said there's someone inside?"

Nodding, I draw in a breath, trying to stop my chin from quivering. "Master bedroom."

"And where is that?"

"Upstairs. End of the hall."

"Which windows?"

I lift my arm and point. "Last three in the front here, and the three opposite them on the back. The window on the side of the house leads to the ensuite bathroom."

He nods curtly, then waves over a man from the ambulance that had just arrived. "Get her checked out."

Before I can protest, he darts off, issuing more orders to the rest of the firefighters on the scene, everyone seeming to know precisely what their job is.

"Come with me, ma'am," the paramedic says, touching my elbow and leading me toward the idling ambulance.

"I'm fine," I insist. "I wasn't inside."

"It's just a precaution. Now, any shortness of breath?" he asks, going through a series of questions I answer absent-mindedly, my eyes focused on the house, every second that passes without seeing the firefighters appear with Wes making my hope dwindle more and more.

This is all my fault. Grady all but threatened he'd do something like this. We should have taken him more seriously. Shouldn't have brushed off his threats as just meaningless words, as all his other threats have been. This time, he followed through.

And now Wes will pay the price.

"Oh, my god, Londyn," I hear a familiar voice call out as the paramedic checks my breathing, a stethoscope pressed against my back. I look up to see Miss Clara rushing toward me from her car parked several yards away. She takes my hands in hers, squeezing them tightly. "When George's radio went off and I heard about the fire, I didn't want to believe it. Wanted to think they got the wrong address."

"George's radio?" I furrow my brow. "What are you talking about?"

"My son is a volunteer firefighter. Normally, his radio only goes off every now and then, and usually with false alarms. But this…" She shifts her gaze back to the house, her lower lip trembling. "I really didn't want it to be true." She takes a minute to get her emotions under control, then looks at me again. "Where's Wes?"

I pull my lips between my teeth, not saying a word. I don't have to.

Her eyes widen as she looks at the burning house again. "Oh Lord, no."

My chin trembles as a new wave of tears threatens to spill forward. "I was out in the old stables that Wes had turned into a workshop when Zeus alerted me to the fire." I inhale a sharp breath. "Oh god. Zeus."

I step away from the paramedic and Clara, ignoring his protests that he wasn't done checking me out.

"Zeus!" I shout, darting along the property for any sign of the dog, Miss Clara joining me in the search. I'll never forgive myself if he ran into the house. I wouldn't put it past him. That dog would do anything to protect Wes. "Zeus, where are you?!" I scream, tears streaming down my face as my world falls apart around me.

I'm on the brink of collapsing to the ground and willing it to swallow me up when I feel a hand on my shoulder. I whirl around, staring into Clara's eyes.

She nods toward the front of the ladder truck. "Is that who you're looking for?"

I look in that direction, relief filling me when I notice Zeus sitting by the front wheels, as if supervising. The second he spies me, he trots over, rubbing his nose against my leg and whimpering.

"I know, boy. I know." I scratch his head between his ears, offering him the same comfort he offers me. "He'll be okay. I know it. He has to be."

Clara rubs my back reassuringly, then grabs my hand in hers once more. She closes her eyes and mutters the words to a prayer.

I tighten my hold on Clara's hands, allowing her words to lift me up and give me hope in one of the most hopeless moments I've ever experienced.

"I need a medic!" a booming voice calls out.

I rip my gaze back to the house as several firefighters emerge, two carrying a limp body between them.

Not hesitating, I rush toward them. "Is he okay? Is he alive?" I'm in hysterics, desperate for some sort of reassurance that I'm not responsible for his death.

"Give him some space," one man answers gruffly.

I stumble back, my lungs struggling to take in air as I watch them carry Wes' unconscious body toward the ambulance, a stretcher meeting them halfway. I don't even know how I find the strength to put one foot in front of the other and follow them, my legs weak and brain fuzzy, but I do.

As I get close enough to take a good look at Wes, his left leg and foot a mangled mess of red and pink flesh, some of it charred black, I release a strangled sob, shoving a fist against my mouth.

"Oh god," Miss Clara exhales as she joins me. "Please, Lord." She wraps her arm around my waist to help support me when it feels like the world's about to give out beneath me. "Show mercy."

"I've got a pulse," the paramedic shouts, then places an oxygen mask over Wes' face before glancing at me. "We're taking him to Trinity Hospital, then he'll most likely need to be airlifted to Atlanta. You can ride up front."

I look at Clara, then Zeus. I can't just leave the dog, but I can't leave Wes, either.

"You go, sweetie." She squeezes my bicep. "I'll take Zeus to our place. We have a fenced-in yard. He can stay with us as long as you need."

"Thank you." I hug her tightly, then rush to jump into the front seat of the ambulance.

The second the paramedic treating Wes knocks on the wall separating the front cab from the back, the driver pulls away, sirens blaring and lights flashing.

I glance in the side-view mirror, watching as the firefighters struggle to get the flames under control.

All I can do is pray that the house isn't the only thing I'll lose tonight.

# CHAPTER THIRTY

*Londyn*

I should be exhausted.

In a way, I suppose I am. Since I stepped off the medevac helicopter and they rushed Wes into the burn unit at the hospital here in Atlanta twelve hours ago, I've been running on fumes.

The nurses told me it would be a while before I could see him. That it would take the doctor several hours to clean the burn area, then even longer to perform the skin graft. But I refused to leave. I abandoned him in the house earlier and look what happened. I can't abandon him again.

Not when I should be the one undergoing surgery instead of Wes.

A hand squeezes mine and I glance at my dad. When I called him in the middle of the night to tell him what happened, he didn't hesitate. He hurried out of bed to be here for me. So did Hazel and Diego, the three of them taking turns to sit with me.

"He'll be okay, lollipop," he assures me.

I'd like to believe he's right. According to the nurses, this surgery is fairly typical for burn victims. He was lucky his severe burns were limited to only fifteen percent of his body, isolated to his left lower leg and foot. As I was informed, the major concern right now is preventing any possible bacteria from getting into the wound, causing an infection that could turn deadly if it enters the bloodstream.

Which is why my anxiety is through the roof. Every minute that passes makes my worry increase. I haven't had the best of luck lately. Why should the tides turn now?

"I hope so," I mutter as I check the clock on the wall of the waiting room to see it's nearly four in the afternoon. My eyelids droop, the only thing keeping me going the ridiculous amount of caffeine that's been my diet the past twelve hours.

"Why don't you go get some rest, sweetie?" Dad suggests. "I'll stay here and call you the second I hear anything."

I vehemently shake my head. "I can't leave until I see him. Until I know he's okay."

He nods in understanding. After all, he was once in my shoes. Unfortunately, he didn't get the outcome he'd hoped for when the paramedics wheeled my mother into the trauma unit for emergency surgery.

I pray I do.

"Another coffee then?" He stands. "Maybe some food? There's a barbecue place around the corner."

At the suggestion, my stomach rumbles, alerting me to the fact that I haven't eaten in almost twenty-four hours. "That actually sounds really good."

"I'll be right back." He leans down and presses a kiss to my forehead. Just as he's about to walk away, a nurse enters the waiting room.

"Ms. Bennett?"

"Yes?" I shoot to my feet, heart hammering in my chest, praying she's not about to deliver bad news. Sensing my nerves, Dad grabs my hand, linking his fingers with mine.

"Mr. Bradford's surgery is complete and he's in one of the recovery rooms."

I close my eyes, my muscles relaxing for the first time since I saw the house engulfed in flames.

"That's wonderful news," Dad says, pulling me in for a hug. "Thank the Lord."

I remain in his embrace for a beat, sending up a prayer myself. Although, over the past several hours, my father's done enough praying for the two of us, having spent quite a bit of time in the hospital's chapel.

Once he releases me, I return my eager eyes to the petite nurse. "Can I see him?"

"He *is* heavily sedated."

"I'd still like to see him, if that's okay. Please."

"Of course. Right this way." She gestures toward a pair of automatic doors.

I glance back at my dad, who gives me an encouraging smile. "I'll be here when you're done. Then maybe you'll be ready for a nap."

"Thanks, Dad. I can't tell you how much I appreciate you being here."

"It's the least I can do for you, lollipop."

I nod, then hurry to join the nurse, following her as she leads me through a maze of corridors. I try to take note of my surroundings, worried I'll never find my way out afterward.

"When do you think he'll wake up?" I ask.

"It's hard to say. Our goal is to make it so our patients can't remember their first few days here all that much. It's too painful otherwise."

A vice squeezes my heart at the idea of Wes experiencing any pain. "And how long will he be here?"

"It all depends on how well he recovers and responds to the skin graft. Once we're able to step down his meds and bring him out of his sedation, he'll begin physical therapy."

"For a burn?"

"Burn victims are left with a great deal of scar tissue. With Mr. Bradford's being on his foot and lower leg, he'll have to retrain his muscles how to walk. The new skin over the area will make it difficult until he gets accustomed to the sensation. That's why we start physical therapy as soon as possible."

She leads me to a pair of double doors, *Recovery* written over the top, and gestures to a bin holding green protective gowns, yellow latex gloves, and blue surgical masks.

"Every time you visit him, you need to put on a gown, gloves, and mask before entering this area," she explains as she dons her own. "As I'm sure the nurses have advised you, bacterial infections are our biggest concern at this stage."

I nod, grabbing a gown and putting one on, then sliding on a pair of latex gloves before covering my nose and mouth with a mask. "They did."

"This protects everyone in the ward from being exposed to any outside bacteria or germs." She steps up to the door, which automatically opens.

As I follow her down more hallways, I peek into a few rooms, spying some patients with most of their bodies bandaged, including faces.

"Like I said, Mr. Bradford was extremely lucky. It could have been a lot worse."

"Yes, it could have," I admit through the thickness in my throat, not wanting to think what could have happened if Zeus hadn't alerted me to something wrong. I may have happily stayed in my workshop for hours. Zeus certainly earned a hero badge last night. Or at the very least, the steak dinner I told Diego to feed him after he picked him up from Miss Clara's.

Finally, the nurse comes to a stop outside a room and opens the door, holding it for me to walk in ahead of her. My attention immediately shifts to the bed, swallowing down a sob that threatens to escape.

From the moment we met, I've always viewed Wes as a confident, determined man. Even when he begged me to not push him away, he was still in complete control, even if he was falling apart on the inside.

That's why it crushes me to see him lying in a hospital bed, unconscious, his arms, abdomen, and legs covered in bandages, the little amount of skin visible on his face and chest pale.

"I thought his burns were only on his leg and foot," I manage to say.

"The severe burns were isolated to his leg and foot," the nurse explains. "But there were some first- and second-degree burns on other parts of his body we treated and bandaged in order to ward off any possible infection."

I nod, absorbing this new information.

"We've also started him on a course of medication for the smoke inhalation. Once he wakes up, he'll have to take it easy. There's some scarring in his lungs, so he can expect to experience shortness of breath for a bit. That's why we have him propped up." She nods toward his bed, and I note the slight incline. "He'll likely need to sleep like this for a while. It makes breathing easier. But we'll also have a respiratory therapist work with him."

She walks up to the machines attached to him that measure his heartbeat and lung function…I assume.

After making a quick note on her tablet, she turns to me. "I'll let you have some time with him."

"Thank you."

"Of course." With a smile, she retreats toward the door, stopping just before opening it. "He'll be fine. He's been treated by one of the top burn specialists in the country, if not the world."

All I can do is nod. I won't be able to breathe again until I see Wes' eyes open and hear him tell me he's okay. Until then, I can't find comfort in her words, no matter how reassuring they are.

Once she closes the door behind her, I walk toward the bed, doing my best to keep my tears at bay, but it's impossible, a few sliding down my cheeks now that I have a moment to myself and can let go of everything I've kept inside the past several hours. Hell, the past several weeks.

From learning who Julia's husband truly is. To being arrested for defending myself. To Sawyer making a sudden reappearance in my life, then going on national television to paint me a liar. To the run-in with Grady. To the fire.

I'm emotionally drained.

Lowering myself into the chair beside the bed, I gently wrap my glove-covered hand around Wes' bandaged one, wishing I could feel his skin on mine.

"I'm so sorry, Wes," I choke out. "I should have been with you. Should have been the one in that house." I take in his slumbering form, the subtle rise and fall of his chest offering me some semblance of comfort.

"But I know if you were awake, you'd tell me you're glad I wasn't." Sniffling, I swipe at my tears with the sleeve of my protective gown. "Which is ridiculous, but that's just the type of person you are. You'd happily suffer third-degree burns to prevent me from experiencing a single iota of pain. And that's why you don't deserve this, Wes. Why you don't deserve any of the shit you've been through the past few months. Because you are such a good person." I lean over the bed, resting my forehead on his hand, lowering my mask and feathering a soft kiss on his bandaged knuckles. "And I'll forever be grateful our paths crossed back in June, despite the shitstorm that's happened since then."

I close my eyes, basking in the warmth coming off his body. It's exactly what I need right now. What I've always needed. His warmth. His affection. His love. He may be unconscious, but I can feel his love.

The door flies open, interrupting my moment, and I shoot my gaze toward it, expecting to see one of the nurses coming in to check on him again. Instead, I jump to my feet when Julia rushes into the room wearing the same protective gear as me, eyes bloodshot and expression frantic.

"Is he okay?" she asks, her voice heavy with emotion.

I freeze, unsure what to do. I should leave, stick to the terms of the court order. But Wes is her brother. If I were in her shoes, I'd want to know. So instead of walking away, as I'm supposed to, I do what I feel in my heart is the right thing.

"There was a fire," I tell her, although she must already know that. She wouldn't be here if she didn't.

"Miss Clara called early this morning. I didn't recognize the number, so I didn't pick up. Otherwise I would have been here sooner."

I blink, glancing at Wes. "I'm sorry. I didn't even think to call anyone. I just…" My voice hitches.

She reaches for my hand and squeezes it. "It's okay."

I shift my eyes toward our joined hands. There was once a time this woman was a huge part of my life. Even when she'd gone back to Charleston after the summer, we remained in touch, constantly FaceTiming and texting. Now it feels strained, a giant elephant in the room neither one of us wants to talk about.

Clearing my throat, I pull away, stepping back. "Do your parents know?"

"They left yesterday for the opening of a hotel Wes designed in Australia."

I furrow my brow. This is news to me. "Why didn't Wes go?" He typically went to all the grand openings.

"He asked Dad to attend in his place so he could stay here with you. He's canceled all his out-of-state travel since, well…"

"Of course," I respond, not needing her to explain.

"They're not expected to land for another eight hours or so," she continues. "Once they do, I'm sure they'll want to get back here as soon as possible. Still, it's about fifteen hours to LA from there. Then another five or so to Atlanta. I don't foresee them being able to get back for at least two days."

I nod, finding relief in the short reprieve from having to explain this to his parents. It's bad enough that this happened. I can only imagine what choice words Mrs. Bradford will have for me once she returns. She'll blame it all on me. Then again, isn't it my fault?

"Miss Clara mentioned it was arson?" Julia remarks when I don't immediately say anything.

"It appears so. The investigator called me a few hours ago to ask questions. They found an ignition point. Looks like the exterior was doused with white gas, so it went up in flames pretty quickly, based on how flammable that stuff is."

"Did they mention who they thought was behind it?"

"No arrests yet, but when Wes and I went to Clara's diner yesterday, there was an incident."

She offers me a sad smile. "I know. Wes called yesterday

afternoon to tell me what happened. And to ask if Gampy and Meemaw had ever talked to me about Penny."

"Did they?"

"No." She slowly shakes her head. "This was all news to me, too."

I shift my gaze back to Wes, the ache returning to my chest. "I should have known it was only a matter of time."

"Londyn, it's not—"

"I should go," I interrupt before she can finish her statement, not sure I can handle anyone else telling me it's not my fault when I know this never would have happened if Grady Stowe hadn't seen us together.

It's the Butterfly Effect in action yet again. One seemingly innocent lunch together at Miss Clara's diner. Normally a completely uneventful occurrence. But it set into motion events that have changed everything.

"He'll be okay, right?" Julia asks in a shaky voice as I hurry away from her. "He'll be the same Wes, right?"

Reaching the door, I pause and glance over my shoulder. "He'll recover. But will he be the same?" I slowly shake my head. "There's no guarantee. Take it from me. Going through a traumatic event like this messes with your head. It's a good thing the doctors are keeping him heavily sedated because I imagine once he's conscious, every time he closes his eyes, he'll see the flames that almost took his life."

"You sound like you're speaking from experience. *Recent* experience." She lifts her gaze to mine.

"I am."

She exhales and nods, something bordering on resignation crossing her expression.

I'm about to open the door when she calls out once more.

"Hey, Londyn?"

I look back at her.

"I'm really sorry. About everything. About…" She trails off, seemingly struggling to figure out what to say. "Well, everything." She pushes out a long breath. "I miss you."

I part my lips, on the verge of telling her I miss her, too. But does it matter? Will it change anything? I doubt it.

Instead, I lower my head and continue out of Wes' room, a weight trampling my heart.

# CHAPTER THIRTY-ONE

*Weston*

"Vitals look good," the older man checking me says, marking something on his tablet. He'd introduced himself as Doctor Carlisle, a burn specialist. "On a scale of one to ten, how's your pain?"

When I'd woken up earlier this morning, I was completely disoriented, wondering where I was, how I'd gotten here. But as I slowly took in my surroundings and realized I was in a hospital room, the events of the past several days came rushing back.

Sawyer's interview that painted Londyn as a troubled woman with a propensity to lie. Getting her out of the city to escape it all for a few days. Going to Miss Clara's diner and running into Grady Stowe, who reminded us of the hatred we'd tried to escape. Being woken up by the smoke detectors blaring.

After that, it's all still a blur, except for the fact that I needed to find Londyn. Needed to make sure she was okay.

When the fog of the drugs lifted, the only thing that calmed me down was the nurse's assurance that Londyn was okay and had been practically living at my bedside during visiting hours.

I wince, attempting to move my leg, but my muscles don't seem to work like they once did. "I'd say a solid eight."

"Take it easy," he tells me. "I'll have the nurse get you some more pain killers, but we want to try and keep you off the sedatives now. The sooner we can work on some physical therapy on that leg, the better. Now, lean forward a little for me." He places his hand on my shoulder, helping me curve my body forward, and brings the stethoscope to my back. "Deep breath in."

I do as instructed, then succumb to yet another coughing fit.

"That's going to happen for a while due to the smoke inhalation you suffered. We'll do a respiratory treatment later this afternoon. But, all things considered, your lungs sound good." He steps back. "If you notice you cough up any mucus that's black or red, make sure you tell a nurse right away. Got it?"

"Got it."

"Good. I'll send someone in to give you some more pain killers."

"What about Londyn?"

The doctor lowers his tablet. "Visiting hours start at eight…" He smirks, "so my guess is she'll be here any minute."

As if on cue, the door flies open, Londyn rushing in wearing the protective gear I've seen everyone else wear who comes into the room. When she notices the doctor, she comes to an abrupt stop.

"I'm sorry. I didn't—"

"It's quite all right, Londyn," Doctor Carlisle says, stepping to the side.

Tears dot her eyes as they lock with mine for the first time in what feels like an eternity. "You're awake."

I smile, my heart warming at the obvious mixture of concern and relief covering her face. "I'm awake," I reply, drinking her in. From the mess of curls piled on top of her head. To the deep pools of her eyes. To her powdery fresh scent that wraps around me, even from the few feet separating us. I've never been so happy to see another person in my life.

"I was just finishing up," the doctor says, making his way toward Londyn. "He's all yours. But only for a little bit. The nurses need to change his bandages today."

"Of course." She swipes at her tears. "Thank you, Doctor."

He nods, then leaves. The instant the door clicks closed behind him, Londyn rushes toward me, not pausing as she lowers her face mask and touches her lips to mine.

I sigh, reaching for her, wanting to rip the bandages off my palms so I can feel more of her skin on mine. At least my fingers are no longer wrapped like they were when I first woke up.

"I didn't think I'd feel this again," I murmur in a scratchy voice, mouth hovering over hers. "Didn't think I'd ever taste your lips again. That's all I wanted. Just one more kiss."

I press my lips back to hers, breathing her in. But with my lungs not functioning like I'm used to, I break into a coughing fit.

"I'm sorry," I choke out.

"Don't be. The doc warned me this would probably happen." She grabs the pitcher of water on the bedside table and fills my cup, bringing it to my mouth. "Drink this. It'll help."

I take the cup from her. As the cool liquid travels down my throat, the fire within is momentarily relieved. Once I return the cup to the table, I extend my hand to hers, desperate to feel her warmth, even if there's a layer of bandages and latex separating most of us.

"I was so worried about you, Lo."

"Me?"

"Of course." I reach for her face, cupping it. "I was so disoriented when I woke up this morning. But once I started to remember, I panicked, worried they'd tell me you didn't make it. I can handle the pain of these burns. But I couldn't handle it if something happened to you."

"I'm okay. I wasn't even in the house. I couldn't sleep, so I got up in the middle of the night to go to my workshop."

"Thank God for that. At least someone was watching over us."

"And I think his name is Zeus."

"Zeus?"

She nods. "He came with me out to the workshop. After a while, he grabbed my pants and started barking, rushing back and forth to the door. If he hadn't…" She trails off, her lower lip trembling. "Well, I don't want to think what would have happened."

"Maybe we can call it even now?" I suggest in a light-hearted voice, trying to cut through the solemn atmosphere.

She tilts her head. "Even?"

"Yeah. I saved you from becoming roadkill. You saved me from becoming ashes."

Laughing through her tears, she brings her mouth to mine. "I guess we are even."

She feathers her lips against mine, and I drink in the

sweet nectar of her kiss. I wish it were deeper, but I'm not sure my lungs can handle too much excitement right now.

When she pulls back and returns to her seat, I take her hand in mine again. "Do they know what happened?"

Once the nurses filled me in on the fire, I was desperate for more information. But they didn't have any, other than that I nearly died.

"Arson."

I feared that would be the case. I just didn't want to think it could be true.

"Grady?" I ask.

She nods. "I got a call from Miss Clara on my way over here. They arrested him this morning. The police found four big cans of camp fuel in the dumpster behind the auto shop where he works. He claimed ignorance, but no one uses that much gas at once. Couple that with a diner full of people who overheard him threaten us, and it was a fairly open-and-shut case."

I close my eyes. I should be relieved that he won't get away with his actions, but something doesn't sit right with me.

Grady's been in and out of trouble his whole life. That's nothing new. His rap sheet boasts a multitude of burglaries and the occasional bar fight. But that's as far as it ever went. All bark and no bite. What changed this time?

"And the house?"

She subtly shakes her head, seemingly incapable of saying the words. She doesn't have to. I know it's gone.

I lean back against the pillow, staring at the ceiling.

In the grand scheme of things, the house doesn't matter. Londyn is okay. Zeus is okay. The house is just a building. But in that building live so many memories. Not just of growing up with Gampy and Meemaw, but of the early days of my relationship with Londyn.

"I'm so sorry, Wes," she offers, her voice wavering. "I know how much that house meant to you. All the memories it holds. Maybe if I hadn't gotten up, I would have—"

"Don't even think about blaming yourself for this. *You're* not to blame. And the person who is will spend the rest of his life in prison," I declare, although my words come out weak. I hope she doesn't pick up on the fact that I question whether Grady truly *is* the one responsible.

"He did this *because* of me."

"No." I squeeze her hand as hard as I can through the pain. "He did it because of *me*. Not you. And who cares about his reasoning anyway? I won't let you accept blame. Won't let you burden yourself with this. Not when you bear absolutely no responsibility."

She peers into the distance, her eyes clouded with tears. "What if Julia and Imogene were there?"

"They weren't. Thank God for small miracles."

"But what if they were? What if someone else tries something in the future and someone else gets hurt?"

"If you're trying to get me to leave you, you're going to have to try a hell of a lot harder, Londyn. I won't. I told you from the beginning that I'd fight for you. Even if it means battling flames, I'll do it. I'm more than aware that this won't be easy, that we may face even greater challenges down the road, but I don't care. Do you hear me?" I cup the back of her neck, forcing her eyes to mine. "I. Don't. Care," I emphasize. "All I do care about is you. Being with you." I brush her tears away with my thumb. "*Loving* you." My lips hover over hers, the sweetness of her breath intoxicating me. "For the rest of my life."

I cover her lips with mine, coaxing them open, to hell

with any potential coughing. I hesitantly swipe my tongue against hers, grateful when she doesn't immediately push me away. My pulse kicks up. As do the heart monitors attached to me.

She giggles against my mouth, then slowly pulls away. "Something excite you?"

"Maybe." I force her lips back to mine, the rhythm of the heart monitor increasing yet again.

We both still, then burst out laughing, a welcome sound. She's the only woman I know who can go from one extreme to the next in a blink of an eye. And I wouldn't have it any other way.

"Do you think they'll let us take one of these home?" she jokes, sitting back in her chair. "It'll be a sure indicator you're excited about something."

Grinning deviously, I grab her hand and press it against my groin. "Don't need a heart rate monitor to do that."

She averts her gaze, fighting against a smile. "You really are shameless."

"It helps me forget about the pain," I admit honestly.

"Does it hurt a lot?" she asks quietly.

"A little." I shrug, downplaying how uncomfortable I truly am. The last thing I want is for her to feel even more guilty about what happened. "It's better now that you're here. You're the best medicine I could ask for."

"Knock, knock," a voice sings as the door swings open, a chipper blonde in blue scrubs sauntering into the room. Londyn quickly replaces her face mask. "How's our patient holding up, Londyn?"

"Great." She stands, winking at me as I attempt to adjust myself, using the blanket to cover up any lingering proof of my erection. "All things considered, of course."

"Good to hear. Doc wants his bandages changed. It's a

bit of a process, so it might take around an hour. Maybe longer. The staff will buzz you when you can come back."

"No need." She reaches into her purse and retrieves a cell phone and charging cord, setting it on the bedside table. "It's still the same number as you had, Wes. Mia took care of setting it up for you. If you ask me, that girl deserves a raise."

"Duly noted."

She starts to step away from me, but I grab her arm, stopping her.

"I love you."

Something flickers in her gaze as she peers at me. I can't quite explain it. Not sadness, but it's not the same carefree feeling we enjoyed mere seconds ago. Or at least that I thought we enjoyed.

"I love you, too." But there's an emptiness in her tone as she says those words. Like they physically pain her.

She grits a half-hearted smile, then makes her way out of the room, an unsettling premonition forming in the pit of my stomach.

# CHAPTER THIRTY-TWO

## *Londyn*

I lean against the wall right outside Wes' room, squeezing my eyes shut and blowing out the breath I'd been holding. I've endured a lot of shit in my life, faced my fair share of difficult situations. None compared to looking into Wes' eyes, knowing he's currently in pain because of me. He doesn't want me to blame myself, but it's impossible not to.

From the instant I stepped out of my workshop and saw the house engulfed in flames, I knew I had something to do with it. A part of me hoped the investigators would uncover a different cause of the fire, like faulty wiring or electrical, even though it had all been replaced and was up to code. So when Miss Clara called to let me know about Grady's arrest, it took the breath out of me. Reminded me I *am* to blame.

How much more can I endure? How much more suffering can I force Wes to endure? Hasn't he been through enough?

As much as I want to fight for this, for us, I fear it's a battle we'll never win. That not even the strongest love can overcome the forces constantly threatening us.

And it won't ever stop. Wes may not see it, but I do. Today it was a house fire. What will it be tomorrow? Even with Grady behind bars, that doesn't mean we're safe. There will be another Grady. There always is.

"You okay, Londyn dear?"

When a hand touches my arm, I open my eyes. Gemma, one of the nurses, stands in front of me, brows creased in concern.

I blink back my tears, clearing my throat and nodding. "Of course. Just a bit…overwhelmed."

"That's to be expected. Why don't you get out of this place? Relax. I understand your need to be here as much as you can, but you're worn down. You won't be any good to Wes once he's released if you don't take care of yourself, too."

I suck in a deep breath and nod. "You're right. Thanks," I say blankly as I push away from the wall.

I've never felt so exhausted before in my life. And it's not only due to the lack of sleep the past few days.

I'm emotionally drained.

Just when I think things will be okay, that our love is strong enough to endure any obstacle, something is thrown in our path, reminding us it's a fool's wish.

Things will never be okay.

There will always be something standing in our way.

We were naïve to think otherwise.

"How is he?" Hazel asks, approaching me once I walk into the waiting area.

I smile sadly. "The same old Wes."

I should be thrilled he's awake. That he doesn't appear to

be suffering from any of the psychological effects they warned me about. That he still has so much love for me.

But it's hard to be happy at a time like this.

"That's good, right?"

"Of course. I just…" I trail off, struggling to put everything I'm feeling into words.

"Londyn, sweetie," Hazel soothes, running her hands down my arms. "What is it? You can—"

"*You!*" a shrill voice interrupts, startling me.

I jump back, whipping my head toward the source as an irate Mrs. Bradford storms toward me. The man I recognize as Wes' father trails behind her, almost reluctantly.

"This is all *your* fault. You did this to him. You just had to rope him into your life, didn't you?"

"Lydia, please," Mr. Bradford says in a deep, commanding voice. "Now isn't the time. Emotions are running high." He looks at me. "On both sides, I'm sure."

"My emotions are *not* running high," she insists. "It's the truth. She may not have lit the match that nearly took my baby boy from me, but she's just as responsible for almost killing him."

I should argue, tell her I'm no more at fault than Wes, but I don't have it in me. Not when her words mirror my own thoughts.

"How would you feel if he *did* die?" she continues. "Would you even care? Or is he just someone else you'll toss aside, like your *husband*? Are you already sleeping around behind his back, like you did with Nick? The minute I saw you, I knew you were bad news. Then the truth of what you did came out."

"Which were all lies," Hazel says in my defense.

"You've caused nothing but destruction in my son's life. And I won't have it anymore. I don't care what I have to do.

I *will* make sure you spend the rest of your life behind bars. Where you belong for nearly killing the father of my granddaughter!"

With every word she speaks that echoes the exact thoughts I've struggled with, my blood pressure rises. It feels like the walls are closing in on me, accusatory eyes torturing me, reminding me I *am* at fault. I *am* to blame. I *did* almost cost Wes his life. There's only so much one person can endure before they reach their breaking point.

And I've hit mine.

"*I know!*" I shriek, my voice echoing in the waiting room, catching the attention of some of the nurses.

One of them gives me a questioning look, as if asking if I need security to intervene. But I know they'll only kick me out after Mrs. Bradford has her way. It's not worth it. If I'm being forced out, I want to leave on my own terms. No one else's.

Drawing in a deep breath, I refocus my stare on Mrs. Bradford. "I know it's my fault. Okay? Is that what you want to hear? Do you think this has been a walk in the park for me? It hasn't. And every day, I've wondered when the other shoe would finally drop. I was too blind, and maybe a little selfish, because I wanted to keep him mine for just a little bit longer. Because, as much as you don't want to hear it, I *love* him. He is the first man I've been with who's fought for me. Who makes me feel loved. Who gives me that love without conditions. Without strings attached. Which is why it pains me to do this…"

"Londyn," Hazel warns, sensing what I'm about to say.

"But you're right," I continue, ignoring her. "I'll only keep bringing harm to your son. I love him with everything I have. But I love him enough to walk away when it can spare his life. So that's what I'll do. Okay? You win." I swipe at my tears, my voice catching. "You win," I whisper.

Mrs. Bradford blinks, almost taken aback by my statement. She obviously didn't expect me to concede so easily. I'm surprised by it, too. But for the first time in a while, I finally see things clearly.

Snapping out of her momentary shock, she clears her throat, straightening her posture, expression exuding that of superiority. "It's about time one of you came to your senses." She spins on her heels, holding her head high as she makes her way toward the nurses station.

Mr. Bradford follows, but he glances over his shoulder at me. I expect him to shoot me a warning glare. Instead, there's something else in his gaze. Remorse. Regret. Maybe even an apology?

"You're not serious, are you?" Hazel whispers, forcing my attention away from Mr. Bradford as a nurse leads them toward the administrative wing, presumably to speak with the doctor while Wes has his bandages changed.

"I think I am," I say weakly. "It's probably best for all involved."

"Best?" Hazel shoots back, crossing her arms in front of her chest, her expression heavy with disbelief. "How the hell is walking away from a man who'd do anything for you 'best for all involved'?" She uses air quotes, then recrosses her arms.

"Have you seen the shit people are saying online about my case? Especially after Sawyer's interview?" I dig my fingers through my hair, tugging at it, my throat tightening with emotion. "Every day…hell, every minute, keyboard warriors leave comments saying I'd be better off dead. And Grady, the guy they arrested for the fire? He's like every single other person online. Except he had the opportunity to do something and took it. He could have killed us. Almost killed Wes. And Grady's just *one* person out of thousands. Have you read some of comments on the article about his arrest?"

She slowly shakes her head.

"They're calling him a patriot. A hero. They just wish the fire department hadn't gotten there so quickly because, and I quote, 'Nigger lovers deserve the same fate as niggers.'"

Her eyes glisten with tears. "You said it yourself, Londyn. They're keyboard warriors. Hiding behind their computers."

"For now. But it's only a matter of time before someone decides to try something else. What happens if they *do* kill him next time? Or you? Or Diego?" I swipe at my tears, an excruciating pain squeezing my chest. "I can't have that on my conscience." I hesitate, then add, "Sawyer called the other night."

"And you answered?"

"I'd spent all day here and was exhausted by the time I got home. When I didn't recognize the number, I worried it might be the hospital. I was operating on zero sleep."

"What did he say?" she asks pointedly.

I snort. "Asked how I liked his interview last week."

"Ass," Hazel snips out.

"He also told me he'd agreed to assist the prosecution with their case and would testify if it came to that. Reminded me that he couldn't claim spousal immunity and refuse to testify if he signed the divorce papers I'd served him. Then he said his offer was still on the table."

She blinks, jaw dropping, eyes wide. "You're not seriously considering that, are you?"

"Maybe I should."

When I spoke to him the other night, I made it clear I wasn't interested. Maybe I shouldn't have been so rash. It's not what I want, but if taking Sawyer up on his offer means I can keep Wes safe, why wouldn't I do it?

"So you're just going to give up? Go back to your old life? Go back to being the old Londyn?"

"I'm not giving up," I argue.

"No? What do you call this? Because from where I'm standing, that's exactly what you're doing."

"You may think I'm giving up. But I know when it's time to throw in the towel. And it's time. It's *been* time, but I stupidly believed people were better than this." I hang my head, a profound exhaustion settling in my bones, making even breathing a laborious process. "I guess I was wrong."

Her lips pinched into a tight line, she leans into me, her eyes on fire. "I thought you were stronger than this. I thought…" Her voice catches. "I thought you wanted to rise above, like your mama taught you." She pins me with a stare. "I guess *I* was wrong." She whirls around, storming inside a waiting elevator, the doors sliding closed.

I exhale deeply and collapse onto a nearby chair, defeated. I pinch the bridge of my nose, wondering if Hazel's right. Maybe I am giving up too quickly. Wes said he'd fight for me. Why can't I fight for him?

Or maybe this *is* me fighting for him. Like I told Mrs. Bradford, I love him enough to leave him in order to keep him safe.

"You're really walking away?"

I snap my head up, my breath hitching when I see Julia standing a few feet away, her sad eyes trained on me. There's no question in my mind she overheard my conversation with Hazel.

I should leave, keep my distance. But I'm too tired to care about a bullshit protective order right now.

"What choice do I have?" I say through the painful lump

in my throat, in my chest, in my soul. "I need to do something. So I either go back to my ex or take the latest plea deal and spend what I think is now up to five years in prison. Either way, I'm away from Wes, so he won't get caught up in my path of destruction."

"Londyn, I—"

"I'm sure Nick will be thrilled to learn this," I interrupt, jumping to my feet. "He won. That's *all* he's ever cared about. The win. You may refuse to see it, refuse to see that he's a master manipulator who will do and say anything he needs in order to maintain the upper hand over everything."

I should stop, should walk away, but I can't control the words flowing out of me, saying everything I've kept locked inside for weeks.

"I used to think you were this amazing, strong woman who broke free from her past to go her own way. But I was wrong. The Julia I met last summer wouldn't put up with someone like Nick. Wouldn't allow him to dictate her every move." I pull my bottom lip between my teeth. "I guess I misjudged you."

Tears streaming down my face, I push past her and scurry toward the elevator, needing to get as far away from this family as possible. I jam my finger against the call button, wanting to scream in frustration when it seems to take forever for a car to arrive. When one finally does, I rush inside, keeping my eyes lowered.

"You'll break his heart," I hear as the doors start to slide closed.

A voice tells me to let it go. But I can't. I thrust my arm forward, pushing the doors back open, and meet Julia's gaze once more.

"But at least it'll still be beating. At least people who think I should pay for hurting an 'innocent' man won't harm him in the process." I pause, cocking a brow. "Unless you have a better idea?"

She parts her lips, as if wanting to confess her deepest secrets. But as always, something holds her back. *Nick* holds her back.

She lowers her head, remaining silent, despite her eyes screaming at someone to finally help. I can't blame her. I was once her, too. And that's what's so sad about this. Because as much as I want to shake her, scream at her, hate her, I can't.

"That's what I thought." I allow the doors to slide closed.

# CHAPTER THIRTY-THREE

## *Weston*

"You know…"

At the sound of the familiar, teasing voice, I look up from reviewing emails on my phone. I can't help the smile that tugs on my lips at the sight of my sister.

"If you wanted to get out of coming up with a good toast for our dinner Monday night, you could have just said something."

I blow out a small laugh, extending my arms. Julia rushes into them, squeezing me tightly. I wince slightly from the pain, but I don't care. I'll gladly suffer through the mild discomfort just to feel my sister in my embrace.

"I'm so glad you're okay," she sobs against my chest before pulling back. "If we had stayed…"

"No," I say sternly. "Don't even go there, Jules. You weren't there. I was. And I am so glad it was me. You know I'd do anything for you."

She nods. "I know. But maybe we can cross 'walk through fire' off your list now."

"Sounds like a plan to me," I say with a smile.

She squeezes my hand as she sits in the chair beside me, a flicker of something in her expression. If I didn't know her as well as I do, I probably wouldn't notice it.

"What is it?" I ask.

"What do you mean?"

"You want to tell me something. What is it?"

"Wes, I—"

"My poor baby!"

We both snap our eyes toward the door where my mother stands, protective gear covering her pant suit, tears welling in her eyes. I'd like to think her reaction is genuine, but after everything she's put Londyn through, after the act she put on just to turn the public against her, I know it's all a show.

I grit out a smile. "It looks worse than it is."

It's not a complete fabrication. While quite a bit of my body is currently covered in bandages, most of the burns are no worse than a bad sunburn. It's my leg and foot that are in rough shape. If the medical staff weren't taking every precaution to prevent any sort of infection whatsoever, my mother probably wouldn't even notice anything's wrong with me, apart from the skin on my face being slightly red, as if I spent too much time in the sun.

In the middle of the winter.

Then again, it is Atlanta. Anything's possible.

"It doesn't make this right, Weston." She rushes toward the bed. Practically tossing Julia out of the chair, she sits in it and grabs my hand in hers. My dad follows behind, observing, calculating, analyzing.

Just as he always did in chess.

"I never said it was. It could have been a lot worse. Londyn could have been in the house, too," I say as a test.

"It would serve her right if she were. This *is* all her fault, after all," she snips out, failing my test miserably. I shouldn't be surprised, but it still disappoints me.

"Lydia," Dad cautions, placing his hand on her shoulder, narrowing his eyes on her. "Wes' girlfriend had nothing to do with this. The person responsible has been arrested. Justice has been served. We should be thankful for the police department's quick investigation into this matter."

"I had a bad feeling something like this would happen," she mutters, ignoring my father's statement. Which only serves to irritate me more.

"Why?" I shoot back. "Because of what happened to Penny?"

My mother's eyes widen as she inhales sharply, every inch of her stiffening. The room grows eerily silent, apart from the steady beeping from the machines monitoring my vitals. Even my father, the perpetual mediator and peacemaker, remains quiet.

"What did you say?" she asks softly.

"I know all about her."

"How?"

I hesitate, not wanting to throw Miss Clara to the proverbial wolves. But my mother will figure it out eventually. She always does.

"Grady made a few threats when we were at Miss Clara's diner on Saturday. Warned us it would be a real shame if history repeated itself. I had no idea what he was talking about, so Miss Clara told me." I furrow my brow. "Why didn't you ever talk about her or what happened?"

"And what?" she shoots back. "Encourage you to make the same bad decisions Penny did? Your gampy and meemaw warned her people in town might have something to say about being seen around town with a negro."

"Black man," Julia corrects.

Mom waves her off. "But she didn't care. And look what happened to her. Penny's the exact reason I didn't want you to get involved with that girl. I knew the minute I laid eyes on her she was bad news. And I was right. She shot your brother-in-law, for crying out loud." She glances at Julia.

"Because he *raped* her," I remind her.

I expect Julia to protest or argue to the contrary, but she doesn't.

"And look what she's done to you." My mother gestures down my body, ignoring my previous comment. "Like I said, that girl is nothing but trouble."

"And what about Samuel?" I retort, not backing down. "Did you think Samuel was trouble, too? Think the mob was justified when they beat him to death, then torched his family's house, killing his little sister?"

"I'm not the one at fault here, Wes. I'm not the bad guy. I did what I had to in order to give you the life you deserved."

"Don't play the martyr now. It's too late for that." I laugh to myself, looking up at the ceiling. "You know, I hoped this might force you to open your eyes. To see what your hate has caused."

"I—"

I hold up my hand, cutting her off. "You may not have lit the match, but it's because of people like you this kind of thing keeps happening. And it will keep happening because people like you refuse to see the way you've been living is wrong. Isn't necessary. And maybe that's where I made a mistake.

"There's this part of me that always wanted to think there was a good person buried deep inside you somewhere.

One who used to play hide-and-seek with me. Who used to push me on the swing in the back yard. Who used to beam with love whenever I opened presents on Christmas morning. You were once a good person. I know you were. I saw glimpses of that person at one point." I shake my head.

"But I haven't in years. I'm done waiting for you to change. Because I don't think you ever will. I don't think you'll ever see the damage your hate has caused. Not just to Londyn, but also to me. To Julia. To Imogene. Until you can finally accept Londyn and me as a couple, until you make amends for the way you've treated her, I can't have you in my life. I *won't* have you in my life."

Her eyes flame as she rises to her feet, ripping off her face mask. "You're choosing *her* over your own mother?" Her voice grows louder with every syllable. "I gave birth to you." She jabs a finger at Julia. "Raised her. Hell, just spent the past three days on and off airplanes to get back to you! And this is the thanks I get?"

"Do you think this was an easy decision for me? I shouldn't have to choose between anyone. You should support me in whatever relationship I want to pursue. I plan on marrying Londyn. Bought her a ring back in December. So she *will* be a part of my life, whether you like it or not. If you can't support that, I don't want you in my life. Starting now."

Her mouth agape, she stares at me for several long moments, as if I'll change my mind. But I won't. Not when it comes to Londyn.

Huffing, she turns her ire onto my father. "James, talk some sense into your son. He's being ridiculous."

He looks from my mother to me before returning his attention to her. Stepping away, he places a hand on my shoulder. "If anyone's being ridiculous, it's you, Lydia."

Her eyes bulge. "What do you—"

He holds up his hand, stopping her. "Maybe I'm partially to blame for how out of control things have gotten. Lord knows my parents weren't the most accepting of people from different backgrounds. Like you, I went along with it because it was just the way things were. But unlike you, I didn't make it my mission to ruin people's lives. I eventually realized what's on the outside has no bearing to what's on the inside. Look at you." He gestures down her frame. "To the uninformed observer, you'd come off as attractive. Maybe even beautiful." Then his voice drops to barely a whisper. "But I know just how ugly your soul is." He pauses, inhaling a shaky breath. "And I'm done."

"Done?" Mom blinks, obviously surprised by this.

I'm a bit surprised, too, considering the last time I had a meaningful conversation with my father, he made it appear he had no intention of leaving my mother. Now it sounds as if he's changed his position on that.

"Yes, Lydia. I've put up with a lot over the years. From the way you treat women you claim are your friends, then stab them in the back the second they do something you don't approve of. To the way you've tried to control every aspect of Wes' and Julia's lives, including whom they date and marry. I let it all slide, knowing they had a wonderful upbringing, thanks to your parents. That they'd be able to stand up to you, despite your repeated attempts to sabotage their personal lives. But this… Having so much hate in your heart that you insist on blaming an innocent woman for a crime she didn't commit…"

He floats his gaze to mine and gives me a look, as if telling me he's not only talking about the fire, but also the aggravated assault charges stemming from Nick's attack. Then he levels his glare back on my mother.

"This is the last straw."

"Last straw?" she shoots back, crossing her arms in front of her chest. "What are you talking about?"

"Divorce, Lydia. I'm talking about divorce, something we should have discussed years ago."

She blinks repeatedly, incensed. "You're divorcing me? After everything?"

"It appears that way," he replies, as if talking about something as mundane as the score of an inconsequential football game, not ending his marriage of over thirty years. "It's not like we've ever really cared for each other. Perhaps that's my fault. But my parents thought you were a good match for me, so I didn't protest. Maybe I should have insisted on marrying for love, not someone whose family had the right connections. I can't change my past mistakes. But I *can* change my course going forward. And that starts today. So the question remains. Can you change *your* course? Will you accept Wes' decision to be with the woman he loves? Or is your heart too clouded with hate?"

"I…" She shakes her head, indignant. "You'll regret this, James. Trust me on that."

"Maybe," he admits with a sigh. "But the older I get, the fewer fucks I have to give."

I fling my wide eyes to Julia, the sound of my father swearing as out of place as a palm tree in the North Pole.

"And right now, I don't give a fuck. The only thing I *do* care about is giving my children the support they need. If you can't support them, including everyone in *their* lives, then I refuse to support you. Emotionally *and* financially."

My mother stews, jaw agape. I'm not sure what has her more upset — my father's words or the calm tone in which he speaks them.

Seemingly unable to come up with a response, she spins on her heels, storming out of the hospital room.

No one speaks for several moments, all of us staring at the door, expecting her to walk back into the room so she can have the last word. But she never does.

"I guess that means you win the bet," Julia tells me, breaking the silence.

"Bet?" Dad looks between us. "What bet?"

"We made a wager a few years back," she explains. "After Lydia blew up at Brooklyn when she called off the wedding. Wes insisted it was only a matter of time until she did something to push you over the edge. I guess he was right."

"I'm just sorry it took me this long."

"Better late than never." Julia slings an arm around him, hugging him before pulling back. "I'm happy for you, Dad."

"Thanks, buttercup." He glances at me. "A wise man once said, 'Sometimes the right path isn't always the easiest.'"

I smile at his statement.

"I'd like to think it's never too late to change course and get on the right path."

He narrows his eyes at Julia, almost as if telling her it's not too late for her to take the right path, too.

# CHAPTER THIRTY-FOUR

## *Julia*

"**M**ama!" Imogene's sweet voice calls out the second I enter the foyer of my parents' house after leaving the hospital.

I wasn't sure what I'd walk into, if Lydia had come straight here to take out her anger on her household staff. But as I continue into the open living area, everything's just as it was when I left earlier today. It's peaceful, apart from the tug-of-war plaguing me, my father's words seeming to play on repeat in my mind, as they have since he uttered them.

*It's never too late to change course and get on the right path.*

Sure, he made it seem like he was talking about his situation, but the way he narrowed his gaze, a silent admonishment within, I know he said them for me. To remind me it's not too late to change *my* course. That perhaps it's time I get on the right path, too.

But what *is* the right path?

"How's Uncle Wes?"

I snap out of my thoughts, focusing on my daughter, just as I have since she was born.

"He's doing so much better, sweetie." I tousle her blonde curls, her blue eyes peering at me with concern and innocence.

"Look what I made!" She holds up a folded piece of construction paper, a drawing of a bandaged man on the front. "It's a get-well card for Uncle Wes. Can I go with you the next time you visit him so I can give it to him?"

I sigh, my heart breaking a little at her request. "I wish you could." I cup her cheek. "But you have to be a little older to visit someone where your uncle is. They have to keep his area of the hospital extremely sterile. Even I have to wear a hospital gown, gloves, and a face mask to go into his room."

"Sterile?" She pinches her brows together, tilting her head. "What's that?"

"Clean. Free of germs. Uncle Wes has some pretty big boo-boos. And if germs get into those boo-boos, he could get really sick. Little kids tend to carry lots of germs." I touch her nose. "So right now, only grownups can visit him."

Her expression falls, shoulders drooping. "Okay."

I hate seeing her so upset. It seems like I haven't seen her smile in ages. At least not a true smile.

I don't think I've smiled in ages, either.

"But when I go back to check on him tomorrow morning, I'll give him the card," I offer. "He can't have any flowers in his room, so your card will brighten up his day."

Her eyes light up with excitement. "Do you think so?"

"Of course. He'll love it. He loves everything you make

for him."

She flings her arms around me, squeezing tightly. "Thank you, Mama!"

I close my eyes, basking in my daughter's love. She may have been a bit of a surprise, considering I was on birth control at the time, but I'm forever grateful she came into my life. Whenever I feel like I'm losing my grip on everything, all I need is to look into my daughter's eyes and I remember my purpose in life.

"You're home," a deep voice cuts through.

I stiffen, snapping my head up as Nick saunters from the den and into the living room area like he owns the place instead of simply being a guest. Then again, he's made himself at home here in the main house, while Imogene and I prefer the privacy of the guest house. But the guest house doesn't come with a household staff, which Nick seems to have taken to rather quickly.

"I am."

"A bit late, don't you think?"

I swallow hard, taking a moment to contemplate my answer. This could be a test. *Everything's* a test to him. A game. A chess match to see who can outsmart whom.

"What makes you say that?"

"Your mother returned several hours ago before leaving again."

I part my lips, on the brink of telling him about the divorce, but stop myself, not wanting to upset Imogene. She's had enough bad news lately. Although I struggle to call this bad news. Still, I prefer to explain what's happening without Nick present.

"I stayed with Wes a little longer."

He arches a brow, eyes raking over me, as if looking for evidence of deception. Too bad for him I've become a master at lying over the years, even before I met him. That's the one thing Lydia taught me. I can make even the most observant person believe I'm being truthful.

"Was his girlfriend there?"

I fight the urge to shift on my feet.

"Imogene, sweetie…"

I look up as Lila emerges from the kitchen. She gives me a smile, obviously picking up on the tension between Nick and me.

"Why don't you come help me with the dough for the chicken pot pie?"

"Okay!" she says excitedly, darting from me and taking Lila's outstretched hand.

"Have fun, peanut!" Nick calls out joyfully, playing the part of the affectionate father, his fond gaze focused upon her.

Despite our differences, I can't discount the fact that he's always been good to our daughter. It's probably why I've stayed whenever I've been tempted to leave, to flip the chessboard and let the pieces fall where they may. But I haven't. I've stuck it out. For Imogene. I wanted to give her the normal childhood I never had.

Now I wonder if, by staying, I've ruined her chances at having one.

Once Lila and Imogene disappear from view, Nick's expression transforms into the one I've become accustomed to over the past several years. At least in private. Calculating. Cold. Contemptuous.

"Was *she* there?" He widens his stance, rubbing his hand against his shoulder, his injured arm still in a sling.

"By the time I got there, she'd already left," I lie.

He studies me for several more moments, assessing my response. My pulse kicks up, but I do everything to keep my demeanor calm. He wouldn't call the hospital to verify my story. Would he?

I'd like to say he wouldn't. But lately, I can't be sure of anything.

"Good." He exhales a breath, something that resembles relief replacing the annoyed look on his face. He wraps his uninjured arm around me and pulls me into his body. "I just worry about you, Julia." He brings his hand to my chin, forcing my gaze to his, sincerity etched in the strong lines of his face. "My queen." His lips descend toward mine. "My Hera," he murmurs against my mouth before kissing me.

I try to feign enthusiasm and be the dutiful wife I've been the past eight years. But with my father's words ringing in my brain, I can't seem to muster the need he requires.

Pulling back, he narrows his gaze on me. "What aren't you telling me?" His grip on my hip tightens, becoming painful as he leans closer and lowers his voice. But even with the low tone, I still hear the threat in his timbre. "We're not supposed to have any secrets between us. That's the only way this works."

I open my mouth, struggling to come up with something to explain my odd behavior, then blurt out, "My parents are getting a divorce."

He blinks, brows raised in surprise. "They are?"

I nod quickly, taking advantage of his loosening hold to rid myself of his touch.

"What happened?"

I pause, debating how to proceed. I'm not sure I want to tell him my dad essentially chose Londyn's side over my mother's, which was the tipping point in him finally suggesting divorce.

Blowing out a long breath, I shake my head. "I'd rather not get into it right now. It's still a little...new."

"Of course. I can only imagine how you must feel." He curves toward me, kissing my forehead. "Why don't you go relax? It's been a trying several days, what with losing Gampy and Meemaw's house in that fire."

I note how Nick doesn't mention Wes being in the hospital. He must hate that he's no longer the center of attention.

"I'll be working on edits for the next few hours. Then maybe I'll see if your father can watch Imogene tonight and I'll come and massage every inch of your body. How does that sound?"

I drape an arm over his shoulder, toying with a few tendrils of his blond hair. "That sounds great." I grit out a smile.

I once craved him, the way he seemed to know what to do and say making me think we knew each other in another life. But lately, I have to force myself not to flinch when he brushes my skin, his touch stirring feelings I can't quite explain.

"Good. I'm going to get back to work. Go relax. Take a long bath." His lips curve into a sly smile. "Maybe shave."

"Shave?"

"You know what I like, Julia. Let's just say you left a bit to be desired on New Year's." He winks, then spins around before I can ask how he knows I haven't taken the time to groom myself, considering it's been ages since we've been intimate.

Heat washes over me, bile rising in my throat. I push it down, though, coming up with every excuse about how he'd know that. He probably just noticed me getting dressed or something.

Ignoring the voice screaming at me that's not the case, I continue through the house, stopping by the kitchen to see Imogene briefly before heading out to the guest house.

The second I close the door behind me, I exhale my held breath, reveling in the brief moment of peace. I'd love nothing more than to crawl into bed and forget about everything for a minute. But Nick expects me to be fresh and well-groomed. So that's what I need to give him.

I drop my bag and slide off my flats, then pad into the bathroom. I'm about to turn on the bath, then stop, remembering I haven't unpacked my bath salts yet. Straightening, I walk toward the far wall of the bedroom where several of the boxes I'd brought from Charleston still sit.

Nick had put together quite the extensive list of items he wanted me to bring, claiming they'd offer him comfort during his recovery. I wasn't about to argue. It was simply another one of his tests. So I packed everything he asked for, regardless of how absurd. Like the dozen or so small, wooden boxes that held the ashes of his childhood pets. Or the myriad of journals containing years of research on dozens of characters in Greek mythology. If bringing them made my life easier, I was only too happy to do it.

Moving the boxes around, one topples onto the floor, causing some of the contents to spill out.

"Shit," I mutter, scrambling when I spy a wooden box holding one of his dog's ashes crack open, the lock breaking. I hurry to re-secure the latch, praying Nick never notices, but stop, seeing a delicate chain sticking out.

I pick up the box, noting it's remarkably light for supposedly containing a dog's ashes. Maybe it was a small dog.

I run my fingers over the gold plaque on the top, Hera etched in it. According to Nick, it was his first rescue. I found it endearing he felt so attached to each of the animals he saved and kept their remains with him. I've often walked into his office, where he displays them prominently, listening to him talk to them, as if they were still alive.

He can't be that bad of a guy, can he? He's an animal lover. It takes a special type of person to rescue dogs.

At least that's what I try to tell myself as a nagging voice questions whether these boxes hold ashes at all. And it's that nagging voice that has me cracking the lid of the box instead of returning it to its place.

When my gaze falls on the contents, my grip loosens. The box clatters to the floor, trinkets I recognize spilling out around me. My skin heats, heart hammering in my chest, hundreds of questions swirling in my brain.

A glimmer catches my attention and I lower myself to the floor, wrapping my fingers around a gold locket I didn't think I'd ever see again. One I couldn't find when my foster mom helped me pack up my things before coming to live with the Bradfords.

How did Nick get it?

I want to believe he tracked it down because he'd heard me talk about how it was the only piece of my birth mother I had left. But when I look at the rest of the contents of this box, I know this goes far beyond that. Why else would he have Meemaw and Gampy's obituary? Or newspaper clippings of stories I was featured in throughout my adolescence?

Maybe he was just interested in my past. Something I rarely speak about. I can somewhat rationalize that.

But I can't rationalize why he has the perfume I wore during my teenage years. Or the brand of razor I used during college. One that, upon closer examination, had been used. Or why he has my sports bra that went missing from my dorm's shower. I figured it would eventually turn up somewhere. I didn't expect it to do so over ten years later.

I glance toward the moving box holding the rest of what I thought were ashes, each of them named for another character from Greek mythology. I never paid much attention to them before. Now, my mind is reeling.

I grab a different container, this one with Europa etched in the gold plate on top. I yank on the lock, but it won't budge. Jumping to my feet, I glance out the window to make sure no one's walking down the path toward the guest house, then rush into the kitchen. Meat tenderizer in my hand, I return to the box and smash off the lock, praying all I'll find are ashes.

But I don't, this one containing personal items belonging to another woman. Another necklace. More perfume. Chapstick.

I continue ripping through the boxes, becoming increasingly nauseated with everything I discover. All these things belonged to someone, but who? Who's Europa? Who's Persephone? Who's Callisto? Who's Danae? Or Semele? Or Io? Or Philomela?

When I come to the final box, my breath hitches, dread settling in the pit of my stomach.

I stare at the gold plaque with Medusa etched in it. I almost don't want to open it. Don't want confirmation of what I've known all along. What Nick convinced me was a lie.

Bringing the meat tenderizer up to the lock, I smash it off and open the box.

I'm not sure what I expected to find. Probably just more stolen jewelry or pens, as in the previous boxes.

But this one is different, only containing a single item.

A lock of hair.

A lock of a dark ringlet I recognize.

I sit back on my heels, squinting, wondering what this means, my eyes glossing over all the names etched on each dismantled box. That's when it hits me why these names in particular stick out in my mind. Because each one matches that of the multitude of journals Nick had me pack up.

Journals I thought simply contained research he'd conducted on various characters in Greek mythology.

Journals I fear contain something else.

Scrambling to open the remainder of the moving boxes, I find the one I'm looking for, grabbing the journal with "Hera: Volume One" printed on the binding. Without hesitation, I open to the first page, my heart caught in my throat as I read what sounds like scientific observations. But between the lines, it's there. My husband's true nature.

*September 20th*

*Subject presents with a classic vulnerability she masks with an outgoing and vibrant personality. She's friends with everyone. Not because she genuinely likes them, but because of her desperate need to be accepted by everyone. To be loved.*

*Based on my research, I imagine it has to do with her childhood. Born to a drug addict. No known father. Sent to foster care at the age of four, where I'd argue she had a shot at a decent life. Taken from the loving care of her foster parents when adopted by a couple who didn't seem interested in her. At least her adoptive mother didn't. Her adoptive father did show interest, but his true passion was his work. Subject constantly strove to do everything to make her mother happy, but nothing was ever good enough.*

*Subject now often struggles to voice her own needs and wants for fear her social circle will shun her. She's easily manipulated.*

*Thus can be easily groomed.*

My hands shake as I frantically flip through the pages, every word I read making me even sicker.

I'd met Nick my freshman year of college when he was a graduate student teaching assistant in my English class. After the semester was over, we remained somewhat friendly, but he was never in my inner circle. He was always…different. Smart and charming, but different. From the beginning of our friendship, I felt like I could tell him anything about me and he wouldn't judge.

Now I see why he always seemed so interested in me. Always seemed to know what to say to get me to talk about things I preferred to keep to myself. He was *researching* me. But for what?

I wrack my brain for a reason, a memory from my sophomore year rushing back. Of going to a party after yet another fight with Lydia about how I'm a failure and can't do anything right. Of getting roped into a juvenile game of "Suck, Suck, Blow" I had no interest in but hated disappointing people. Of Maddox Finn purposefully dropping the card when he turned to me, covering my lips with his and shoving his tongue down my throat. Of everyone laughing and cheering as he slid his hands up my shirt, ignoring the fight I put up.

Of watching Nick appear out of nowhere and throwing Maddox to the floor, breaking his nose before ushering me out of the house. Of him driving me back to my dorm.

I'd invited him up, not wanting to be alone. He was hesitant, but eventually agreed. I was still a little buzzed from the multiple beers I'd consumed at the party, so he'd ordered us a pizza and grabbed some sodas from the vending machine. But even the food didn't stop the dizzy spells. In fact, it made them worse.

I squeeze my eyes shut, doing my best to bring forward memories that have been fuzzy for years now, everything like a dream. But as I draw in a deep breath, surrounded by the perfume I'd worn back then, more and more pieces snap into place.

I remember thinking I must be coming down with something. That I normally didn't feel so dizzy after four or five beers.

I remember needing to lay down, unable to keep my head up, even though hours had passed since I'd had my last drink.

I remember Nick helping me into bed.

I remember the compassionate smile on his face as he helped me take off my shoes.

I remember how that compassion morphed into something different when he didn't stop at just my shoes.

I snap my eyes open, the memory hitting me hard. For years, that night had been foggy. I'd tried to piece it together, but I couldn't remember what happened between getting into my bed and my roommate frantically calling for our resident advisor when she came home the following morning to find me in a pool of my own vomit.

It was the final straw, an incident that eventually led to my dismissal from college. At the time, it was the worst thing to happen to me, knowing I'd never be able to win Lydia's approval. But when my path crossed Nick's again several years later, he made me see it for what it truly was. The push I needed to finally forge my own course in life. To stop making decisions based on whether Lydia would finally approve.

Now I can't help but question if Nick played a bigger role in that night than I'd been led to believe.

Desperate for answers, I flip through the pages, skimming the entries that seem to get increasingly irritated as time goes on, complaining that I'm going on another date with another loser who is leagues below me. It goes on and on, each entry becoming more incoherent and angry.

*March 28<sup>th</sup>*

*Subject had another fight with her mother and, being the predictable college student she is, has agreed to go out with her roommate to a party at the soccer house. At this point, I'm losing all patience. I've done everything right. Shown an interest in her so-called hobbies, although it's more than obvious she hates meditation and paint night. However, since all her "friends" insist the benefits of both are "amazing" and "transcendental", she goes along. That's the sad thing about observing her for what feels like the better part of my life. Subject doesn't have an identity. She is whoever she feels she needs to be. She would never tell any of her cliché friends she has no interest in meditating. Or going on a trip to India to "center her chi".*

*I fear my original plan is no longer enough. She needs an intervention. She needs to be set free. And I need to give her her wings.*

The more I read his account of the actual events of that night, the more my stomach churns. I don't want to believe it, but here it is in black and white. He planned this. He watched me and took copious notes on every aspect of my life, so he knew what to do and say to get me to leave that party. He even made me feel comfortable enough with him to invite him up to my dorm. I thought he was being a good friend when he ordered pizza and grabbed us some sodas. But he had an ulterior motive.

He tricked me.

He drugged me.

He *raped* me.

Just like Zeus tricked Hera.

According to Nick's journal entry, he didn't intend to. He simply wanted to make it look like I'd had too much to drink and broke the school's strict no-tolerance policy. But when he helped me out of my jeans and shirt, he claimed he couldn't help himself.

Sick fuck.

I should stop reading, put the journal away, but this is only volume one. Meaning there are more.

More observations.

More assessments.

More…assaults?

Picking up the box, I flip it upside down, dozens of journals identical to this one cascading onto the floor. I shift them all around, finding one titled "Hera: Volume Two". I flip it open. I expect it to pick up years later at the time our paths crossed again.

It doesn't.

The first entry is dated only a few weeks later and chronicles his observations of me over the years I had no contact with him. That I thought he was just a part of my past.

But he wasn't.

He was still watching me. Observing. Calculating. Planning.

I toss the book onto the floor, grabbing "Hera: Volume Three" and turning to the first page, which details our initial meeting again after all those years. One that was planned, not pure coincidence as he'd led me to believe. I keep reading. Keep drowning in a truth that sickens me.

This man preyed on me. *Groomed* me. Then manipulated me into believing him to be a good person.

Glancing at the journals scattered before me, desperate for even more answers, I spy one labeled "Medusa: Volume One".

My heartbeat thrashes in my ears as I slowly reach for it, knowing this journal may contain a truth I've been too happy to ignore the past several weeks.

When Wes had first confronted me, demanding to know if Nick had ever hurt me, I was caught off guard. There was this part of me that wanted to tell him about the questionable things Nick had done. All the times I woke up sore and couldn't remember the night before.

How I couldn't remember getting into bed on New Year's Eve.

How I couldn't remember sleeping with him in the few months before I learned I was pregnant.

But the words never came. I'd convinced myself I was imagining things.

Correction... *Nick* convinced me I was imagining things. Made me think I was losing my mind. That there was something wrong with me and perhaps I should seek psychiatric care.

But there's never been anything wrong with me.

When Wes told me exactly what Nick had done to Londyn, I'd like to say I didn't believe it could be true, and that's why I've stayed silent.

But I *do* believe it to be true.

I have from the beginning.

And now, as I read Nick's supposed research on Medusa, I have proof that Londyn's telling the truth, too.

# CHAPTER THIRTY-FIVE

*Londyn*

My limbs heavy and soul torn, I make my way through Wes' house, packing a few things to take him. Socks. Briefs. Toothbrush. Even a photo of him and Imogene he keeps on his desk in his home office. Anything to make his hospital room feel as close to home as possible.

He deserves to be surrounded by comfort, affection…love.

I'm just not sure he needs *my* love anymore.

Since leaving the hospital a few hours ago, I've been riding a perpetual rollercoaster of emotions. Up one second, down the next. When I'm down, I convince myself I'm doing the right thing, that I'll only bring more harm to him by staying. Then a memory will return, pulling me from the depths, convincing me that maybe Hazel's right. Maybe I am giving up too easily. That, against all odds, Wes and I have survived this long. That we'll get through whatever the future holds, too.

These are the thoughts that run through my mind on a constant spin cycle as I continue through the house, every room, every photo forcing more and more memories to return, breaking my heart and shredding my soul.

When I think I can no longer take the crushing pain at the thought of not having Wes in my life, I make out what sounds like someone inserting a key into the front door. Stopping in my tracks by the kitchen island, I slowly look toward the foyer as the door opens, then closes, light steps echoing against the high ceiling.

I try to remember what day it is, wondering if perhaps it's Wes' housekeeper. But she comes on Fridays. It's only Wednesday.

Not wanting to take any chances, especially after the last few days, I lunge for the knife block on the counter and whirl around, knife held in front of me, eyes going wide when a familiar silhouette comes to an abrupt stop a few feet away, arms raised, body stiff.

"It's just me," Julia says cautiously, gaze unwavering. "I came to talk."

I take a few calming breaths to settle my nerves, then lower the knife and return it to the block. "I'm not so sure—"

"I believe you."

I snap my mouth shut, sucking in a breath. "You... believe me?"

"I do. I've believed you from the beginning. But I..." She trails off, struggling to find the words.

"You were too scared," I finish, knowing all too well what she's going through. I went through it myself.

Even after I found the strength to go to the police all

those years ago, I still questioned my sanity. Questioned whether Nick was right. That maybe he *hadn't* done anything I didn't want him to. It was the most confusing and frightening time of my life.

It wasn't until I attended my first self-defense class and met Hazel that I allowed myself to finally see the truth. But poor Julia hasn't had that opportunity. She's been married to him for years. If he was able to control and manipulate my behavior from across the coffee shop, I can only imagine what he's done to her over the course of their marriage.

Nick is the epitome of a lie parading around as the truth.

"Yes, I was scared, terrified. I still am. But Dad said something today that stuck with me. 'It's never too late to get on the right path.' So that's what I'm doing. Getting on the right path. And hopefully this will help you get on *your* right path, too." She reaches into her purse and produces a leather-bound journal, handing it to me.

"What's this?" I ask hesitantly, my eyes skating over Nick's familiar scrawl on the front, spelling out the name of the mythological creature from which I've drawn strength these past few weeks.

"Proof."

"Proof?" My breathing grows more uneven, my fingers trembling slightly as I run them along the surface.

"Yes. It's all in there. Everything you need to back up your claims. And probably things you never even knew about."

I stare at the journal, a bout of dizziness overtaking me. "Is it bad?"

"It's not easy to read. At least mine wasn't."

I dart my eyes to hers. "Yours?"

"Yeah." She smiles sadly. "Hera. There are others, too."

"Others?"

"Over a dozen, all named after a different character from mythology." She draws in a deep breath. "Many of whom were raped."

"Just like Hera," I exhale.

"And Medusa." She extends her hand.

Without hesitating, I take it in mine, no longer caring about any protective order. Like I suspected, it was a ploy to keep us from figuring out the truth. But that's the thing about the truth. It can only stay hidden for so long.

Steeling myself, I pull my hand from hers and set the journal on the island, opening it. My face heats as I'm bombarded with Nick's meticulous observations of me. But that's not what has me on the brink of purging the contents of my stomach. It's the fact that this predates our first encounter by over a year.

A year he spent watching me, unbeknownst to me.

A year he stood in the shadows.

A year he learned everything he could about me.

Julia wraps an arm around my shoulders, supporting me when I feel like the floor is about to disappear from under me. Pressure builds in my chest, my mind numb as I read how he'd first noticed me sitting in the quad on campus with my sketch pad. How I immediately caught his attention, standing out from a sea of conformity. How he became infatuated with me, even going so far as to find out where I lived when not at school, traveling to the house I shared with Sawyer just to watch me over the summer.

"It went on for so long," I manage to say as I flip through the pages, not having even reached our first meeting.

How could I have been so blind? How could I have not noticed him observing my every move?

The more I read, the more my stomach churns with every rationalization of his actions.

And the sickening part? He truly believes he didn't do anything wrong. That he actually helped me. He was so convinced I needed him, to the point of obsession. He claimed I was trapped in a world I wanted no part of. That I deserved to be free. That he was the only one who could free me.

I slam the cover closed, my jaw clenching as I shake my head, rage seeping through every inch of me. I want to scream, cry, punch a hole in the wall.

But mostly, I want vengeance. For me. For Julia. For all the other women Nick did this to.

We deserve that much.

"Come on." I clutch the book and spin abruptly, slinging the duffle bag and my purse over my shoulder before making my way toward the front door.

"Where are we going?" she asks, catching up to me.

"To show this to my lawyer." I wave the journal in front of her. "You say there are more?"

"Dozens. And then there are the urns."

I stop before opening the door. "Urns?"

"Maybe urn isn't the right word. They're wooden boxes. He told me they contained his pets' remains." She laughs under her breath. "I suppose he didn't exactly lie about that. I'd assumed he was talking about cats or dogs."

"He wasn't?"

She slowly shakes her head. "Each box has a gold plate with a name that matches one of his journals."

"And inside?" I ask, although I'm not sure I want to know the answer.

"Tokens. Things he stole. Jewelry. Perfume. A piece of clothing. A lock of hair. That's what's in yours."

"What?"

"A lock of hair."

I didn't think I could feel any more violated than I did the night Nick forced himself on me. But I do. The knowledge that he did all of this without me knowing makes me question everything. He stalked me. Observed me from afar. Entered my home and cut off a lock of my hair without me even knowing.

"This needs to stop," I say with determination. "Before he adds another box to his collection."

Julia nods and extends her hand toward me. Meeting her intense gaze, I take it, drawing strength from the fact that I'm no longer alone in this battle. She opens the door, both of us stepping into the bright sunlight. And that's what it feels like. Like I'm finally stepping out of the darkness of my past and into my future.

I only make it a feet few before a sharp pain hits the side of my head, everything going dark.

# CHAPTER THIRTY-SIX

## *Londyn*

A throbbing ache pulses in my head when I come out of whatever state I've been in for however long. I feel some sort of wetness on my temple, which I assume must be blood. But I can't move my arms to verify that. I blink my eyes open, disoriented, despite the familiar surroundings of Wes' garage.

Over the past several weeks, I've spent hours out here, transforming dilapidated pieces of furniture into something usable. Now I can't shake the feeling it may be the place where I draw my final breath. Why else would my wrists and ankles be bound, preventing escape?

But escape from whom?

Who was the shadow that came out of nowhere, attacking me and Julia?

*Julia...*

I squint, searching for any sign of her, breath hitching when I spot her a few feet away. Her wrists and ankles are bound like mine, her body propped against a dresser, head hanging, everything about her lifeless.

*Oh god. Please no…*

"Julia," I whisper-shout, but she doesn't move.

I attempt to wiggle closer to her, but my restraints make it impossible. I try to make out the rise and fall of her chest, praying she's still alive. But I see no motion. No life. Nothing.

"Julia," I say again, this time louder, my voice more urgent. "Julia, please…"

Finally, I notice a slight movement and expel a small breath.

She lifts her head, tears streaming down her cheeks. "I'm so sorry, Londyn," she manages to say. "I should have been more careful. Shouldn't have left everything out for Nick to find."

I swallow hard. Of course the shadow was Nick. He's been a shadow in my existence for years now.

"It's okay." I force a smile, although nothing about this situation is okay. "We'll be okay."

"How?"

I open my mouth, unsure what to tell her.

When I first met her, I thought her to be a strong, tenacious woman. Even after everything went down, there was still a fire in her eyes, giving me hope that she'd find a way to break free. But now, it's gone.

Nick's finally succeeded in doing what he set out to do from the beginning.

He broke her, like he did me.

But buried inside me somewhere was a fighter. Like I know there's a fighter inside Julia. She just needs to realize it.

"Because you're Hera. You don't take shit from anyone," I insist. "Zeus may have been the king of the gods, but there was only one being he feared. And it wasn't Hades."

The defeat that had covered her expression wanes. "It was Hera," she exhales.

"Exactly. Nick may worship and idolize you. But he also *fears* you. Don't forget that."

"He fears me," she tests the words, almost as in affirmation.

Suddenly, the door flings open with a loud bang, like a formidable clap of thunder. We simultaneously whip our gazes toward Nick as he saunters down the short flight of stairs from the laundry room and into the garage.

"Well, well, well…," he begins slyly. "Look who's finally awake. I was beginning to worry I caused more damage than I intended and would miss out on some playtime."

His cruel voice forces a shiver down my spine. Julia's eyes lock with mine, wide with panic and fear. But I give her an encouraging nod, silently reminding her exactly who she is. Who she needs to be if we're to make it out of this.

Nick crouches in front of Julia, swiping away the few tears on her cheeks. "My sweet, sweet girl. Do you know how much it pains me to see you like this?"

"Then why are you doing this?" she demands. Her words come out stronger than I expected.

Stronger than Nick expected, too.

But it's not the tone Julia uses that catches him off guard. It's the disappointment laced within that probably sends him over the edge.

He shoots to his feet, his demeanor shifting from calm and collected to agitated and distressed. "What choice did you leave me?" He paces, digging his fingers into his blond hair, the sling he wore now nothing more than a memory.

I wouldn't be surprised to learn he never needed it to begin with. Like I doubt he needed the wheelchair during Lydia's press conference.

"Do you think I *wanted* things to go this way? It wasn't supposed to. It was never part of the plan."

"Then tell me why. Help me understand."

"You wouldn't. You never could. You've always been happy to live in your own little bubble, haven't you?"

"I don't know what you mean. I—"

"It's who you are. Who *they* turned you into. I tried to help, tried to set you free. Make you remember the girl you used to be before you were taken away from me."

"What are you talking about?" Julia asks cautiously. "When was I taken away from you?"

"My point exactly," he barks out. "*You don't remember.* You didn't care anymore. Not once you had your nice new family with tons of money. You no longer had any use for the foster family that saved you from being abused by a drug addict and her dealers."

"I didn't know you back then, Nick. I—"

He widens his stance, lips pinched. "Are you sure about that, Juju Bear?"

"Juju Bear…," she repeats deliberately, her voice low. She blinks slowly, brow pinched in contemplation. Then her gaze widens. "That was you."

It's not a question, but a statement, one that leaves me more and more confused as I attempt to unravel this mystery.

"You were that quiet boy. You looked out for me. Kept all the mean kids at school in line."

"Exactly." His eyes awash with a nostalgic gleam, he kneels, cupping her cheeks in his hands. "We may have only been kids, but I knew there was something about you. I knew you *needed* me to save you…" He brushes his thumb along her bottom lip. "My Hera."

She closes her eyes, basking in his touch. Even *I* can't tell if she's acting. It feels so real.

"I watched what these people did to you, how they transformed you from this innocent little girl into a jaded woman who would do anything anyone asked just for something I would freely give you."

"And what's that?" she asks with a hard swallow.

"Love. And it was because of my love that I knew I had to set you free."

"By drugging me, then assaulting me and making me think I'd lost my mind?" she asks with a quiver.

If she expected her words to have any impact on him, she's mistaken. As I gathered from reading his journal entries, Nick honestly believes his actions were justified. That he helped her. Helped me. Helped every single woman he victimized.

"I understand how difficult this must be for you to wrap your head around, but trust me when I say you needed me to do that. You needed me to make you aware of how vulnerable you'd become. Only when one faces their weakness can they find their strength. That's what I did. Gave you the strength to leave your old life behind." His grip on her face tightens, his voice becoming deeper with passion. "If I didn't do what I did, you would have drowned in your desperate need for approval. I *saved* you."

She stares ahead, her expression unreadable. "And the others?" Her lips form into a tight line, her jaw tightening. "Did you *save* all of them by raping them, too?"

"Don't cheapen what I've done." He rises to stand, indignant at her accusation. "I did what all those women needed…" He looks in my direction. "Take Miss Bennett over here."

He stalks toward me. When he brings his hand to my

cheek, I stiffen, holding my breath. The mere idea of his skin on mine churns my stomach. But Julia endured. I can, too.

"She was so weak, forced to marry a man she'd never love because of some misguided need to never disappoint her father, thinking he'd only love her if she did everything he asked of her."

I part my lips, about to argue he's wrong, that I had other reasons for marrying Sawyer. But that's not true. I know it's not. Worse, Nick knows it's not.

"Like Julia, you needed to be saved. To be set free. So that's what I did. I *saved* you," he emphasizes, his eyes filled with compassion before darkening. "And how do you repay me for everything I've done?" He jumps to standing, the wild pendulum of his mania swinging once more. "Attempt to turn me into campus police. Thankfully, I'd already alerted your department head to your infatuation with me."

"I wasn't infatuated," I argue. "You were the one who stalked me. Who broke into my home and cut off a lock of my hair!"

"Don't fool yourself. You were just as infatuated with me. You never frequented the coffee shop with much regularity until you kept running into me there. You never spent much time in the English building until we became more friendly. And let's not even talk about the dress you chose to wear to the masquerade ball."

"So is that all it takes for you to believe your actions were justified?" I counter harshly, blood rushing through my veins. "A short dress and a few chance encounters? I can't be the only one who ever questioned you. Who ever said enough is enough and decided to seek justice. I get why Julia never did," I continue, giving her a reassuring smile. "She's been imprisoned under your constant influence and control. You can't honestly tell me no one else has stood up to you."

"Unlike you, most women are thankful I helped them."

"*Most* women?"

He flinches, obviously not expecting me to read between the lines. But thanks to him, I've learned to analyze everything a person says and does. It's the only way I've been able to protect myself from history repeating itself.

"Yes."

"And those who saw you for who you are?"

He doesn't utter a single syllable in response, simply glowers at me with a sinister glare. In that one look, I know precisely what he's done. It's what he threatened to do to me.

What I fear he's about to do now that he has the chance again.

"You're lucky you got away with it," I comment, knowing my remark will incense him. My insinuation that his ability to walk free has to do with luck and not his intelligence obviously eats away at him. To the point of him spilling his secrets.

"I don't do anything without careful planning," he retorts smugly. "All the months I'd spent observing you, finding out your likes, dislikes, dreams, ambitions, fears... It was all for a reason. By the time I finally approached you, I knew everything about you. I probably knew you better than you knew yourself. So disposing of someone who threatens everything I've built?" He shrugs nonchalantly. "It's easy if you pay attention. Look how easy it was to pin the house fire on Grady Stowe."

My eyes widen at the same time as Julia's jaw drops. I was so confident it was Grady. Everyone was. He'd all but threatened to set the house on fire in front of a diner full of people. It couldn't be anyone else. Could it?

"See?" Nick says through our utter surprise. "That's the problem with society. Everyone is so focused on social media, on how many likes they got on their latest Instagram post that they ignore the world around them. But not me. I observe. I listen. Then I act."

In one swift move, he reaches into his back pocket and draws out a utility knife with a curved blade I use for cutting carpet or linoleum. When he brings it up to my throat, I stiffen, the hair on the back of my neck rising, tremors rippling through me. Through everything, I've tried to maintain my composure, give the impression of the intrepid Medusa he turned me into.

Now I fear this is the scene where Perseus sacrifices her.

"What are you going to do?" I ask.

"You know the answer to that."

I briefly close my eyes in resignation, then return them to his. "I do," I say calmly.

He probably expected me to put up a fight or beg for my life. But after years of analyzing every single one of our interactions, I've come to the conclusion that the best way to outsmart Nick is to not play into his hand. To change the rules. To act out of character.

"So get on with it then."

I catch Julia's stare out of the corner of my eye, giving her a look I hope she can understand. I *need* her to understand, to read my mind. It's the only way we'll both walk out of this alive.

"You're not going to fight?"

"What's the use? You have me tied up. I can't fight you. You win. So go on." I tilt my head back, presenting my neck to him. "Do it."

On a long exhale, he runs the blade along my skin, a chill trickling through me. I've never really thought about how I would die, but I never could have imagined it would be like this, a blade cutting my throat until I bleed out.

"Such a pity, really. To ruin such a beautiful neck. It's like destroying a priceless piece of art. But it's sometimes necessary. For the greater good."

I can't fight him off when he leans closer, dragging his tongue along my throat, the sensation like tiny daggers stabbing me. I squeeze my eyes shut, muscles tightening.

"Just needed one last taste," he explains as he pulls back. I snap my gaze to his as he lifts the knife back to me.

My chest rises and falls in a faster pattern, my heart thundering in my ears. All I can do is stare at him, wishing with everything for Medusa's ability to turn him into stone. But I'm not her. I never have been, despite Nick's insistence to the contrary. I have no way of defending myself. My only chance is that Julia assumes the role of Hera and becomes who she needs to be.

Nick keeps his gaze trained on mine, almost amused that I don't look away and instead glare at him as he presses the blade into my skin, a droplet of blood escaping.

"Let me do it!" Julia finally demands, her voice stark against the silence in the garage, causing Nick to stop.

I blow out a breath, sending up a prayer.

He blinks, taken aback by her command. And that's precisely what it was. Gone is the scared, confused woman she's been these past few weeks. In her place is a strong, confident woman. Like the goddess Hera herself. And like Hera, she holds immense power over Zeus.

"You want to do it?"

"I understand now," she says evenly, peering into his eyes. "I was scared. Seeing all that stuff from my past, reading about myself from your eyes..." Licking her lips, she shakes her head. "I didn't know what to think. But like always, you've helped me see what's important. What matters. Everything you did was to protect me. Like you did at the foster home when you always gave me your apple slices."

He exhales, dropping his hold on me. "You remember." In awe, he stands, taking several slow steps toward her.

She nods. "I do. And when they wanted to cut my hair, you intervened on my behalf, convinced them to let me keep my curls."

Kneeling before her, he wraps a strand of golden blonde hair around a single finger, bringing it up to his nose and inhaling. "I couldn't let them do that. Couldn't let them do anything to destroy your beauty. After all, it was your perfect blonde hair that drew me to you. Like the goddess Hera herself. It's how I knew we were meant to be, even as kids."

"See? You've always had my best interests in mind, even when I didn't know what I needed myself. My king. My Zeus." She cranes her head back, her lips seeking his.

He covers her mouth in a soft kiss. "My Hera."

"Which is why I should be the one to silence her," she sneers in my direction. "I'm your Hera. It's my duty to punish any woman who dares consort with my king. Who dares steal my love from me."

He searches her eyes for a beat, looking for any deception. Finding none, he slams his lips against hers, seemingly getting off on every manipulative word she feeds him. I can't help but marvel at how easily he believes her without even a single doubt about her devotion. I guess when you want to believe something so badly, you're more inclined to ignore reality.

Then again, I'm fairly certain Nick's never lived in reality. Not based on what I've seen today.

"We're in this together, my love," Julia whispers huskily. "We are one. Inseparable. Impenetrable."

"Together," Nick mutters as he feathers another kiss to her mouth.

"Forever," she promises.

"Forever."

Reaching behind her, he slices the rope binding her wrists before doing the same to the restraints around her ankles. After pressing another kiss to her lips, he helps her to her feet, beaming down on her with a creepy sort of pride, as if the years and years of hard work have finally paid off.

"I knew you'd come around once you saw things from my perspective. You always do."

"I just needed you to show me the way. I'll always need you to show me the way."

"And I'll always be here to do that." He tugs her body back into his, groaning as he coaxes her mouth open. She stands on her toes to meet his height, digging her fingernails into his scalp before pulling back.

"May I?" She extends her hands, gaze focused on the knife Nick holds.

"This may be the sexiest thing I've ever seen you do." He passes me a sinister look as he places the knife into Julia's open palm.

"Wow." She shivers, eyes gleaming as she turns from him, moving toward me. "It's so small, but I don't think I've ever felt so powerful."

"It's a rush, isn't it?" Nick remarks. "Holding someone's life in your hands?"

"It certainly is." She slowly nods, stare focused solely on me as her lips quirk into a smile, not breaking character once. Neither do I, considering my life depends on both of us playing the roles he's given us. "Now it's time to atone for your sins."

She shifts toward Nick, gaze darkening as she tightens her grip on the handle of the knife.

Before he has a chance to fully understand what she's about to do, she plunges the blade into his groin. A strangled cry pierces the air as he falls to the floor, clutching himself.

I gasp, jaw dropping. I knew she'd have to resort to harming him in some way in order for us to make our escape. I didn't expect this. Didn't think Julia had it in her.

"That's for making me question everything in my life, even my own brother, you fucking asshole!" she shrieks, her entire body vibrating with fury. "You preyed on my weakness, my vulnerability…" She brings her foot up to where the knife protrudes from his body, a fear unlike any I've seen flashing in his eyes. "*Now* who's the weak one?" She presses her foot down, forcing the blade to dig in even deeper, a pained cry reverberating in the space until his eyes close. His body goes limp, the agony probably too much for him to remain conscious.

Spinning from him, she rushes toward me, struggling to undo my bindings with her shaky, blood-covered hands.

"In the toolbox." I nod at the far wall. "There are more utility knives. Hurry."

She darts toward it while I keep an eye on Nick, worried he might somehow miraculously spring back to life like the true immortal Zeus was. But he's no god. Just a pitiful man who used these characters he obsessed over to validate his behavior.

"Got one," she announces, whirling around and scurrying across the garage back to me.

Once my wrists and ankles are free, she drops the knife, helping me to my feet. I loop my arm through hers, both of us supporting each other as we struggle to put as much space between Nick and us as possible.

I fumble for the garage door opener on the side of the wall, repeatedly smashing the button. Finally, after what feels like an eternity, the mechanism kicks in and the door slowly slides open.

I breathe in the fresh air, placing my hand on the exterior wall to steady myself, a dizzy spell overtaking me. The events of the past few hours seem to catch up to me, spots obscuring my vision as I struggle to maintain my balance.

But I can't, collapsing to the ground in a heap.

# CHAPTER THIRTY-SEVEN

## *Londyn*

"There you go," the nurse says brightly, smoothing her hand over the bandage she just applied to the side of my head.

I bring my hand up to it, feeling the large bump and gash Nick left, which required five stitches. I'm lucky he didn't do more damage than that. At least not physically.

Emotionally, though…

Those scars will take a lot more than a few stitches to heal.

But I've done it before. And I'll do it again.

"You'll want to make an appointment with your personal physician soon, preferably this week."

"I will. Thank you."

"Of course, sweetie."

She leans toward me, dropping her voice to a whisper. "I have to say, I've been following your case."

"You have?"

"Sure have." She turns to the cart, arranging the bandages into some semblance of order. "If you ask me, that bastard got what he deserved."

I can't stop the smile from tugging on my lips.

In the four hours since I arrived in the emergency room, undergoing a myriad of tests to figure out what caused my fainting spell, the story about what happened to Nick has made the headlines. I should feel vindication that the truth has finally been revealed, but it's a little bittersweet. I wish Wes were here to celebrate with me. After all, he stood by my side, his support unwavering, regardless of the obstacles we faced.

"Bet you wish you could have been the one to stab him."

I look at the blue privacy curtain separating me from all the other patients. Then I turn my eyes back to the nurse, offering her a small smile. "Actually, it needed to be his wife. She's suffered the longest."

"Well, I'm glad he won't be able to hurt anyone else ever again." She lowers her voice once more. "And according to some of my colleagues in critical care, he may never be able to get it up again, either. If you know what I mean." She playfully nudges me. "He got exactly what he deserves. Poetic justice."

I couldn't agree more. A knife to the groin is a fitting punishment for a man who lived his life thinking the stories in Greek mythology were real.

She squeezes my arm. "I'll get started on your discharge papers." She starts to pull back the privacy curtain, coming to an abrupt stop when a nurse pushing a wheelchair lingers just outside, about to open the curtain herself.

My focus immediately goes to the man in the wheelchair, eyes awash with concern, tension oozing from every pore.

I slowly sit up in the hospital bed. "Wes…"

"You're…" He licks his lips. "You're okay."

"I'm okay."

"You must be the boyfriend," my nurse teases.

"I am," Wes answers, turning his attention toward her.

"Well then. I'll give y'all some time together. Miss Londyn here couldn't stop talking about you, made sure we sent word over to the burn unit to let you know she's okay."

"These two are perfect for each other," Gemma, Wes' nurse, says. "Because this one threw a right fit once he heard the news. Threatened to get out of bed and find her if that's what it took. Not sure how far he'd get since he can't exactly walk, but he's determined. That's for sure." She turns her attention to Wes. "You've got ten minutes before I need to get you back."

"I'll take whatever I can get," he responds, not so much as glancing at her, his focus on me and me alone.

She nods, pushing his chair toward my bed. Then she follows my nurse into the ER, closing the privacy curtain behind her.

Wes doesn't hesitate, taking my hand in his and bringing it to his mouth. I sigh, relishing in the warmth of his skin on mine now that his hand is no longer bandaged.

"You're okay," he says again, almost as if he needs the confirmation.

"I'm okay," I say once more.

"Do you have any idea how worried I was? When I saw the news alert pop up on my phone, I thought I was going to die, Lo. Especially when I couldn't reach you." He cups my cheek. "It was like New Year's Day all over again."

I lean into his touch, basking in the love that pours from the connection. There was a time I didn't think I'd ever feel his skin on mine again. That Nick would be the last person to touch me. But for once, luck was on my side.

Or at least Julia was.

"I didn't mean to worry you. I can only imagine the hell you gave your nurses."

"They pretty much had to restrain me." He laughs. "I didn't care. I'd do whatever it took to get to you. Still will." He draws my lips to his, and I melt into his kiss. It's exactly what I need.

He once told me I was the medicine for his soul. He's also mine. In this one kiss, all my indecision is gone. In this one kiss, I remember what's important. In this one kiss, I know the path I'm meant to take. And that's with Wes. We're stronger together. And we'll get through whatever the future holds. I was foolish to think otherwise, my fear getting the better of me. No more.

Pulling back, he surveys my body, starting with the bandage on my temple, continuing down my torso, his jaw clenching when he sees the heavy bruising on my wrists.

"How…," he begins, shaking his head. "How did this happen?"

Taking his hand, I draw in a deep breath, then recount the events of the afternoon.

How I'd stopped by his place to gather a few of his things to make his lengthy hospital stay more comfortable. How Julia came by and said she believed me. How she showed me a journal Nick kept that detailed his observations of me, predating our first encounter by over a year. How Julia had found dozens of similar journals, all supposedly research on various characters in Greek mythology. In reality, they were his stalking chronicles, including one that detailed Nick's obsession with Julia from an early age. How the journal Julia brought me corroborated my story. Not only back in college, but also on New Year's Day.

Then how we were about to take the journal to Sophia

when a figure came out of the shadows and knocked me out. How I woke up in the garage, bound and unable to move. How I learned Julia and Nick actually knew each other when they were kids, that they were at the same foster home together. How Nick was the one responsible for the fire at Gampy and Meemaw's house, having set it in the hopes of silencing me, then pinned it on Grady, a tactic he confessed to using with several of the other women he'd stalked and assaulted.

How Julia was the real hero of the afternoon, playing the role of Hera perfectly, tricking Nick into believing she wanted to be the one to kill me. How she turned on him and stabbed him in the groin. Then how, once she freed me and we were out of the garage, I passed out.

Blinking, he pinches the bridge of his nose, processing everything. "Is Julia okay?"

"She's fine. The police took her statement, then went with her to your parents' house to collect all the journals and keepsake boxes as evidence."

"And Nick?" he asks hesitantly, as if expecting him to escape justice yet again.

"In surgery. With two cops stationed outside. They'll stay with him until he's released, at which point he'll be taken into custody."

"What about the charges against you?"

"Sophia is already in talks with the DA. It sounds like they'll be dropping them within the next few days. And as of right now, they have no intention of pursuing any charges against Julia for her actions today."

"Thank God." He exhales a relieved breath. "I can't believe she knew him growing up."

"I doubt she has many clear memories of him. Not like

he does of her. He *is* six years older than her. She was, what? Five or six when your parents adopted her?"

He nods, staring into the distance for a few seconds before looking back at me. "How are *you* doing? You said you fainted. Did they check you for a concussion?"

I part my lips to answer, but he won't let me, his worry for my well-being obvious.

"Have they done an MRI or CAT scan?" he continues.

"Wes, I—"

"I don't think you should leave until they do. You fainted, for crying out loud. I've had concussions before and fainted. You can't be alone."

"Wes," I say again, and yet again, his concern over-shadows my protest as he frantically scans every part of my body. It reminds me of our first meeting, how he just wanted to make sure I was okay.

"You need someone with you to check you out every two hours. If you go to sleep and you really do have a concussion, you might not—"

"I'm pregnant!" I shout to put an end to this.

He stiffens, jaw dropping as he gapes at me, my words echoing around us. The chaotic atmosphere in the emergency room seems to disappear, everything going still. This isn't how I imagined telling him. I kind of wanted to wait until he was out of the hospital to spring this on him.

"That's why I fainted," I continue in a small voice. "Because I'm pregnant and haven't exactly been taking care of myself lately."

He stares at me in wonder, shifting his gaze to my stomach. His Adam's apple bobs up and down. "Is... Is the baby okay? With everything that happened, did—"

"The baby is fine."

He blows out a breath, relief covering his expression. "How far along?"

"About eight weeks. With all the craziness lately, I hadn't realized when I missed a period."

"A baby." He places his hand over my stomach, tears welling in his eyes.

"A baby." I cover his hand with mine. "It's still early. The risk of miscarriage in the first trimester is pretty high, but—"

He cuts me off with a kiss. Gentle, yet intense. Swiping his tongue along my lips, he coaxes my mouth open, the feel of his breath intermingling with mine setting me aflame. I moan, drowning in all he is. And for the first time, I don't want to come up for air. Not anymore.

He pulls back, leaning his forehead on mine. "Everything's going to work out. I feel it."

"So you're not upset?"

"Upset?" He cocks his head to the side. "What could I possibly be upset about?"

I fidget with my hands in my lap. "I'm sure this must come as a surprise to you. It surprised me," I say, talking fast. "When I told the nurse my symptoms, insisting it had to be a concussion, like you did, she asked if I was pregnant. I thought she was crazy, but when I couldn't remember when my last cycle was, she had me give her a urine sample. Sure enough…"

He touches his lips to mine. "Are you kidding me? It might be a surprise, but it's the best kind of surprise. *You* are the best kind of surprise. A plot twist." He floats his eyes to my stomach. "And now we get to share our love with our child. You for me, Lo."

A warmth flows through me, my heart expanding in my chest. "Me for you."

"For the rest of our lives."

"The rest of our lives." I bask in the exchange we've said countless times over the past few weeks. But this time, it has a different meaning. A *deeper* meaning.

For the longest time, the future was just an abstract idea in my mind, something I never gave much thought to. Not when the shadows of my past constantly pulled me down.

Now I look forward to a future. And no matter what it brings, no matter the obstacles we'll face, this man will be exactly where he has been since he brought me in out of the rain…

By my side.

Supporting me.

Loving me.

# CHAPTER THIRTY-EIGHT

## *Weston*

A heaviness weighs on my chest as Londyn drives my Range Rover along the familiar dirt path leading to Gampy and Meemaw's property, a solemn air in the car. Even Zeus picks up on it. While he'd normally perk up, tail wagging at the prospect of chasing birds and squirrels all weekend, he sits stoically in the back seat, eyes trained forward.

As we round the bend and the remains of the house come into view, I push down the lump building in my throat. I thought there'd still be something standing. But there isn't, the frame collapsed from the extensive damage caused by the fire. The only thing still intact is the fireplace in the living room.

My father offered to have everything cleaned up before I was released from the hospital yesterday after a three-week stay. I told him no, insisted I wanted to be part of the process. Wanted to come out here before anything was removed to see it all for myself.

Londyn parks and glances at me. "Are you sure about this?"

I grab her hand, bringing it to my lips. "I am. This is important to me. To us."

"Okay." She pulls her hand from mine, then kills the ignition, jumping out of the car and running around to my side to help me.

While I've regained most of my strength and motion in my injured leg, it's still stiff. At least I can finally walk again, albeit with a slight limp. But my physical therapist assured me, with time and exercise, that will disappear.

I link my fingers with Londyn's as we walk along the property, Zeus following dutifully behind us. I had spent the past few days mentally preparing myself for this, but I don't think I truly anticipated the myriad of feelings filling me over the destruction.

All I can do is find comfort in the fact that the man responsible is now behind bars and will finally pay for all his crimes. Not just for the arson, but for everything he did to Londyn, Julia, and the dozens of other women who came forward once news of his arrest broke. With all the charges filed against Nick, he'll spend the rest of his life in prison. Regardless of all the evidence and testimony against him, though, he's maintained his innocence, claiming he was completely justified in his actions.

I doubt he'll ever be able to admit he was wrong.

I doubt he'll ever be able to *see* he was wrong.

"Are you sure you want to do this?" Londyn asks after we've finished our brief survey of the charred remains. "It'll be a lot of work."

"When has that ever stopped me before?" I counter.

She smiles shyly. "Never."

"Exactly. So I'm not going to let it stop me now. This is important to me. Thanks to you…" I playfully nudge her.

"Me?"

I fully face her, taking her hands in mine. "Yes, you. You taught me the importance of rebuilding after tragedy. That's what you did all those years ago. It would have been so easy for you to give up, crawl under the rubble, let the world forget about you. But you didn't. You rebuilt who you were brick by brick. It wasn't easy. And I'm sure there were more than a few days you wanted to give up."

She laughs under her breath. "You've got that right."

"But through it all, you persevered." I hook my arm around her waist, drawing her body into mine. "So that's what we're going to do here. We're going to rebuild. Together." I press my lips to hers, sealing my vow with a kiss.

There was a time I worried each kiss might be our last. But now I can relish in the fact that we'll have a lifetime of kisses. No more Nick looming in the shadows. No more threat of going to prison for a crime she was justified in committing. Just years and years of loving each other.

When our kiss comes to an end, I drop my hold on her, placing my hand on the small of her back as I lead her toward the remains of the master bedroom. The only reason I can tell is because of the iron bed frame, the mattress barely anything more than a tattered shell. I try not to consider that, had Zeus not alerted Londyn, my ashes could have been in that pile, too.

I look down, Zeus staring back at me, as if thinking the same thing. I scratch his head between his ears, his tail wagging. "Good boy. I promise to make you a steak to reward you."

"Already done," Londyn remarks.

I shift my eyes toward hers, a single brow arched in question.

"What?" She shrugs. "I've fed him steak at least twice since you were in the hospital. Figured he deserved it."

"He certainly does."

I look over the debris, grateful to have survived this with minimal damage to my body. When something underneath the charred frame of the mattress catches my attention, I squint.

Cautiously stepping on a few of the blackened wood planks, I limp toward it.

"What are you doing?" Londyn asks worriedly, following me.

"I'm fine."

"Just be careful. Don't want you ripping something and needing to go back to the hospital. I've had my fair share of hospitals lately."

"You and me both." I roll my eyes before bending down, wincing slightly.

"What is it?" Londyn presses, noticing my attention drawn to something.

I stare, almost in disbelief. Once I regained consciousness and learned about the fire, I didn't care about what was lost, only that Londyn was safe and I was alive. But there was one thing I wished I hadn't lost. I didn't think it would turn up. Assumed it would simply become a casualty of the fire.

I should have known otherwise. After all, there's a reason diamonds have become the symbol of love. They're impenetrable. Nearly indestructible. And when I flip open the black box that's covered with ash and soot, I confirm that to be true. The rest of the house may have perished. But this ring survived.

Our *love* survived.

Twisting toward her, I place my injured foot on the rubble, putting my weight on my opposite knee.

"Wes, what are——"

I reach for Londyn's hand, tugging her toward me.

"I promised when this was all over, the first thing I would do is propose."

"I know, but——"

"And it's over. The DA dropped all charges against you over a week ago."

"True, but I don't see how it's really over." She glances around. "Not with all of this."

"But if it's not this, it will be something else. That's how it seems to go with us."

"I can't argue with that," she retorts with a laugh.

"Exactly. And if the last few months have taught me anything, it's that there may never be a perfect time for us. There may always be some obstacle we'll have to overcome. But we *will* overcome them. Together."

She swallows hard, a lone tear trickling down her cheek as she subtly nods, giving me permission to continue.

I briefly look into the distance, collecting my thoughts before returning my gaze to her.

"A few months ago, I had this whole speech prepared. Planned to bring you to the intersection where we first met, get down on one knee, and ask you to spend the rest of your life with me. At the time, I didn't think there was a more appropriate place to propose." I glance around me. "I was wrong. To most people, this may not be the ideal location. But we're not most people. Never have been."

She swipes at her tears, shaking her head. "You're right about that."

"So, in the rubble of our former lives, I want to make you a promise, Londyn Jade Bennett. I promise to love you so fiercely that you'll have no choice but to be consumed by it every second of every day. I promise to listen whenever you need to talk. I promise to support every single one of your dreams, no matter how big or small."

I bring my free hand to her stomach, marveling at the idea of a life we created growing within. "And I promise to love this child, and any other children we're blessed enough to have. To raise him or her to be the best person. To teach him or her about respect, acceptance...love. And that's the truth about us, Londyn. We *are* a love story. At least you're mine. You're my beginning. My ending. My everything in between. And the only woman I want by my side.

"I thought I knew what love was. Thought I'd already experienced it, so I didn't think I'd ever find it again. But I was wrong. What I thought was love..." I shake my head. "It didn't even come close. There's no doubt in my mind that this is love." I gesture between our two bodies. "*We* are love. And I want nothing more than to surround you with this love for the rest of our lives. And even after."

Carefully removing the ring from the box, I bring it up to her finger. "So please, Londyn Jade Bennett, will you do me the honor of marrying me?"

"How could I even think to say no to that?" she chokes out as she clutches my face in her hands.

Tears falling steadily down her cheeks, she pulls my lips toward hers, forcing me to my feet. I slide the ring onto her finger, then succumb to her kiss, blocking out everything. Nothing else matters right now. Not our past. Not our trials. Not our struggles. All that matters is this moment. It didn't come easy. But like Gampy said... "Sometimes the right path isn't always the easiest." But when you're on that right path, it's pure magic. And Londyn is magic.

When the sound of tires crunching against dirt cuts

through, I pull out of the kiss, looking toward the driveway as a car parks behind mine, Imogene jumping out.

I shoot Londyn a confused look as we carefully walk toward her.

"Uncle Wes!" she exclaims, wrapping her arms around me in a tight hug.

"Hiya, peanut. What are you doing here?"

"Mama and Pappy said we're here to help you."

"Help me?" I snap my head up as Julia and my father walk up behind Imogene.

Despite everything that's happened, Imogene's bounced back better than any of us thought she would. After years of keeping Nick's true personality from everyone, Julia insisted on being honest with her daughter. About everything. Even the things no six-year-old girl should have to learn about her father. While Imogene was upset at first, she's starting to understand why she can no longer see her daddy. The therapist our father recommended has helped immeasurably in that regard, as well.

It's also helped that Julia has agreed they'd stay in Atlanta, taking up residence in my house. I don't mind. I've been in the hospital anyway. Even if I hadn't been, I'm thrilled to have them back in my home.

"Can't let you do all this on your own." Dad pulls me in for a brief hug. "Truthfully, I'm looking forward to getting my hands dirty. I think it'll be good for my soul. Help me remember where I come from."

I nod, giving him a smile. "Thanks, Dad."

"You bet, son." There's a twinkle in his eye I haven't seen in years.

While my mother certainly made a stink once the attorneys officially served her with divorce papers, my dad took it all in stride, letting it all roll off him. As he said repeatedly over the past few weeks, he's too old to care what people think or say about him. I'm glad he finally realized this.

After news of Nick's arrest made headlines, my mother tried to save face for taking his side. But as my father told me back in January, her Danish Gambit would either end in a quick victory or utter failure. And this certainly ended in utter failure. While the police never found any wrongdoing on her part, she may as well be sitting in prison for all she's concerned, all her society friends effectively cutting ties with her.

Now she's just a lonely, pathetic woman with nothing but her hate to keep her company.

At the sound of more tires on dirt, I look away to see several more cars making their way along the drive, more and more people stepping out. Londyn's dad. Miss Clara. Hazel and Diego. Even a few volunteers from the charity house-building program I founded a few years back. All of them here to help us pick up the pieces of our life.

As I stand back with an arm around Londyn, watching the several dozen people who volunteered their time to lend a hand, I feel like things have finally clicked into place.

Sure, our future may not always be sunshine and rainbows. We may face many more obstacles, especially as parents. But there's one certainty in my life.

No matter what the world tries to throw at us, Londyn and I will get through it. Together.

Me for her.

Her for me.

For the rest of our lives.

# CHAPTER THIRTY-NINE

## *Londyn*

"Nervous?" Hazel asks as she makes a few final adjustments to the back of my gown.

I look at my reflection in the mirror, smoothing a hand down my torso.

My body has a few more curves since the last time I wore a wedding dress. Then again, I'd be hard-pressed to call that simple white dress I found at a thrift store a wedding dress.

For that reason, I decided this time around, I'd finally have the dress of my dreams. An off-the-shoulder, form-fitting, sheath bridal gown with a lace appliqué overlay that accentuates all my curves, especially the new ones I've grown over the past year-and-a-half from not only my pregnancy, but also nursing little Elijah James. Who, at nine months old, isn't all that little anymore.

"Not a bit." I turn around, meeting her eyes. "Should I be?"

She runs her hands down my arms. "If it's right, you won't be."

"And this is right. Without a doubt."

She pulls me in for a hug. "I'm happy for you. You deserve this."

"Thanks, Haze."

"Oh, Auntie Londyn!" a small voice squeals. "You look so pretty."

I pull away from Hazel as Imogene walks into the master bedroom of Gampy and Meemaw's old house, Julia behind her carrying Elijah.

It doesn't matter that we spent the past eighteen months rebuilding this house from the foundation, only able to salvage a few original pieces. This will always be Gampy and Meemaw's house.

"You look beautiful, too, sweetie," I say, taking in her simple ivory lace dress with a silk belt that matches the violet hue of both Hazel's and Julia's tea-length dresses. "Have you been taking good care of Elijah?"

"Of course!" She scrunches up her nose. "But I think he went poo."

I roll my eyes. "Of course he did." I reach to take him from Julia, but she waves me off.

"I'll take care of it. I just wanted to come and see if you need anything before I head out there. Best person duties, and all that." She winks.

"We're ready," I tell her with a confident smile.

A gentle knocking on the open door interrupts, followed by my father peeking his head inside. "How are we doing in here?"

Julia steps back, allowing him to enter. The instant Elijah sees him, he reaches for him.

"There's my adorable grandson." With a gleam in his

eyes, he takes him from Julia and bounces him in his arms, showering him with kisses. "Are you ready to be the cutest ring bearer we've ever seen this side of the Mason-Dixon?"

Elijah coos, his tiny hands reaching for my dad's face, squeezing his nose.

"We just need to keep him from putting them into his mouth," I laugh, only half-joking.

"That's my job," Imogene says proudly.

"Yes, it is." My dad smiles at Imogene, then clears his throat. "If y'all are ready, I'd like a minute alone with my daughter." He glances at Hazel, then Julia.

"Of course," Hazel says. "We'll head downstairs."

"Thank you." He kisses her cheek before handing Elijah to her.

Once we're alone, he turns toward me, unshed tears glistening in his eyes. It's a different look than the one he gave me when he came to talk to me before my sham of a wedding to Sawyer. But I no longer hold any grudges against my father for the role he played in that. After all, everything that's happened in my life has led me to this moment.

And it doesn't hurt that Sawyer was finally exposed for the fraud he truly is.

After Nick's arrest, things took a turn for Sawyer. The board of his church voted to remove him for not being transparent with them regarding the true nature of our relationship, as well as the lies he spewed on national TV, a fact they corroborated when the contents of Nick's journals were made public. From there, things only got worse, especially once the church board did some digging into their finances and learned that Sawyer had been embezzling donations. And not just small amounts. When all was said and done, they discovered he'd stolen over eight figures from the church's coffers.

Despite his threats that I'd be spending the next few decades of my life behind bars if I didn't accept his offer, he's now the one behind bars, serving a fifteen-year sentence.

"You look just like your mama did on our wedding day," Dad says, his voice wavering.

I smile, reaching for his hand and squeezing. "I wish she could be here."

"She is, baby girl." He looks up at the ceiling. "She's always been here, looking out for you. Even when I didn't." He meets my gaze for a moment, then steps back, clearing his throat. "I got you a little something." He reaches into the inside pocket of his suit jacket and hands me a small, velvet box.

"What is it?" I ask as I pop open the lid, my gaze settling on a small opal ring.

"It was your mother's. We never had a lot of money, and I couldn't afford a diamond when I proposed. But she deserved something, so I got her this ring. And even when I had the money for a proper diamond ring, she refused, said this held more meaning." He looks down at the simple piece of jewelry, nostalgia flickering in his eyes as he removes it from the box. "She'd be happy to know you wore it on your own wedding day."

I swallow hard, allowing him to slide it onto the fourth finger of my right hand. "It's beautiful. Thank you."

"Thank *you*, lollipop." He wraps his arms around me, holding me tightly in his embrace. "For giving me a second chance to be a better man."

"Everyone deserves a second chance."

"Well, I'm still grateful you found it in your heart to give me one." He holds me for a moment before pulling back. "Now, why don't we go get you married? And for real this time."

"I'd like that."

I hook my arm through his, allowing him to lead me from the master bedroom and down the stairs where Hazel, Diego, and Imogene wait, everyone else already out in the meadow.

When Wes and I began planning this day, we knew we wanted it to be here. Of course, there were a few complications, most notably the fact we had to rebuild from the ground up before we could even think about hosting a wedding.

But that didn't matter.

We'd both waited our entire lives to find each other. What was a couple more years?

"See ya out there." Dad brushes a kiss to my cheek before retreating out the back door.

"Any last-minute change of heart?" Hazel jokes, looking my way.

"Not a chance," I answer with certainty.

"Good. Then let's start this show." She hugs me one last time, then hands Elijah to Imogene. Her bouquet in hand, she slowly makes her way out of the house and toward the meadow where my dad, Wes, and Julia are already waiting at the makeshift altar I'd constructed with Imogene's help.

"Can we go now?" Imogene asks excitedly.

"Do you need help putting Eli in his wagon?"

She shakes her head, carrying him with ease, as if she's done it her entire life, then straps him into the wagon before pulling him along the path.

From the minute Eli was born, Imogene couldn't get enough of her little cousin. And Elijah certainly took a liking to Imogene. At times, she's the only one who can make him stop crying. They share a bond I hope will continue all their lives.

Just like Wes and Julia.

"Ready?" Diego asks, glancing at me.

I nod quickly. "Of course."

He offers me his elbow, and I hook my arm through it. "Congrats, Lo," he murmurs against my temple.

"Thanks, D."

With a heartfelt smile, he leads me down the stairs and along the path. When the guitar duo transitions from "Canon in D" to "What a Wonderful World", everyone in attendance rises to their feet.

I swallow hard through the lump in my throat, over-whelmed with a myriad of emotions at the significance of this day. One that's a lifetime in the making.

Diego squeezes my hand, and we turn toward the altar, my eyes immediately finding Wes'. My heart expands at the love and admiration in his gaze as I slowly walk toward him. I've never questioned his devotion. Never thought he looked upon me with anything short of adoration.

But right now, as Diego takes my hand and places it in Wes', there's something so much more powerful and poignant than love in his eyes. Awe. Wonder. Esteem.

"You look…" Wes begins once the music comes to an end, struggling to find his words. "Wow.

My face heats. "I like wow. You look wow, too," I say as I take in his navy suit.

His mother would have lost her mind if she knew he was getting married wearing anything other than a designer tux. Then again, she would have lost her mind if she learned he was getting married in the meadow at Gampy and Meemaw's property, too. Which is why she's not here. It was a difficult decision for Wes to make, considering she is his mother, but he didn't want any bad energy today. Only support and acceptance. Two things his mother is still incapable of providing.

"Ready?" Dad asks in a whisper, forcing our eyes away from each other. But only for a split second.

Once we nod and he starts the ceremony, I look back at Wes as my father talks about the importance of love, respect, and acceptance.

"The couple has written their own vows, which they will now share with each other," Dad says after offering his own advice. Then he steps aside, allowing us to have the floor.

Wes takes my hands in his, running his thumb along the fourth finger where his wedding band will soon sit.

"They say love is blind, but I disagree. Maybe *lust* is blind. In my opinion, love is all-seeing and tolerant. It's seeing every flaw and imperfection, yet staying the course despite them. Maybe even *because* of them. It's embracing each scar, learning the story behind every one, and doing everything to help heal them. It's seeing behind the mask." He swallows hard. "It's seeing something in them, something you can't put into words. But you still know it's different. From the very beginning, I knew you were different. I knew I'd gladly overcome any obstacle or scale any wall just to know you. Just to be with you. Just to love you."

I blink away my tears, grateful Hazel insisted I wear waterproof mascara. I didn't think I'd need it. Didn't think I'd be so emotional. But I underestimated myself. Or maybe I underestimated Wes.

He briefly drops his hold on me, smiling and nodding at Imogene, who grabs the box from Elijah's wagon and hands him my ring. He brings it up to my finger.

"All my life, I feel like I've been searching for something just out of reach. Until you. You're my missing piece. My anchor. My beginning and end. Our road hasn't always been easy. We've endured more struggles than most couples. But that's just it. We've endured, Londyn. Even when it would have been so easy to give up. There's no doubt in my mind that those words you told me all those years ago are true. You *are* made for me. And I'm made for you. For the rest of our lives."

I watch as he slides the wedding band into place, like the last piece to the puzzle of my life. "I should have made you go last," I say through my sobs. "Then you could be the blubbering mess."

He blows out a laugh. "I'll probably still be a blubbering mess."

I shift toward Imogene and take Wes' titanium wedding band from her, then turn toward him, bringing it up to his hand. I hesitate, a single brow cocked, as if telling him he has one last chance to back out.

But he remains steadfast, his brilliant, blue eyes unwavering. Those same eyes I saw in my dreams after our first encounter. Those same eyes that have always been my solace, my salvation, my grace.

"I fell in love with you because you taught me how to love myself. I fell in love with you because you saw my scars, yet didn't flinch. I fell in love with you because you stayed by my side even when the world seemed to abandon me." I pause, offering him a small smile. "I fell in love with you because you stood in the rain with me."

His composure cracks, a single tear sliding down his cheek at the memory my words evoke in him.

"You called me a storm. Or, if I recall correctly, a goddamn hurricane."

I wince, glancing at my father, who gives me a playful look of reproach before smiling. He may still be a pastor, but like Wes' father, he's also realized what's important in life. Family.

"But if I'm a storm, you're my calm. We may be as opposite as two people can be, but to understand one, you must have the other. If we didn't endure storms, we'd never appreciate the beauty of a sunny day. If we didn't have pain, we'd never appreciate happiness. If we didn't endure hatred, we'd never appreciate love. And that's exactly what you've done for me. You taught me the beauty in the small things. In having paint fights on a random Sunday. In sitting on a porch and listening to nature. In surviving a near-death experience on a Ferris wheel."

Everyone laughs, causing a break in the tension.

"And you taught me the beauty of dancing in the rain. From this day forward, I will always stand in the rain with you. You for me. Me for you. For the rest of our lives."

I slide the ring onto his finger, where it will remain until he draws his last breath. And even after.

"By the power vested in me by God, I am thrilled to declare you husband and wife. You may now kiss the—"

My dad doesn't even finish his statement before Wes cups my cheeks, drawing my mouth toward his. He breathes into me, his kiss filled with passion, but still respectful for the occasion. Sparks ignite in me, this man's kisses the perfect drug. The only thing that makes me feel this euphoria and bliss I didn't think possible.

When he pulls back, he winks.

"Bride," my father finishes with a smile, which elicits a laugh. "Ladies and gentlemen, I present Mr. and Mrs. Bradford."

Everyone claps and cheers as we face all the people who've come to mean the world to us. Wes brushes his lips against mine once more, then grabs my hand, leading me down the makeshift aisle.

As we pass his father, Elijah reaches for us from his arms.

Unable to walk by him without picking him up and smothering him with kisses, Wes grabs him, nuzzling him. "You hear that, bud. We're finally a family."

"We've always been a family," I remind him.

He lowers his lips to mine, kissing me once more, wrapping little Elijah in all the love we share.

A wise man once said, "Sometimes the right path isn't always the easiest."

My path to this place has been anything but easy.

But there's no doubt in my mind all the struggles we've encountered have been worth it to finally be in this place. To have love. To have hope.

To have a home.

Thank you so much for reading Atonement. I hope you enjoyed the conclusion to Wes & Londyn's story.

Wondering if Julia ever finds her own happiness after finally standing up to Nick? Find out today in Temptation, an epic older woman, younger man romance filled with mystery, suspense, and steam!

https://www.tkleighauthor.com/t-k-s-books/temptation

I appreciate your help in spreading the word about my books. Please leave a review on your favorite book site.

# TEMPTATION

**He was her addiction.**
**But she was the object of another man's obsession.**

It was supposed to be a typical business trip to Hawaii.

During the day, I'd promote the new location of my bakery. At night, I'd relax on the lanai while sipping a glass of wine.

But that all changed when I met *him*.

*Sexy. Intriguing. Haunted.*

And easily fifteen years younger than me.

I should walk away. The last thing I need after turning forty is a middle-age crisis in the form of an Australian Adonis.

But something keeps drawing me back to him.

So I make a proposition.

**One week. No names. No expectations.**

It was the perfect plan…

Until I learned the true identity of my vacation fling.

They say temptation can be dangerous.
*I didn't realize it could be so deadly.*

Scan below or type the address into your web browser.

https://www.tkleighauthor.com/t-k-s-books/temptation

# PLAYLIST

*Moment* - Noah Guthrie

*Disconnected* - Jazz Morley

*Been A Long Day* - Rosi Golan

*The Hollow in Retrospect* - Corey Kilgannon featuring Liza Anne

*Far Away* - Matthew Nolan

*Maple Whisky* - James Spaite

*Calm Down* - Sonny

*Break My Heart Right* - James Bay

*By My Side* - The Paper Kites featuring Rosie Carney

*Texas Wildflower Honey* - Ron Pope

*If I Have A Son* - Ruth B.

*Grace* - Rachel Platton

*Courage to Change* - Sia

*I'll Be There* - Hadley Hanson

*Naked* - Brielle Von Hugel

*My Sweet Refuge* - Roo Panes

*My Love Will Never Die* - Claire Wyndham

*Pictures of You* - Lauren Ruth Ward

*Sinnerman* - Nina Simone

*Darkside* - Oshins
*Things We Lost in the Fire* - Janet Devlin
*Something in the Rain* - Rachael Yamagata
*Better Days* - Judith Hill
*What A Wonderful World* - Louis Armstrong
*I Can't Wait* - Micky Skeel

# ACKNOWLEDGMENTS

Can I just take a minute to take a big breath? Man, this was a tough one for me. This entire duet was extremely draining. I've written close to thirty books by now, but this story hit me hard. There were so many times I felt like pulling back and not going in the direction I knew in my soul this story needed to go, worried it was too much.

But I needed this story to have truth. I needed it to be real. I needed it to accurately display the struggles black people face in this country. And the struggles women who attempt to come forward regarding sexual assault also face.

So on that note, I must first thank all my incredible sensitivity readers for taking the time to read this and offer me feedback — Renita, Curtis, Crystal, and Keeana. You all rock my world. Thank you for supporting this project from the day I first mentioned wanting to write an interracial romance to the moment you read the final word.

A big thank you to my husband, Stan, for supporting this crazy profession of mine from day one.

To little Harper Leigh — I hope you'll grow up in a world without hate.

To my Dad, a career fire fighter of over forty years — thanks for all your expertise in making sure I accurately portrayed the fire scene. Some of my favorite memories of my childhood still remain visiting you at the station and playing on the fire engines.

To my incredible PA, Melissa Crump. That you for all your support and encouragement. And for taking care of all my social media so I can hide in my writing cave for days on end.

To my BFF, A.D. Justice. Thanks for always being a quick message away whenever I need to talk out plot points. Or just complain about things. You get me.

To my beta team - Melissa, Lin, Stacy, and Vicky. Thanks for all your helpful feedback.

To my admin team — Melissa, Joelle, Lin, Vicky, and Lea. Thanks for all you do for me.

To my fantastic promo team! Thanks for always helping to share my books with the world. I can't tell you how much I appreciate everything you do for me.

To my review team — thanks for taking the time to review each and every one of my books, regardless of the subject matter. I appreciate each and every one of you!

To my reader group. Thanks for giving me a fun space to disappear to when I need a laugh.

And last but not least, thank you to YOU! Thanks so much for taking a chance on my books. Whether you're new to me or have been with me for years, I appreciate each and every one of you. Stay tuned… I've got lots more planned. Pretty sure Julia deserves to find a happily ever after. ;-)

Love & Peace,
~ T.K.

# ABOUT THE AUTHOR

T.K. Leigh is a *USA Today* Bestselling author of romance ranging from fun and flirty to sexy and suspenseful.

Originally from New England, she now resides just outside of Raleigh with her husband, beautiful daughter, rescued special needs dog, and three cats. When she's not writing, she can be found training for her next marathon or chasing her daughter around the house.

facebook.com/tkleighauthor

instagram.com/tkleigh

tiktok.com/@tkleigh

bookbub.com/authors/t-k-leigh

pinterest.com/tkleighauthor

Printed in Great Britain
by Amazon